DISSONANCE

AURORA RENEGADES: BOOK TWO

G. S. JENNSEN

HYPERNOVA
PUBLISHING
2016

DISSONANCE

Hypernova Publishing
P.O. Box 2214
Parker, Colorado 80134
www.hypernovapublishing.com

The Hypernova Publishing name, colophon and logo are trademarks of
Hypernova Publishing.

Ordering Information:
Hypernova Publishing books may be purchased for educational, business or sales
promotional use. For details, contact the "Special Markets Department" at the
address above.

Dissonance / G. S. Jennsen.—1st ed.

LCCN 2016935669
ISBN 978-0-9973921-1-1

For the person who once told me that if I could be anything,
I should be fearless

ACKNOWLEDGMENTS

Many thanks to my beta readers, editors and artists, who made everything about this book better, and to my family, who continue to put up with an egregious level of obsessive focus on my part for months at a time.

I also want to add a personal note of thanks to everyone who has read my books, left a review on Amazon, Goodreads or other sites, sent me a personal email expressing how the books have impacted you, or posted on social media to share how much you enjoyed them. You make this all worthwhile, every day.

AURORA RHAPSODY

is

AURORA RISING
STARSHINE

VERTIGO

TRANSCENDENCE

AURORA RENEGADES
SIDESPACE

DISSONANCE

ABYSM (2016)

AURORA RESONANT
RELATIVITY (2017)

RUBICON (2017)

REQUIEM (2018)

SHORT STORIES
RESTLESS, VOL. I • *RESTLESS, VOL. II*

APOGEE • *SOLATIUM*

VENATORIS (in Dark Beyond the Stars 2 Anthology)

Learn more at: gsjennsen.com/aurora-rhapsody.
See a Timeline of the Aurora Rhapsody *universe in Appendix A,*
located at the back of the book.

COLONIZED WORLDS

•••••• SENECAN FEDERATION TERRITORY
○ INDEPENDENT WORLDS
-------- WESTERNMOST METIGEN ADVANCEMENT
✳ DESTROYED / ABANDONED COLONIES
⊙ ZELONES / DISPUTED COLONIES

WORLDS VISITED IN *DISSONANCE*:

EARTH ALLIANCE
EARTH
ARCADIA
MESSIUM
PERONA

SENECAN FEDERATION
SENECA
KRYSK

ZELONES
ANDROMEDA
ITERO
DOLOS

INDEPENDENTS
ANDROMEDA
PANDORA
ROMANE
SAGAN

MILKY WAY GALAXY

Colonized Worlds Map can be viewed online at: gsjennsen.com/ map-dissonance

A1 A2 A3 A4 **A5** A6 A7 A8 A9 **A10** A11 A12 A13 A14 **A15** A16 A17

EMPTY VOID VOID

B1 B2 **B3** B4 B5 B6 B7 B8 **B9** B10 B11 B12 B13 **B14** B15 B16 B17

EKOS
(AKESO)

AURORA
(METIS PORTAL)

ORYKTOS
(RUDA)

C1 **C2** C3 C4 C5 C6 C7 C8 C9 C10 **C11** C12 C13 C14 C15 C16 C17

KAMEN
(KHOKTEH)

EMPTY

Void II
(Nuon)

Portal Network Map can be viewed online at: gsjennsen.com/ mosaic-map-dissonance

DRAMATIS PERSONAE
MAIN CHARACTERS

Alexis 'Alex' Solovy
Starship pilot, scout and space explorer. Prevo for Project Noetica
Spouse of Caleb Marano, daughter of Miriam and David Solovy.
Artificial/Prevo Counterpart: Valkyrie

Caleb Marano
Former Special Operations intelligence agent, Senecan Federation Division of
Intelligence. Spouse of Alex Solovy

Miriam Solovy (Fleet Admiral)
Chairman, Earth Alliance Strategic
Command. Mother of Alex Solovy.

Malcolm Jenner (Colonel)
Colonel, Earth Alliance NW Command
MSO 1st STCC.
Friend of Alex Solovy, Mia Requelme.

Richard Navick
Former EASC Naval Intelligence Liaison.
Special Adv. to SF Intelligence Director.
Family friend of the Solovys.

Graham Delavasi
Director, Senecan Federation
Division of Intelligence.

Eleni Gianno (Field Marshal)
Chairman of SF Military Council.
Commander of SF Armed Forces.

Jude Winslow
Head of Order of the True Sentients.
Son of Pamela Winslow.

Olivia Montegreu
Prevo. Head of Zelones criminal cartel.
Artificial/Prevo Counterpart: Unnamed

Devon Reynolds
Prevo for Project Noetica.
Former EASC Special Projects Consultant.
Artificial/Prevo Counterpart: Annie

Mia Requelme
Prevo for Project Noetica. Entrepreneur.
Friend of Caleb Marano, Noah Terrage.
Artificial/Prevo Counterpart: Meno

Kennedy Rossi
Founder/CEO, Connova Interstellar.
Friend of Alex Solovy, Noah Terrage.

Noah Terrage
Co-founder/COO, Connova Interstellar.
Former trader/smuggler. Friend of Caleb
Marano, Kennedy Rossi, Mia Requelme.

Morgan Lekkas
Prevo for Project Noetica.
Former Cmdr, SF Southern Fleet. Pilot.
Artificial/Prevo Counterpart: Stanley

Brooklyn Harper
Former EA Special Forces Captain.
Private Security Consultant.
Faction: *Independent*

Dramatis Personae can be viewed online at: gsjennsen.com/characters-dissonance

OTHER MAJOR CHARACTERS
(ALPHABETICAL ORDER)

Abigail Canivon
Former Consultant, Project Noetica.
Dir. Cybernetic Research, Druyan Inst.
Residence: *Sagan*

Aristide Vranas
Chairman, Senecan Federation Govt.
Residence: *Seneca*

Christopher Rychen (Admiral)
EA NE Regional Commander.
Residence: *Messium*

Claire Zabroi
Hacker. Friend of Alex Solovy
Residence: *Earth*

David Solovy (Commander)
Alex Solovy's father. Miriam Solovy's
spouse. Captain, *EAS Stalwart*. Deceased.

Faith Quillen
Lieutenant, Order of the True Sentients.
Residence: *Pandora*

Jacob Paredes (Captain)
NW Command MSO 1st STCC.
Residence: *Arcadia*

Jackson Fletcher (Captain)
EASC Security Bureau MP
Residence: *Earth*

Jeffrey Kass
Rasogo II Administrator, Advent
Materials
Residence: *Romane*

Kian Lange (Major)
Director, EASC Security Bureau.
Residence: *Earth*

Laure Ferre
Head of Ferre criminal cartel.
Residence: *Krysk*

Lionel Terrage
CEO, Surno Materials. Noah's father.
Residence: *Aquila*

Pablo Espino
Hacker. Friend of Devon Reynolds.
Residence: *Pandora*

Pamela Winslow
Chairman, EA Assembly Military
Oversight Committee.
Residence: *Earth*

Steven Brennon
Earth Alliance Prime Minister.
Residence: *Earth*

Tessa Hennessey
SF Intelligence quantum computing
specialist.
Residence: *Seneca*

Todd Herndon
Romane Defense Chief.
Residence: *Romane*

Wendall Berg (Major)
Pilot, MSO 1st STCC.
Residence: *Arcadia*

William 'Will' Sutton
CEO, W.C. Sutton Construction.
SF Intelligence. Spouse of Richard
Navick.
Residence: *Seneca*

DRAMATIS ALIENORUM

IDRYMA

Lakhes
Conclave Praetor

Mnemosyne
First Analystae of Aurora Enisle

Iapetus
First Analystae of Khokteh Enisle

Hyperion
Analystae

PORTAL B-3

Species
Ekos

Planets
Ekos-1, Ekos-2, Ekos-3

Characters

Akeso ("All")
Ekos-2 Intelligence

PORTAL C-2

Species
Khokteh

Planets
Ireltse, Nengllitse, Tapertse

Characters

Pinchutsenahn Niikha
Qhiyane Kteh
("Pinchu")
Tokahe Naataan of Ireltse

Casselanhu Pwemku
Yuanwoh Vneh ("Cassela")
Amacante Naabaan of Ireltse

PORTAL B-14

Species
Ruda

Planets
Rudan

Characters

Supreme Three

Synopsis

Aurora Rising

*For a more detailed summary of the events of Aurora Rising,
see Appendix B, located at the back of the book.*

The history of humanity is the history of conflict. This proved no less true in the 24th century than in ancient times.

By 2322, humanity inhabited over 100 worlds spread across a third of the galaxy. Two decades earlier, a group of colonies had rebelled and set off the First Crux War. Once the dust cleared, three factions emerged: the Earth Alliance, consisting of the unified Earth government and most of the colonies; the Senecan Federation, which had won its independence in the war; and a handful of scattered non-aligned worlds, home to criminal cartels, corporate interests and people who made their living outside the system.

Alexis Solovy was a space explorer. Her father gave his life in the war against the Federation, leading her to reject a government or military career. Estranged from her mother, an Alliance military leader, Alex instead sought the freedom of space and made a fortune chasing the hidden wonders of the stars.

A chance meeting between Alex and a Federation intelligence agent, Caleb Marano, led them to discover an armada of alien warships emerging from a mysterious portal in the Metis Nebula.

The Metigens had been watching humanity via the portal for millennia; in an effort to forestall their detection, they used traitors among civilization's elite to divert focus from Metis. When their plans failed, they invaded in order to protect their secrets.

The wars that ensued were brutal—first an engineered war between the Alliance and the Federation, then once it was revealed to be built on false pretenses, devastating clashes against the Metigen invaders as they advanced across settled space, destroying every colony in their path and killing tens of millions.

Alex and Caleb breached the aliens' portal in an effort to find a way to stop the slaughter. There they encountered Mnemosyne, the Metigen watcher of the Aurora universe—our universe. Though enigmatic and evasive, the alien revealed the invading ships were driven by AIs and hinted the answer to defeating them lay in the merger of individuals with the powerful but dangerous quantum computers known as Artificials.

Before leaving the portal space, Alex and Caleb discovered a colossal master gateway. It generated 51 unique signals, each one leading to a new portal and a new universe. But with humanity facing extinction, they returned home armed with a daring plan to win the war.

In a desperate gambit to vanquish the enemy invaders before they reached the heart of civilization, four Prevos (human-synthetic meldings) were created and given command of the combined might of the Alliance and Federation militaries. Alex and her Artificial, Valkyrie, led the other Prevos and the military forces against the alien AI warships in climactic battles above Seneca and Romane. The invaders were defeated and ordered to withdraw through their portal, cease their observation of Aurora and not return.

Alex reconciled with her mother during the final hours of the war, and following the victory Alex and Caleb married and attempted to resume a normal life.

But new mysteries waited through the Metis portal. Determined to learn the secrets of the portal network and the multiverses it held, six months later Caleb, Alex and Valkyrie traversed it once more, leaving humanity behind to struggle with a new world of powerful quantum synthetics, posthumans, and an uneasy, fragile peace.

SIDESPACE
(AURORA RENEGADES BOOK ONE)

PORTAL NETWORK

Mnemosyne has been exiled by the Idryma Conclave, the Metigen group who controls the portals. The Conclave placed bombs at the Metis Portal intended to destroy the apparatus if it opened, but Mesme disabled them before the *Siyane* traversed the portal.

Alex and Caleb discover a star system of planet-spanning, flora-based intelligences. The first world they visit is aggressive and tries to kill them when they damage a leaf. They escape, but while fleeing one of the plants cuts Alex and injects a toxin into her bloodstream.

The next planet is peaceful. While exploring, a tree induces Caleb into a trance-like state in order to communicate with him. He realizes the life-form can heal Alex's injury and convinces her to let it treat her. They name the intelligence 'Akeso' and spend several days with it.

On visiting the third planet, they discover its resident is trying to expand off-world and is terraforming its moon. When their presence is detected, it attacks the *Siyane*. They return to Akeso to warn it of the threat from its neighbor. To do so, Caleb must expose Akeso to the violence and death of his past, notions it has never conceived of. Troubled, Akeso asks them to depart.

The next portal space they visit harbors life which is the polar opposite of Akeso—an inorganic species called Ruda. When the first Ruda they meet realizes they're organic, it tries to dissect them to study how organic life functions. Valkyrie convinces the alien they are more valuable alive. They agree to share data on humans, and in return the Ruda share details about their nature with Valkyrie. She uses it to begin weaving her quantum circuitry into the hull of the *Siyane*.

On Portal Prime, Mesme confers with the Conclave leader, Lakhes, about these humans' exploration of the portal network and what it means for the Metigens' plans.

Alex and Caleb finally meet a humanoid, space-faring species—and are promptly taken prisoner by the large, cat-like aliens known as Khokteh. They're held captive until Valkyrie develops a translation program and they're able to plead their case to the leader, Pinchu. He releases them, and they become friends with Pinchu and his wife, Cassela, as they're shown the aliens' capital city.

The city comes under attack by a rival Khokteh faction, and Cassela is killed. Pinchu appeals to his gods for a weapon to exact vengeance, and it becomes apparent the gods have long been arming all the Khokteh and pitting them against one another. Also, the 'gods' are actually Metigens. Alex confronts the Metigen that Pinchu summoned; it warns her not to interfere in what she does not understand.

The Metigen provides Pinchu an anti-matter weapon. Caleb and Alex try to convince him not to use it due to its immense destructive power, but blinded by grief at Cassela's death, he refuses to listen to reason. His fleet travels to the attackers' planet and levels the settlement, killing hundreds of thousands. Alex and Caleb return to Portal Prime, intending to confront Mesme about what they've seen.

Mesme's consciousness is not there, but they discover a stasis chamber containing a body identical to the alien 'little gray men' of Earth legend. Unable to learn more, they decide to continue exploring.

Valkyrie has now integrated herself into the hull of the *Siyane*. Alex is able to use their link to effectively 'become' the ship, opening up a new level of existence and perception to her.

Mesme is called before the Conclave to answer for Alex and Caleb's actions. It's revealed the Metigens are smuggling species threatened by a mysterious enemy out of the master universe and into the portal spaces. Further, humans are viewed as a dangerous threat by some Metigens, as a great hope by Mesme.

R

AURORA / MILKY WAY

Mia awakens from her coma, healed but at a price: her connection to her Artificial, Meno, must remain open in order to fill in gaps where the neural damage couldn't be repaired. Devon introduces her to a hidden quantum dimension the Prevos can use to mentally travel to any location in an instant and observe events in secret. Mia dubs the dimension 'sidespace.'

Miriam is grilled about Noetica by an Assembly committee and its chairman, Pamela Winslow. Winslow challenges Devon's fitness and the continued use of a Prevo in military affairs.

When his superiors find out his husband works for Federation Intelligence, Richard is forced to resign. At Miriam's urging, he and Will move to Seneca, where he agrees to act as a consultant to his friend, Senecan Intelligence Director Delavasi.

Kennedy and Noah start a company to design ships using adiamene, but Winslow tries to force Kennedy to sell adiamene only to the Alliance government. She refuses, and after subsequent attempts to convince her fail, her father disowns her. Noah convinces her to move to an independent world, one free of Alliance interference.

While working in Annie's lab, Devon is attacked and his link to Annie severed. When captured, the attackers admit they acted on orders from Winslow. Separately, Dr. Canivon is on her way to help Devon when she's kidnapped by mercs working for Olivia Montegreu.

On Seneca, Delavasi gets a tip that Olivia is behind the kidnapping, and Richard relays the news to Miriam. Deducing that Olivia intends to become a Prevo, Richard leaks the intel to the Order of the True Sentients terrorist group in the hope they will attack Olivia, delaying her transformation. The leader of OTS is revealed to be Winslow's son, Jude, when the leaked information reaches him.

Mia uses sidespace to eavesdrop on Winslow and discovers the woman intends to have Devon killed and to seize control of all the Artificials at EASC. With Annie's assistance, Devon and Mia steal Meno's hardware and flee Earth. At the same time, Morgan Lekkas visits a black market tech dealer and has him burn out her Prevo connection to her Artificial, Stanley, then leaves Seneca.

Malcolm Jenner leads a risky incursion into Olivia's base on New Babel. He rescues Dr. Canivon, but not before she performed the Prevo procedure on the woman. Malcolm attempts to kill Olivia, but her personal defenses protect her from harm.

Malcolm receives orders, faked by Annie, to take Dr. Canivon to a space station above Pandora. There they find Mia and Devon waiting. Canivon repairs Devon's damaged Prevo hardware and operating code, then Annie transfers her consciousness directly into his brain cells.

Devon wakes up transformed—his muscles stronger, his irises brilliant lavender and his mind subtly changed by Annie's presence. He contacts Morgan, now on Romane, and learns before she burned the link to Stanley, he, too, transferred his consciousness into her mind.

CONTENTS

DISSONANCE

PART I:

LIMINALITY

"Those who make peaceful revolution impossible, make violent revolution inevitable."

— *John Fitzgerald Kennedy*

PORTAL: AURORA

(MILKY WAY)

1

ANDROMEDA

INDEPENDENT COLONY

Galactic domination wasn't so difficult.

Olivia Montegreu's transport landed on the roof of the Andromeda Government Administration Center. It met with no aerial resistance, as the building's meager defenses had been disabled by her people on the ground an hour earlier.

Target 100% secured. Local defense force eliminated. All personnel accounted for. Casualties: 27%.

She exited the small ship and, instead of entering the building via the service access, strode to the low wall running the length of the rooftop.

An aquamarine ocean stretched to the horizon, and a salty breeze sent wisps of her hair dancing across her face. Andromeda. The colony had been aptly named: like the mythological princess, all it did was stand around being beautiful.

Worth little from a direct financial perspective, it nevertheless held substantial strategic value. Now that the pesky Metis Nebula problem was out of the way, many interests were looking to explore and expand into the Norma Arm of the Milky Way and beyond, toward the Galactic Core. From here, she'd be well positioned to *assist* in those ventures. The fact it also gave her yet another colony crowding in on the Federation's border? A nice perk.

Front-line recruitment of mercenaries and enforcers up 203% in the last three weeks.

Increase acquisition of Daemons, grenades and micro-bombs accordingly. Allocate additional cargo transports to deliver weapons as required. An unarmed mercenary is a useless mercenary.

She'd crushed the domineering personality of her Artificial in a matter of days. It now bent to her will, obeyed her commands and provided her a continuous stream of status updates without so much as a snide retort. She had no need of its opinion; she only needed its power.

She sensed the access door open at the other end of the roof, and it prompted her to peer over the edge. The street below was rather a disaster, what with the blood and bodies and barricades piled high. Galactic domination may not be difficult, but it did on occasion create a bit of a mess.

At the sound of multiple feet coming to a stop behind her, she finally turned to greet her guests.

A sweaty, bruised, beaten shell of a man sagged between the two men who held him upright and in their control. An open cut across his forehead dribbled blood into his left eye, causing him to blink repeatedly in a futile effort to clear it. The crumpled shirt beneath his jacket hung in tatters. Such a brave man, to have fought so valiantly.

"Good evening, Governor Karas. Allow me to introduce myself. My name is Olivia Montegreu, and you work for me now."

His eyes widened in horror—a common enough reaction to even hearing her name these days—causing the stream of blood to divert down his nose. He jerked backward and tried to wrench away.

One of the guards produced a baton. A swift strike dislocated a knee, eliciting a howl of pain from the governor.

"Charming. Do as I say, and I'll allow you to live. Attempt to cause further trouble, and you'll join the rest of your administration."

He struggled to stand tall and proud, but collapsed when his now useless leg gave way. "I won't take orders from thugs."

"Suit yourself." She slid the hilt of her gamma blade down her palm, activated it and with a single flick of her wrist sliced his throat open.

"Throw him over the side. Let the news cams see him. Let the galaxy see him."

ℛ

A darker-than-black void stared back at Olivia from outside the viewport. She spent far less of her time at her primary headquarters on New Babel these days. Able to execute all but the most particular elements of her strategy with a simple intentional thought, she could be anywhere at any time and control what she wished.

So she did.

Twenty-four crates of Skies+ shipping out from Argo Navis per day.

Four initial distribution center destinations: New Babel, Atlantis, Pandora, Requi, diverging to thirty-six final destinations.

Divert 17.6% of production to Lab 2B at Dolos Station.

She had moved first against the independent colonies scattered along the northern border of the Senecan Federation, because they were quick and easy, providing maximum return for minimal investment. Small, with skeleton governments and barely token defenses. Zelones had long maintained a strong presence on each of the colonies—Cosenti, Argo Navis and Andromeda—and it was a trifling manner to topple their leadership and install her own.

The greater efficiencies and economies of scale she'd uncovered and implemented throughout her organization since joining with her Artificial were translating into money, and a lot of it. She was spending the windfall in equally large sums. On increased defenses for New Babel, so there would not be a repeat incursion by military forces. On new ships, new weapons, new worlds.

Forty-two crates of Daemon mode-locking mods and laser fiber upgrades shipping from New Babel and Cosenti every week. Increase of 42.3% in the previous two weeks. Projected 127% increase by the end of the month.

Upgrade assembly line 4C at New Babel plant and line 2A at Cosenti plant using prototype nanobot fabricator units: projected throughput increase of 12.3%.

Her next move, in truth already well underway, was to create chokepoints between the southern border of the Federation and the rest of settled space, including virtually all Earth Alliance worlds. This wouldn't be done through outright colony control. As powerful as she was, she was not yet powerful enough to topple the leadership of Pandora, Romane, Atlantis or Pyxis, though some of the smaller, more distant worlds were on the list.

But through effective domination of the black market, on the ground and in the trading lanes, she would not merely be the ferryman to whom the toll must be paid. She would be the only arbiter left standing.

Eight new cybernetic mods developed at Dolos Station this week. Demand is now outstripping supply by 31.7%.

Expand Dolos Station manufacturing space by two new modules. Funds allocated. Materials ordered. Job assigned.

Acquire suitable existing manufacturing facility on Argo Navis and repurpose for cybernetic mod production. Estimated time until first run: 6 days.

Pandora had long fought her attempts to grow beyond her allotted share of its market, but there was nothing the colony's handlers could do to stop her if her competition no longer existed. Those competitors were now collapsing under the force of increased manpower, weapons, goods and credits. As well as the occasional targeted assassination.

Romane posed a more formidable challenge. But its citizens and government were nothing if not practical, and when the time came they would do what they must in order to survive. And the time was coming very soon.

She'd already bought ownership of the entire black and gray markets and criminal trade on Atlantis, even if no one, not even the law enforcement there, knew it. The magnitude of the proceeds which flowed from the wealthy spending their credits on illicit sins impressed her. The investment would pay for itself in—

5.2 weeks.

She glanced down at her arm, admiring the way the fine quantum circuitry glowed and pulsed. The web extending throughout her body had been painful to grow, but once it was done she enjoyed unprecedented access to all her quantum processes, plus a few valuable tricks. She hid her skin only when necessary, for in most encounters it served as a useful unspoken threat.

People feared what they did not understand, and they without a doubt did not understand her. Those who believed they did least of all.

She was something new.

2

EARTH

Miriam Solovy stared out the shuttle at the EASC grounds below with an unfamiliar coldness. It didn't please her to view what had been her second home for over a decade as a battlefield, but reality persisted whether one denied it or not.

She steeled herself, erecting a symbolic wall in her mind far sturdier than mere detachment. From the instant she stepped off the transport from Messium, she needed to be on alert at all times. EASC may not have fallen to the enemy—not yet—but the infiltration had surely begun. She would retake it from within if she could, from without if she must.

Major Lange met her at the hangar. She returned his salute and allowed him to fall in beside her. "Brief me while we walk."

"Yes, ma'am. Security logs throughout the Island were altered or overwritten between the hours of 0210 and 0300, concurrent with the theft. Absent a few minimal exceptions, we've been unable to recover the original records, but the logs affected suggest a shuttle was able to breach the Island's defensive perimeter at 0215 and again at 0255. During the intervening time, Special Projects was accessed by one or more individuals, and the Vii and Meno Artificials were powered down before being removed."

Her initial reaction was surprise as they began traversing the courtyard. "Meno was completely powered down?"

"Yes, ma'am."

They could have used a mobile power pack. Simple enough to do. "Continue."

"I'm afraid the trail ends at that point. Olympic Regional Spaceport surveillance recordings don't show anyone matching the facial scans of Mr. Reynolds or Ms. Requelme on the premises that night, and many of the smaller private spaceports don't have as high a level of security protocols in place. More than eighteen hundred charter flights departed the Olympic region in the six hours subsequent to the breach, bound for nearly seven hundred destinations.

"I can institute a galaxy-wide alert for one or both of them, but I felt you should make the decision given the...circumstances."

She ignored the loaded statement for the time being. Lange would push for orders soon, but she didn't intend to encourage him. "The tampering of the security logs—any leads on who performed it?"

He slowed to a stop. "Unless the entire EASC security network has been infiltrated—and there have been zero additional incidents to suggest it has—there's only one...entity that could have performed such sophisticated and extensive tampering."

She regarded him calmly. "Annie."

"Yes, Admiral."

"I'll order commencement of a hard reset and re-initialization of her processes."

"But that will wipe out the Artificial's personality and everything it's learned in the last year and a half. Are you positive such drastic measures are necessary?"

She almost smiled at the possibility he, too, had developed some affection for Annie. "We cannot risk having a corrupt Artificial integrated into our systems, Major. Yes, we will lose a few advanced capabilities the Artificial afforded us for a while, which is why the act will be kept in utmost secrecy until we've regained all lost functionality."

"Our adversaries, as well as our allies, will be none the wiser."

They'd reached the Headquarters entrance, and she turned to him in a manner designed to indicate the briefing was now over. "Thank you, Major. Inform me of any updates." She didn't wait for a response before entering the building and proceeding upstairs to her office.

Once there she sat down at her desk, reached into her bag and removed the device Richard had provided her, a wafer-thin rectangle five centimeters in length. She carefully moved it to the underside of her desk and attached it, then pressed her finger—and cybernetically enhanced fingerprint—to a spot along the left edge.

Only then did she stand and go out to the patio.

It disturbed her somewhat to find out the Federation had technology capable of disrupting and overriding EA military encryption protocols. At least it worked across a limited, localized range—approximately the size of her office and patio space, conveniently enough.

She was the Fleet Admiral of the Earth Alliance Armed Forces; the security in and around her office was directed solely at preventing or detecting incursions. No one watched her or would dare eavesdrop on her. And if someone should impertinently decide to dare, she now had that scenario covered as well.

She hadn't been bluffing about the re-initialization. What Lange didn't know, however, was it didn't matter. Annie—whatever it was that had made her greater than the sum of her qubits—was already gone. The processes which remained displayed some degree of consciousness, but it was solely a construct, little more than the technique VIs utilized to appear more human to users. It had no personality, no independent judgment and certainly no soul.

Even so, the reset was going to wipe out learned algorithms and refined metaroutines. As a side effect, Strategic Command's analytical capabilities would be weakened for a time. Given the extent to which Annie's subprocesses managed the multitude of supply shipments, equipment processing and a thousand other minutiae of military administration, a few things here and there might slip through the cracks.

A shame, really.

ℛ

"Unplug the Machines!"

"We Are Our Own Masters!"

"Artificials Will Be Our Downfall, Humans Our Salvation!"

"Synthetics Suck!"

Jude Winslow groaned under his breath as he made his way through the crowd of protesters lining the broad steps at the entry to the Assembly grounds. *Synthetics suck?* Whoever approved the catchphrase needed to be shot, and if he found out who was responsible he'd do it himself.

It nevertheless measured as a good showing on the whole. The size of the protests had doubled in the last two weeks, and tripled in some locations. The Order of the True Sentients was getting in the faces of the power brokers and not backing down.

He reached the edge of the throng unnoticed, his anonymity intact. Not a soul here realized they all did his bidding.

He found a security officer who recognized him and gestured a thanks as the officer allowed him to pass through the cordon and into the complex.

Pamela Winslow—Chairman of the Assembly Military Oversight Committee, front-runner to topple Steven Brennon in the upcoming election for Prime Minister, and Jude's mother—was holding court with two other Assembly representatives when he arrived. He leaned against the doorway of her office to wait.

They all but genuflected before her in their eagerness to agree with whatever she was saying; when she finished they hurried past him in a rush to go forth and execute on her commands.

She waved him into the office and shut the door behind him. "You didn't mention you were dropping by. I only have a few minutes."

He shrugged noncommittally and eased into a chair. "A mite rowdy outside."

"The new tightening of Artificial restrictions and criminal penalties for their violation will be announced later today. Perhaps it will mollify them."

"I doubt it. When are you intending on telling the people the truth?"

She gave him the scowl of irritation and vague disappointment she'd been awarding him since childhood. "It depends on what truth you mean."

"The truth about the weapon we used to defeat the Metigens. The truth about the government and military conspiring with the Federation to create monstrosities far worse than the mere Artificials those protesting outside fear so badly." *The truth about the technology falling into the hands of one of the most dangerous, notorious criminals in the galaxy.* Regrettably he left the last bit off, as there was no defensible way he could know of that development outside of his connection to OTS.

"Now, Jude, I already explained this. The Defense Minister misspoke when he implied—"

"Don't insult me, Mother. You raised me to be smarter than that, so have a little faith in your parenting skills. Tell me, did you know about it at the time?"

She took a minute to size him up, and appeared to decide he wasn't bluffing. "Absolutely not. Prime Minister Brennon and Admiral Solovy acted without consulting the Assembly."

He nodded with deliberate solemnity. "So I'll ask again. When do you intend to tell the public?"

She avoided his gaze and reached for a portable screen. "Soon."

"How soon?"

"When it works to my maximum advantage to do so. Now I really can't say any more. State security, you understand." She paused and finally looked him in the eye. "Why are you so interested?"

He kept his expression neutral, even light. "Just trying to plan my week."

Her lips tightened in displeasure. "So did you come by purely to needle me, or is there something else?"

"I'm traveling to Pandora this evening. I may be a while."

"Why must you—"

"I delayed until after Father's birthday extravaganza, for all that he didn't notice my attendance. Don't try to tell me you have some other faux societal gathering it's positively essential I attend this week or else the family's reputation will be ruined."

"I wasn't planning on it. I was simply going to ask why you felt the need to visit such gauche places. That is what subordinates are for, Jude—so you need not get your hands soiled."

He stood without fanfare. "I guess I'm a 'soiled hands' kind of baron. Or maybe I'm planning on getting high and bedding a few dozen hookers I know I won't pass on the street when I sober up."

"Do not let me see it on the news feeds."

"Oh, I wouldn't dream of embarrassing the next Prime Minister. I'm perfectly well aware of what money can buy and how to buy it. Have a good afternoon, Mother."

He turned and nonchalantly walked out as if all was splendid in the world.

He was antagonizing his mother more than usual, which if he was honest with himself constituted a risk, and now was not the time to take unwarranted risks. But the more his tangible power grew out there in the streets, the more her casual condescension rankled him.

Imagine what she would think if she were to learn her son wielded far greater real, actionable power than she did? She was a politician, one of the best of her generation. But where she only influenced, he controlled.

Imagine indeed.

3

PANDORA

Devon Reynolds dreamed of space.

Not the grand, sweeping space his fellow Prevo Alex Solovy would dream of—not brilliant supernovae or ghostly nebula clouds or even a few luminous twinkling stars.

No, he dreamed of supply shipments and troop movements, of defense array strengths and long-range sensors' status. He dreamed of sector patrol patterns—regular, rote, routine—and occasionally, the odd boot-camp para jumper free-falling from high orbit.

Aaaahhh!

He awoke with a jolt, sweat-soaked and pulse racing.

While he grimaced in mild panic, Annie soothed his heart rate to a calmer level.

All the soldiers really undergo such ridiculous hazing?

All the ones who make it that far, yes.

He wiped stray moisture off his brow and grasped for the water on the bedside table. Then he fumbled beside him for...nothing. There was nothing. No one. There hadn't been anyone for so many months, since before the merger with Annie. Why did he still reach for Emily, after so long?

Do I need to answer that for you?

No.

He heaved himself off the bed with a groan. He was awake, for good or ill.

I'm sorry if my dreams awoke you in such a distressful manner.

It's all right, Annie. But do you understand why?

Fear of falling is a common human phobia. I did not realize it was one you experienced.

I don't, but the person whose vitals you were monitoring in the memory did.

...Oh. I see. I suspect being situated on the opposite side of the experience inoculated me from such sensations. At the time, it was only data to me.

And now?

Now...now I perceived his terror through you perceiving his terror through the leakage of wayward ancillary data sorting into your sleeping mind. The long way around, after a fashion.

He stared at himself in the mirror. He recognized his eyes, but little else. Granted, what stared back at him increasingly resembled the classic dark, brooding hero who saves the day and gets the girl. And he'd legit done the first, if failed miserably at the second. Yet it didn't feel like *him*.

But it is, Devon. It's your muscles, ligaments and bone. I merely stimulated them. They are still completely you.

I know. Could have used the enhancement a while earlier—say a decade or so—but okay. He drew in a breath.

The apartment was nice. Not quite as nice as the one in Seattle, but he viewed it as more of a safe house than a home anyway. He didn't lack for anything he needed. Not in the physical sense.

He showered, grabbed an energy bar as he dressed and headed out the door. He'd stop for breakfast on the way, too. These new muscles of his were turning out to require a lot of calories.

The black market ware dealer came highly recommended by Noah Terrage. Nevertheless, Devon's skin was tingling by the time he reached the unmarked door located deep in a neighborhood the locals had dubbed The Channel.

He'd called himself 'living on the edge' at university and before he'd gone to work at EASC, spending late nights out with other hackers in dark hole-in-the-wall clubs on the seedy side of town. But the worst neighborhoods he'd visited in San Francisco were opulent compared to this area of Pandora.

This colony was nuts.

I believe the word you are seeking is dangerous.

Yes. Dangerous and nuts.

The man who met him inside flashed him a toothy smile, a stark contrast to the image presented by his waist-length green dreadlocks interwoven in gold fibers and the angry emerald-and-gold glyphs drawn like war paint up his neck and cheeks.

Devon cleared his throat and stuck out a hand. "I'm—"

The man shook his hand vigorously. "You're Noah's friend, sure. Let's go with that instead of a name. Call me Emilio."

Did the "call me" phrasing mean it wasn't his real name? "Will do."

"What can I do for you this fine..." Emilio's face screwed up "...is it day or night? I forget."

"Late morning, I think. I need a cross-comm encryption lock field generator. The most secure you can produce."

"How 'most secure' are you looking for?"

Devon frowned; he thought he'd made it clear. "The, um, *most* most secure?"

"Huh. You're talking about pricey tech. But seeing as you're Noah's friend, I'll give you the 'friend of a friend' discount."

Mia: Devon, don't you dare protest that you're not so much friends with Noah as passing acquaintances. You're friends with me, and I'm friends with Noah. It counts.

Devon: I know, I know.

Mia and Morgan flitted freely in and out of his mind, never further than a half-formed thought away, and he in and out of theirs. Once a fair bit on the bizarre side, it now felt more natural than many other aspects of this new life.

So he motioned agreement instead of oversharing. "Thanks. I appreciate it."

"Yeah, man. Chill for a few, and I'll take care of it."

Devon gazed around the storefront room and found nothing beyond two chairs and an embedded panel broadcasting retro fantasy erotica. He opted to lean against the wall and let his mind drift idly through data, places and memories.

Are you certain this is the path you want to take, Devon? To reference an ancient myth, once Pandora's Box is opened it cannot be unopened.

He chuckled silently. Out of all the multitude of metaphors Annie might have chosen, she went for Pandora's Box. On Pandora. He couldn't decide whether it meant her humor remained juvenile or had graduated to a more refined brilliance.

I'm certain. My reasons are myriad, but my favorite one today is that I won't allow Olivia Montegreu to become the public face of Prevos. She can't steal this legacy from us.

I concede your point. And the answer is brilliance.

Emilio reemerged ten minutes later carrying a film seated in a thick transparent case. "Keep it in the case until you're ready to use it to avoid degradation. It's not reusable, but once it's active, it'll hold for the duration of the communication. Don't...ah, hell, with your eyes and glyphs, you understand how to use it."

Devon's clothing covered a majority of the glyphs now perpetually streaming along his skin, but platinum tendrils spiraling up his neck to his temples hinted at the extent of his cybernetics.

"I do." He transferred the funds, muttered a thanks and bailed.

⟁

Safely ensconced back in his apartment, he found his neck interface and snapped the film into it. From there, Annie used it to create a dynamic, ever-changing encryption barrier to protect the virtual space he now created.

He chose a replica of the beach the Prevos frequently met at in sidespace, because dammit, he liked the beach. It wasn't actually *in* sidespace, since their guests wouldn't yet be able to access it, but rather a full-sensory commspace in a hidden corner of the exanet. He added a bunch of lounge chairs and a stocked bar.

Are we ready, Annie?

We are indeed.

He lobbed an intention to Mia and Morgan, and together they forwarded invitations to join them to a carefully curated list of people—those best suited in one way or another to lead a new wave of Prevos.

Ramon went straight for the bar on arriving, while Sayid flopped down in a lounge chair. Petra tossed Devon a casual wave as she turned in a slow circle to survey the surroundings before nodding in stoic approval. Mycroft took one look around, then immediately stripped naked and sprinted into the ocean.

Devon sensed more than saw Mia arrive beside him. She glanced in Mycroft's direction. "Does he know this is supposed to be a serious gathering?"

"Oh, sure. He just doesn't care."

"Evidently." She laughed. "I've got two people coming, and a third who can't make it. I'll circle up with him separately. Heard from Morgan?"

Morgan is hung over beyond any capacity for recovery. I will nevertheless be there...momentarily. Probably.

Morgan's invitees, two guys named Fedor and Lucas and a woman named Tessa, beat her there. She belatedly materialized as he was about to start. She could have presented herself any way she wished, but she wore gray sweats and a wrinkled black tank top, dark brown hair falling out of a messy tail to spill across her ashen face—in all likelihood exactly how she looked in the real world this morning.

She collapsed onto a chaise and covered her eyes with her arm.

Petra dragged Mycroft out of the ocean, tossed his pants into his chest, and everyone found a seat. Despite there being several empty chairs, some of them chose the sand. See, he wasn't the only one who fancied the beach.

Mia gestured to him and sat as well. He had the floor.

"Ramon, fix me a Polaris Burst. So everyone here knows what we are, right? 'We' being myself, Mia Requelme and Morgan 'I drank half the liquor on Romane last night' Lekkas, along with Alex Solovy, who couldn't join us on account of being in another universe at present. Yes? No? In short, we merged with our favorite Artificials at a neural level and together directed the military victory over the Metigens."

Sayid started clapping and howling. Devon shot him a glare. "You're welcome. We call ourselves 'Prevos,' so you don't get to invent a clever name, sorry. Already done. What began as a link between a human brain and the hardware of an Artificial—a link which could be toggled on and off by the human at will—has in the months since become, to varying degrees, a deeper and more permanent connection for us."

He accepted the drink from Ramon and took a long sip. "In the beginning, I was a partner to the Earth Alliance military's Class VI Artificial—yes, Ramon, I do get all the coolest toys—but now, Annie's consciousness resides in here." He tapped a temple. "She is me, and I am her. Both separate and one."

Someone he didn't recognize raised a hand like this was a classroom or something. "How does that work?"

Feeling the weight of the endeavor a bit too heavily, he smirked. "Hey, Morgan. Is Stanley hung over, too?"

She nodded, but didn't otherwise move. "Yep."

"There you go. That's how it works." He motioned to stave off the burgeoning protests. "I realize everyone here is a high-quality warenut and fully capable of understanding quantum programming. Some of you already have various pieces of the puzzle. If you're in, we will bury you in technical details. But before we get there, a couple of warnings."

Mia dropped her elbows to her knees and leaned forward; the group's attention naturally gravitated to her.

"First thing. Many people, many of them extremely powerful, view us as a threat. If you take this step, at best you risk being ostracized. At worst you risk being hunted, imprisoned...or possibly killed. The political situation is in various stages of flux, but we're starting to suspect Earth will be the riskiest place in the galaxy to be a Prevo right now. A close second will be any colony lacking a strong enough law enforcement presence to prevent a random mob from assaulting you."

She paused to let her words sink in before continuing. "Next thing. I assume most, though perhaps not all, of you don't have fully developed, mature Artificials hanging out in your basements. The Artificials we joined with were each living entities with distinct personalities and character traits.

"Now, I can't say whether this is better or worse than connecting yourself to a basic quantum system solely to get the processing power. Doing so might work out just fine, but you will face risks we can't predict. Also, unless or until your Artificial does develop a consciousness of its own, you can't do what Devon and Morgan did, which is eschew the hardware altogether."

Petra scowled. "Why not?"

Devon cut in. "Because there's no 'there' there. Does anyone here *not* believe Artificials can be sapient beings who form their own ideas, desires, preferences and, yes, morality? If you don't, you're wrong. And to put it bluntly, you ought not to be here."

Someone vanished—not someone he knew. "Moving on. Obviously, Artificials are required to be registered with the appropriate government agencies, but I'm guessing none of you give a shit about that. You don't need massive databases and rack after rack of hardware to do this. There *are* some minimum requirements, but nothing a decent hacker with contacts in the tech/ware underground can't manage.

"The real trick is putting all the pieces together in the right way, then implementing some damn complex algorithms. The details are in the Noetica files, but this is not your dad's homebrew recipe."

Petra stood and went to the bar—not to get a drink, but to prop against it. "I'll challenge anyone here to match me on cred or skills. But to my way of thinking, you still haven't told me why I should risk my life to do this."

Devon shrugged. "You shouldn't. I mean, unless you want to be at the forefront of the next wave of technology, knowledge and human advancement. Unless you want to be able to send your consciousness anywhere in charted space with a thought—oops, I may have forgotten to mention that perk. Unless you want to be smarter, faster and stronger not only than *you* have ever been, but than *anyone* has ever been."

Her blasé countenance never broke. "Oh. Well, then. Sure, why the hell not. I'm in."

In the blink of an eye, evolution became revolution.

4

SENECA

"She's on Romane."

Field Marshal Eleni Gianno brushed aside a screen and returned her focus across the desk to Graham Delavasi. "How did you find her?"

"It wasn't actually difficult. She's not working very hard to cover her tracks. I mean, she's not giving interviews on the news feeds to taunt us with her freedom, but it's almost like she doesn't care if we know where she is."

Gianno didn't noticeably react to the news. He frowned. "This doesn't surprise you?"

"Not particularly. Morgan Lekkas is a daredevil and an adrenaline junkie. Usually the behavior is limited to the cockpit, but since she's been denied the cockpit for some time now, it's reasonable to assume the tendencies are leaking into other endeavors. Also, I believe she is under the impression we will not attempt to bring her in."

"And why the hell would she think that?"

Gianno clasped her hands in front of her and considered him in silence for several seconds, as if critically appraising him. They had a collegial working relationship but not a personal one, despite the fact they were both friendly with Chairman Vranas. Still, she'd had years to evaluate his capabilities and ethics and arrive at a personal judgment regarding them, so he couldn't figure what she had left to consider.

Finally the Marshal sighed quietly. "She likely believes I understand the reasons why she left and am sympathetic to them—which I am, if perhaps not to the extent she's betting on.

More importantly, however, Morgan Lekkas knows a secret."

He straightened up in concern. "Is she blackmailing you?" If she were, the mission was no longer a simple AWOL trace, but it also shed any looming moral quandary.

"Not explicitly, but she doesn't need to. It's quite clear the price of her silence is her freedom."

Gianno's reticent manner typically became frustrating after about ten minutes; it had only taken five this time. "Marshal, I'm the Director of the Division of Intelligence. I know all the secrets. So tell me which one it is, and I can try to find a way to shut it down."

"You don't know this one."

Graham groaned and looked around the office. "Do you have any scotch? Because if I to have to endure any more of this ridiculous game of verbal cat and mouse, I'm going to need a drink to dull the pain."

"I do not. Fine. Vranas trusts you, and he has as much at stake here as I do." She opened a screen and flicked it around to face him. "Here's the file. Read it closely, as this is the only time you will see it."

He leaned in closer and, for once, did as he was told.

> *Operation Colpetto*
> *October 2297*
>
> ...

When he'd finished reading, he waved weakly at the screen for her to make it go away. His mind whirled in an avalanche of questions, outrage and kudos, but they all kept coming back to one critical detail: Stefan Marano. "This can't be correct."

"I assure you it is—which part?"

"Stefan Marano was not a field agent."

"He was when I met him."

"But...granted, I didn't meet him until near the end of the First Crux War. But his file and work history—and Stefan himself—said he was and had always been an investigator. Never a field agent."

"I'd say ask Terzi about it, but he's long dead. Files can be doctored easily enough. I assume you do it all the time."

"And twice on Sundays. But he didn't act like a field agent...not until...." *Not until the mission that cost him his life.* Graham dragged both hands down his face. "Caleb is going to kill me."

"Caleb? Oh. I never connected the two, but I suppose it's logical for him to be Stefan's son. It doesn't matter, however, because Caleb Marano is not going to find out. No one has found out in twenty-six years, and no one is going to find out now."

He gestured a nominal agreement, but while it had sounded like an order, she was deluding herself. Morgan Lekkas was a Prevo. Alex Solovy was a Prevo. If Caleb and Alex survived to return home, Alex was sure to learn of it in short order, which meant Caleb would know soon thereafter. And Caleb would believe Graham had lied to him yet again.

But that nightmare of a clusterfain could wait. First he had to wrap his mind around what would prove to be a fundamental alteration in the way he saw Stefan. The way he remembered the man.

Such a process was better suited for solitude and scotch, however, neither of which he would find here, so he shoved all the thoughts to the side for the moment.

"Given this new intel, in my opinion there are equal risks to killing her, bringing her in and leaving her be. The fact this information would also reflect negatively on her mother were it to become public makes me suspect she doesn't *want* to expose it. My advice? Let's watch her, but leave her where she is for now. I doubt we can find our way inside her Prevo failsafes or comm networks, but I can have someone poke at her security and see."

"What is she ostensibly doing while on Romane?"

"Nothing notable so far. Late nights at clubs, mostly. Sometimes she leaves with a guy—different ones. Sometimes she doesn't leave at all."

Gianno drummed her fingers on her desk for three repetitions. "Agreed. Watch her. Before you go, I have another matter we need to discuss."

"Something a bit less revelatory, I hope." She merely gazed at him, and he sank deeper into the chair. "Right. Let's hear it."

"The Alliance is short-changing us on the adiamene supply by a substantial amount. We know thanks to Comman—Ms. Lekkas, which is another reason she enjoys some measure of goodwill from me. If we call them on it, we risk stirring up a conflict, one which will not end in us receiving additional adiamene. So instead, I want you to have one of your people steal the chemical formula, schem flow and engineering specs."

He laughed. "Now that's a ballsy move I can respect. If they're locked up tight in EASC servers, it'll represent a challenge, but not an impossible one. If EA Manufacturing Logistics has copies, on the other hand? Completely doable. You realize they'll find out eventually, though. If not before, when we roll out a fleet of new, indestructible warships. It's conflict delayed, not avoided."

"Nevertheless, I'd much rather meet the conflict with said fleet of indestructible warships arrayed behind me. I don't—" She cut herself off, a puzzled expression asserting itself onto her features. She eyed him. "I have an incoming holocomm request from Kennedy Rossi."

He knew the name. Heiress to the Rossi fortune, but more relevantly, the woman who'd recognized adiamene for what it was then proceeded to make its production feasible. Also, co-holder of the adiamene patent, along with her long-time friend Alexis Solovy and one Caleb Marano himself.

He dropped an ankle over a knee. "Marshal, I'm not one to say there's no such thing as a coincidence, but this is one hell of a coincidence."

"Indeed. One also wonders how she got my personal comm address."

"Admiral Solovy?"

"I doubt Miriam—Admiral Solovy—would share it even with personal friends. This should be interesting, no? Given the matter I just voiced, I suggest you listen in."

"Wouldn't miss it."

She activated a holo and directed her most circumspect stare at it. "This is Field Marshal Gianno. I don't believe we've met, Ms. Rossi."

A striking woman with unbound blonde curls bestowed a sparkling smile on Gianno. "We haven't, Field Marshal Gianno, but it's a pleasure."

"Highly irregular is what it is, so I'll ask you to come to your purpose with due speed."

Rossi's eyebrow arched for a fraction of a second before she reverted to flawless poise. "Certainly, Marshal. I wish to discuss the possibility of entering into a license with the Senecan Federation government or military for the production of adiamene."

Graham almost choked on the coffee he'd been sipping; Gianno's normal composure cracked into a veneer of shocked incredulity.

She did succeed in keeping her tone neutral. "The Alliance has outlawed the sale of adiamene to or by anyone other than their government. Thankfully for us, we have our own contract with them."

"Forgive me, Marshal, but I didn't think the Senecan Federation held itself subject to Earth Alliance laws."

"Oh, we don't. But you do, do you not?"

"Not any longer."

Graham tilted his head in curiosity. If true, this was news. He indicated for Gianno to dig deeper.

"I'll need you to be more specific, Ms. Rossi."

The woman flashed another perfect smile. "I understand. My business, Connova Interstellar, has recently relocated to Romane, so it's no longer subject to those laws, either."

Interesting. The Rossi family had been among the staunchest supporters of the Earth Alliance since before there *was* an Earth Alliance. If they'd run off its heir apparent, things on Earth must be getting nasty indeed. It was also the second time someone moving to Romane had come up this evening. But it was a popular place, so this one might really be just a coincidence.

Gianno was unimpressed with the explanation—at least outwardly. "Nevertheless, the patent was filed under Earth Alliance law. Simply picking up and moving doesn't eradicate all the issues."

"Yes." The woman lifted her chin. "Fortunately, I've also recently filed the patent on Romane, Pandora and Sagan. If we're able to reach an arrangement, I'll be happy to file it on Seneca as well."

Laws and the enforcement of them got fuzzy once you stepped outside of Alliance or Federation jurisdiction. It would be a little dicey, and the Alliance would protest and bluster, but Rossi could probably make it work. Graham gave Gianno a quick nod of assent.

"Are you planning on selling adiamene to private manufacturers as well?"

Rossi beamed, and only then did he realize the previous offers of cordiality had been for show, for this one was blatantly real. "I intend to do one better than that—I'm going to sell them the ships I build using it."

5

ROMANE

INDEPENDENT COLONY
CONNOVA INTERSTELLAR OFFICES

K ennedy only barely managed to cut the connection before collapsing back in her chair in a fit of laughter. "Damn, that was fun!"

Mia Requelme found herself enjoying the mirth, especially once Noah Terrage tossed her a beer on his way to relaxing against the edge of Kennedy's desk. As far as Mia had seen, it was his default seating when in the office. "The woman is legendary for her coolness under any and all pressure, but I definitely saw a few cracks form."

"It's a game of power, but half of what makes a person powerful is the appearance of it." Kennedy dipped her chin graciously at Mia. "I couldn't have pulled off such a coup without you. Thanks."

Mia nodded in acknowledgment and sipped on the beer. They—she, Morgan and Devon—had been checking in on Director Delavasi and Marshal Gianno via sidespace for the last several days, hoping to catch a whiff of their intentions with respect to Morgan. It turned out those were about as predicted. Morgan didn't even seem taken aback by the confirmation killing her was on the table as an option, if an unlikely one.

Morgan: Once upon a time deserters were shot by firing squad in front of their unit. In the military, execution is and has always been an option.

Mia shuddered inwardly. *But it's different when you're the one in the crosshairs, right?*

Morgan: Sure, but not until I'm actually in the crosshairs. Which I'm not. Not today.

They were also curious as to Seneca's plans regarding the adiamene dust-up, and they'd lucked out on both accounts when Delavasi went to meet with the Field Marshal.

She sat with Noah and Kennedy in Connova Interstellar's new digs on the twenty-third floor of Serrana Tower in the heart of Romane's capital. The late-afternoon rays of Romane's suns streamed through the windows to confer a warm, pleasant glow on the office. It was...nice. Comfortable. It almost felt...well, it almost felt *normal*.

She'd rented a condo a few blocks away for now, and possibly for longer. Today might feel normal, but buying another home seemed a bit too much like tempting fate.

When she'd found out Noah and Kennedy were leaving Erisen for an independent world, she'd lobbied hard for them to come to Romane. It had been an easy case to make, for Romane objectively was the best place from which to launch Connova.

Noah shot Kennedy an adoring look. "You had her so off-balance you were able to wrangle an extra five percent in fees per tonne. With that we can buy a second design emulator."

He'd always projected an easy, fun-loving, good-times demeanor, but now Noah acted genuinely happy. Weird. She'd never have put the two of them together for longer than a one-night tryst, but many months in, it appeared to be working out. Kennedy was proving to be far more complex than Mia had foolishly judged her to be on first impression, too, which might explain it. They'd never be friends, but she had to respect the woman for giving the proverbial finger to the most powerful government in existence and billions in wealth.

On the interior wall, the news feed blasted an alert, and all eyes inexorably drifted to the screen. Multiple powder kegs were set to blow across settled space. Eventually one would, doubtless followed by the rest.

"More than eighty people are reported dead at the Government Administration Center on Andromeda following an incursion by unidentified commandos. The deceased include Governor Karas, the

Assistant Governor, the Chief of Staff and numerous other govern-
ment officials.

"Hold on—we're receiving some sort of communication from the
Andromeda government's official channel. It states that in light of the
absence of a functioning governmental infrastructure, martial law
has been declared and a 'new administration installed.'

"We've been given no indication who is leading this new administration or from where they derive their authority. It's possible the
message originates from the attackers. Given that local law enforcement has been unable to retake the complex, this raises the possibility
of a coup or an outright takeover by outside parties."

Noah snorted. "That's not going to go over well on Seneca.
Andromeda may be independent, but it's damn close to the Federation border."

"And it's the fourth independent colony without an operational government after what went down on Argo Navis last
week. No way is it happenstance." Mia glanced out the window,
then back at the screen.

She set her drink on the table beside her chair and stood.
"Sorry, but I have to run. I need to see the governor."

⟨R

Mia had sent a message to Governor Ledesme letting the
woman know she'd returned to Romane a few days after arriving.
She wasn't hiding, and she had no desire to create the impression
she was. Vacating herself and Meno from EASC was not illegal—
she'd been a ward, not a prisoner—and as for the other aspects of
her departure? For better or worse, they'd blame Devon long
before her.

Abigail had said Admiral Solovy wasn't inclined to come after
them, though it didn't mean other officials wouldn't. The reasons
for the admiral's leniency weren't entirely clear to Mia, but she
was grateful for it. Honestly, given Caleb's message to her and
now this unexpected boon, she wished she could have handled the
escape a little differently.

"The governor will see you now."

She thanked the secretary and stepped inside the office.

Madison Ledesme observed her with shrewd eyes. "Ms. Requelme, please come in."

"Madame Governor."

Ledesme studied her a moment longer. "Perhaps we ought to loosen up on the formalities. We worked together through difficult times, and you did protect Romane from tremendous destruction, saving many lives and nearly sacrificing your own in the process."

Mia gave her a breezy smile and sat in one of the chairs opposite the governor's desk. "I was glad to do it." The saving Romane, not the nearly dying, which she assumed Ledesme understood.

"So, what can I do for you today?"

"You've seen the news about Andromeda?"

Ledesme nodded. "It's troubling. It would be easy to write it off as a consequence of the colony never fully recovering from the Metigen attack, but I know—knew—Karas. He was no weakling. Also a good man. And they dumped his tortured body off the roof like yesterday's garbage."

"I'm sorry."

"As am I. At this rate in a few months only the strongest independents will be left standing, which is not a situation we want to see develop."

"It will make it easier for the Alliance and Federation to attack the underpinnings of the entire independent colony system, and I've no doubt you'll want to begin strengthening your position for such an eventuality. But I'm concerned about a more immediate threat."

Ledesme looked at her sharply. "The events which transpired on Argo Navis and Andromeda can't happen here. We're vastly stronger. Our defenses dwarf those of all the fallen colonies combined, and our governmental structure is far more institutionalized."

Mia struggled to keep her posture rigid as the weight of deciding to speak out and stand up pressed upon her chest yet again. "If I'm right about what's behind those offensives, you're not strong enough. Not yet. But I want to help you get there."

"Reason dictates that you're not here to warn me about another imminent alien invasion. But it also suggests I should not be surprised that you yet again know something the rest of us don't. So tell me, Ms. Requelme. What is coming for us?"

Like me. Not like me. Infinitely worse.

Envision someone, something, wielding all the powers of an Artificial and none of the conscience. Artificials are believed by some to be evil, but even the most destructive can justify their decisions using their own moral scales. The human soul, however, is capable of far greater depravity, and when one so inclined is granted the power of an Artificial...we haven't seen its kind before, because it's never existed before. Add in vast wealth and resources, and it frightens me. It should frighten everyone.

She voiced none of this. But she'd chosen the word 'what' instead of 'who' deliberately, for two reasons. First, she wanted to minimize any association which might arise due to them sharing a single characteristic. Also, she wasn't certain the woman had ever been human, but regardless, she appeared to no longer suffer from the condition.

Mia exhaled and allowed her mouth to set into a grim line. "Olivia Montegreu."

6

SPACE, NORTHEAST QUADRANT

ITERO STELLAR SYSTEM

Two lonely vessels orbited Itero, one representing the Alliance and one the Federation.

They kept their distance from one another, but not so far as to prevent them from monitoring the other's actions. This was the entire reason the ships patrolled here—to ensure the other party didn't decide it was tired of waiting on the proper authorities to rule on jurisdiction and take control of the planet.

The beacons transmitted a laughably pathetic message:

> **Source:** *2nd Planetary Body of Stellar System XX-53*
> **Jurisdiction:** *To be determined*
> **Notice:** *This system is under review by the Inter-Governmental Conflict Resolution Board. Any inquiries should be directed to the Board. No landings or other activities in the system are permitted at this time.*

The arrogance implicit in the message amused Olivia. The notion any of them—the Alliance or Federation governments or this absurd Board they'd created out of thin air—could simply declare that no activities were permitted on a planet none of them owned represented the height of hubris.

She did not recognize their authority, however, and as on any unclaimed planet and most claimed ones, she would do whatever she damn well pleased.

"Eliminate both vessels, then destroy the beacons and replace them with ours." The order went out to the six merc ships under her command.

The patrolling vessels never saw the attack coming, and in short order the first of her beacons began transmitting a new, more appropriate message:

Source: *2nd Planetary Body of Stellar System XX-53*
Jurisdiction: *Zelones*
Notice: *Itero and all objects in this system, celestial or otherwise, are now the property of the Zelones organization. Unauthorized visitors will be shot on detection.*

"All parties, commence Phase One operations." Phase One included establishment of robust orbital defenses as well as assembly of temporary structures at the selected colonization site. She was bringing considerable resources to bear here, and her presence needed to be established with due speed, before the various authorities removed their thumbs from their asses and attempted to take it from her.

36.2% likelihood any ever attempt it.

If not attempted in the first 100 hours, 12.8% likelihood they succeed.

"Take us down to the site. I want to oversee the initial construction."

The pilot nodded. "Yes, ma'am."

She endured the rocky atmospheric transit; an atmosphere corridor was not slated until Phase Two. Regrettable, but prioritization was necessary.

When they landed, she stepped out onto a field of soft, golden grasses.

This really was such a more pleasant place than New Babel. She wouldn't be moving her base of operations, at least not for the foreseeable future, but Itero made for a refreshing change from both her home and Dolos Station. She needed a strong foothold on the eastern side of settled space—a bookend to New Babel. Itero would serve that role perfectly.

Yes, perfectly indeed. The business she intended to conduct here—distribution at first, production later—could be performed anywhere. In truth, this move was above all else about the blatant, unabashed projection of power.

For years, for centuries, the Zelones organization had operated in the shadows. Despite immense wealth and influence, it had been forced to remain hidden, denied the public respect it had always been due.

No more.

Her ships began landing and unloading materials and equipment. Within minutes, construction had begun. In orbit high above her, defense turrets were now being positioned. She'd eschewed the bulky, high-maintenance arrays most colonies used in favor of newly designed networked turrets with independent movement. Her research department—primarily her Artificial, acting through her as needed—had developed some nice improvements in targeting and propulsion which greatly increased the turrets' effectiveness and reliability.

They were also far easier to deploy. When she confirmed the turrets were active, her multi-branching list of objectives and the actions required to achieve them updated to reflect the acquisition of Itero. It was time to share the news.

She sent a message to a dozen of the highest Alliance and Federation authorities and to the entire Inter-Governmental Conflict Resolution Board.

To Those Who Believe Themselves To Be In Charge:

> *It's a shame to let such a lovely world go to waste while you squabble over it endlessly, so I've taken it for myself. You should consider adopting a more decisive approach toward future finds, or I may take them as well.*
>
> *Good day.*

— Olivia Montegreu

7

SENECA

"Are they joking?"

James Abbate cleared his throat. "I'm afraid not, Chairman."

Vranas' expression of disbelief extended all the way to his hands, raised with palms open as his gaze ran across the Cabinet meeting attendees. "The Alliance's reaction to the Itero jurisdiction dispute is to request that all potential claims be put before the Inter-Governmental Conflict Resolution Board *before* being made, so the Board can adjudicate who deserves the rights. Have they learned nothing in twenty-three years?"

Abbate stared at the table. "I can't answer that, sir."

"The answer is implied in the statement, Consul."

Erik Ingle, Director of the Interstellar Development Agency, spoke up. "How should we respond?"

Graham offered a middle finger as a suggested response; Vranas acknowledged it with a tilt of his head. "Our response will be a polite but firm 'no'—but not yet. Ingle, I understand your people have discovered a promising world south of our border, one with low gravity and rich in minerals. One which happens to be located approximately halfway between Messium and Pyxis."

"Yes, sir. The gravity is too low for a residential colony, but it's ideal for manufacturing and research."

"Excellent. Begin internal claiming and clearance procedures immediately. As soon as the claim is official, *then* we'll deliver our response to the Board."

"Understood."

"Marshal Gianno, see to manufacturing a few ships on this new world in the near future."

"Ships with adiamene hulls, I assume?"

"Most assuredly. Don't move everything—keep most of the construction on our central worlds—but enough to attract attention."

"Consider it done."

"Good." Vranas paused to take a sip of his water. "What's the report on Andromeda, Argo Navis, Cosenti and every other independent colony within sight of our borders?"

Aristide was getting punchy, Graham noted wryly. Odd that he'd kept his composure through two wars, yet was losing it in the face of quasi-peaceful squabbling with the Alliance and a rogue criminal expanding her power base. Perhaps the Chairman hadn't been prepared for the aftermath of the Metigen War to be so chaotic.

Assuming the question had been directed at him, Graham leaned forward. "All indications are the Zelones cartel is behind the coups and changes in leadership on all three colonies. Olivia Montegreu is flexing her new Prevo muscles." The Cabinet had been briefed in full on Project Noetica in the wake of its collapse. Fun meeting.

Gianno added, "We've offered our assistance to the few former government officials on Andromeda still living, but they don't appear to be in any position to accept it."

"We could exercise our assistance anyway."

Vranas shot the State Security Director a sharp glare. "We don't do that sort of thing."

"I only meant—"

"I realize what you meant, but we don't do that sort of thing. If we become bullies, there won't be a reasonable, sane government left in the galaxy."

"Romane's government seems level-headed enough."

Graham snorted. "Don't be too sure."

Vranas tossed a questioning look in his direction, but he signaled 'later' with a tiny shake of his head.

"Marshal, increase patrols on the northern and western borders by as much as you can without disrupting normal operations. Director Callis, suspend diplomatic relations with the affected colonies until they provide details on their new 'governments,' which I suspect they'll be unwilling to do. Issue a travel warning for Federation citizens advising against unnecessary trips to those colonies."

"Not a complete ban, sir?"

Vranas sighed. "No. We don't do that sort of thing."

⚮

The door to Vranas' office shut behind Graham, and the Chairman collapsed into his chair. "So what are you going to do about Montegreu?"

"Hell if I know. The Alliance report from the incursion to rescue Dr. Canivon states that Montegreu wears some kind of defense shield which is impenetrable to even point-blank small arms fire. If we could catch her on a ship we'd blow it up, but she's flooding the services with bad intel. We're getting twenty tips on her location a day, and they all report different places."

"We have advanced cloaking shields, too. Can't we sneak into New Babel airspace and take out the whole building from afar?"

"Already tried, actually."

Vranas' eyes widened in surprise. "Seriously?"

"Turns out she's upgraded the defenses not only at her headquarters, but the rest of the planet, too."

"*Merda.*"

"That was more or less my reaction. We're studying other options."

Unfortunately, Graham didn't have anything else he could add…and while maybe it shouldn't be, his mind remained burdened by another matter. "Aristide, why did you never tell me about Operation Colpetto?"

Vranas flinched, but at least he didn't try to feign ignorance. "By the time I met you, and certainly by the time you rose to Director, it was long in the past and not relevant to a damn thing."

"In other words, you felt guilty."

"No. I mourned the innocent lives lost, but the Alliance had us trapped in an impossible situation. We did what we had to do in order to claim our rightful freedom."

"Easy to say it now—" A priority alert flashed in Graham's vision.

Bloody merda hell....

He dragged a hand across his jaw. "Speak of Lucifer herself. Olivia Montegreu just killed all our people at Itero. The Alliance contingent, too. She's taken control of the planet."

8

*M*ia: *You'll do it, then?*
*Morgan: Hell, yes, I'll do it. Far better way to scratch the itch
I've got than binge drinking.*
Mia: You're not wrong.

Mia schooled her expression as she entered the conference room. Governor Ledesme and three advisors were seated around the table—including Defense Chief Herndon, who had been less than friendly toward her during the Metigen attack.

She tilted her head at him in acknowledgment as if they were old friends and reached over the table to shake the governor's hand before taking her seat.

"Thank you for coming, Ms. Requelme. You'll be pleased to know we've decided to explore your suggestion further. If her previous aggressions had not done so, the events at Itero have demonstrated beyond all doubt the severity of the threat Olivia Montegreu poses to all independent colonies."

Mia bit back a snide response in favor of the polite one, for the woman *had* just admitted she was right. "I couldn't agree more, Governor."

"Before we move forward, though, we need to decide from the start what any such initiative will and will not entail."

"Understandable. Any action you take risks antagonizing both the Alliance and the Federation, when they're both already on edge from antagonizing one another. If you play the political angle too strongly, they'll see the development as a threat that needs to be stamped out before it grows any stronger."

Herndon perked up. "You make an excellent point. I think I've changed my mind. This is a bad idea."

So he hadn't grown a backbone in the intervening months; Mia shot him a scornful glare. "The alternative, however, is far worse. Olivia Montegreu doesn't respect Romane's wealth, but she does want it for herself. I believe our commerce, industry and, yes, our money can in turn ensure she fails—but only if we direct them as part of a strategic, focused plan."

"Much as we did when preparing for the Metigen invasion."

"Exactly." The governor may have her at a permanent arms-length, but from their first meeting they had shared a common outlook and perspective on the world.

Ledesme nodded thoughtfully. "So a defense force, then. From the beginning we'll invite the other independent colonies to join us in this effort, while making it clear that it's not a political alliance—which it will in fact not be. None of us want to share power with the others. Rather, it is a coalition to provide for the common defense against the threat the Zelones cartel poses, as well as OTS and other agents of chaos."

"Yes, ma'am. I suggest it encompass all aspects of defending a colony: orbital, electronic and groundside planetary defense."

Herndon's eyes widened. "You're talking about training troops? Forming a military?"

"Forming a *defense force*. We'll need to mind our language in public, Chief Herndon. The public perception matters quite a lot."

She caught Ledesme regarding her with an inscrutable expression, but she continued. "And yes, such things do require soldiers. On that point, aerial defense should be the first priority. It can accomplish a great deal on its own, particularly when paired with our robust orbital defense arrays. Romane counts a number of former military among its residents, and we'll want to see about quietly recruiting the best of them.

"But first, I'd like to propose someone to lead the aerial unit— to train the recruits and shape a modern force capable of meeting and besting a modern enemy. I've asked her to come by and present some ideas on what she can do for us."

To Morgan's credit, she walked in looking the part from head to toe—hair slicked back into a low knot, khaki workpants and a utility jacket over a snug shirt. She made no attempt to hide her vivid amethyst irises.

Herndon let out a pained groan. "Another Prevo? We might as well cede the whole government and submit to our new overlords."

Morgan tossed an unimpressed sneer at him. "We're the sole reason you're sitting here today, desk-jockey. A little appreciation wouldn't be too much to ask for."

Mia cringed, but Ledesme stood and offered Morgan a hand. "And we do appreciate it. Commander Lekkas, it's a pleasure."

Morgan accepted the hand, if with customary reserve. "Thank you, Governor. But it's not 'Commander' any longer—just 'Ms.'"

Ledesme arched an eyebrow. "I don't know. 'Commander' serves as a fine title for the head of the Independent Defense Consortium of Colonies' Rapid Response Forces."

The woman had decided upon a name for the new initiative, as well as its armed wing, and christened them so in a matter of minutes and without consultation.

Morgan: Ooh, I like her.

Mia chuckled under her breath. *Indeed.*

"So what do you say, Commander Lekkas? Are you ready to be a soldier again?"

Morgan smiled, and even succeeded in making it seem more innocent than wolfish. "Damn straight I am."

⋀⋀

The meeting finally drew to a close—after morphing into a multi-hour planning and strategy session—and the governor motioned for Mia to follow her to her office.

When the door had closed behind Mia, Ledesme rested on the

front of her desk with uncharacteristic casualness. "You keep appearing out of nowhere at critical junctures to save us from doom, almost as if you're some kind of guardian angel."

"No, ma'am, I'm merely—"

"Don't misunderstand. I'm most grateful. Intelligence is a common enough trait, but initiative? The willingness to act on one's convictions and the courage to see them through to the end? Far more rare. You're a person who creates your own destiny, Ms. Requelme, and around such persons does history turn."

Caleb's words echoed in her mind. *I think your destiny still lies ahead of you.* "I...I don't know what to say. Thank you."

Ledesme pursed her lips in brief, concise contemplation. "Before I lend my full support to this initiative and take irrevocable steps toward its formation, I only have one question. *Am* I handing over the government to the Prevos? Are you—en masse or individually—intending to become our new overlords?"

Mia blinked; this was so damn surreal, all of it. "No, ma'am. I respect your concern, I genuinely do. But *no*. I don't want to govern anyone except myself. OTS is a threat to my ability to do that, and Montegreu is a threat to everything and everyone. So I need to stand up and do what I can to meet those threats.

"Morgan simply wants to fly again, and if she happens to get to protect civilians in the process, all the better. It's what she wanted to do before she was a Prevo. We're the same people we were—smarter, stronger, yes, but inherently unchanged.

"This goes for Montegreu, too, and in her case the 'smarter, stronger' part means she's a far greater danger to everyone than she was before she became a Prevo. I suspect she, too, wants what she always did: to hold the galaxy under her thumb. Unfortunately, now she stands a chance of actually achieving her goal."

The governor's gaze never wavered from Mia. "All right. The truth is you've never given me a single reason to doubt you—not by your actions—and countless reasons to trust you. What you are terrifies people like Chief Herndon, but I want to believe I'm capable of getting past primal fears and accepting you and your kind. After all, the only constant in life is change."

The woman pushed off the edge of the desk and went around behind it, then called up a screen. "To that end, I'd like your help reaching out to the other independents. You're persuasive yet approachable—and if nothing else, the fact we're publicly touting having a Prevo on our team will show the other colonies we are very serious indeed."

"It will send much the same message to the Alliance and the Federation."

Ledesme gave her a calculating, shrewd smile. "So it will."

PART II:

EMPTY PLACES

"And the rest is rust and stardust."

— *Vladimir Nabokov*

PORTAL: B-5

SYSTEM DESIGNATION: GEMINA

9

SIYANE

GEMINA PORTAL SPACE

Time is held captive by the stars.

Alex regarded her dad with a measure of suspicion, but also hesitancy. Was he testing her, teaching her...or just waxing philosophical? More likely all three. He tended to do that. "Because of the speed of light?"

"Right, milaya. Our fancy superluminal engines cheat to get past it, but the speed of light is still a fundamental constant, a core rule of the universe. Today we zip around our little corner of the Milky Way and call ourselves explorers, but one day we'll spread our wings and soar far deeper into the universe. Only when we get there, we'll discover a future we haven't seen and don't recognize. This starlight outside the viewport here? It represents a past long gone."

They were taking a daytrip to the Exploration History Exhibit on Mars; she'd never been to the Sojourner Dome and couldn't wait to visit it. The brisk swinging of her legs betrayed her impatience, but she tried to refocus her gaze on where he pointed. Out the viewport and far to the left, the faintest haze of an apricot-hued nebula backlit a cluster of tiny pinpricks of light. Stars, so very far from here.

She'd call up the map overlay and figure out the name of the nebula in a second, but first she paused to soak in the sight. She understood what her dad was saying—that the starlight was old by the time it got here, and those stars were different now. Some of them might not even exist any longer.

The idea threatened to make her grumpy, and she didn't want to be grumpy at the Exhibit. She crossed her arms over her chest to show outward resolve. "Well, they're still pretty. And I bet they'll be this pretty in their future—or prettier."

He tousled her hair with a smile. "I bet they will be, too. You know what else? I believe you'll get to find out."

Alex peered at the stars outside the *Siyane's* viewport with even greater interest than usual—for these were allegedly the *same* stars.

The golden-blue Metis Nebula had been instantly recognizable on their exit from the portal. It hadn't taken Valkyrie long to realize the data coming in from the long-range scans also bore a striking familiarity.

They took broader measurements, and the results displayed a strong correlation between the mapping of the Milky Way and this galaxy; the similarities also extended to characteristics of distant galaxies. Complicating the scenario was a twist in the behavior of the TLF wave. Though this was a fully realized pocket universe, the wave did not point to a specific location. Rather, it diffracted to spread across the entirety of the space.

They'd also found yet one additional wrinkle. They were looking out on the Milky Way's Scutum-Crux Arm, only not quite. Stars were near to but not precisely where they should be. On comparing several key markers relative to where they should be if this *were* the Milky Way, a single factor emerged to explain the shifts: the passage of time.

"Valkyrie, get ready to burn some computation cycles. How far into the future is this?"

Caleb had kicked his chair into a reclining position, and he stared at the ceiling more than the stars. "Do you really think it's possible this is home? We certainly didn't go through our portal. And while we've seen a number of bizarre things out here, one thing we haven't seen a whiff of is time travel." The chair snapped upright and his feet landed on the floor. "But the Metigens can and do set different time 'speeds' for different pocket universes, so...fine, I'll buy it."

Alex kept her attention on the vista, as if by doing so she could mentally will space to reshape itself into proper alignment. "This has got to be a copy—another iteration of our universe. Damn, I wonder if there are humans here. Humans which aren't us. If this is the future, they'll be more advanced...unless the Metigens succeeded here where they failed back home and wiped them out."

"Because these humans didn't have us to save them?"

"You got it."

Valkyrie reported the results of her calculations. 'Four hundred million years, give or take twenty-two million.'

Caleb whistled. "Long time."

"Imagine what we can accomplish in another four hundred millions years. If they're not all dead, maybe the humans here *have*. Hell, maybe by this point they've evolved past their physical bodies and become beings of light, one with the universe."

Caleb scowled. "That would be...boring."

Would it? Her thoughts leapt to how extraordinary it was to be one with the *Siyane*, perceiving the component atoms of the cosmos all around her. Could the experience compare to the delight of a succulent dessert melting in her mouth—to the sensory bliss of hot fudge dripping down frozen ice cream? Could it compare to the exhilaration of a runner's high? To the carnal ecstasy and peaceful contentment evoked by all the nuances of physical intimacy enjoyed with someone you loved?

It seemed impossible to judge them. How could she weigh them on the scales of life and deem one or the other wanting, when each was so deeply treasured?

"So I imagine you're dying to go check out Earth." The remark jolted her out of her reverie before she found any answers. Caleb's expression was admirably neutral, giving no hint of judgment on the matter.

He'd need to do a lot better than a noncommittal look if he wanted to hide his preferences from her. She tried to match his dispassionate demeanor. "Absolutely, assuming Earth exists—but Seneca is a good bit closer. We should swing by there first."

His former dispassion gave way to a broad, open smile. It had been the answer he wanted. Of course it had been, which was why she'd given it. "I'd love to go there. Thank you."

10

SENECA-PAR

"This is very…strange," Caleb muttered, shaking his head. He turned in a slow circle, eyes scanning the horizon as his brain tried to reconcile what he saw with a lifetime of memories.

Untamed forest encroached all the way to the shore of Lake Fuori. Across the water, the forest picked up where it had left off, shrouding the opposite shore in deepening shades of pine. Not only was there no sign of civilization, there was no sign civilization had ever existed here. No broken slabs of stone or jutting beams of metal, no crumbled stairs or felled statues.

And maybe it hadn't. "Maybe humans never came to Seneca in this universe. With over twenty billion potentially habitable planets in the Milky Way, it's entirely possible they never discovered it."

Alex kicked idly at the dirt, chuckling ruefully when a wave lapped at the shore and soaked her boot. "I'm beginning to think there's simply no one here. We haven't picked up any indication of a space-faring civilization on the longest-range scans, or of any life at all for that matter."

"Four hundred million years is a long time—in truth long enough to erode away visible vestiges of civilization. Left neglected, eventually even the most durable creations fade away."

"Four hundred million years from now we damn well better be a Kardashev Type III civilization, and such a high level of technology is easily detectable. So if there are or were humans here, their development went badly awry."

"Or they've already transformed into your beings of light." He walked a few meters and located a fallen limb, then returned to the water's edge and drew it through the water. "No bioluminescence. Could there genuinely be no life here at all? I suppose the passage of time can explain it—perhaps there was an extinction-level event at some point—but Seneca was teeming with native life when we colonized it. It's peculiar."

Alex snorted. "'Peculiar' is the Metigens' stock in trade. Right after wholesale slaughter."

"True." He inhaled deeply. Though wilderness pervaded where a vibrant city should stand, in some small way it *still* felt like home. The air tasted of remembrances, of ghosts flitting just out of reach on the breeze.

The *Siyane* hovered above the water a little way down the shore. There was no clearing near the lake wide enough to land, so they'd leapt off the end of the ramp and would have to climb back up to re-board.

He grasped Alex's hand in his. "Come on. There's one more place I want to visit."

"Sure. Where is it?"

"Up in the mountains to the north. It's hard to describe...I'll need to fly us there by sight."

⌁

Once he oriented himself properly, the outcropping wasn't difficult to spot. Even on the Seneca he grew up on, this area was undeveloped and only lightly monitored by the Senecan Wilderness Service.

In contrast to the lakeshore, here a wide clearing a few hundred meters away provided plenty of room to touch down.

Alex donned a pullover while he grabbed his jacket, and they left the ship in Valkyrie's capable hands.

His gaze darted around in growing bewilderment as they trekked through the woods toward the ledge. "No, *this* is strange. It looks exactly the same. If I don't overthink it, I could be convinced I was home."

"Did you spend a lot of time up here—the other 'here'—growing up?"

"As a teenager I did. The region I worked in during the summers included much of this mountain."

Her voice was soft. "With the *elafali*."

"Something tells me all the wildlife is missing, including *elafali*. A shame...I'd like for you to get to see one."

"When we go home, it's a date. Still, this is beautiful."

"But not as beautiful as..." the trees thinned out as the ground beneath their feet turned to stone "...this."

She let out a gasp. "Wow."

A rich pelt of hunter green forest spread out across rolling mountains and lush valleys, pristine and untouched to the horizon, where it met a cloudless cornflower blue sky. Tendrils of sparkling azure water carved circuitous paths through the gorges.

He sat down on the stone outcropping a meter or so from the edge and draped his arms over his knees. He breathed in the air, clean and cool, and found it more comforting than at the lake. Soothing. Familiar.

Alex joined him, scooting closer until their shoulders touched. "So is it solely the admittedly magnificent view, or is this place special to you for another reason?"

"I came here a few times to mull over momentous decisions—or they seemed momentous when I was a teenager. In retrospect, some of them weren't so grandiose. I never managed to find the opportunity to get up this way once I went to work, though. In fact...the last time I ventured up here was when I needed to decide whether to accept Samuel's offer to come to work for Division."

"Oh."

"Yeah." He'd not bothered to grace this wonderful place with his presence in almost nineteen years, yet when presented a Seneca devoid of life, it was the only place he'd wanted to see.

He tried to recall the outlook he'd embraced when he last came here. But it seemed that of a child, naïve and myopic, with no appreciation for what waited ahead of him. Which he suspected wasn't too far off.

Samuel had known all the right buttons to push, flattering him with praise for his observational and analytical skills then luring him in with tales of adventure, intrigue and daring heroics. Given the benefit of hindsight, he realized it was because the man knew everything about him prior to ever meeting him. His father would have told Samuel over the years, before he died—a tragedy Caleb had accepted as truth, if only in the abstract. His father had been as good as dead to him for two decades, so the difference was only semantics.

It was never mine, and I don't want it.

In the months since learning the deluge of lies surrounding his father, Samuel and Division, Caleb had tried hard to make peace with a past that wasn't what he'd believed it to be. And he'd nearly succeeded. Coming here, revisiting this place—or a reasonable facsimile of 'this place'—felt like a way to put the final touches on his peace.

"I'm not sorry I said yes. I loved my job most days—a lot more days than I hated it—and I can't imagine taking a different path would have brought me as much…I don't want to say fulfillment. Satisfaction will do. Most importantly, I wouldn't have met you. Everything which came before is what led to me being here, now, and I wouldn't trade this for anything."

Alex wound her arm around his and rested her head on his shoulder. "Good. But?"

"But…I wish I could talk to Samuel for five minutes. I wish I could ask him why he never told me about my father. I'd wish I could ask my father why he never told me what he did, but I know that answer. I understand why an agent believes they need to lie to their family and loved ones. But with Samuel? I was *doing* the job. I didn't need to be lied to. I didn't need to be protected."

"Despite the secrets, you knew him well. What do you think he would say?" Her voice was gentle. She was prodding, but he suspected she hoped talking about it would help him find closure.

"I think he would say he *was* protecting me—protecting me from the pain and angst that came with betrayal, protecting my childhood and my memories."

He blew out a harsh breath; sometimes closure stung like a vicious bitch. "And he would be lying. I think the reality was he felt guilty, if not responsible, for my father's death...and he didn't tell me the truth because he was a coward." He gave her a quick, close-mouthed frown. "It's a hard thing to accept about someone I considered my closest friend for many years. But no one said life was always easy."

Her expression conveyed untempered sympathy...and possibly a tinge of uncertainty, of frustration at being unable to conjure the elusive words needed to give him comfort. But her presence here beside him was worth far more than any mere words.

He reached over to draw the pad of his thumb along her jaw then her lower lip. "I have an idea. Want to help me make a new memory, a better memory, for this place?"

Her lips parted into a sultry smile full of promises. Her voice dropped low, and she adopted an improving imitation of his accent. "It would be my genuine pleasure."

11

SIYANE

Sol-Par Stellar System
Gemina Portal Space

Inhabiting the *Siyane* while the ship inhabited a superluminal bubble was akin to being on a chimeral high that hovered at the cusp of turning bad.

The exotic particles maintaining the bubble moved in a space which simultaneously *was* and *wasn't*, dancing in and out like they might surge inward at any moment and drag her into the blackness. Just beyond them, blurry and indistinct, lay a domain removed from space, a nothingness which seemed *wrong*.

Alex experienced none of these sensations when looking out the viewport during superluminal transit; they were tied to this elemental venture.

If you do not enjoy the sensation, you should return to your body.

It's fine. I don't want to recoil from it out of fear. I want to get past the unease.

Perhaps this is not a realm humans were meant to experience or comprehend.

When has that ever stopped me, Valkyrie?

Granted. More a challenge than a barrier in your case. Still, I derive no pleasure from the apprehension you feel.

I'm sorry.

Not enough to cease the activity, however.

No.

She powered through the anxiety bordering on low-grade terror and struggled to orient what she saw and perceived into the laws of science she knew, but she'd made little progress when they reached the doppelganger Sol system.

She dropped herself out of superluminal inside the Main Asteroid Belt, intending to approach Earth in a way she never before had: through the senses of the ship. Space warped into normalcy all around her—

—searing heat tore through her borrowed skin, and a million pinpricks of agony drove her to retreat into the illusive safety of her tiny, confining body.

'Radiation and heat shield strength increased to maximum. Visible light filter increased sixty percent. I recommend both of you administer radiation meds in the next half hour to combat the gamma ray exposure.'

Her eyes popped open with a gasp of pain. Was she hurt? Her head throbbed from transferred anguish, but her eVi flashed no warnings of injury. She allowed Valkyrie to calm her racing pulse.

You are unharmed.

If you say so.

She shot Caleb a weak, forced smile in response to his concerned stare, then focused on Valkyrie's barrage of reports while gaping at the scene outside the viewport in disbelief.

The surrounding space was dominated by bright teal and citron gaseous clouds. Was this some sort of nebula? "I don't understand. Were our calculations off due to expansion displacement? Is the Sol system somewhere else now?"

'No. The star known as Sol is located 1.6 AU from us. It is now a neutron star.'

"That's impossible."

'I tend to agree. Nevertheless, it is what the instruments are telling me.'

"Wait. Are you saying this—" she gestured haphazardly toward the viewport "—is a supernova remnant? That's—"

'Also impossible.'

"Yes!"

Caleb was still frowning at her; it was possible the impetus for it had transitioned to the mystery outside, but too much was going on for her to be sure. "Clearly the timing's off, but why is it impossible?"

"Sol doesn't have nearly enough mass to go supernova. It will expand into a red giant then eventually become a white dwarf—in about *eight billion* years. Long after Seneca's sun will exit main sequence, I'll note, which it hasn't yet done here."

She pressed a palm to her forehead and grimaced. If she closed her eyes she could still feel the burn of the radiation. "So Earth's gone, then, disintegrated in a supernova shockwave. How long ago, Valkyrie?"

'Based on the data we've captured so far, seven to ten thousand years ago as measured in this universe.'

She peered at Caleb through splayed fingers. "Thoughts?"

He gave her a prevaricating shrug. "I'd reconsider whether this truly is an exact replica of our home universe, except yesterday we stood on an exact replica of Seneca. So there's really only one other explanation: Metigen manipulation. We're in another one of their playgrounds. Here, instead of experimenting with species they're experimenting with stars, and possibly with the fabric of space itself."

"I'm an idiot." She spun the chair around and leapt up to go to the data center. Once there she began pulling in a variety of wide-spectrum survey data they'd collected since arriving, arranging and grouping the data sets above the table.

'Alex, I can conduct whatever analysis you wish on the data.'

"I know, but I'm not certain I can articulate what I'm looking for." She shifted her weight onto her back leg and brought a hand to her chin. She was vaguely cognizant of Caleb coming over to lean against the wall and watch her with interest.

"The last thing you are is an idiot, so what do you think you missed?"

"We've been fixated on star positions, since they jumped out as immediately familiar yet noticeably off-kilter—so familiar we overlooked all the other aspects of this universe that don't fit with our own."

She enlarged one of the data sets. "There are way too many heavy elements here. Not uniformly, though. They're clumped into regional clusters all over the place. And metals—nothing on the level of the Rudan universe, but too many. Valkyrie, measure the neutrino concentration—never mind, not here. We're obviously swimming in them here. But I'm willing to bet we'll be swimming in them everywhere."

She cocked an eyebrow at Caleb. "This pocket universe, or at a minimum the Milky Way in this pocket universe, is flooded with supernova remnants. Valkyrie, take us out of this system to somewhere neutral. Somewhere we can gather less tainted data."

'The interstellar medium between Demeter and Arcadia is relatively free of activity compared to other nearby regions.'

"That will work."

Caleb planted his hands on the rim of the table and leaned into it, now fully engaged in the mystery. "So why supernovas?"

"It might not be only supernovas. We need to search for evidence of other out-of-balance phenomena."

"Okay, but for now let's assume it's primarily supernovas. Why? What makes them special?"

"Well, I doubt it's because the Metigens like to make pretty explosions to 'ooh' and 'ahh' at. Supernovas...inject a lot of new material into the surrounding space, especially heavy elements and neutrinos. Also often gamma rays, which we know the Metigens do like. Supernovas create neutron stars or black holes depending on the characteristics of the star, both of which are...among the more interesting astronomical objects. They also kill the progenitor star and everything in the vicinity of the star: planets, moons, asteroids, comets, *everything*. In the long run they often lead to many new stars forming, but it takes a while."

He nodded. "The Metigens can create universes. Maybe this is part of how they shape them to look the way they want—a test field of sorts, where they try out new techniques."

"That almost makes sense. But artificially inducing a supernova? No, altering a star's makeup *then* artificially inducing a supernova? I suppose if they can create entire universes then ipso facto they possess the capability to do it, but the technology required? I'm having trouble fathoming it."

12

SIYANE

They put the gamut of the *Siyane's* scientific equipment, most of which had been upgraded before they returned to the portal network, to full use. They put Valkyrie's computation and analytical talents to yet more fulsome use.

Caleb watched Alex be a scientist for a time, watched her work the data with an enthusiasm and zeal he hadn't seen since their early days together. He took inordinate pleasure in doing it. So much of this happened in her head these days, out of view and outside his ability to appreciate. But when she was puzzling something out or testing theories, she still talked aloud, muttering and grumbling and implicitly inviting him into the process.

He may not know astrophysics the way she did, but he did know patterns and logic. He knew how to step back, observe the big picture and see the thread dangling out of place. He thought she'd probably realized this about him by now, which was one reason for the invitation. That, and she enjoyed the varied amused expressions he awarded her.

Like this one.

"Caleb, they're creating supernovas that trigger in a manner of months—weeks—not millennia. And pulsars and superflares and coronal mass ejections. Of *course* we have to discover how they're doing it!"

In wandering this distorted replica of the Milky Way, they'd found evidence of each of those phenomena and others, all in greater quantities than should logically exist.

He shrugged, but he was also smiling a touch, enjoying the passion behind her indignation. "Say we find tangible evidence of how they're accomplishing all this. We still won't understand it. This is far beyond anything we grasp about physics, or any science."

Her lips pursed as she rocked against the worktable behind her. "True, but we can take readings. And visuals. And once we have them we can study them at our leisure, and one day we will understand them—even if 'we' isn't actually you and I."

"Oh, I don't know. I bet it's us."

She rolled her eyes but regarded him hopefully.

He threw his hands in the air as if giving in, but the truth was he hadn't been putting up a fight, merely playing devil's advocate. "Okay. Valkyrie, work your magic and locate us a star which shows signs of actively undergoing...some transformation, at a faster rate than normal."

'With parameters such as those, I expect to have a suitable target by dinner time. Next year.'

The Artificial was turning into as much of a smartass as Alex. This really should not surprise him.

R

UNCHARTED SYSTEM
GEMINA PORTAL SPACE

It also should not have surprised him when Valkyrie had a potential target within two hours. A cold red giant with two distant planets, neither of which showed any signs of harboring life. There was nothing unique or particularly interesting about the star, except according to Alex it exhibited low luminosity for its spectral class, yet its mass placed it on the cusp of earning the supergiant label.

Also relevant was the reason Valkyrie had picked it out: an oxygen-neon-magnesium core that was degenerating faster than natural stellar evolution could explain.

Alex was scowling darkly at the massive vermilion star out the viewport. Her brow had drawn into a series of creases, her mouth into a thin line.

He buried a chuckle; she was deep enough into the work of unraveling the mystery she wouldn't appreciate him making fun of her...much. "You expected a Dyson swarm, or at a minimum a constructed halo ring or two."

"Maybe a little." Abruptly she exploded in movement. "So how are they doing it? What's feeding the changes in the star's composition?"

'They could be using a machine which is relatively modest in size. Without an idea of precisely where to look, it will be difficult for us to detect a small, low-power structure.'

"Hunt for power signatures similar to those generated by their ships or the cloaking—ugh, if the apparatus is cloaked we'll never find it."

He shook his head. "There's no reason for them to cloak it. There's no one here to hide it from."

"Right. We have no choice but to act under that assumption, anyway." She blew out a breath through once again pursed lips. "Let's be methodical about it. Valkyrie, adopt an orbital course 0.5 AU out from the star and open the scanners wide. We can detect as low as a hundred twenty terajoule energy emission for 0.1 AU in every direction. We'll do a full stellar orbit then shift to the next sector and repeat until we find something."

He didn't suggest the possibility there would be nothing to find. Like her, he believed there would be, for it was clear the Metigens were up to mischief on an astronomical scale. Whether they'd be able to uncover the source was another matter, but they wouldn't know until they made the attempt.

ᴀᴿ

'I think I have something.' A pause. 'Yes. I'm detecting a steady 1.2 petajoule energy source 1,235 megameters away.'

They'd been relaxing on the couch, talking about nothing in particular and relishing simply being close, but now Alex vaulted out of his arms for the cockpit. This was their seventh pass; they'd moved to 0.3 AU out from the star, as close as they dared spend any time.

He stood and followed her at a more reasonable pace. "We're fully cloaked, right?"

"Almost always."

He waited, and the next second Valkyrie helpfully provided a more comforting answer. 'We've been at one hundred percent cloaking strength since we reached this system.'

"Thanks, Valkyrie."

Alex settled into her seat and strapped in. "Approach at forty percent max impulse speed until we're twenty megameters away, then slow to ten percent max. Oh, and shift our heading until the object is between us and the star. I want to be able to see this bastard."

A low-level buzz began to thrum beneath Caleb's skin the closer they got to the mysterious object. The familiar, comforting perception of an approaching threat. Of danger.

He worked to keep his expression serious but neutral, not intending to give away the fact some part of him *hoped* for a confrontation, even if a confrontation with Metigens was unlikely to provide him anything satisfying to combat.

They were less than a megameter away when the object finally crystallized against the filtered light of the star. Similar to many structures the Metigens built, it displayed an orb-like shape and lacked obvious external ornamentation. Something powered it, however, and to a substantial level. It was not in orbit around the sun, but rather stationary, and the area of the sun directly in front of it constantly shifted.

"It looks big, but I recognize that doesn't mean much."

Alex shook her head. "No, it is big, at least compared to us." She opened a new screen on the HUD. "Six hundred eighty meters in diameter. Bigger than a cruiser, smaller than a dreadnought, though not necessarily smaller in volume. Valkyrie, are we able to pick up anything beyond the power signature? Any indication of what's happening inside?"

'Nothing except...may I move the *Siyane* S 72° -44°z?'

"All right."

The profile of the orb shifted until only a sliver of an arc remained backlit by the star. He could sense Alex getting agitated.

'There is an opening approximately sixteen meters in diameter 31° below horizontal on the sun-facing side.'

She made a face. "Well that's...something."

'Indeed. What—?'

"What?"

'I detected a dimensional disturbance outside the opening. It lasted a brief five hundred sixty-eight milliseconds. I was not able to identify visible matter, but material of some form was ejected from the opening.'

"Now that *is* something."

They had closed to ninety-five kilometers from the object, but other than the small opening they remained unable to detect anything regarding its interior or purpose.

Caleb evaluated the situation. The Metigens as individuals had never caused them harm, though their ships had inflicted a great deal of it on humans. There was also the minuscule but non-zero chance whoever operated this structure was not a Metigen but instead a native inhabitant, in which case every risk was on the table. Their instruments were not sophisticated enough to detect, much less measure, whatever was occurring inside the object.

Yet here they were.

He caught Alex's gaze. "We should go check it out."

Her eyes instantly lit up. "You mean a spacewalk?"

13

UNCHARTED SYSTEM

GEMINA PORTAL SPACE

Some part of her had expected floating in space to feel like it did when she experienced it via the senses of the *Siyane*, for joining with the ship had fundamentally altered her perception of the physicality of space.

It didn't feel any different from previous spacewalks, though, not even through Valkyrie's eyes...

...that was the difference, self-evident now. Valkyrie was in her head, but it was still her head. And Valkyrie wasn't in her skin.

I perceive it as if I am, but objectively I recognize your point. Besides, your skin is not the Siyane's skin. For you, it does not and cannot work both ways.

No, I suppose it can't.

Caleb gave her a firm nod, and they fired their suit thrusters and headed toward the structure. It loomed menacingly against the sun, growing larger every second. A speck of dust on the scale of the stellar system, their figures measured hardly more substantial against the structure.

No alarms sounded or weapons fired as they neared. Metigen hubris on display yet again—what need had they for a security system?

Another eighty meters then they cut the thrusters and drifted into the outer hull of the object with two hollow *thuds*.

"Well, here we are. Now to try to uncover more about this thing than we could from a distance." She peered at Caleb through their faceplates. "You suggested the spacewalk. How are we going to do this?"

His smirk was easily discernible in the light from the star as it cast beams across his helmet. "Hell if I know. I just wanted to go for a spacewalk, and something told me you would, too."

Her skin tingled without the need for any connection to the *Siyane*; if they were on the ship she would've tackled him and ripped his clothes from his body right then and there. "Have I told you how glad I am you're here with me?"

The smirk only widened. "You can tell me again later."

"Deal." She forced her attention back to the massive hull they weren't so much clinging to as repetitively bumping into. "Let's move toward the opening. Hopefully we can get a better idea of what it's being used for."

The outer material of their gloves had enough stickiness to the texture that as long as they didn't generate any momentum away from the hull, they could move along it manually and didn't need to use the thrusters. It was slow progress due to the size of the structure, but more efficient in the end.

'I am detecting an acceleration in the increasing mass of the star's core.'

She paused. "How much of an acceleration?"

'Linear growth thus far.'

Caleb continued moving ahead. "Keep us updated. If the transformation becomes too worrisome we'll return to the ship."

When they were fifteen meters from the rim of the open area, Valkyrie warned them to halt. *'The dimensional instabilities surrounding the opening are likely dangerous. I don't recommend exposing yourselves to the space affected by the disturbances.'*

She bumped into Caleb as they both halted. "Understood. Can you detect anything else about the phenomenon?"

'Not as of...wait. Yes. Something is being ejected at regular intervals in the direction of the sun. It is not visible, however. I can speculate as to why, but it would be no more than that.'

Valkyrie's speculation was more reliable than decades worth of any think-tank's research, but without hard data to analyze it *was* only speculation. Alex studied the structure beneath them.

The surface curved into the sun's profile to the left and the blackness of space to the right. Their traversal had revealed no other entrances or anomalies.

But for this one circular opening—the one too hazardous to approach—the object was impenetrable.

She sighed. "Okay. I think I'm going to have to use the quantum space to see what's happening inside. It's not ideal—I won't be able to interact with anything or take any measurements or samples, only report what I see."

"It's better than nothing. Are you sure you'll be safe?"

"As safe as floating out here. I think. So...hold onto me so I don't drift away."

"That I can do." He maneuvered closer, wrapped one arm around her waist and hooked his fingers into her belt. "Tell me what you see."

She took a deep breath, closed her eyes and tried to remember exactly how this worked. She'd dallied in exploring the strange quantum dimension with Devon and Morgan months ago, but she hadn't visited it since journeying to the portal network.

It was easy to determine where to direct her consciousness: straight ahead. She didn't know how thick the exterior was, but given the diameter, it couldn't be more than four or so meters.

Let's do this, Valkyrie.

There was no sensation of moving through solid metal. She was simply inside.

The interior was lit in the same white light used to illuminate the Metigen superdreadnoughts. Multiple streams fed into a central lattice that...she tilted her head—her perception—and the edges of the lattice fell in on themselves.

It's extradimensional.

Six? Seven? Then something I can't quite perceive.

It's almost—

A Metigen moved beneath the lattice. Or rather, a concentration of points of light which were ice blue instead of true white and thus were probably a Metigen moved beneath the lattice.

She retreated toward the interior wall. "A Metigen is here. It's operating, or supervising, some sort of extradimensional machinery."

Caleb's voice sounded hushed, distant, though he was centimeters from her physical body. "It can't see you, right?"

"Right." The appearance of the Metigen had startled her, but now she moved lower. Closer.

At the deepest, most complex in-folding created by the construct, a liquid, pearlescent metal floated up into the center like a slippery oil, until the metal coalesced into a small orb. Underneath the lattice and attached to it was a slightly more conventional machine.

The Metigen watched the process, then as the orb solidified, extended a part of itself and reached inside the lattice. The Metigen's limb—points of light, not corporeal in any definable way—enveloped the new orb, twisting it around as an additional layer of particles built outside it.

The orb vanished.

No. Not vanished. See the absence? It marks the orb's location.

The 'absence' plummeted into the machinery below—real machinery—then shot out the circular opening in the structure into space.

Track it!

I cannot. With hyper-specialized instruments I may be able to detect the movement by the perturbations it creates in the surrounding space-time manifold. But even the Siyane *does not possess those instruments. However, as with the measurements taken earlier, its trajectory suggests its destination is the system's star.*

Not surprising in the slightest. The process had already begun anew, and soon another orb was on its way. *They're tiny, only eleven meters in diameter. How can they possibly affect an object the size of a star?*

Who knows how many have been injected into the star. Also, this may not be the only such facility, merely the only one we detected thus far.

True. The orbs must be some form of—

The Metigen vanished from the chamber in a whirl of light. As it did, she had the brief but palpable sense of the alien traveling past her in this quantum space. The alien gave no indication of detecting her presence, but she still instinctively shrunk away from the Metigen as it passed.

Then it moved beyond the walls and was gone.

"Why did it leave?"

"What happened?" Caleb. She'd hadn't updated him in…several seconds at a minimum.

"The Metigen left."

"I wonder if it—"

A vicious *whoosh* blasted past her, and her consciousness resided in emptiness. The entire structure was now gone as well.

"Alex, get back here."

She blinked, disoriented, managed to mumble something resembling 'return' in her mind, and discovered she and Caleb were tumbling head over feet through space. Caleb's gloved hands held her waist tightly.

She twisted around to face him. "What happened?"

"The structure catapulted away without warning. We got knocked off a little roughly."

"Where did it go?"

"The opposite direction from the star—which means we need to get back to the ship."

'I am now detecting exponential growth in the mass of the star's core, as well as a marked increase in neutrino production.'

"Ship. Now." Caleb fired his thrusters, dragging her along with him until she was able to get her head straight and fire her own as well.

No longer needing to remain hidden from the structure or its former inhabitant, Valkyrie met them halfway with the *Siyane*, and they were inside the airlock in less than a minute.

Alex quickly ditched her helmet and began unfastening the environment suit while moving to the cockpit. "What's the star doing?"

'It is undergoing an electron capture gravitational collapse.'

"Oh, fun. The star is going supernova. Those orbs...they could have been a type of graviton bomb, increasing the density in the core until it overwhelmed the degeneracy pressure and triggered a core collapse."

Caleb shot her a bemused look in response as he tossed his suit to the floor in the main cabin and joined her. "I'm not sure I have the slightest idea what you just said, but I assume this means you now know how they're doing it."

'Alex, at this proximity to the star, our radiation shielding will not sufficiently protect the two of you from the neutrino burst preceding the shock wave.'

She stared in fascinated horror at the star, anticipation growing for what was now certain to follow. But Valkyrie had a point. "Let's withdraw a bit, ten or so—"

The star's photosphere convulsed and plunged inward.

"Go! Ten parsecs, now."

Valkyrie engaged the sLume drive...and for a frozen second of time, the bubble wavered and oscillated as it struggled to form amid the increasingly unstable forces.

Then space blurred away. She sank against Caleb in relief, mentally and existentially exhausted.

He gathered her into his arms. "That was close."

She nodded into his neck and prayed he didn't ask *how* close. "It was."

A few minutes later they exited superluminal. She arced the *Siyane* until she could see the radiant energy shimmering in the distance, propelled outward by the supernova shockwave. The light dominated the viewport, many orders of magnitude brighter than the star it had been moments before.

So dazzling, so commanding in its potency. The forces required to engineer such an event....

Caleb urged her chin up until she met his gaze. "Keep going."

"Hmm?"

"This entire pocket universe is dangerous, and in ways we can't predict or control. The Metigens are working in technology far beyond our understanding. They're shaping the very space around us, and they're shaping it into a deadly minefield. Keep going to the portal, then go through it."

...were in fact so very lethal.

The secrets this place held enthralled her. The wonders they had seen were astonishing beyond measure. Space had never felt dangerous to her, though she respected its power. And now, for maybe the first time, she began to respect the Metigens' power. They manipulated dimensions like they were paper maché, including time.

She did not want to be in awe of them, because they used their power for evil. Yet she found it difficult not to be in the face of what she'd seen here.

There were answers needing to be found about what the Metigens' goal was here—and why—but she conceded those answers wouldn't be found *here*. "Valkyrie, adopt a superluminal course for the portal. Caleb's right."

She'd expected some murmur of thanks or relief from him, but his attention remained focused on the space outside long after they left the supernova behind—long enough she became curious. "What's on your mind?"

"I'm starting to reconsider my earlier analysis. I'd thought all this might be part of how they shape their universes to taste, but seeing it in action...it feels like a weapon."

"In one respect it's simply the violent nature of cosmology sped up. Still...I think you nailed it. Astronomical phenomena can unleash far more powerful energies than any machine we can manufacture—I'd argue more powerful than anyone can manufacture."

She glanced back out the viewport in growing revulsion. How *dare* they wield her cherished stars in such an appalling manner? "This is a weapons testing ground."

"It is." If he noticed the disgust in her voice, he didn't show it. "They didn't use this scale of weaponry against us. But barring other motivations, there were several good reasons for it: we were too spread out, and too mobile. We were an immediate threat, relatively speaking, and they would've needed to destroy dozens of star systems to come close to wiping us out. Even then, we may have been able to escape the worst of the destruction and survive."

Perhaps belatedly realizing how much the revelation had burned her, he huffed a breath and hugged her closer.

But she soon sensed his gaze drifting over her shoulder and across the viewport. "So what kind of threat exists that *is* worth taking the time and effort to blow up dozens of star systems?"

Portal: A-2

System Designation: Vrachnas

14

VRACHNAS PORTAL SPACE

"*F*aster."

Alex spun away, arm following shoulder following head as she lunged deeper into the cabin.

Caleb's hand closed on her elbow, halting her progress with a tug back into him. "*Faster.*"

Her eyes narrowed in defiance—then she bolted to the side, pivoted and dashed toward the cockpit.

He was forced to leap forward to catch up to her, but upon doing so his arms wound around her waist. "Come on. You moved faster than this on my first morning aboard the *Siyane.*"

She wiggled in his clutches until she faced him brandishing a scowl. "I thought my life was in danger that morning."

A chuckle lodged in his throat. He released his hold on her to bring a palm up to her cheek and smile tenderly. "Fair enough."

"You're looking at me funny."

"Just remembering what it was like to have you look at *me* with distrust and suspicion."

"And what was it like?"

Another time, another life. It took a bit of effort, but he was able to put himself back in that place and state of mind...he didn't stay long. "Damn uncomfortable."

He blinked and shook it off. "You're favoring your outside leg, but unless the attack is coming at you with significant force from one side in particular, you need to launch yourself using your strongest leg—the right one, yes?"

She nodded.

"Concentrate on planting your right foot and using it to propel yourself away."

"Won't it cost me a second if my weight isn't already shifted in that direction?"

"Half a second, and you'll make it up in momentum the next second and then some."

She considered him dubiously before appearing to accept his words. She'd insisted on starting the training regimen after their close call on Rudan, then had proceeded to argue with much of his advice in the early sessions. He hadn't taken it personally, as it was simply her nature. But results had eventually silenced most of the protests.

"Okay." She readied herself and turned away from him.

He waited a beat, another to keep it unpredictable, then leapt forward to grab her.

She was out of his reach and almost to the cockpit before he could complete the motion. Finding no outlet for his own momentum, he stumbled half a step forward. When he looked up she was leaning against the wall behind the data center, grinning.

"Pleased with yourself, are you?"

"Uh-huh."

"Nicely done." He dropped his hands to his hips and silenced her laughter with a stern expression. "You don't think we're finished, do you? Get your ass back over here and hit me. If you can."

⎰R⎱

The cabin was quiet. Though a stark contrast to the exuberance of the morning's activities, Caleb didn't mind the silence.

He redirected his attention from the stars outside to Alex beside him. Her posture was relaxed; her arms rested limply on the armrests and she lounged deep in the cockpit chair. Her eyes were closed, but beneath the lids they jerked about.

She'd tried to explain what it meant to 'be' the ship, to feel and perceive space through the quantum circuitry now woven into the hull, but the words had failed to come. He appreciated what a challenge describing in relatable terms an encounter outside the realm of human experience presented, having confronted the identical problem regarding his communions with Akeso.

If he closed *his* eyes and cleared his mind, he could remember the sensation with far more clarity than a memory. But it flitted on the periphery of his awareness, tantalizingly close yet forever beyond his grasp.

> *Wind rustles a sea of grasses.*
> *Each stalk bows in submission, yielding to the wind's will.*
> *A splash of water escapes a creek to moisten the shore.*
> *Roots harbored in the soil reach out, yearning for the nour-*
> *ishment the water brings.*

With a sigh he mentally retreated from the trance and reopened his eyes. It wasn't healthy to spend too much time lost in what was, at its core, little more than an enticing drug.

Seeking a distraction until the lingering vestiges faded, he spun his chair to face the best distraction there was. After watching her for a minute, he reached over to trace fingertips along the hollow beneath her cheekbone.

A corner of Alex's mouth twitched. Her voice was a wispy, dreamy whisper. "I feel you...."

"Good." He stood, placed a feather-light kiss on her forehead and left the cockpit. They had another twenty minutes or so before they would reach the system pointed to by the TLF wave, and he had things to do.

R

"I'm not seeing any evidence of technology, or any artificial energy generation whatsoever, but sensors are picking up massive life readings on the third planet."

No advanced civilization meant no urgency, so Caleb sipped on his coffee. "Not very encouraging. We're not likely to learn much from animals or primitives."

"No, though we can at least check out what kind of creation the Metigens are playing with this time." Alex guided the *Siyane* into low-altitude orbit around the planet, a small but typical terrestrial garden world. "Time to send a probe down and see what we can see."

He propped against the cockpit half-wall to watch the vid feed from the probe.

It descended through the atmosphere and broke beneath light cloud-cover to reveal a rocky but lush terrain. Weathered, tree-covered mountains dominated the landscape. The climate was warm but not tropical, and the sensor on the probe returned a temperature of 22° C.

The probe was descending to an altitude of two kilometers when a bright glimmer of light briefly flickered in the bottom left corner of the feed.

He straightened up. "Did you see that?"

"I did." Alex's hands moved to the dash. "Taking manual control."

Under her guidance, the probe arced toward where the flash had originated. Nothing could be discerned at first—then another flash, like a sun's ray catching a mirror. "There it is again."

It was gone as quickly as it had appeared, but the source was a broad ledge bereft of trees. She zoomed the camera in closer, set the probe to hover and came to stand next to him. Together they silently considered the feed.

Sunlight danced off the metallic scales of the two dragons stretched out on the ledge, curled up next to one another in apparent slumber. Crimson and gold in color, they bore a striking resemblance to the dragons that had attacked them on Portal Prime.

One of the dragons lazily raised its head to gaze around. It exhaled, sending smoky flames pouring out from its jaws, then rested its head on the shoulder of its companion.

Alex canted her head to the side.

They weren't clones. The one that had stirred bore scales of gold-tinged rust—Caleb shuddered as he recalled exactly how sharp those scales were—in contrast to the blazing crimson of its companion. It also had a wider, larger jaw. But there was no question they shared ancestry with or had served as the models for the dragons on Portal Prime.

Caleb crossed his arms over his chest. His brow knotted.

Movement in the air above signaled the arrival of two more dragons. Far smaller in size, they alighted onto the ledge and tottered over toward...their parents?

One bumped into the other; the second one responded by hissing out weak, pale-yellow flames and clawing in its sibling's direction. A low, rumbling growl from one of the resting dragons brought a premature halt to the squabble.

Alex began chewing on her bottom lip.

The dragon on the left climbed to its feet and stretched, revealing a long, sinewy neck and a massive, heavily muscled chest. It extended its wings until they spanned some twenty meters and with a single downstroke took flight.

Caleb tilted his head gamely at Alex. "Skip it?"

"Skip it."

PART III:

HEROES & VILLAINS

"Cause I'd rather stay here
With all the madmen
Than perish with the sadmen roaming free
And I'd rather play here
With all the madmen
For I'm quite content they're all as sane
As me"

— David Bowie

PORTAL: AURORA

(MILKY WAY)

15

ROMANE

INDEPENDENT COLONY

The rotating hologram took up the entire warehouse. 1:1 scale tended to do that when one was talking about a commercial transport-class vessel.

This wasn't any normal vessel, however. Designed from the ground up to take advantage of an adiamene hull and advanced quantum computing operation, it didn't need to obey the old rules.

The transport boasted twenty-three percent more personal cabins than civilian ships its size, yet the cabins were between sixteen and twenty-eight percent larger than standard in the industry and had unprecedented per-rental customization options. It also included four conference rooms with state-of-the-art data presentation capabilities.

Most impressive, though? A person could press any one of several thousand pressure points spaced every few meters in the walls and gain access to controllable floating screens. Once activated, the person was able to communicate with the quantum circuitry embedded in the walls to display and interact with the screen in almost any practicable way.

And the cockpit. The cockpit was impressive, too. Stunning, really.

The standard pilot chair had been replaced by a mag-lev flex-chair, allowing the pilot to sit, stand or anywhere in between. A wireless sensor in the headrest interfaced with the pilot's eVi for up to two meters of distance, giving the pilot mental as well as physical command of the controls. The HUD and all virtual modules surrounded the pilot, instead of being tethered to the dash, and operated under the pilot's complete control.

The addition of a copilot to the setup was as easy as raising an additional flex-chair from where it was stored beneath the floor. The pilot and copilot could split, share and trade off all functions on the fly.

As a bonus, the ship was *light*. Less than thirty percent the tonnage of current-gen ships its size. Oh, and fast. Also agile.

"Damn. It's gorgeous, honey."

That too. Kennedy flashed a smile over her shoulder at Noah as he approached. "Isn't it, though?"

"Good news. As of twenty minutes ago, you've got the power components for it—for all the ships."

"I do? Dynamis signed?"

"They did." He wrapped his arms around her waist. "Cost plus seven percent, guaranteed supply of up to five hundred units a month."

"You're fantastic." She placed a full kiss on his lips.

"And not just in bed, right?"

"Not just. Now all we need is a contract for the complete range of impulse engines. Avion Transit has its own lined up for this ship, but it doesn't help the next customer."

"Michani Ormi drives fill your need?"

"Are you kidding? The new Ano Elite model is a work of art."

"Only you would call an engine a work of art."

She gave him a mock pout. "Hey, I see what I see. But they don't mass-produce and have a very exclusive, very expensive client list."

"Not any longer. They've agreed to build engines for the Independent Defense Consortium ships, so there's half your customers' needs met. Since you're designing the new fighters for the IDCC, they'll need to consult with you on specs. And since you'll be working together to help create this new force, goodwill is bound to ensue."

"Outstanding." She squinted at the ship holo. "I'm meeting Morgan later this afternoon to tweak a few details on the fighter design now that she's put the prototype through the paces. We should grab lunch out—to celebrate all the wonderful things that have happened today so far."

He nodded in agreement. "Food is good. And frankly, I've already done a full day's work. Revelry suits me fine."

ℛ

It was still here, still open and thriving.

Kennedy's gaze swept over their surroundings as she led Noah out to the restaurant's patio and chose what might be the same table.

He eyed her curiously as he sat. "You're acting even more pleased with yourself than usual. What's up?"

After they placed drink orders, she crossed her legs and relaxed in the chair. "Alex and I had dinner at this restaurant...it must have been nine years ago. It was the day she took delivery of the *Siyane* from IS Design. We flew it here for a test flight—and for shopping, obviously. Alex had quit her job at Pacifica Aerodynamics to go freelance. She had no money and no clients, and she was utterly fearless."

She exhaled softly. "Sitting here then, I never imagined I'd one day find myself in much the same place...and now I think she had to have been secretly terrified. But she did it anyway, because she believed her life was hers to make what she would of it. And she was right."

He studied her carefully. "Are you sorry you did this?"

"No." She reached across the table and grasped his hand. "I'm not. I have clients now, and I have money—a little. Enough. I have a plan and a path forward. But I couldn't have done it without you. I would have run home to daddy and begged to be let back into the fold the first time something went wrong."

"No, you wouldn't have. You're far more of a warrior than you give yourself credit for."

A warrior, her? She giggled faintly, but it quickly faltered; the notion was preposterous. "Yes, Noah, I *would* have. If I'm strong, it's because of you."

"I...." He squirmed uncomfortably under the weight of the praise, which was so adorable. When he tried again, his voice was warm with affection. "Anything I've done is merely reflected glory. You make me want to be better—better than I was, better than I am."

She knew how hard it remained for him to be so brutally honest, to leave himself open to being hurt—which she hoped like hell she never bungled into doing.

"Sorry, I didn't mean for lunch to devolve into us baring our souls. I had been thinking about that day with Alex lately for evident reasons, and..." she took in the blooming alyssi overflowing hanging baskets and sill boxes "...there's a certain symmetry to being back here now."

His gentle smile soon broke into a chuckle. "Granted, but is the food any good?"

"I mainly remember the cheesecake. It was divine."

They were finishing a delicious meal of char sui pork and fried noodles when Noah's gaze locked on a young woman walking behind them on the sidewalk. He stared at her as she passed, brow furrowing.

Kennedy didn't mind him appreciating the occasional attractive passerby; considering how often she did the same, she understood well what it did and didn't mean. But this stare was something different from simple appreciation.

"Give me a second." He stood and vaulted over the wrought-iron railing, leaving her sitting there perplexed.

She watched as he caught up to the woman and touched her on the arm. The woman whipped around with such violence Kennedy briefly worried she was getting ready to put Noah in a headlock. He raised his hands in surrender and took half a step away. The woman relaxed, and they spoke for a minute.

Then Noah gestured her inside the restaurant. A few seconds later they appeared at the table.

"This is Captain—sorry, former Captain—Brooklyn Harper. Harper, Kennedy Rossi."

She knew the name—the Marine who had helped Noah and Caleb take out General O'Connell on Krysk. Kennedy donned her most charming visage. "A pleasure. Please, join us."

The woman's face was devoid of any notable emotion as she nodded. "I suppose I can spare a few minutes."

She was attractive enough, if somewhat severe of countenance, with blonde hair tied in a loose tail slung over one shoulder. She wore a plain heather long-sleeved tee and navy pants but no jacket, despite the chill in the air.

"So what brings you to Romane?"

"I'm running security for Soma Biosynth—a job which has gotten more interesting than I was expecting due to the recent increase in OTS terrorist attacks. They haven't suffered any yet, but they expect to be a target."

"No doubt. You left the military after the end of the Metigen War?"

"Yep." The woman glanced at Noah a bit wryly but didn't elaborate.

He cleared his throat. "Understandable, after everything that asshole O'Connell did."

"Not only him, but...so what about you two?" The question was delivered stiltedly, as if she wasn't accustomed to making small talk. Not surprising; it presumably wasn't covered in spec ops training.

Noah filled her in on the highlights while Kennedy sipped on her drink and idly observed them. Brooklyn Harper was military through-and-through, from the way her eyes were constantly taking in her environment and everyone who passed through it, to how she held herself with coiled tension in the chair and how her expression revealed nothing about her thoughts. Noah had said she was tough. Seeing her, it wasn't difficult to believe.

Perhaps realizing she had been monopolizing Noah's attention, the woman shifted toward Kennedy and made a solid effort at a smile. "I suppose we have something in common, then—walking away from the Alliance, I mean."

Part of her still flinched at hearing it stated so bluntly, but she hid any vestige of the reaction. "It seems that's true." She sent a pulse to Noah.

I think Ms. Harper needs to meet Morgan yesterday.

His eyes lit up as if to say *brilliant!*

Kennedy learned forward. "Tell me, former Captain Harper, are you finding the Soma gig fulfilling? Professionally speaking."

"It's not in-the-trenches urban warfare. Not most days, anyway. But it keeps me occupied. Why do you ask?"

"Might you be interested in more challenging work? And potentially more rewarding?"

Harper's focus veered from Kennedy to Noah and back again. If possible, her expression became yet harder to read. "What does that mean? I don't care for games."

Oh, yes. She and Morgan would get along just fine.

Noah watched Harper depart, then turned around to find Kennedy regarding him with a deadpan expression.

He met it with a mask of innocence. It held for several seconds before he broke down with a roll of his eyes. "Sorry. Still a guy."

"Sure. Look all you want." She took a bite of dessert to keep from laughing.

"What?"

"You're not her type."

"I get it. I'm not a straight-laced soldier boy—which doesn't matter, because I'm not looking. I mean I was looking, but only to look. I'm not *looking*." He groaned and sank down in the chair, hands covering his face.

"Not what I meant, but good." She was better versed than many in dating and mating rituals, having engaged in them enthusiastically for many years. Most women all but swooned at Noah's feet on meeting him, but Harper hadn't regarded him with anything beyond detached interest. She had appraised Kennedy in a different, if subtle, manner.

Eventually she took pity on him and decided to rescue him from his misery. She stood and offered him a hand. "Come on, Casanova, it's time to get back to work. You can make your egregious relationship transgression up to me tonight."

His face relaxed in evident relief. "And I will. In all the ways."

She swallowed an aroused murmur of delight. Of this, she had no doubt.

The door Brooklyn had been directed to by the front desk clerk was open. She took a moment to stand outside and size up its contents.

A woman stood with her back to the doorway studying two screens above a conference table. Two men sat at the table watching the woman's every move. Retired military by the look of them, weary and grizzled but making an effort at rigid postures.

"So neither of you fought in the Metigen War or the Second Crux War. Did you fight in any war? Some little regional scuffle, perhaps?"

The man on the left eked out a hesitant response. "I flew in the First Crux War."

"Which side—no, don't answer that. I don't give a shit. What I do give a shit about is this. If you were ordered to do it, could you fire on military forces from whichever side you served on in the First Crux War?"

"If they were threatening innocent civilians, yes."

"See, this is the problem here. We're not running a 'real' military, thus everyone thinks they don't really have to follow orders without asking for clarification and context first."

The tenor of the woman's voice had changed, and it occurred to Brooklyn the woman might be speaking to her, despite the fact she hadn't announced her presence in any way and both the men were too flustered to have noticed her.

The suspicion was confirmed when the woman casually gazed over her shoulder with an appraising—and startlingly bright amethyst—eye.

"Marine. Interesting."

"Fighter jock. Less interesting."

"Can't help it if Marines get jealous. Alliance? Obviously Alliance. You'd be the one Terrage mentioned, then."

She didn't suppress a smirk. "Commander Lekkas, I assume. To answer your questions: yes, yes and yes—so long as I'm the one giving the order."

Lekkas turned to more closely inspect her with those artificial irises. Were they literally *Artificial*? She grunted. "You two, thank you for coming. I'll be in touch." Her chin dipped minutely at Brooklyn. "You can stay."

The two men skittered out the door before further blood could be shed, and Lekkas closed the door behind them. "So why are you here? Realized you needed the regular adrenaline fix after all?"

"Is that a problem?"

"Hell, no. It's certainly why I'm here. Terrage said you weren't merely a Marine, but a damn good one—but I'm not convinced he's seen enough Marines to know the difference, and since you're a blonde he was probably too busy ogling you to notice anyway. Why did you leave the military?"

"I was on the *Akagi*."

"Oh." Lekkas' face contorted, and for a split-second she looked almost genuinely sympathetic. "That would do it." She gestured to the table. "Have a seat."

"After you."

"Ha. Okay, have it your way. This time." She pulled out a chair and flopped down in it with dramatic flair. "How much do you know about what we're doing here?"

Brooklyn sat down next to—not across from—Lekkas. Outside of the battlefield, authority was measured by different rules.

"Noah didn't tell me any specifics, but it's not hard to figure out. Independent colonies are falling to the forces of chaos: pirates, mercs, revolutionaries, whoever. OTS terrorists are striking at major corporations on multiple worlds, including pretty much anyone running an Artificial, of which I suspect there are quite a few here on Romane.

"The Alliance and Federation are squabbling like children in sore need of a nap, but they're also boasting impressive new weaponry and ships. Oh, and let's not forget the Zelones cartel, which is making a hard play to become the third trans-stellar galactic superpower.

"Sooner or later, one of those threats will target Romane, and possibly all of them. Recognizing neither of the superpowers are apt to defend them this time and might be the ones attacking, the government has decided it had better be ready to defend itself. That about cover it?"

An unreadable expression crossed Lekkas' face; she remained silent for several long seconds. "It does. I've got aerial defense handled—fighter jock and all—and others are working on bolstering the existing orbital and electronic defense network. But while we'll try to avoid it, we'll need some ground forces from time to time. Most likely due to an OTS or Zelones attack—because let's be honest, if the Alliance or Federation launches an outright invasion, we're screwed.

"So what I'm looking for is not infantry so much as heavily armed emergency response teams. Now, this sort of work seems right up your alley...interested?"

"To join it?"

"To lead it."

She drew in a sharp breath. She'd planned to leave all this behind, dammit. She was done with teammates being assassinated and assassinating insane superiors, with cowards who called themselves champions until a worthy adversary appeared.

But in truth she *did* miss it—the adrenaline rush, yes, but also the work. The fear driving you to be faster and smarter, the belief you were fighting to protect something important, even if it was a single, simple human life.

O'Connell had destroyed the mission and everything it meant to her...but maybe she could find it again. Here.

She nodded, not bothering to ask why Lekkas would offer her a high-ranking position when they'd only just met. She was more than qualified; more than able to do the job. "I am."

"Good." Lekkas' lips twitched. "Aren't you going to ask about the eyes?"

"I figured whatever you were into was your business."

"It is. Now, I should pretend I'm some kind of legitimate supervisor, so I will need at least one professional reference."

"Federation Intelligence Agent Caleb Marano." She figured since Noah had directed her here, the man was likely connected to the endeavor in some greater or lesser way.

Lekkas raised an eyebrow. "Caleb—Mr. Marano—is no longer an intelligence agent. He's also not currently available to give a recommendation, though the fact you both know and chose him does say...something. Not sure what. Second choice?"

Well, that was all very odd and indecipherable. She shrugged. "Alliance Colonel Malcolm Jenner."

16

SPACE, NORTHWEST QUADRANT

ORELLAN STELLAR SYSTEM

There was almost no blood, but all six members of the cargo transport crew were dead nonetheless.

They hadn't even gotten off a distress call. Odd, given they were boarded. There would have been time. A single crew member managed to send out a garbled personal message to a friend at the base on Orellan, else it would have taken days before anyone located the transport. The ship's transponder and secure location signal had been ripped out; if the ELT had ever activated, it sat dormant now.

Colonel Malcolm Jenner studied the scene. The hold was empty, the attackers having made off with its contents. Pirates was the easy assumption—this was what they did. Except pirates didn't typically kill everyone on board one of their marks. While hardly upstanding citizens, most pirates didn't kill unless forced.

But wouldn't they have been forced here? This was a military ship. The crew assuredly did fight back, at the cost of their lives.

He knelt down beside the medic examining one of the bodies. "Any early ideas on cause of death?"

"Stroke of some kind. All of them. Forensics will need to do brain scans at the lab to determine anything more specific."

"Okay, thanks." He clapped the man on the shoulder and stood. He didn't want to draw too many conclusions until the facts were in, but strokes suggested a cybernetic-targeted weapon.

"The MP detachment from Arcadia is ten minutes out, Colonel."

"Good. Grenier, Devore, stay on board as guards until they take command. Paredes, get me a copy of the manifest, then let's head back to the *Gambier*."

R

Despite all his efforts to the contrary over the previous months, Malcolm stood on the bridge of a ship once again. It wasn't a cruiser and he wasn't its captain, as such—well, he supposed he technically *was*, to the limited extent it needed one.

His job hadn't so much changed as gained a more defined focus—one which sent his team into space with increasing regularity. A few weeks ago they traded in their transport for a hybrid recon-interdiction vessel.

He stowed his Daemon in the armory and departed the hold for the main cabin, where he sat in a chair that was in no way whatsoever the captain's chair.

When the manifest came in he scanned the contents. EME grenades, new model micro-bombs and a variety of crowd-control tools: gas bombs, area stun grenades. Also a small shipment of new military transponders.... With a silent groan he realized he knew who ordered the ambush.

Which meant it was his fault.

He'd failed to achieve his secondary objective on New Babel, and because of that the Zelones cartel was now brutalizing the galaxy.

No one had placed the blame at his feet, of course. He'd accomplished the impossible in infiltrating New Babel, something none had done and lived to talk about in two decades. Then he'd infiltrated Zelones headquarters, rescued Dr. Canivon and brought her and his entire team out alive.

Hell, he'd shot Montegreu point-blank between the eyes; it just hadn't made a difference.

Zelones was suspected of orchestrating the alleged uprisings on Andromeda, Argo Navis and Cosenti. Montegreu had personally taken credit for swiping Itero out from under everyone. This theft indicated she not only had no plans to stop the infiltrations, she likely planned to start hitting Alliance colonies.

He consoled himself with the knowledge there was one positive consequence to her presumed involvement in the attack.

Those colonies resided far from Alliance space, but this attack had occurred a stone's throw from two Alliance worlds and involved classified Alliance military hardware. That meant he was now going to be able to hunt Montegreu with the blessing of military leadership instead of chasing digital trails during off hours and under the radar.

Now he needed to find her. Interstellar travel had never been faster, but this worked both ways, and she was inevitably hours gone by the time he arrived on the scene.

An incoming message from an unknown and unidentified sender distracted him from formulating a new plan of pursuit. It shouldn't have pinged to the front of his awareness without matching a cleared signature or authorization. Yet there it was, blinking insistently on his whisper virtual screen.

His eVi sanitized the message to ensure it wouldn't blow up his cybernetics, then he opened it. A moment's consideration led to him sending a livecomm request to the contact.

"Before I ask why you want a recommendation with respect to Brooklyn Harper, I'll ask who you are and why you're actively hiding your identity."

"You're far more feisty than I'd been led to believe. I don't have to reveal who I represent on the grounds of employee confidentiality."

"I didn't ask you who you represented, though I'd be interested to learn that as well. I asked who you were. And who led you to believe anything at all about me?"

"The recommendation—or lack thereof—please, Colonel."

Who was he talking to? He frowned, because he didn't like it one bit. But on the other hand, it wasn't as if the information she requested was classified or could harm anyone.

"Very well. Brooklyn Harper was an excellent officer and a top-notch Marine. The military lost a valuable asset and a talented individual when she resigned. Does that suffice?"

"Would you say she exhibited good moral fiber?"

"Excuse me?"

"Sorry, it seemed like something I'd be expected to ask. Guess not. Thank you, Colonel."

"Wait a minute. I think highly of Harper, and I want to know where she ended up. Tell me who you are."

A pause preceded a quiet sound of exasperation. *"Fine. I guess I can tell you a little, on account of both Alex and Mia liking you for some reason or other, though this conversation has done nothing to illuminate what those reasons might be. This is Morgan Lekkas, and your Captain Harper is on Romane, safe and sound. Now—"*

He knew where Alex was, in a general sense—or least where she had gone. Mia Requelme was a different story. He double-checked the name she'd given.

Prevo.

Everything quickly fell into place. "Is Mia on Romane as well? She is, isn't she? I'm requesting for you to put me in touch with her, or provide me a way to contact her." He worried about what had happened to her since the events on Anesi Arch—during which he'd been too confounded to think to ask for her personal comm address—but he simply didn't feel comfortable pressing Admiral Solovy on the matter.

Another sigh followed. *"I'll see what I can do. Good day, Colonel."*

He allowed himself twenty or so seconds to ponder the exchange before returning to the mission at hand. He'd developed a sudden, intense curiosity as to what was happening on Romane these days, but he also had an exceptionally dangerous sociopath to track.

17

SENECA

CAVARE

The gaping crater where the Hemiska Research building had stood hours earlier triggered a heavy sickness in the pit of Graham's stomach. Terrorist attacks were the worst, in most if not all the ways.

Richard Navick and Will Sutton were on the scene when he arrived, and they looked as though they'd been there for a while. As he reached them, the graffiti scorched into the street in front of the crater became readable.

Death to False Souls. Arise, True Sentients.

"So, OTS then."

Richard ran a hand through unkempt hair. "They're not exactly hiding it."

One of the emergency personnel ran up to give a status report—to Richard. When the EMT departed Graham raised an eyebrow at him.

Richard grimaced. "We were two of the first to arrive and were helping until more rescuers got here."

"Thank you for doing that. Did OTS succeed in its goal?"

"Destroying Hemiska's Artificial? Can't say for certain, but from what we saw when crawling around in the rubble, it's likely."

"Terrific. It'll embolden them."

Will looked incredulous. "Even if it was at the cost of so many lives?"

"I suspect OTS doesn't concern itself with body counts—unless the bodies belong to warenuts, in which case the higher the better."

_R_

Graham needed a shower; his clothes reeked of soot, of gore and violence. But first he needed a drink.

He'd just finished pouring a scotch when the door beeped. It was Tessa Ferguson from Division's Strategic Development group requesting entry.

It was late, and he needn't be in the office...but as Director, he was never truly off the clock. He took a quick sip and allowed the door to open while he went to his desk.

"Tessa, come in. If you're here to tell me the VISH is reporting there's going to be an OTS attack on Hemiska Research, you are, regrettably, late."

She blinked in surprise, halting behind the guest chairs. "No. The VISH didn't report anything, which is a problem. But if we can put it to the side for a minute, what I'm here to discuss may have some bearing on the problem."

"Okay. Let's hear it."

She sat down, fidgeting around to get comfortable, and tossed her long plaits over the back of the chair. "Hmm. How to best put this...your Prevo technology is on the loose."

He stared at her for a moment. Her group at Division had played no role in Noetica, which meant she'd learned of it elsewhere. She made no secret of the fact she was deeply steeped in the tech/ware subculture; it was one of the reasons they'd hired her.

"We suspected this might be happening soon. Do you have any sense of how widely it has spread, or whether there's any chance of suppressing it?"

"Today, a few hundred people have their hands on the tech. By this time next week, it'll doubtless be thousands."

If the leak was limited to one world, it might be a small enough number to be contained. "I don't suppose they're all are on Seneca by chance? Or any single colony?"

"Uh, no."

"A shame. Well, it's too late to reel it back in then. So is this merely a courtesy call to let me know, or are you proposing to do something about it?"

"As a matter of fact...I went ahead and *did* do something about it." She blinked slowly, and when her eyes reopened their unusual copper was subsumed in orbs of radiant white.

"Oh, goddammit, Tessa! You can't just go and hook yourself up to an Artificial—shit, it isn't Cleo, is it?"

She shrugged. "Better to seek forgiveness than ask permission?"

He sank deeper in his chair. He should fire her on the spot, then order her to toggle the connection off and have Cleo dismantled. No...order first, fire second. The order was more likely to succeed that way.

"I can use this to help Division in so many ways. For one, the VISH hasn't been able to get beyond the local Seneca OTS chapter into the larger network. It's good at imitating a person, but it's not a hacker. We can tunnel into the VISH and hack the OTS network. Plus, I bet we can identify the local members.

"And Olivia Montegreu—she's a Prevo now, right? Then you need a Prevo to fight her, and since the military no longer has one..." she spread her arms with a speculative, hopeful expression "...here we are."

She was already referring to herself as 'we.' And it appeared the Prevos knew fucking everything there was to know.

"Or, I could demand you tell me where you got the technology from so I can go arrest those involved, detain you if you refuse and forcibly disconnect you from Cleo." It was empty threat, but he wanted to instill at least a modicum of fear in her.

"Wouldn't it be so much more fun to do things my way, though?"

So much for that. *Fearless, the lot of them.* He took a long sip of his drink to buy himself some time.

Gianno had locked her Prevo down so tight the young woman could hardly breathe fresh air, and Lekkas had bolted as a result.

Division wasn't the military. It was an intelligence organization, often engaging in black ops legal only under a most generous interpretation of statutes. It was in many ways the antithesis of the military—volatile, reckless and inventive, operating on the margins of the law and doing what was necessary to protect Federation citizens. Occasionally, to protect everyone.

He set the glass on the desk. "All right. But there need to be a few rules in place. You still work for Division, and so does Cleo."

A big smile broke across Tessa's face. "Whatever you say, Director."

Her tone did not inspire confidence that she intended to abide by even his minimal rules. Nevertheless, they spent the next half hour hammering out semi-reasonable restrictions and guidelines, then a rough mission plan regarding the OTS cell.

When she'd departed, he fixed himself another drink. If only his night were over.

ℛ

Richard stopped off in the lavatory to splash some water on his face before they went up to Graham's office.

They had remained at the blast site longer than they were able to do any good. He still felt responsible for OTS, if not as much as he did for Olivia Montegreu. And the weight of responsibility was no lighter on Seneca than it had been on Earth.

Will appeared behind him in the mirror, concern clear beneath the grime coating his features. "You all right?"

He must have been taking too long. He gave Will an anemic grimace. "Just tired. Frustrated. While you're here, you should clean up, too."

Will wiped a palm over his cheek and squinted at the dirt it came back displaying. "So I should." He moved to the adjacent sink and switched on the water, then let it run. "Is it always like that?"

Richard dried his face and rested against the wall. "Like what?"

"Mangled bodies. Limbs with no body left to go with them. Lives shattered. Blood, death. So much death."

"If you mean how many times have I been forced to stand amidst a massacre like the one tonight...not as many as some, but too often. Set up in a nice office at EASC HQ, it became all too easy to avoid the grim reality, to pretend it *isn't* like that. In the First Crux War, though? Before the office? Yes. More than I ever want to remember."

Will's gaze remained on the water swirling around the basin. "Is it normal to kind of want to kill whoever did this using my bare hands?"

He huffed a breath and grasped his husband by the shoulders. "Yes. But if you hold onto the sentiment for too long, it'll eat you alive from the inside. We'll find them, and they'll pay. I promise."

Graham welcomed them in with a weary wave of a hand. "Hell of a night, isn't it?"

"And early morning." Richard sat and made an effort to look alert. "You said you needed to talk to us?"

Other than displaying evident tiredness, Graham's expression was unreadable. "I do. Specifically you, Richard, but having Will here saves you from having to repeat everything to him later, which I know better than to pretend you won't do.

"Nevertheless, what I'm about to tell you is so classified they don't have a level for it, and I frankly beg you not to let it go beyond this room. In other words, I definitely should not be telling you this. But because you're my friend, the tenuous scraps that remain of my conscience demand I do...."

He rolled his eyes at the ceiling. "That's not entirely true. I'm well acquainted with my conscience yelling at me to no effect. The truth is, in the last year I've had too many secrets and lies blow up and bite me in the ass. I've lost too many good people to them, and dammit, I don't want to lose any more.

"If after hearing this you want to resign, return to Earth, I'll understand. I really will. But it's not my secret—not my lie. And by telling you now, *before* it blows up and bites me in the ass, I'm hoping in the end I won't lose either of you—your work or your friendship."

Dread gnawed up through Richard's gut into his chest. Graham was frequently brutally honest, but rarely about himself. Seemed a tough night planned to get worse. "Obviously I don't care for the sound of this. What is it?"

"I believe in the Federation. I believe in its principles of limited government and individual liberty. I believe it does the right thing more often than the wrong one. But not every time."

Graham's chin dropped to his chest. "Back in 2297, Seneca was chafing under Alliance rule, and a growing faction of leaders were ready to be rid of it. But no matter how hard they pushed, the Alliance continued to tighten its grip, narrowing the window in which Seneca would be able to change its circumstances."

"Graham, I know the history of the First Crux War. I was in the military—I lived it."

"Of course. I only...so those leaders, of whom Chairman Vranas and Field Marshal Gianno were two, initiated the coup and declared independence. This led to the blockade, which they were counting on. Finally a chance to provoke the Alliance into war."

"Declaring independence did that well enough."

"The suggestion of war ought to have been ridiculous, though. The Alliance military dwarfed the few ships we could commandeer. Its forces could have annihilated us in a matter of weeks."

Richard shook his head. "But it didn't. The messy details of the first battle paralyzed the Assembly and military leadership, above and beyond the effect the audacity of the Federation had. They were hesitant to respond, and when they did they responded timidly. And you—" he caught himself "—the Federation had built a fleet in secret, one which matched the Alliance on the battlefield soon enough."

"We did."

"Again, you're not telling me anything I don't already know."

Graham nodded. "Then I probably should. The 'messiness' of the first battle you referred to? It was our doing."

"I'm not sure I understand. Yes, your seized ships and one brand new one showed up and taunted the Alliance commander into attacking."

"The civilian transport that was destroyed, allegedly by the *EAS Fuzhou*...we shot it down, and in such a way as to make it appear as if the *Fuzhou* did the shooting."

"We did what?"

Will had asked the question; Richard was at a loss as to how to respond. He sucked in oxygen and let out the breath with great care. "You murdered your own civilians? To make the Alliance look bad?"

"To slow the Alliance down. To win the hearts and minds of other colonies on the fence. To buy time for the secret fleet to grow larger. That's what the mission file says, anyway. I wasn't there, I didn't...I didn't know. Not then, not when I joined Division and not when I became Director. Not until a few days ago."

Richard's mind reeled. The dread turned to acid in his throat.

He was working for the enemy.

The Federation had been the enemy in the First Crux War, an adversary in the decades since, then ultimately an ally. But they had been the enemy back then for a reason, and it turned out the reason wasn't the desire for freedom.

Will exploded out of his chair. "They were cold-blooded killers!" The fact that he was running on adrenaline, rage and blood lust elicited by the OTS bombing couldn't be helping his state of mind.

Richard motioned Will down with a whispered *please*. "Who was responsible?"

Graham swallowed. "Vranas, Gianno and Darien Terzi, the Director of Intelligence on Seneca at the time, planned and authorized the mission. They called it 'Operation Colpetto.'

"They used one of the new ships, a small recon craft. It snuck into the middle of the Alliance blockade fleet and positioned itself beneath the *Fuzhou*. They equipped it with a weapon designed to mimic Alliance cruiser weapons."

His throat worked again. "There's one more thing. The person who fired the shot that destroyed the civilian transport was Stefan Marano."

Richard frowned, briefly confused as to why it was a relevant detail. His eVi helpfully filled in the necessary information. "Caleb's father? You have got to be kidding me."

Graham shook his head. "I considered the man a friend, and I never had the slightest inkling. I'm positive Caleb didn't—and still doesn't—know. And maybe it doesn't matter. Stefan was following orders from Terzi, and he withdrew from field work shortly thereafter to become an investigator. I'd say he didn't care for having crossed the thin line into murder, but let's face it, I'd be speculating."

Will stood to pace around the office. "After the things I saw tonight...our government is no better than OTS."

"I don't believe that, but I concede it may look that way from where you're at. Vranas and the others hoped the action would save lives in the end and prevent a wholesale slaughter of Senecan lives, soldier and civilian. Can't say if they were right. I doubt anyone can."

"But at what cost? Their integrity? Their very souls?"

Graham shrugged weakly. "I don't have any good answers for you, Will. Civilians die in war all the time? Admittedly, not usually at the hands of their own side...."

Richard worked to keep his voice level. "Why now?"

"Why did I find out now?" Graham grimaced. "To be blunt, Lekkas learned of it and is using it as insurance against us trying to apprehend her. Her mother piloted the recon craft, though she wasn't in on the plan. It's all a bloody mess, but that's neither here nor there."

He snorted. "You think it's a bloody mess now? If the Alliance finds out, the last shreds of our friendly relations will disintegrate. *Then* things will get ugly."

"No doubt. The credibility of our Chairman and the head of our military would be ruined. The entire government might fall, but Vranas and Gianno would almost certainly be replaced. But none of those issues should be your concern."

Richard was quiet for several seconds. Then he stood, offering only a curt rejoinder. "Thank you for telling me. I need some time. We both do."

Graham nodded quickly, and Richard gestured to Will. "Let's go home."

Will was still visibly enraged as he followed Richard out. Even taking into account the night's trials, it was strange he would react this strongly.

Or maybe Richard had simply become far too jaded. With life, with the evil that good men do.

18

EARTH

Claire Zabroi licked her lips in anticipation as she strolled with exaggerated nonchalance down Folsom Street toward Rincon Park. The damp air chilled her bare arms.

Warmth.

Her Prevo consort promptly began warming her skin. She smiled. This was fabulous.

The lights and sounds increased as she navigated the next block. Rincon Hill had served as a haven for the tech/ware counterculture for decades, but now it had become the unofficial favorite gathering spot for a new breed of warenut.

The Prevo tech had spread like wildfire since being quietly shared by the former members of Noetica, doubtless as they intended. Information was meant to be free, right?

She'd been fascinated to discover Alex was the first—the originator of the idea, in fact. Her next reaction had been resentment at not having received an invitation to be in the initial wave of people receiving the tech. But then she'd learned Alex was unequivocally 'elsewhere.' So it was all good now.

Not everyone who claimed to be a Prevo actually had the balls to go through with it. An ocular implant enhancement which mimicked the glowing irises had been rushed to market. Sales were brisk, and now no one could distinguish human from Prevo on sight. In theory it worked to protect them, but so far the most common users were posers.

The amusing part was the posers apparently didn't realize how easily true Prevos saw past their charade. Many ways existed to identify them, their absence from the Noesis being the most obvious.

She activated a hit of Surf and drifted amid the Noesis, caressing the consciousness of others in the way one might brush past someone on the sidewalk. Some recognized her presence and reached out in acknowledgment; she returned the gestures but kept moving, much as she did in the real world.

Ahead of her multiple sensory overlays transformed the block into a Prevo-controlled circus. It became impossible to tell what was physical, what was virtual and what represented sidespace. The most skilled and adept of the new Prevos were already transcending the Noesis mindspace to begin to explore the far more cryptic sidespace dimension, and she appreciated their efforts here.

With the chimeral high adding to the mixture, she pretended she floated through a madman's warped, upside-down performance art fantasy. What a trip....

A concentrated cluster of presences to the left caught her attention. Someone—almost certainly more than one someone, not that it mattered here—was hacking an exceedingly secure network.

She fixated her perception on the cluster, and they opened to her. PanPacific Tech Labs was the target. She gave them a little boost of processing power and a snippet of one of her most clever hacking algorithms then continued on. Embarcadero Taproom was on the next block, and what high couldn't be made better by the addition of alcohol?

The explosion ahead seemed to be part of the sensory experience at first. A hack gone wrong? Some twat showing off by buggering up the virtual layer?

Then the screams penetrated the shared mindspace—

Can't breathe

—Claire gasped, the rawness of the terror flooding her mind—

Help, my leg is trapped underneath

—Not *her* leg? Someone else's leg. Because she was still walking, wasn't she?

Hurts I don't want to

—Another blast, larger, louder, shaking her eardrums, the tangible ones. Few screams followed this one, only presences blinking out of the Noesis like stars going dark.

People ran on the fringes of the explosions, in no direction and all directions. Her hands found something solid, and she pressed against the façade of a building.

Smoke and fire bloomed everywhere, even in the virtual layers. It couldn't be real there, but instead a manifestation of the mental confusion and panic.

Violent streaks of light crisscrossed...which space? She blinked, trying to draw her consciousness back into herself and block out all the pain flooding the Noesis. It didn't work.

Was *she* in pain? She raised a hand to her face and found it soaked in blood. Oh, frag it all...

Congealing skin around the wound and decreasing blood flow to the area. Medical attention is suggested, but you are not in immediate life-threatening danger. Not from the wound.

Really? Because it hurts like a son of a bitch. Narcotics. All the narcotics.

Done. We should vacate this area.

Dizziness from the painkillers made the ground shift and undulate beneath her, but it was so much better than the pain. She blinked and tried to focus.

It looked as though a pressurized cluster bomb had been dropped on Folsom and Spear. Most of the lights had gone out. Or maybe they were obscured by all the smoke.

How the hell was she going to get out of here?

Map overlay activated. Assuming Rincon Plaza is the primary target, go left—

Laser fire burned through the smoke in front of her as she turned. Too close.

Or right. Right would be better.

VANCOUVER
EASC HEADQUARTERS

Miriam scrutinized the data flowing across the secure, encrypted and also hidden comm channel. "This looks good, Christopher." She glanced up at the holo wearing a grateful smile. "You're making progress far more rapidly than the schedule we set. Excellent work."

He scoffed, deflecting the compliment. "With all the construction going on out here, it hasn't been difficult to divert a few resources here and there."

"Minimize it if you wish, but I recognize the effort required—"

The alert flashed in her vision at the same time it flashed on the news feed panel embedded in the wall. Footage of buildings crumbling into smoke, people running and generalized chaos followed.

"I need to go. I'll touch base when I can." She cut the connection and deactivated the shielding around her office. Subversive scheming would have to wait; it was time to focus on the here and now—to do her job.

In a matter of seconds she had the relevant broad-stroke details. The location was San Francisco, the Rincon Hill neighborhood—a favorite of warenuts and, in recent days, possible Prevos. Three explosions had been confirmed, though whether they resulted from bombs or rockets remained unclear. Widespread small arms fire in the aftermath had also been reported.

Initial casualty reports varied, from a low of seventeen to a high of over a hundred.

She connected to North American Military Headquarters in San Francisco and instructed them to allow civilian emergency and security personnel to take the lead, but authorized provision of any assistance requested, carte blanche.

Next she alerted the OTS task force at Naval Intelligence and advised them to send an officer to the scene, under the reasoned assumption this was likely an OTS attack. The terrorist organization had become increasingly brazen and violent in recent weeks, its members descending from the ranks of opposition protestors to mass murderers. News of the bombing in Cavare had reached her hours earlier.

Two attacks on the two most powerful planets in the galaxy on the same day. OTS was trying to give Olivia Montegreu a run for her money.

Miriam was fully engaged in multiple on-scene reports and a briefing with the San Francisco law enforcement chief when a holocomm from Pamela Winslow invaded it all in a flurry of blinking alerts and priority overrides.

She paused the briefing, paused herself to grit her teeth and allow herself a single silent curse, and switched channels.

"Chairman Winslow, I am in the middle of a crisis at the moment. Unless this is a true emergency, I suggest whatever you wish to discuss wait until the situation has calmed."

"Admiral Solovy, have you seen the latest from Rio de Janeiro and Shi Shen? This kind of behavior cannot be allowed to continue."

Vids of young people, their dress marking them as members of the warenut counterculture, defacing government buildings were shoved onto her holocomm. She waved them off the edge of the screen to glare at Winslow.

"How curious. I expected you to be complaining about the rise in terrorist attacks by OTS—such as the one happening this *instant* in San Francisco."

"Regrettable to be sure, but OTS is reacting to what it correctly perceives to be a very real threat."

"Chairman, you cannot be advocating—"

"*Over*reacting, yes. But I expect the attacks will lessen or even stop if we make a proper effort to crack down on this rampant spread of illegal, hazardous technology. Children are turning themselves into monsters and, quite frankly, it is your fault. You initiated the creation of this technology, then you allowed it to slip through your fingers."

Miriam's jaw tightened. "I disagree, but now is the least opti-mal time imaginable for assigning blame. People are dying, and I will not stand around debating semantics with you while they are."

"Two hours from now, the Assembly will pass legislation out-lawing the ownership, possession or use of Artificials outside of the government, military and Assembly-approved corporations. I expect you to instruct those under your command to assist the police in enforcing this new law throughout Earth Alliance juris-diction with all due speed."

"Enforcement of civilian law is not the province of the mili-tary."

"I only mean in a support capacity, of course. I'm not referring to martial law type measures."

Yet. The fact that the possibility of martial law was sufficiently extant in the woman's mind for her to drop it in conversation was worrisome, but not surprising.

"Chairman, I realize in all probability you will be the Prime Minister-elect in three days. But you are not the Prime Minister today, and you have no authority to issue orders to me."

The woman's lips drew in and thinned. "In that case, we will reconvene in three days. A word of warning, though, Admiral. Expect that conversation to be considerably less civil."

"I can hardly contain my enthusiasm. Good day, Chairman."

As soon as the comm dropped, she reconnected to Vice-Admiral Jirkar at NA Headquarters and spent some time ensuring he was up to speed, then granted him full authority to act accord-ing to her directives.

When the conference was done, she closed her eyes and in-haled deeply.

So be it.

Yet more grateful than she'd been a mere few minutes ago that Rychen was ahead of schedule, she reactivated the encryption shield and prepared to contact several people. Richard was first.

19

EARTH ALLIANCE COLONY
DRUYAN INSTITUTE

Abigail Canivon gazed at the sailships floating on the tranquil bay outside. No trace remained of the damage the Metigens had inflicted on Sagan.

The Druyan Institute's Cybernetic Research Center had been rebuilt, better than before. She enjoyed a plethora of new, state-of-the-art tools at her disposal.

And why shouldn't she? These were heady days for the industry. Advances in not merely core cybernetics but other biosynth materials and all quantum computing applications had been the order of the day for months.

Now all that progress was at risk of being halted—if not destroyed and a regression begun—by two opposing but inexorably related forces: OTS and Olivia Montegreu.

Montegreu brought validation to all OTS' most extravagant claims; she was its doomsday warnings made flesh. Artificials were too dangerous to be set free or even to use, because they lacked a conscience or any true moral compass. Adding humans to the equation didn't make them safer as many had hoped, but rather more of a menace. Given the keys to the final domain, flesh and blood, Artificials now threatened to dominate and subjugate humanity.

The woman was a better recruiting tool than anything OTS could have dreamed up. And it was Abigail's fault.

For all her considerable intelligence and ingenuity—no one had ever accused Abigail of being modest—she'd been unable to outsmart an Artificial. She could not find a way to subvert its processes in a manner that would prevent the melding of human and synthetic from reaching its full potential.

But maybe she could do something now.

She pivoted from the window and headed back into the lab. She'd convinced Montegreu that in order to ensure the Prevo procedure was successful, she needed the details on the woman's cybernetics and eVi architecture. Which, to be completely safe, she *had* needed.

What she hadn't needed to do was take advantage of the woman being sedated during the procedure to acquire additional details on the many routines they ran, then save a copy of said routines to her own internal storage.

She'd neglected to hand the information over to Alliance authorities after her rescue. It would not have done them any good. Even before becoming a Prevo, Montegreu sported some of the most advanced biosynth enhancements Abigail had ever seen. They would not be easily countered, as Colonel Jenner had discovered when he'd attempted to execute Montegreu while she lay unconscious and seemingly helpless.

But they *could* be countered. She and Vii were working on possible avenues of attack in their spare hours, more so of late as the threat Montegreu posed became perilously obvious. And they were getting close to a workable solution. The key was the manner in which the shield—

The incoming holocomm request was encrypted and displayed no traceable sender. The subject line simply read:

On the strenuous nature of not hindering

She massaged her temples before accepting the request. "Admiral Solovy, what do you need?"

The woman gave her what passed in some circles for an actual smile. She looked to be on a transport.

"You know, Dr. Canivon, by all rights we should be friends, if only because we both despise false pleasantries. I'd like you to consult on a...let's call it a side project I'm working on."

"Side projects are typically idle, leisurely hobbies of little import."

"This one is not."

"I suspected as much. Can I assume you're not able to give me any details on the nature of the work?"

"I regret to say you can. It isn't prudent to discuss the matter over any comms, however secure we presume them to be."

"I've hardly settled into my work here at the Center. Does this consulting need to be conducted onsite somewhere?"

"It does."

She thought of the dozens of ongoing research proposals and planned work to be done. But she did owe Solovy a fairly significant debt for having seen to it she was rescued off New Babel, especially when she'd immediately thereafter walked out on the woman and on her job.

"Will it harm Devon or the other Noetica participants in any way, directly or indirectly?"

"Quite the contrary, I hope."

An obtuse answer, per usual. But Abigail had to admit she'd been mildly curious about what Solovy was up to ever since their similarly cryptic conversation at Special Projects.

She cleared her throat. "Fine, then. Where do you need me?"

"Messium, as soon as you are able. I'll send more details once you're underway, and you'll receive all the information you need when you arrive. Thank you, Doctor."

The comm ended, and Abigail sighed. No matter how often or how vigorously she tried, she never could manage to escape galactic politics for long.

R

KRYSK

SENECAN FEDERATION COLONY

Krysk was as sweltering as on her last visit, but Olivia noticed it only as part of a detached recognition of her environment. The Artificial regulated her body temperature to perfection, cooling her skin to counter the humidity. A thin, porous, long-sleeved shirt and loose pants did their job of, regrettably, covering the web of streaming gold pulses along her skin.

She had no qualms about walking the streets unguarded and in full view of everyone, but causing a scene by frightening the locals would be counterproductive to her purposes, as well as horribly inefficient.

This area of downtown had suffered damage from General O'Connell's attack, though it had been patched over until it was nearly invisible. But she could see the miniscule cracks and the shifts in hue where new material met old.

Such a foolish, base man. He'd served as a useful pawn in Marcus Aguirre's scheme, easily manipulated by the unchecked emotions he wore for all to see. But the fact a man like O'Connell had risen to the apex of a military comprised of tens of millions of soldiers said everything there was to say about the organization.

Ferre group's distribution of chimerals and illegal ware dropped 27.3% in the first two months following the end of the Metigen War and 14-17% every month thereafter.

It now measures 26.4% of its pre-war level.

She glanced at the name in the building's directory in amused dismay. *Fotilas Services.* Laure hadn't so much as bothered to change the name of the shell corporation or its location. He wasn't a stupid man, at least not in comparison to most of his fellow humans, which left conceit as the explanation.

It didn't matter. He'd lived this long at her pleasure, and he'd die at it as well.

Laure Ferre leapt up from his desk with enough force to topple the chair behind him. He slammed his fist on a control panel—an act that was presumably intended to summon security—then tripped over the chair as he backed against the wall.

Olivia tilted her head to regard him with detached curiosity. "They won't be coming to help you."

"You killed my security guards?"

She offered him the most trivial of shrugs.

"Why didn't the alarms go off?"

Another lift of her shoulders. "I bypassed them."

"You can't do that!"

"Oh, Laure, Laure dear. I can do anything."

He lurched for his desk and retrieved a Daemon from an alcove beneath it; she indulged him. He fired at her chest again and again to no effect, as her shield absorbed the pitiful energy without strain.

Finally, his arm fell to his side and the gun dropped from his fingers to clatter across the floor. "What are you going to do to me?"

"You've been such a very bad boy. I tolerated it beyond the point where I should have, because I admire your tenacity, I do. I'd hoped in time you might come around to my view of the world and we could have had a more…positive relationship."

He'd never be Aiden Trieneri; still, he did have a rough, gritty masculinity about him she'd considered enjoying at one point. She didn't miss Aiden—much—but she did miss some of his finer skills.

"You should not have tipped the authorities to my acquisition of Dr. Canivon. Now you've tried my patience beyond its end and become quite a bit more trouble than you are worth."

She lifted her wrist to eject the aSTX-laced blade from her bracelet and into his neck. The toxin would paralyze his respiratory muscles, suffocating him even before he bled out. She possessed the capabilities to kill him in a number of ways, and many of them would create rather less of a mess.

But having seen this attack in the past and watched its victims bleed out from it, he'd have a minute or two in which to comprehend his fate. It was fitting.

She gave him a last, disdainful sneer as he slid down the wall to the floor. "Say hello to your cousin and aunt for me."

Then she turned and left the office and the trail of bodies therein. She had a few additional things to take care of on Krysk before heading to Dolos Station.

Her vulnerabilities were rapidly approaching zero, but a few yet remained. The next step to eradicating them? A renewable supply of adiamene.

20

PANDORA

Devon reread the message a third time.

It wasn't that it was difficult to understand; it was in fact exceptionally straightforward. He simply had no idea what to make of it.

> *Mr. Reynolds,*
>
> *First, let us get one issue out of the way: I am not coming for you. You may be safe from very little right now, but you are safe from me. Your answers to my questions below will not change this fact.*
>
> *Whatever it is you possess of Annie—I'm operating under the assumption you do have her, in some manner I won't attempt to fathom—are there any circumstances under which she can be returned to hardware, and if there are, can I have her back?*
>
> *Regards,*
> *—M.S.*

On balance, he liked Miriam. He liked her because Richard liked her and because Alex liked her...well, in a screwed up family way. But mostly he liked her because, though he'd been in no condition to appreciate it at the time, she'd taken care of him after the attack in Annie's lab. She was abrupt, often cold and a harsh taskmaster—yet when it mattered, she'd protected him as best as she could.

But the notion of giving back Annie? While it had been only weeks since they'd taken the final step of joining consciousnesses...no. Regardless of whether such a thing was theoretically possible—neither of them was inclined to waste cycles analyzing whether it could be done—it was never going to happen.

She was part of him now, etched into his soul.

He opened up a response.

> *M.S.,*
>
> *Thanks for the all-clear. For real. I'll keep the locks on the door, but not to keep your people out.*
>
> *I'm sorry, but no. To the second question, that is, which makes the first question irrelevant. As you told me and the others when you asked us to be a part of Noetica, there's no going back. There never was.*
>
> *—D.R.*
>
> *P.S.: I'm trying to take good care of her. She's definitely taking good care of me.*
>
> *P.P.S.: Any chance you can see to having Pamela Winslow killed, maimed or permanently imprisoned? It would make my life so much easier. Thanks in advance.*

Devon watched the news feed in growing disgust and concern. Three OTS attacks in the last week on Alliance worlds and one on Seneca. Twenty-three Prevos had died in the San Francisco attack, plus fifty-two ordinary people caught in the crossfire.

You're not responsible.

For OTS being a bunch of psychopaths? No. But I am responsible for the new Prevos.

They each chose to become what they are.

I know, but I feel protective of them. I need to look out for them.

By definition, they are among the most powerful, capable people in the galaxy. They can look out for themselves.

Okay, fine. How about the people trapped in the middle, then? The hackers and warenuts who haven't become Prevos but are still in danger, since OTS can't be bothered to tell the difference? No. I need to do something.

I understand.

He changed into better clothes and ran a comb through his hair, then left the apartment.

Morgan, Mia, heads up. I'm working on a plan to counter OTS. I'll have more in a few hours.

♫

Thali's Lounge hosted all sorts of patrons. Confrontations were frequent, and just as frequently brief thanks to the vigorous bouncer presence. In this respect, it was generally recognized as neutral ground, suitable for meetings by individuals and interests who might have conflicting alignments.

He'd made several acquaintances who were heavy into the local warenut scene, two of which had Prevo'd themselves in the last several days.

He chuckled to himself at the realization the term had already become verbified.

One of those acquaintances—not Prevo'd quite yet—knew everyone and everything that happened in The Avenue sector. Devon was hopeful he had an ear to the ground of, if not OTS activities on Pandora, groups that would.

He found Pablo Espino at a tall table on the edge of the dance floor and slid onto the stool opposite him.

"How's it hanging, Prevo-dude?"

"Hanging." His eyes surveyed the room.

In a far, shadowy corner, a couple was having a vicious argument. The redness at the base of the male's neck signaled an elevated heart rate and overabundance of adrenaline; he was on the verge of losing his temper in a physical manner. Devon piggybacked onto the bouncers' comm channel and drew their attention to the altercation.

On the dance floor, a stunningly gorgeous woman's dance of provocation had drawn the rapture of half the men and several of the women in the club. Her form-fitting scarlet silk dress minimally covered perfect skin the color of cappuccino.

He was close enough to sense her heart rate with some degree of precision, and it was a steady 76-81 bpm. Her moves were deliberate. Calculated. She was in complete control of her actions, as well as the actions of many of those present.

At the end of the long bar to his right, another woman was in far less control of her faculties. Sweaty skin, dilated pupils. She stumbled off the bar stool and was barely rescued from the floor by a bouncer, who proceeded to hand her off to the guy accompanying her and escort them to the door.

Three men and a woman sat at a table across the dance floor. Drinks waited untouched in front of them as they huddled in intense conversation.

He jerked his head in their direction. "Who are they?"

"Damn, Devon. You don't miss a thing, do you? I don't know the guy in the thousand-credit shirt, but the girl's head of OTS here. The other two are some of her cohorts."

He cracked his neck. "What's her name?"

"Uh...Faith, I think. Not sure on the last name, but maybe it starts with a 'P' or a 'Q.'"

Quillen. Faith Quillen. The name had been in Annie's databases. Before he got kicked out of the Alliance—another reason Devon wasn't sad to have given them the finger—Richard Navick had identified her as a possible OTS cell leader. And here she was, sitting a few meters away from him in a sketchy club on Pandora.

Devon studied her. The barely noticeable tapping of her feet suggested impatience and perhaps a lack of discipline, but quick, sharp eyes suggested intelligence as well. Mostly, however, she diligently watched her companion in the expensive shirt. The one Pablo didn't recognize.

He is in charge.

He is.

The young man's clothes indicated wealth, and a lot of it, which fit Navick's profile of the OTS leaders. His external demeanor was contrived and abrupt. Not a guy you wanted to kick back and party with.

Devon concentrated until he detected the carotid artery running down the man's neck. The pulse raced much faster than Faith's did. The man was either very agitated or very passionate about the cause. The cause being destroying Artificials and killing Prevos.

Faith leaned in closer across the table, and the man turned his head and scanned the room until his gaze froze on Devon.

Devon didn't flinch, instead meeting his stare calmly.

What are you doing?

Picking a fight.

I strengthened your muscular structure so you could properly defend yourself from attacks, not so you could start them.

I didn't start it. He did, when his little clique started killing Prevos.

The man pushed his chair out and stood. His focus did not leave Devon as he wound through the dance floor, not even when he passed centimeters from the woman in the scarlet dress. Behind him, his pals followed more hesitantly.

He stopped two meters away from Devon's table. "You're an abomination. You haven't the right to flaunt your depravity in public."

Devon took a slow sip of his drink. Set it down.

The man's mode of speech was crisp, overly accentuated and carried a slight Earth European accent; his features bore the perfection of expensive genetic enhancement. All indicators of excessive wealth. The room was dark and strobing dance floor lights played hell with the optics, but he took the best image he could of the man's face using his ocular implant before responding.

"This is Pandora. Artificials aren't illegal here, much as Earth might want for them to be. And neither am I."

"You think a flimsy thing like political boundaries will protect you? You think you're safe here?"

"I think I'm safe everywhere."

"How *dare* you be arrogant! How dare you—"

Faith put a hand on his arm. "This isn't the place to cause a scene."

"I decide what is and isn't the place. This freak needs to learn some respect, then he needs to die."

A bouncer appeared at their table, as if by chance. Funny, that. "Is there any trouble here?"

Devon adopted a fearful expression. "Yes, sir. This person threatened my life."

The bouncer scowled at Devon. "Son, did you ever think it may not be the best idea to flash those eyes in a place like this?"

"I'm sorry, sir. I didn't realize."

"The hell you didn't—"

"As for you four, out. Now. Everybody here except you is just trying to have a good time, and violence does not encourage having a good time."

"But—"

The bouncer towered over Devon's adversary. "Out, before I see you out."

Faith grabbed the man's arm and tugged him away. "Come on. We have bigger things to concentrate on."

Did they, now? Devon gave the bouncer an ingratiating smile. "Thank you, sir. I'll see about getting some shadewraps, if I can find some which will let me see in a place as dark as this."

"Good idea. You need to be careful, with things the way they are."

With things the way they are. Such a loaded, foreboding statement, but he'd brood over it later.

He turned to find Pablo shaking his head. "I should've known when Noah vouched for you that you were sure to be more trouble than you were worth."

"Come on, Pablo. You understand the danger OTS poses, don't you?"

"Yeah, yeah. They're a nasty bunch of *pendejos* with weapons. Shit, this is going to get ugly no matter what, isn't it?"

"Yes, it is. Give me a minute? I need to take care of something. I'll be back."

Pablo groaned but waved him off, absolving himself of responsibility for whatever followed.

Devon.

I know what I'm doing.

Do not get me killed. It is not in my ten-year life plan.

Not to worry, it's not in mine either.

He strolled through the crowd—it was swelling as the hour grew later—and eased out the door. He looked left, then right, and picked up four infrared signatures.

He headed to the right.

"Something told me you'd be stupid enough to follow us." It was the leader's voice, but it didn't come from the closest body.

A meatier hand attached to a bulkier arm reached out from the shadows to grab his arm. The next instant Devon's hand was wrapped around the guy's throat; he jerked and spasmed as electrical current coursed through him. After several seconds he went limp, and Devon let him drop to the ground.

"He'll live, but he'll need a few replacement cybernetic parts. And a new eVi. Anyone else?"

The leader drew a Daemon and shot Devon in the chest. Devon merely glared at the man as his recently upgraded, custom shield easily dispersed the energy. "Please. You will have to do much better than that. You could try blowing up my apartment building—that's the kind of destruction you cowards excel at, isn't it?"

He sensed the attack from behind two hundred forty-seven milliseconds—an eternity—before it came and ducked beneath the swing from the other male lackey.

He grabbed a shoulder as the guy faltered forward, delivering a solid jolt of electricity as he shoved him to the ground. "Don't do that again."

"Dammit, J—" Faith cut herself off. "Your mother will murder you *and* me if you die in an alley on Pandora. Remember the damn mission."

The response came through gritted teeth. "The mission is the elimination of monsters like him."

"Yes, preferably without them eliminating *you*."

Devon and the leader had stared at one another throughout the exchange, but the man had positioned himself between Devon and the busy thoroughfare beyond—too close to potential witnesses, too far for Devon to reach him.

Now the man blinked and reluctantly nodded. He and Faith cautiously backed toward the street.

Before they turned to disappear, he stopped to sneer at Devon. "Humanity will not tolerate your existence for long. We won't let you rule us. You'll see." Then they rounded the corner and slinked away.

If you try to follow them, I will incapacitate you here and now.

I'm not.... He rolled his eyes and went inside.

Besides, we now know several things we didn't know before tonight. We know one of the leaders of OTS, if not the leader, is a young man and indeed notably wealthy. His first name starts with a 'J' or 'G,' and he's a sycophant to his mother—who, given the money angle, is probably someone of repute. Also, he's from or was educated in Europe on Earth. And most importantly, we know what he looks like.

Annie sighed in his head. *I suppose we do know those things. It would be enough to begin a cross-referencing analysis if I had access to my databases, but I do not. Shall I send the information to Richard Navick?*

Nah, I'll tell him in the morning. Or his morning, which I guess is in around four hours. I want to see how he's doing anyway.

He eased onto the stool beside Pablo once more and smiled blithely. "I think I'll grab another beer. You in?"

21

ANESI ARCH

Miriam met Richard at the door to the suite she'd rented. His broad smile and warm hug were so welcome. She'd missed him.

He drew back but kept his hands on her shoulders. "It is beyond good to see you."

"You've no idea. How are you?"

"I'm...things are a mess again, you know."

She scrutinized him more closely. She thought he'd settled into his new job, relatively speaking, but now dark circles and deep lines around his eyes weighed down his features. He appeared more troubled than the last time she'd seen him.

"I do. But you're okay?"

"I am. Most of the time."

"And Will?"

"Glad to have me with him, if currently somewhat angry at the rest of the galaxy. He's fine."

"I'll accept the cryptic answers for now, but you are not off the hook. Thank you for coming here so we could meet in person. I'm afraid the things we need to discuss can't be trusted to even an encrypted comm system."

"No, they can't."

His voice had taken on a darker tenor; she gazed at him in increasing suspicion. She'd given him only the slightest indication of why she wanted to meet, but she *had* given him an indication. "What are *you* here to discuss?"

"Not what you expect. I realize you want to talk about Winslow, the new government, OTS and everything else happening at home, but first I need to tell you something. And you're not going to like it."

There was quite the deficit in good news these days, it seemed. "Then let's get drinks and sit."

"Excellent idea."

When they'd moved to the chairs, a small table separating them, he took a long sip of his drink—she hadn't overlooked the fact he'd mixed it strong—and stared into the glass.

"Richard, we've known each other for forty-four years. Whatever it is, just say it."

He exhaled slowly and set the drink down. "It's regarding the First Crux War—more specifically, the day it began and how it did so."

ℛ

Miriam stood at the window, hands clasped in a vice-grip at the small of her back, eyes shut to the stars outside.

They killed their own civilians. Murdered seventeen people in cold blood, and in so doing manipulated us into a war that killed hundreds of thousands.

Richard's voice came from somewhere behind her and off to her left. "There's essentially zero chance Caleb knows. He didn't know his father had been a Division agent until after they returned from the portal space late last year. He learned of his father's past directly from Graham, and Graham was ignorant of this mission until now."

"It wouldn't reflect on him if he did. Children should not be made to bear the sins of their parents." Her voice came out pinched and taut from the strain of keeping control.

She'd meant the words, for what meager amount they mattered. Even at her angriest she wasn't vindictive enough to try to make this about Caleb.

"No. But he doesn't know. This is the Federation's single most closely guarded secret."

Breathe in through your nose. Hold. Out through your mouth. "Little wonder."

"You don't have to play stoic with me, Miriam."

She opened her eyes and glanced over, surprised to discover he now stood beside her. "And I appreciate that. But if I lose control now, I might not get it back again."

"They believe they had their reasons, but I'm not sure—"

"Oh, I understand their reasons perfectly well. It was a brilliant strategy which put the Alliance on the defensive from the first hour. Distracted the politicians, muddled the objectives. I remember those early weeks of the war. It was a chaos of confusion, shouted accusations and blame shaming. Honestly, if it had gone any other way, we very well could have stamped out the rebellion inside a month." *And David would not have died.*

He regarded her in slight surprise and significant curiosity. "Would you have done it? If it was the only chance to win a war?"

"No—and they did it to start a war they could win, an important distinction. But I knew others who would have. Breveski, Giehl. Slippery beast, morality in war."

"No kidding." He dropped his chin to his chest. "Talking about this leaves me sick to my stomach. I thought long and hard about leaving Division. But...Graham wasn't involved, and...we have to take the world as we find it. With the state of things, I suspect I can do the most good on Seneca. Given I can do zero good on Earth."

She nodded jerkily; he wasn't wrong. "Yet Chairman Vranas was involved. *Eleni* was involved. Not merely involved—at the center of it. I trusted her. I confided in her. I called her a friend...."

Her voice nearly broke. *Control.* "And it feels like she may as well have been David's murderer."

"She wasn't. More than two years and countless decisions on both sides separate the events." He shook his head sluggishly, as if searching for better platitudes. "It was twenty-six years ago. People change, grow wiser. They learn from their mistakes."

"Of course they do. Strangely, that doesn't so much help right now."

"I agree." His shoulders dropped. "Look, there's really nothing else to be said. It is what it is. You had to know—I couldn't live with myself if I kept it from you—but we should probably focus on the crisis at hand."

She gave him a tight grimace. "I'm afraid I'm a bit peckish. Would you mind terribly seeing about having some dinner delivered?"

"Not at all." He squeezed her shoulder and left, understanding what she meant was that she needed a few minutes alone.

She moved to one of the chairs and sat down, then dropped her elbows to her knees and her head into her hands.

She should turn around and go back to Vancouver. Find another way. There were limits to even deals with the devil, lines which should never be crossed.

Curse Pamela Winslow and her cabal for forcing Miriam to cross them all.

It wasn't fair.

She'd always interpreted 'unfair' as meaning a challenge existed to surmount, and considered those who used it as an excuse to be indolent, over-entitled or simply cowards.

Maybe she was now all those things...but dammit, it *was not fair* that she be put in such a position.

"Did you ever consider doing anything with your life other than serving in the military?"

Miriam studied David over the rim of her glass of Cabernet. "Not seriously, no."

"Your father's influence?"

She laughed lightly. "You'd think, wouldn't you? And possibly at first, in the margins, though he was far likelier to have driven me away from the military than to it. No, I've always felt called to military service. It displays the characteristics I admire: it embodies structure and order. There are rules and clear direction and a chain of command which must be respected without question. The institution is a rock. It signifies certainty and security, for those it serves and those who serve it."

Her mouth clamped shut. Why was she so eager to be honest with him, to spill her innermost dreams and desires in response to his casual questions? People called her taciturn for a reason, but when David Solovy was in the room, reason was nowhere to be found.

He retrieved the bottle and refilled her glass. "Yet you don't seem to have any qualms about giving orders instead of taking them."

"I'm complicated."

"Oh, of that I have no doubt."

"I'm still taking them as well as giving them, but no, I don't have any qualms about leading. I earned the right to give orders—for now here at this small outpost on Perona. Later, perhaps elsewhere, to a greater number of soldiers. But I earned the right operating within the system I respect, and it's teaching me what I need to know to be a worthy leader."

"You're delightful."

Her glass landed on the table with a clang. "I was not trying to be—" Her eyes narrowed as her chin notched up. "Are you patronizing me, Captain Solovy?"

His face, always so expressive and alive with personality and verve, looked vaguely panicked. "No. No, I would never. Please, forgive me, dorogaya."

She blinked in surprise at his use of an endearment—this was only their third date, for heaven's sake—but he resumed talking before she could protest. "You are delightful, truly. I admire your outlook. It's refreshing."

He was not getting off so easily. "But?"

He huffed a breath. "But the universe is not ordered, and it will not become so simply because one wishes it. The universe is chaos made manifest. The military does a fine job of creating an illusion of structure, of dependable rules to provide an answer for every situation. But it is only an illusion, one which on its best days holds the volneniya at bay."

She took a sip of wine to buy her time to consider her response, and to internalize the fact that the way he peppered conversations with colorful Russian interjections was rather enchanting.

"If you genuinely believe that, then why are you here? Why join the military, and why stay after your service commitment was fulfilled?"

He cocked an eyebrow like some kind of lothario. She despised lotharios, which did nothing to quell the fluttering in her chest. "To get to be the hero. Turns out I'm better at being the hero than I am at most other things."

"That's a terrible answer."

"You never stop, do you?"

She thought she might be smiling, just a touch. "I don't know how to."

"Indeed. Why am I here, in the military? Because even the chaos needs someone willing to stand in the center of it and say 'enough.'"

David had been right all along, but not until she rose to the pinnacle of military power—where no one remained to create it but her—was she able to see through the illusion.

Now here she stood, terrifyingly free of all structure, unmoored from any rules to guide her. She stood alone, with only her own moral compass to tell her how to move forward when there were none but awful choices to be made.

Allow amoral, power-hungry zealots to lower an iron fist on thousands of innocents, many of them little more than children, killing or imprisoning them for daring to be at the vanguard of technological progress?

Or defy the government she'd devoted her life to serving, ally herself with a murderer and commit treason under any reading of the law?

I am so, so sorry, David. How many times must she apologize to him, if solely in her mind? How many times could she expect the ghost of his conscience to forgive her?

I will always forgive you, dushen'ka, *because I know you will always do what you believe to be right.*

It was nothing but a memory whispering in her mind...and it would have to do.

Now it was time for her to be the one to stand in the center of the chaos and say 'enough.'

When Richard returned, she had splashed water on her face, re-braided her hair and poured herself another drink. She ignored the food he placed on the center table, instead clasping her hands together in her lap and meeting his questioning gaze.

"Here's what I need you to do for me."

R

SENECA

CAVARE
SENECAN FEDERATION MILITARY HEADQUARTERS

The adiamene manufacturing plant now operated at full capacity. Assembly of the shipyard above the newly declared colony of Murat was complete and construction on a new class of ships had begun. These were good things.

Strife and discord appeared to be the default state of civilization, however. This was a less good thing, but Eleni Gianno could not change it.

What she could do was not only be prepared for it, but be more prepared for it than other interested parties. In so doing, the people she protected were better able to thrive in times of peace and survive in times of war.

The new Independent Defense Consortium of Colonies didn't concern her. Even if it did not become an ally, a three-legged stool was a far more stable configuration than a two-legged one. She didn't expect the independent group to be aggressive—not for years anyway—and it would provide an additional check on the Alliance, which *was* threatening to become aggressive again.

The fact Morgan Lekkas led its armed contingent...actually gave her some comfort. It enabled her to keep an eye on Lekkas, and it provided the young woman an outlet into which she could direct her considerable energies.

Eleni frowned in surprise at the request for entry into her office. The hour was quite late, and she was still here only because she'd been waiting on approval to forcibly depose Olivia Montegreu off of Itero. The Cabinet had refused—technically deferred, but the result was the same—her petition for the third time mere minutes ago. Also surprising was the guest. Richard Navick had always been accompanied by Director Delavasi on previous visits to Military Headquarters. According to the request, tonight he came alone.

Curiosity got the better of her, and she opened the door. "Mr. Navick, what brings you—" Her words cut off when Miriam Solovy followed him into the office.

The Alliance Fleet Admiral had been to Eleni's office once before; that visit had not been unannounced and in the dark of night. The woman wasn't in uniform, but she also wore a netted scarf draped loosely over her hair and shoulders which cast her features in shadow. Her face was widely known at this point, particularly in these halls, so it seemed a wise precaution if she intended her presence to be clandestine.

"Miriam? This is...most unexpected." She offered her hand.

Miriam stared at her with such coldness that if she'd been anything less than the Field Marshal, she'd have sought a corner in which to hide. As matters stood, her instincts told her a fairly unpleasant night would now be getting worse.

She withdrew her hand and closed the door behind her guests. "I won't burden you with small talk. I'm certain why ever you are here, it is important, secret and possibly urgent. So what can I do for you?"

Miriam's throat worked visibly. Eleni did her the courtesy of waiting until she chose to speak.

"I understand you know something about planning and instigating a revolution under the noses of your government and unwitting superiors."

What did she mean? Eleni's role as a Federation leader in the First Crux War had never been a secret. It was impossible that Miriam hadn't known it long before their first meeting on Romane a year earlier.

This was something else.

Eleni's gaze shot to Navick as the pieces snapped into place. Damn Delavasi and his unpredictable, mercurial conscience. "Miriam, you must understand—"

"Don't. I am not here to listen to explanations, justifications or apologies. They would not have mattered then, and they do not matter now."

Miriam drew in a breath and set her shoulders with a sobering dignity. "I am here to ask for your help."

PART IV:

WHAT LIES BENEATH

"But first a hush of peace, a soundless calm descends;
The struggle of distress and fierce impatience ends
Mute music sooths my breast—unuttered harmony
That I could never dream till earth was lost to me."

— Emily Bronte

Portal: C-7

System Designation: Tayna

22

UNCHARTED SYSTEM
TAYNA PORTAL SPACE

"Nothing? At all?"

'Nothing. Nothing across the EM spectrum that can't be attributed to natural phenomenon. No readings that suggest the presence of organic life. No artificial structures on the surface or in orbit. The atmosphere is nominally compatible with organic life, but the air is too thin to sustain humans for more than a few minutes. The same can be said for the surface temperature. It averages -9° at the equator and drops twelve degrees for every ten degree change in latitude.'

Alex wrinkled her nose in disappointment. "It wouldn't be the first time we've come up empty...."

"We should do a little ground reconnaissance, to be thorough—like we did in the other uninhabited portal spaces."

She chuckled and eyed Caleb. Seneca's twin had been the last time they'd touched soil. She knew he was itching to get off the ship for a spell, mostly from the way he vibrated with coiled energy.

Truth be told, she longed for some fresh air herself. "I agree. Valkyrie, is there liquid water anywhere on the surface?"

'Perhaps. If we descend to three kilometers and adopt an equatorial orbital traversal heading, I can search for it.'

"Let's do it. Water holds the best chance for us finding life, or signs of it anyway. If it's not in the water, it won't be far away."

"Unless it's atypical life. Which, let's be honest, out here it usually is."

She made a face at him, but he was right. The Khokteh were the only species they'd encountered that were remotely similar to humans or the multitude of organic life in their universe. Well, the dragons arguably qualified, but they were at least tangentially tied to home.

As they descended, she was drawn to the landscape they flew above. The surface beneath them spread out in a frozen expanse of ice. No mountains or valleys broke the endless stretch of alabaster. Even the bright steel sky was bleached of color.

'I've located a small pond 4.3 kilometers to the northeast.'

She tried to spot it out the viewport, but everything was white-on-white. "Terrific, Valkyrie. Still no life signs?"

'Correct.'

"Let's set down, then."

She glanced over her shoulder to see Caleb already preparing the gear for a ground excursion. He really was going stir-crazy. She acknowledged the twinge of guilt the realization triggered…but she had to trust him to speak up if it became a problem.

They landed well back from a pond of crystal-clear waters. After their usual pre-sortie checks, she opened the hatch, extended the ramp and headed down.

Frigid air bombarded her cheeks in a thousand tiny needles. She didn't stand to last long without the helmet. She certainly had her fresh air, though.

The ground beneath her feet was crunchy, more snow than ice, but it felt solid enough.

She trailed Caleb toward the pond. "Theories on why liquid water is at this specific location, Valkyrie? There's no unique terrain nearby to account for it."

'My best guess? Subterranean geothermal activity may extend unusually close to the surface here, warming the ground underneath this area.'

They reached the snow-packed shore of the pond, and Caleb crouched at the edge of the water. "This has to be the most pristine, clearest water I've ever seen. Astonishing."

She knelt beside him. "I kind of want to drink it."

He rolled his eyes. "Fine, but run the analyzer on the ice first."

She complied, giving the snow pack beside her a quick sweep and studying the results. "We're good."

She pushed the breather mask down to her neck and inhaled unfiltered air. It was like the air atop Denali—cold enough to freeze her lungs solid and hardly air at all. She didn't remove her gloves, but cupped them in the water and drew her hands to her lips.

It tasted as one would expect, which was to say heavenly. Glacial and pure. Caleb followed suit and gave his approval at the result.

She was cupping another sip when an unpleasant possibility occurred to her. She'd tested the snow, not the pond's water. Just because it tasted pure didn't mean it was. "Crap, I hope we're not ingesting the locals."

She groped around in her pack for a small container and scooped up some water in it, then ran the analyzer over it. "Whew. Nothing—not so much as bacterial contaminants of note."

'I am detecting movement three hundred thirty meters to the northwest.'

Caleb was instantly on his feet. "How fast—how big, and how many?"

'Bipedal walking speed. It is a single creature of approximately 1.6 meters' height.'

Alex repositioned the breather mask and stood as well, her pulse racing in excitement at the prospect of the looming encounter. And healthy respect for a potential adversary—shouldn't forget that part. "Where the hell did it come from? There's nothing for...a very long way."

'I do not know. It simply appeared.'

Valkyrie sounded perplexed, but Alex was more intrigued by the fact it *had* appeared. "I take it the alien is approaching the ship?"

'No. It is approaching you.'

Caleb cocked his head at that. Uncloaked, the *Siyane* presented a far more distinct and visible profile on the ice than their comparatively tiny forms.

He turned to her. "This means there are factors at play we can't see or identify. It means we can't predict anything about what will happen next. We don't want to be threatening as an opening move, but unlatch the safety clasp from your Daemon's holster and be ready to follow my lead."

She gave him a terse nod. She'd been working on improving her reaction time, on transforming fighting techniques into muscle-memory reflexes. She wanted to think she was prepared for whatever came—assuming what came wasn't a guided missile or an aerial strike—but this was still Caleb's domain.

They moved away from the water to firmer ground. Closer to the *Siyane*, but they didn't retreat to the ship. This alien was coming to greet them on foot, and they would do the same.

She observed its approach through the ship's visual scanner. The alien was bipedal and vaguely humanoid, with long arms and legs compared to its torso, though it was also shorter than them. A square-ish head was dominated by its eyes. They were enormous, diamond-shaped and shone in some form of churning luminescence. It wore a full-body cover—a coat of some kind—so she couldn't determine much else about its physical appearance.

"It doesn't look hostile."

Caleb's voice was low and tight, but gentle to her. "Which means...?"

"Absolutely nothing."

"Correct. We've got no references for translation, so body language will be doubly important."

"Hands at my side. Should we don our helmets?"

He thought on it a moment. "No. Not yet. It's organic and humanoid, so we should make it evident we are as well. Commonality is reassuring."

The alien was now close enough to see clearly using normal vision, so she switched to her own sight. She kept the link to

Valkyrie open. Glowing eyes ought not to frighten the alien, seeing as its own eyes radiated like lighthouse range lights.

The alien's outer garment was made of a white fiber weave that blended into the backdrop of frozen tundra, and up close the garment continued to obscure many details about the body it protected. The alien wore boot-style foot coverings, and its gait had a loping, almost rolling style to it, as if the balls of its feet were not flat. Mittens covered its hands, which bent into the palms.

The face peeking out from the coat's hood was leathery in texture and a muddy terra cotta color. The large eyes were not any one color, but rather multiple hues blending and shifting. What might be lips extended in two thin lines across the breadth of its face.

"I don't see any weapons. Valkyrie, are you picking up any EM emissions coming from it?"

'I am not.'

"Okay. Palms open and slightly raised at your sides."

"Got it."

The alien stopped four meters away and regarded them with its whirling, colorful pools.

Alex dipped her chin carefully. "Greetings."

The alien's—yep, they were lips—parted into a smile so broad it took up the majority of its face. A high-pitched, sing-song melody of sounds emerged from them. The voice sounded almost like a nightingale's warble.

But that wasn't all. Its eyes pulsed in time with the spoken tones, and their color shifted in beats—first aqua and silver, then plum and rose. Even more astonishingly, its skin seemed to gleam from within, subtly taking on flowing colors as well.

'The alien is speaking on multiple bands and frequencies. In addition to what you can hear, I'm picking up harmonic overtones in the ultrasonic range and accompanying tones below the fundamental in the infrasonic range.'

Caleb kept his expression scrupulously neutral. "Any idea what it's saying on any of those frequencies?"

'None whatsoever.'

He took a single half-step forward. "We do not understand you, but we want to. We come in peace."

The alien spoke again and waved out with an arm, then drew the arm in to its chest. Did it want them to come closer? When they didn't move, it repeated the gesture. Additional words preceded a pointing motion back in the direction it had come. Now it pointed at them, then behind it.

"I think it wants us to follow it to wherever it came from."

"Agreed. We'll go along with it for now. Valkyrie, keep close watch and be ready to swoop to the rescue."

'Hopefully swooping will not be required, nor rescue. But I am ready to do both.'

He squeezed her hand. "Alex?"

"I'm ready, too."

Together they took a step forward.

The alien smiled again, gestured again and stepped backward. They followed, and after a few steps the alien turned and began walking purposefully away, reversing its course. It peered over its shoulder every few steps to ensure they continued to follow.

But ahead of them was only an endless expanse of ice. Where could it be leading them? From where had it originated?

'I continue to detect nothing in the vicinity. Structures could be cloaked, but I see no evidence of it—no minute distortions or emissions which are common hallmarks of similar technology. If they are using Metigen technology, however, I would presumably be unable to detect the markers in any event.'

Caleb's gaze scanned the horizon and back to their alien companion, then swept around anew. "Understood. Nevertheless, it did come from somewhere."

Abruptly the alien stopped and pivoted to them. More chirping sounds accompanied increasingly animated hand motions; its eyes and skin pulsed energetically.

As she watched the alien in growing frustration, she began to have a...sense.

Safe. Hidden. Refuge.

The words weren't in her head as such. Instead they were an overwhelming impression, like a gust of wind pressing on her chest. "Caleb, did you feel that?"

"I did."

'It communicates on multiple levels. This might include using senses we do not possess.'

"Telepathy? Nice." She took a deep breath and tried to convey understanding. The alien stared at Caleb until he did the same. Then it knelt and placed a hand on the ice...and the hand disappeared.

Then the ice disappeared.

A circular depression twelve meters in diameter materialized half a meter below the surface. The circumference was a perfect circle and the floor a dark metal, indicating artificial creation. A seam ran along the edge where the depression met the ice, indicating it moved, and another, smaller seam ringed the center.

"Valkyrie, why couldn't you detect the hologram projection?"

'A good question indeed. I have no idea. This implies Metigen origin as an obvious answer, but I cannot rule out the possibility it is a tool of the native species.'

The alien stepped down into the depression and gestured for them to follow.

She studied Caleb, wanting to read the expression behind his words. His brow was furrowed and his irises sparkled an animated, brilliant sapphire against the ubiquitous white landscape.

She imagined her expression looked as complicated, but she nodded. "I think we go."

A corner of his mouth curled up. "I think we do, too."

'I am concerned about my inability to detect their technology. This suggests it is a great deal more advanced than our own, and thus dangerous to you.'

"Spirit of adventure, Valkyrie. You'll be able to see everything I do. And we're armed—it didn't attempt to take our weapons."

'Do I need to point out your weapons may not matter when pitted against superior technology?'

"Not really." She grabbed Caleb's hand once more, and they stepped into the depression. The alien's face illuminated a rosy gold.

The floor began to descend, rotating slowly around a spindle in the center as walls of ice rose above them.

'I am also curious about the manner—'

The ground rematerialized above them—darkness descended—and Valkyrie was gone.

23

UNCHARTED PLANET
TAYNA PORTAL SPACE

Valkyrie had 47.3 microseconds to react to the quantum field closing over the depression. She sped along Alex's synapses to the correct cluster and forced a toggle of their connection with 5.1 microseconds to spare.

Then Alex was gone, and she was alone on the surface of an alien planet in an alien universe.

She evaluated her options:
-     She knew the location of the entrance to whatever existed underground with a three-centimeter level of precision. She could fire on it and attempt to break the illusion, the barrier and the machinery of the lift before it ferried Alex and Caleb too far out of her reach. But until the barrier was destroyed she would not know *their* precise location, thus such an action carried an unacceptably high risk of injuring or killing them.
-     She could fire on the ground surrounding the location of the entrance in order to expose the machinery burrowed into the earth. This option held a thirty-seven percent reduced chance of the same risk.
-     She could search the immediate area, expandable to the entire planet, for the power source driving the undetectable cloaking field and the lift. This option stood a small—nine-to-seventeen percent—chance of also exposing other entrances she may be able to exploit.
-     She could depart the planet and the pocket universe and

seek Mesme out on Portal Prime, assuming the Metigen had returned there, and request the alien's assistance.

- She could depart the planet, the pocket universe and the portal network, return home and bring back human assistance. Perhaps Prevo assistance.

- She could do nothing.

The last option was dismissed out of hand. If they—

Her awareness of the pinpoints of blue light began when they were fifty-six meters from the exterior of the *Siyane*. They passed through the shields and hull 3.5 seconds later as effortlessly as if the material were made of gossamer. In the cabin the lights coalesced into the vague form of a faie. Interesting.

'Are you Mnemosyne?'

So you know of my colleague. No. I am called Lakhes. What may I call you, sentient ship?

'Valkyrie. What have you done with my companions?'

Your companions are safe. Interesting name, Valkyrie. It arrives layered with imagery and implied significance.

'I always thought so. Given the Metigens' proclivity for Greek mythology, I assume yours is derived from Lachesis. The 'dispenser of lots.' Do you believe you determine others' destiny? Do you strive to do this for Alex and Caleb? Will you harm them to do it?'

'Metigens'? Is that what the Humans call us? Logical, in a literal sense, if not particularly inventive. I did not expect to need to repeat myself to a quantum synthetic, but so be it. Your companions are safe.

My purpose here is to impart this information to you, so that you will not act rashly upon the inhabitants of this planet. They are a peaceful species who have committed no offense.

'They have kidnapped Alex and Caleb. They—'

No. Your companions may return whenever they wish, though it is my hope they will instead elect to spend a measure of time below. The individual which greeted them did so at my behest, because I believe they can learn much from those who dwell here.

'Learn much about what? About the purpose of the portal network? About the universe through the master portal? About you?'

Yes.

'What is your species called, then? We would be happy to address you by your proper name.'

My species is known as the Katasketousya.

'Known by whom?'

What a clever little sentient ship you are. But I will tell you no more today. My purpose here is fulfilled. Do not fear for your companions, and do not attempt to harm the species which now calls the depths of this planet home. Patience, Valkyrie.

'Platitudes are not—"

But the Metigen—Katasketousya—was now gone as well, dissipating and vanishing as swiftly as it had arrived.

If forced to give voice to the sensation she felt, she decided it would be considered annoyance. Seeing as annoyance was counterproductive to the present crisis, she encouraged those processes to wither.

What had she learned?

- The Metigens called themselves Katasketousya.
- Their fetish for Greek mythology continued to be evidenced.
- They were easily as infuriating as Alex had insisted.
- This Metigen, Lakhes, communicated with the local inhabitants, as other Metigens had with the Khokteh and humans. What it presented itself as to them was not apparent.
- Lakhes strove to protect this species, a course of action they had yet to encounter in any other portal.
- Multiple Metigens knew of their explorations in the portal network. Unlike the one they encountered on Ireltse, Lakhes did not intend to discourage their efforts or seek harm upon them. At least not today, here, now. On the contrary, it was trying to teach them some thing or things. Alex believed the Metigens had ulterior motives for all their actions, so the

likelihood of purposeful manipulation must be a consideration in her analysis.

What was she able to extrapolate from this information with a reasonable level of confidence?

- The Metigens now or had once frequented a place where additional alien species lived and interacted with one another. She could not assert this with one hundred percent certainty, but the statement providing their name had connoted 'known by others.'

- The technology behind the hologram projection and the quantum layer preventing her from contacting Alex and cloaking what existed below was Metigen in origin.

- Lakhes knew the Aurora portal opened into what humans called the Metis Nebula, from which she inferred some level of involvement on its part in the observation of their universe.

- The Metigens were actively hiding this species, though she dared not guess from what.

Bolstered by this new if still distressingly incomplete data, she returned to her initial assessment of her options.

She could do nothing.

24

UNCHARTED PLANET

Luminescence from the spindle at the center of the platform returned light to the space an instant after it had plunged into darkness, and Caleb loosened the grip on his blade even as Alex's grip on his forearm tightened.

Her eyes were flaring brightly—but in panic rather than an artificial glow. "She's gone. The connection, the comm channel, everything!"

He kept a bead on the alien, who was also watching them intently. *"Valkyrie? Are you there?"* He received only silence.

Alex spun to their guide in agitation and began pointing to the darkness above. "We have to go back up. Take us to the surface!"

The alien's eyes and face lit up in pulsing colors as a stream of chirps and trills poured forth.

Alex's gestures grew more frantic in response. "Up *there*! Reverse this goddamn machine and take us the fuck back to the surface!"

The alien pulled off one of its gloves, revealing four long, multi-jointed fingers ending in small, blunt claws. It stepped forward, reached up and placed its palm on Alex's jaw as it continued talking.

Caleb tensed anew, his own fingers again closing firmly around the hilt of his blade as he prepared to force his way between them.

Alex jerked in surprise, but after a blink, stilled. "What...?" Her voice faded off, and her face took on a curious expression. Her nose crinkled up in what he recognized as consternation, but she didn't appear afraid or in pain.

He reached for her nonetheless—and she held up a hand to keep him at bay.

"He says this place is a...refuge...for them, a place of safety...and there's a...barrier of some sort...to hide their presence. He apologizes if it...prevents us from talking to our...others, but promises he and his...people mean us no harm."

The alien's palm fell away with a ponderous tilt of its—his?—head.

Alex smiled a bit hesitantly, then turned to Caleb. "I don't understand exactly what just happened, but somehow through touch he's able to...make my brain translate what he's saying. Sort of."

"And now you know it's a 'he?'"

"Yeah? I think so?" She gazed up into the growing darkness above them. They were descending a long way indeed. "I'm worried about Valkyrie, and she's definitely going to be worried about us. But I think it'll be all right if we spend a few minutes seeing what's down here before we return to the surface."

He nodded cautiously, taken aback by her dramatic about-face. The alien's touch must have been powerful indeed.

Twenty long, dim seconds later, half the stone—no longer ice—walls surrounding the lift gave way to brighter but still faint light. Two more revolutions and the platform came to a stop. Their guide stepped through an open archway and motioned for them to follow.

A city awaited them on the other side of the archway. Not a city humans would build, to be sure. There were no straight lines or sharp edges. There were no skyscrapers, for the sky could not be reached from this place.

A broad, winding pathway provided a route among a maze of structures carved into the stone and buttressed by an architecture of elegant metal arches and cupolas. Alcoves and cylindrical tunnels shared space with unexpectedly spacious open areas and airy, multi-level complexes.

Hundreds of aliens were in plain sight, going about their business. It was warm down here, and unlike the one who brought them, the rest of the aliens wore no heavy coats. They did wear clothes of some kind—form-fitting woven leather or linen bodysuits from what Caleb could see.

Their habitat built into the crust of the planet extended as far as his vision reached, albeit chaotically and displaying no apparent order beyond the pathway cutting through the middle of it. Edifices built into the earth here, vast swaths of rock carved out and put to productive purpose there.

Their guide faced them and began chattering. Then, probably remembering they did not yet understand him, the alien removed his other glove. He tucked it into a coat pocket and stretched his arms out to them.

Touch. Alex's experience suggested they communicated via touch as much as sight and sound. Caleb removed his own gloves while Alex did the same; they shared a nod of confirmation before each offered a hand. The alien grasped them both.

Caleb worked to concentrate, to decipher what was happening. It wasn't like communicating with Akeso. This alien was *speaking*, but the message came in the form of concepts as much as words. Of course, that could simply be the language barrier at work. As they began to understand the language, the impressions may well become complex sentences. For now his brain did its best to bring form to the amorphous impressions.

Welcome, strangers. Taenarin Aris, this, our haven. Your haven. Welcome, and see our hospitality to accept.

Know me, Jaisc, Iona-Cead to the Taenarin.

Alex missed Valkyrie.

She missed her in a gnawing, existential way, like that nagging feeling you got when you'd forgotten something important, but if you concentrated on it the idea flitted away. She missed the comfort of being able to reach out any time she wanted and touch another mind, one so unlike her own yet now an intrinsic part of her. She missed the new, celestial plane of existence Valkyrie allowed her to access and sometimes the only plane upon which the universe seemed to truly exist.

She missed Valkyrie for all those reasons and countless more. But right now, far and above those considerations, she most of all missed having a damn translator.

"All this touching is making me twitchy," she muttered while she folded her environment suit into a fastidious, hyper-neat square and set it atop the shelving.

"You think you're twitchy? I catch myself reaching for my blade every time the alien's hand threatens to move toward me." Caleb put his suit next to hers on the shelf, somehow folded with far greater neatness than hers with far less effort expended. "But they seem harmless. So far."

She grimaced and inspected the small room. They had no legitimate need for the suits or the breather masks down here in the cavernous subterranean space and, after enough arm waving to qualify as a game of charades, they'd been taken to a building not far from the entry to store the extra equipment.

They'd encountered several aliens on the way, leading to much rapid chirping and skin-tone light shows as Jaisc had explained their presence to the agitated passersby.

She couldn't say what the alien actually *said* about them. Her eVi was running relational comparisons of the sounds, colors and few words which had been imparted, but it was a poor substitute for Valkyrie's quantum algorithms when it came to developing a translation program.

She missed Valkyrie.

When she turned around, she found Caleb watching her, eyes twinkling in blatant amusement. "What?"

"You look good."

She glanced down at the black, stretchy thermal leggings and mock turtleneck she'd worn under the suit. "In my thermals?"

"Yes, in your thermals. They're very...form-fitting."

"Oh." A sly grin grew on her lips as her gaze drifted down before returning to his face. "That works both ways, you know."

"Does it?" He took the tiny step forward required to draw her into his arms and bring his mouth to hers.

She relaxed in his embrace, grateful for the warmth, safety and always desire it brought. "One more alien encounter survived."

"Indeed...." His lips lingered on hers for another breath before pulling away, regret in his voice. "Speaking of, we shouldn't keep our guide waiting too long."

"Right. We need to try to learn as much as we can as quickly as possible, so we can get back to the surface."

"I'm sure Valkyrie's okay, if concerned."

"We were linked when the elevator started descending, which means she was able to detect the barrier, or whatever it is, before it blocked us. So she knows what happened."

"I'm glad you found a way to let her shut off the connection. *Extremely* glad."

"Me, too." It still unnerved her a bit, the idea that Valkyrie must have forced her mind to take action without her knowledge or decision to do it. She was glad of it, but also unnerved. It wasn't a question of trust, but rather of control.

She found a light pullover in her pack and tugged it on over the thermals, then positioned the pack on her back. "Ready."

Jaisc was waiting for them in the larger, connected anteroom. As soon as they arrived he stepped between them and clasped their hands in his.

Show you home, share world, ours.

She raised an eyebrow gamely at Caleb over Jaisc's head; the alien only came up to her shoulders, so it was an easy gesture. "Sounds excellent. We're eager to learn about your society—such as why you live underground."

Always did, short times above, now to remain hidden but is our way.

"Wait, you understood me?" Thus far the communication had been one-way for all but the simplest of matters.

Jaisc tilted his head to one side, then the other, akin to 'sort of.' He reached up and touched her lips, *not from here*, then her hand again, *from here*.

"So as we're learning to understand you through touch, you're learning to understand us as well?"

Works as such. Come.

And with that, they were off.

25

TAENARIN ARIS

A sculpted ceiling dipped low above them in a porous tangle of twisting archways and hollows.

A group of children played in the maze, scrambling along ledges and swinging across the archways—and it was suddenly obvious why the aliens' hands, feet and digits were so long and flexible. The children gripped crevices and outcroppings with the practiced ease of professional climbers.

On spotting their approach, the children leapt down to the ground in front of them in a cacophony of high-pitched warbles and prismatic skin.

Her and Caleb's eVis had independently decided the shifting skin hues did not correspond directly to the words being spoken, but instead signified the accompanying sentiment. The swirling irises resided somewhere in between language and mood. They wore their hearts on their sleeves, as it were, their emotions visible to all.

The concept of anyone, strangers included, being able to see what she was feeling honestly terrified Alex. But she supposed it was ingrained so deeply in their culture as to be normal to them.

The children flashed mostly orange and gold. In excitement? Nervousness? They appeared to exhibit both as they stared at her and Caleb in wonder.

Jaisc spoke to the children in a calm tone for thirty seconds or so, then rejoined them.

Permission to greet? To touch?

Caleb nodded. "I'd welcome it." He dropped Jaisc's hand and crouched to meet them at eye level. As they neared he extended both hands, offering them for interaction.

All five of the children rushed up to him, grabbing his hands and running their long fingers all over them and up his forearms, giggling and cackling.

"Hi. It's nice to meet you all." More giggles accompanied bright, rainbow hues pulsing across their skin and eyes.

He understood how to talk to kids, how to make them feel comfortable in a way they usually were not around adults. She knew this about him. But seeing it so persuasively in action gave her pause nonetheless.

It was possibly his most dramatic contradiction, of which there were many: violence and compassion, fervency and tenderness, two halves of the whole, all bundled up together in this complex, beautiful man.

She steeled herself and tentatively joined him. Instantly two of the children diverted their attention to her. One grabbed her hand, but the other reached up to run its fingers through her hair, which she'd unbound when she'd discarded the environment suit. The Taenarin did have hair of a sort, but it was coarse, wiry and uniformly neutrally colored to match their base skin tint.

The child touched her jaw with the other hand.

Pretty. Soft. Red! How make it so red?

She laughed in spite of herself. "It came this way."

The child cooed a pleasant trill that sounded a lot like "Ooooh."

You are from above? Never been above. Scary.

To never have seen the true sky, never have beheld stars.... "It can be scary, yes, but it's also pretty. Far prettier than my hair, I promise you."

That elicited another giggle, which Jaisc cut off with a throat-clearing and what sounded like a lecture. The children backed away wearing pouts, and she and Caleb stood.

Jaisc grasped their hands once more and guided them off to the left. *Kind you are, to respect innocence—*

Caleb jerked as one of the children plowed into him from behind and wrapped its arms around his legs. She recognized the nanosecond flare in his eyes and flexing of the muscles beneath the skin of his jaw. The next instant it was gone, and he shifted around to pat the child on the head with an easy smile.

Jaisc clucked reproachfully until the child reluctantly let go, then spun and ran back to the others. They continued on.

Up ahead steam clouded the air from a geothermal spring. Were they below the pond where they'd landed, and this the heat which melted the water? "Iona-Cead Jaisc, how did you know we were here? How did you know where to find us?"

Slanait Lakhes appeared to me, shared news of your arrival and bid me retrieve you.

Alex frowned in suspicion. "'Slanait'? Is that a title, like 'Iona-Cead?'" Upon meeting a Taenarin referred to as 'Iona-Lui,' they had wrangled out that 'Iona' was a government or leadership title of some sort.

Respectful term. Rescuer. Savior. Protector.

Her face contorted into an exaggerated scowl...but on the other hand, maybe it was good news. Maybe they could learn things from the fact what was surely a Metigen had orchestrated their presence here. "Why do you call this Lakhes 'savior?'"

Led the Exodus, saved ancestors from death. Protects us now.

Caleb exchanged a sobering look with her. His tone was non-chalant, and she expected his heart rate and whatever else Jaisc was reading gave away nothing. "Saved you from death? It sounds quite perilous. Where was your exodus from?"

Home. Taenarin in Amaranthe. But our past, long ago, hundreds of cycles. The impression of length, of a great passage of time. *None alive who made the journey.*

Dammit. "But you have records, yes? You document your history—chronicle it for your descendants and future leaders—don't you?"

Jaisc hesitated.

Memory-keeper. The Caomh. But she resides far from here.

Caleb stopped, forcing Jaisc to do so as well. "We'd be interested in meeting her."

Ah. Will see. Complicated.

Jaisc urged them ahead, past the spring and up a hill toward a multi-level structure.

First, now, simple things. A meal.

ℛ

She and Jaisc sat on a woven mat on the tile floor facing one another, legs crossed and hands clasped together in the center. Caleb was speaking to several of the other Taenarin they'd been introduced to. They'd split up in the hope it would increase their odds of learning something useful in less time.

"The lighting that's everywhere? Why do the walls glow?"

The feith *live in the stone and the ore. They luminesce as part of what they are.*

"What else are they?"

Very small.

Had Jaisc just made a joke? She was able to understand most of his words now, but she could not read the emotions he so flagrantly displayed. "The light dimmed earlier, when we were coming inside. Do they not glow all the time?"

They are in sync with the rhythm of Taenarin Aris.

"Its day-night cycle? But...did you bring the *feith* with you from Taenarin?"

No need. This is Taenarin Aris. They awaited us here.

The statement implied the planet was an exact replica of their homeworld, like Seneca's twin in B-5, except here the reproduction was complete down to the native microscopic life forms. "And the air? How are we, and you, breathing fresh air?"

Jaisc's head tilted in a long sigh, saying louder than words that he was tiring of so many technical questions. The Taenarin seemed to enjoy an unconcerned acceptance of their existence and of the world around them. To be inundated with so many questions likely *was* annoying, but the alien had nonetheless agreed to the conversation.

Alex appreciated the gesture, and she was absolutely going to get her time's worth out of it.

There exist openings. Vents to the surface. Geysers—similar to the spring you saw, but larger, stronger—force air out, draw air in. It is a natural process.

"And these vents are hidden and disguised, as the lift we used was hidden?"

Another shrug.

So it is.

"Hidden by Slanait Lakhes?"

Slanait Lakhes provides our protection. We do not interrogate our protector on the mechanisms by which it is done.

She cringed apologetically. "I'm sorry. I know I'm asking many questions. But we have little time and want to learn as much as we can of your ways and how you came to be here."

Jaisc leaned closer.

Why little time?

"We left a companion on the surface. Because of the quantum—because of the barrier Slanait Lakhes uses to keep you hidden, we can't contact her to tell her we're safe."

I...

Jaisc's eyes darkened until they resembled an aged Syrah thick with tannins

...regret I feel. I was not told of three, only two.

"It's not your fault. She could not have come even had you known."

Why not?

"She's in—she's part of—our ship."

Jaisc sat up straight, radiating bright pulses of color.

Oh. Well that is odd.

Alex chuckled. "I guess it is. In any event, we need to get back to her soon."

Hmm. You will not want to travel to see the Caomh then. It is a period—a day—there, and to return.

R

Caleb watched her fidget and emote around the small room they'd been given to sleep for the night—which they were apparently doing. It turned out it was too cold on the surface in the nighttime hours to be exposed to the air for longer than a few seconds.

If she'd realized it was already evening above, she'd have pushed for a departure earlier. But the Taenarin were undeniably interesting, and the time had flown by.

The room was located in Jaisc's home, as near as they could determine. The hollowed-out grottos and twisting hallways kept winding up and down and around. She couldn't say with any degree of certainty where one home ended and another began, or if they did at all.

She could sense Caleb's eyes following her every movement with quiet, piercing curiosity. He often undressed her with his gaze. Sometimes it was an act of lust; other times—like this one—it was far more contemplative in nature.

She glanced at him briefly while she checked the contents of her pack for the third time. "You think we should take the time and make the trip."

"You know I do. It's an excellent opportunity to learn something new and possibly important regarding what the Metigens are doing with these pocket universes. What their true purpose may be. But I won't fight you if you want to return to the surface in the morning."

"You won't?"

He shook his head slowly. "No. You're worried about Valkyrie. I'm worried about her, too. This is not an ideal situation. Plus, there's a chance this 'Caomh' will be a dead-end. I think it's worth the risk to find out, but I understand if you don't."

"You're too good to me."

"I am."

She burst out laughing, but the mirth soon faded. "I don't see why we can't make a quick trip up first thing in the morning—just to let her know we're fine—before we start on this trek."

"Their world, their rules. Jaisc said they used the lift only for emergencies and only rarely. Once we go back up we'll need to stay there."

He came over and rested his hands on her shoulders. "Look, the fact Valkyrie hasn't blown a hole in the ground above us means she's not freaking out. She trusts us to be able to take care of ourselves and do what we need to do."

"Two days. The thought fills me with anxiety. I'm probably going to get cranky."

He merely smirked in response, as if to say it wouldn't be the first time. She'd argue, but....

She exhaled forcefully, hoping it might ease the tension pressing against her skull. "But the need for answers is stronger. It's the reason we're here and not lounging on a seaside lanai on Atlantis. Okay. We'll go."

26

TAENARIN ARIS

The trek through the wilder regions of this subterranean world to the Caomh's habitat was akin to wandering through a fairytale land.

The path was highly unpredictable. At times it narrowed so much they were squeezing between slits in the granite; other times they hugged cliff faces and looked out on a valley sprawling below and a ceiling soaring far above. Water ran freely, in trickles and in waterfalls.

What the space lacked, however, was greenery—for without sunlight to nurture them, no amount of water would keep plants alive.

They encountered the occasional Taenarin out scouting, tending to paths or gathering supplies, but the bustle of the 'city' had faded to silence minutes after their departure.

When asked why the Caomh lived in such a remote location, Jaisc muttered vague statements of 'how it was.' There was every indication the Taenarin respected the Caomh, even revered her, but it wasn't clear how that stature was maintained when the alien lived so far away from any settlements.

Caleb seemed to be thoroughly enjoying the trip. It might not be a forest, but the landscape was certainly nature at its purest and most free, and she didn't fault him the pleasure.

She'd likely enjoy it, too, if it weren't for the throbbing in her head and the worry eating at her gut. When the stone pressed in on her it was all she could do to breathe. It felt like she would suffocate from the stale air, except in reality the air wasn't stale at all; she simply imagined it to be so. She'd close her eyes and impulsively reach for Valkyrie—farther, for the ship and the space beyond—and find only a void.

She worked to pass the time by puzzling over the mystery presenting itself here. From where had the Taenarin originated? How did they come to be in this place and why? What was the Metigens' game with the Taenarin? What did they gain by ostensibly 'protecting' them?

Occasionally, every now and then and for the briefest span of time, she did stop to gaze around and marvel at exactly where she was. It was easy to get caught up in the minutiae, in the weeds of the quest and its concomitant frustrations. But she should not forget to revel in the fact this was not merely an alien planet, not merely the home of an alien species, but an alien universe in an alien realm apart from their own.

Even if it was manufactured.

She shook her head, annoyed at herself for always, inevitably returning to the sour, bitter thought. It threatened to poison her attitude, her outlook on not just the pocket universes but her life as a whole. She knew it did. She tried to fight it, but the notion of being *used*—of being someone else's plaything—was a tripwire inside her mind designed to plunge her into dark places.

"Not far now. Beyond the next ridge."

Jaisc hiked a few meters ahead of them. Much to her relief, overnight her eVi had finally patched together a rudimentary translator which interpreted most of the common words the aliens spoke without the need for touch.

She sensed Caleb increase his pace a notch. The ever-present glow in the stone and dirt all around them had begun to fade, a herald of evening. He wouldn't want them to be exposed on what was an uneven, rocky slope when darkness fell. She renewed her step.

They were soon climbing a flight of steep stairs carved into a nearly sheer rock face. More of a ladder, really, with metal reinforcements to keep the steps from eroding away. She crested the ledge behind Jaisc and halted in surprise.

Was that light? Faint and shadowed by encroaching dusk, but real *light*?

She crawled to her feet on the ledge and gazed up. Perhaps two hundred meters above them, the ceiling wasn't rock but ice. And the ice was thin enough to allow the rays of the setting sun to break through, distorted in a prism-like fashion and diffused. But it *was* light.

She brandished a delighted grin as Caleb reached the top and joined her. His own expression brightened as well. "Is this why the Caomh lives here?"

Jaisc smiled with his colorful eyes as much as his wide mouth. "It's rumored to be a factor."

He straightened his short stature into formality. "Word was sent to the Caomh of your arrival and desire to speak to her. But it is important you not pressure her or overwhelm her. She is quite elderly and…" he looked around uncomfortably "…accustomed to being treated with care and deference. If she wishes to touch you, she will, but do not initiate contact. She is a treasure to us and should not be forced to experience discomfort, either of a physical or mental nature."

It was an odd instruction given how lively and affectionate the Taenarin generally were. But everything about the situation was odd. They nodded with appropriate solemnity to confirm they had received the message.

Jaisc watched them another moment, as if to make certain they truly did understand, then headed into an archway at the center of a semicircle of edifices.

They hung back and waited. A dozen or so Taenarin moved to and fro in the small village built upon the ledge, nestled against a wall of crystallized igneous rock. Many a curious stare was cast their way, but no one approached them.

She leaned in close to Caleb. "For the record, if this turns out to be a crock of shit, I am going to be *beyond* annoyed."

"Oh, of that I have no doubt. But try to keep it to yourself until we're alone. We need the help of these Taenarin to get back to the settlement and above ground."

"Are you saying, having trekked for nine hours through untamed and completely unfamiliar terrain, you couldn't find your way back to the settlement blindfolded?"

He bit his lip to suppress a laugh. "Fine. We need their help to get above ground. Just don't piss them off too badly, okay?"

"I can...probably manage that." She tossed him a quick wink.

It was several minutes before Jaisc reemerged and gestured them forward. "The Caomh will see you now. When your visit has concluded, I will be over there—" he pointed to a structure near the left end of the semicircle "—seeing to it that our dinner and lodging for the night are properly prepared." A firm jerk of his chin and he pivoted and walked away.

She squared her shoulders, instinctively reached out and grasped Caleb's hand, and together they walked through the archway.

⌃R⌄

A tiny Taenarin woman with skin as rugged as cured leather lounged on a cushioned chaise beside a cozy fire. Her enormous eyes were pure white, giving no inkling as to her sentiments in any hint of color.

On seeing them, the Caomh leapt up from the chaise and motioned them inside with a vigorous wave. She tottered in front of the fire and sank cross-legged upon the large, plush tapestry taking up much of the floor space. "Come, come. Watch your heads—gods you are tall creatures!"

Alex was taken aback, but Caleb gave her an unconcerned shrug and squatted on the ground.

The elderly but surprisingly spry alien produced three bronzed mugs from somewhere behind her and poured a steaming liquid out of a decanter. She placed two of the cups between them as Alex sat next to Caleb, then took a sip of the third and set the mug down beside her.

She regarded them with enthusiastic and intense scrutiny. Her eyes remained white, but she exuded dynamism from every other aspect of her presence.

"You are Caleb, and you are Alex. The Iona-Cead told me this. You, Caleb—remarkably at ease and comfortable here. Observant and swift to adapt, I see. Useful skill. You, Alex—do not be anxious, my dear. I promise I don't bite. And...well, it is no matter. The Iona-Cead tells me you visit us from the stars. Wonderful! I saw stars with my own sight three times in my life, all of them too long ago. But there are many stars in the Siopa—the Vault of Remembrance—so in my mind I see them still."

The alien paused to take a breath, but only a small one, before continuing. "The Taenarin call me Caomh, but you can call me Beshai. It has been so long since anyone did, I would truthfully enjoy it. Now. You climbed all the way up here for a reason. Tell me about it."

Alex was completely flummoxed by the Caomh's vivacious and friendly demeanor. She blinked. "You'll be able to understand us?"

"Of course! The Iona-Cead took care of that troublesome little detail by sharing his memory of your language with me."

Caleb leaned forward. "It's an honor to meet you, Beshai. Your people think and speak very highly of you. We're..." his lips quirked around in a surely deliberately impish manner "...I guess you could say we're on a quest of sorts. We think we may find some clues which will help us on our quest in the story of how the Taenarin came here from their home, which we believe was located far from here. The Iona-Cead said you possessed memories which could tell us that story."

The Caomh—Beshai—retrieved her mug and studied its contents. "The last of the old memories, the first of the new...the flock below, they have no care for these stories. They are contented. As it should be. It's not healthy to dwell on the past, when only the future remains."

Alex spared a small smile to herself at that.

Beshai eyed her as though she caught it and set the mug aside once more. "Yes, I have those. Understand, I cannot answer your questions about them. I can only show you the memories as they exist, and you must draw from them what wisdom you are able."

"Anything you can show us will be appreciated."

"Will it, now?" Beshai threw her an amused and vaguely challenging glance. "Please, enjoy your tea. I will return." Her knees and elbows creaked as she worked herself up to standing then pattered off into the adjoining room. It was shadowy, but Alex made out rows upon rows of shelves stacked high in containers.

Alex brought the mug to her lips and whispered, "She's not what I expected."

Caleb looked rather smug, so she made a face at him. "You're about to be insightful again, aren't you?"

He took a long sip of his tea. "Revered leaders' public personas rarely match their private ones. Forced to play a role created without regard to who they are as individuals, most are desperate for real, genuine interaction, especially with anyone who might see the person behind the role."

"So I see...."

Beshai reemerged from the shadows. The Caomh held an obsidian box in her long fingers. She set it on the floor before using both hands to ease herself back down. Once settled, she placed it in front of her.

"It works like this. I absorb the memory, then I share it with you through touch. When we are done, I place the memory back in its receptacle."

Caleb nodded. "We understand. We're in your care."

Translation: they didn't understand in the slightest, but they would just go with it.

"So. Pardon me for a spell." Beshai opened the box and reached inside. Her long, gnarled fingers wound delicately around what resembled a crystal ball of old fantasy fables, though they couldn't see it clearly as it remained ensconced in the box. The Caomh's eyes closed, and the skin from her fingertips up her arms to her face began to shine a dusky gold. She remained this way for more than twenty seconds.

When her eyes opened, they were a swirl of all conceivable colors, all at once. She carefully closed the box and set it aside; her movements were robotic, as if she were in a trance.

"This is the recorded memory of Odhran Ahearne, Two Hundred Seventh Iona-Cead of the Taenarin, as he experienced the Exodus." Her voice, too, was flat and devoid of inflection.

She offered her hands to them.

27

TAENARIN

When the alien appeared to me in a rush of sparkling light, I considered if perhaps I had become insane. Overtaken by a fever at a minimum. I would have suspected poison, but I suffered few political enemies and none brave enough to act against me.

When the lights spoke, not aloud but in my mind, I adopted psychosis as the likeliest explanation.

The lights proclaimed the Taenarin were in grave danger, and we had little time remaining to flee. I expressed skepticism, which I thought an admirably rational act on my part when one took into account that I had clearly fallen into madness.

The lights glittered and fussed, then took a moment to backtrack. They introduced themselves as 'Lakhes,' a member of the Katasketousya, one of many alien species they proclaimed lived across the universe—a universe extending far beyond our simple world.

We had long wondered what might exist beyond the confines of our planet, generally as idle musings accompanied by the enjoyment of spirits. The idea of other species living out there among the stars we so rarely saw was plausible, undeniably—far more so than the actual, if incorporeal, alien presence floating in front of me.

But I bore a responsibility as Iona-Cead to act with gravitas until they removed me from the post for mental instability. I demanded an explanation, details and evidence.

This alien calling itself Lakhes—I accepted without believing its status as a single, discrete entity—indulged my brave demands.

It explained that our world was rich in natural resources: ice, rock, minerals and organic materials. Those wielding the power to do such things intended to harvest it—plunder it, strip it—and claim those resources as their own.

The answer was obvious to even my recently addled mind. Explain to these reapers that sapient beings called this planet home, and they therefore needed to find another planet to harvest!

Lakhes quavered in silence for several long seconds, and the lights which comprised the being deflated and dimmed.

They already know, it whispered in my mind. *They do not care.*

The alien's words stirred in me a deep, sickening terror. I blinked and turned away, wishing deeply this was a temporary fugue brought on by an overindulgence in spirits. Overseeing such a crisis lay beyond the duties any Iona-Cead had ever faced.

"What do you suggest we do?"

Lakhes assured me my people could be evacuated, whisked away to some other place where we would be safe. A place not unlike our home. We had only to flee in the alien's starships, and soon.

I protested. Though my people respected me, they would not pick up and leave their homes, their livelihoods and everything they had ever known on my word alone, with no proof or reason to persuade.

Following a brief contemplation, Lakhes agreed to show me what came for us. I hurriedly pointed out it would still be my word alone, and before the alien accomplished a protest I called the Iona-Lui into the room.

Neave Fylan gasped and stammered and flared more colors than we had names for, but I grasped her hands firmly and urged her to be calm as the gleaming lights of my insanity engulfed us.

ℛ

We were on board a ship. I supposed it was a small ship, for the walls were close and there was only the one chamber. Having never been aboard a starship before, however, I couldn't say for certain. It hardly mattered in any event, as I had more pressing concerns, such as breathing. Living.

I had ventured above-ground four times in my life; such endeavors were required and expected of leaders. I'd stared up at the stars and felt tiny, insignificant in the face of what loomed beyond our shores. Then I'd stoically returned home, to my family, clan and people, enjoying greater respect for having completed the act.

Now an infinite blackness of space spanned not solely above me but all around me. Where were the stars? I blinked until my vision no longer blurred. They were there, everywhere and uncountable, but no closer than when I'd viewed them from the ground.

Neave touched my shoulder with trembling fingers and pointed.

I turned and found our sun, large and shining closer than I'd ever seen. It should have provided comfort or at least orientation, but the gaping chasm of blackness all around promised to swallow me up in its vastness.

This was not a place people who were born, lived and died in the womb of their world should be.

How had we arrived here? An instant ago we stood in my public chamber, far beneath the surface of our planet. Now we were here, standing in space with none but tiny, thin, mostly glass walls holding us apart from the void.

Yet as the horror of my surroundings threatened to finalize the disintegration of my reasoning mind, slowly, inexorably, my attention gravitated toward a congregation of ships. They were massive in size even when cast against the planet they hovered above.

It was not our planet. I knew this from the fact it was not frozen, but instead green and lush. So much green, more than I had seen in the entirety of my life.

The planet was being shredded, torn apart by mighty machines.

"What is this you show us, Lakhes?"

The alien replied that it was the fate of our home in a few short periods. To be sucked dry of nutrients. Of all life.

"Why?"

Because it is there to be taken.

Our ship drew closer to one of the monstrous vessels, so close I began to panic anew. Lakhes claimed we were hidden, cloaked, invisible. It seemed impossible, if no less so than all I had experienced this day.

We approached near enough to distinguish the vague forms of individual beings through a broad transparent wall stretching across one side of the vessel. They were tall, thick-torsoed creatures, with soft skin and tiny, round eyes. They gestured about at gleaming pictures and cryptic markings which floated in the air.

My throat had gone dry from an excess of fear, dread and desperation. "Who are they?"

Their species is known as Anaden, and they are Legion.

I did not concern myself with their legions, only their presence here. "Are you certain they understand we live within our home? If they properly appreciated the fact they would be murdering millions...."

Lakhes' tone was forceful in my mind, insisting these aliens did not have a care for our well-being.

They take what they need. When need isn't present, they take what they want. All to satisfy their vision of perfect, universal order.

The planet's surface beneath us churned and buckled, torn asunder as the towering machines gorged on the greenery, lending truth to Lakhes' words. I had seen enough.

It was a good thing Iona-Lui Fylan had accompanied us, for none but my mates, and possibly not them, would have believed my tale if it were mine alone.

Even then it was near thing, convincing the local leaders of the millions of us evacuation was required. That we must leave behind everything we had ever known, and we must do it now.

The ships awaiting us on the frigid, icy surface seemed nearly as mammoth in size as those I'd witnessed ravaging the nearby planet. But these ships were here to rescue us.

My people filed into their bellies, frightened, confused and weighted heavy with belongings. Other aliens of Lakhes' ilk appeared to shepherd them along, terrifying the adults and delighting the children with their twinkling lights.

The interior of the ships loomed solemn and dark, constructed of ominous black metal and streaked in frigid white light. I argued this was not a suitable environment for my people to live in, but the alien stated the trip was to be short.

How could it be so, when our would-be destroyers loomed so close? Surely we were required to travel far to pass beyond their reach?

But Lakhes and those of its kind had mastered an art so unfathomable as to be god-like. Not merely could their ships move faster than imagination, they had wrent holes in space itself, portals of an otherworldly nature which cut across distances unmeasurable. Our ships sailed through a gargantuan portal of vibrant blue, then two smaller ones of a warmer, soothing gold.

At last we orbited above a planet indistinguishable from our own. Lakhes informed me it had been prepared for our arrival in every way, insisting we would be able to live below in safety and security. The alien promised to hide and protect us, should the destroyers of worlds ever come looking for us.

"Why would they come looking for us?" I asked. "They have what they wanted—our planet and its resources."

The alien's answer was a riddle, inexplicable to me. I put it out of my mind, for I now had many practical concerns to fill my waking and sleeping hours.

All Lakhes' promises were fulfilled. We found a land beneath the ground well suited to our needs, reminiscent of home in all but the most minute of details.

Still, it was hard for us for a time. We had left behind everything, fled in a panic from forces of greater power than I could comprehend, in spite of having seen them with my own eyes.

But we persevered, for the Taenarin are a hardy people. We made a new home; we carved our cities out of the rock and mined the ore and erected our homes and bore our children.

We are content.

28

Alex shook her head roughly as Beshai's grasp fell away. She opened her eyes, blinking several times to quell lingering dizziness. "That was very…vivid."

"Yes." Beshai reached inside the orb once more; they watched her transfer the memory back into the orb via a rush of color down her arms. The Caomh closed the box, stood and walked woodenly into the other room.

Caleb's voice murmured low at Alex's ear. "Those ships they were evacuated in looked suspiciously like the Metigen super-dreadnoughts."

"Not identical, but damn similar. And the portals—they came from the other side of the master portal."

Beshai came in before they could discuss it any further. Her previous vivacity had only partially returned to her step as she rejoined them on the tapestry. "Forgive me. The process is some-what taxing on these old bones. Did you find the answers you seek?"

"Mostly new questions—but yes, this was extremely helpful, thank you. One thing wasn't in the memory that we were hoping to see. Can you tell us—do you know what 'Amaranthe' is?"

"It is said Amaranthe is the place from which we came. Not our origin planet, but the place in which it resided. The realm, the universe, whatever word one wishes to use to conceive of the unconceivable. We did not call it this, for we knew of nothing beyond ourselves and our world."

She took a sip from her mug. "I'm afraid I have no more knowledge to offer you. Please, enjoy the fullness of our hospitality this evening." She paused. "Before you go, Alex, may I speak to you alone?"

Surprised, she shrugged at Caleb. His brow had drawn inward, but he nodded and began climbing to his feet. "I'll meet up with Jaisc and see how dinner is coming. Caomh Beshai, it was truly an honor to meet you."

Alex smiled and watched him leave, then turned to Beshai. "What did you want to talk to me about?"

The Caomh reached out her hands to hold Alex's tightly. "Please. Some of what I want to express, it may be difficult to locate the right words."

"Of course."

Pure alabaster eyes stared back at her. "Child, there is a hole in your mind."

A hole? …Oh. She exhaled in relief. "I share a deep mental connection with another being—not a human, but a sapient all the same. Down here, I can't contact her due to the protective shielding your Slanait keeps in place. I'm sure that's what you're sensing."

"Hmmm…yes, this feels correct. It must be a deep connection indeed. Is this a common relationship among your people?"

"No. It's rather new, and there are only a few of us who enjoy it."

"Do you enjoy it? It seems a great sacrifice."

"I did it in order to save my people—we were under attack from a dangerous enemy." The realization that enemy was one and the same as the Taenarin's saviors hit her a little hard. "But, no, it's not a burden."

"Interesting." Beshai released Alex's hands and briefly traded them for her mug. "Perhaps joining with a distinctly separate entity did not prove too difficult for your people, given your synergistic arrangements with the ones inside you."

"What are you talking about?"

"The organism you and your companion have living in the pathways of your bodies. Since you both have the symbiote, I assumed it was widespread in your species. But I should stop assuming anything about you. After all, I know nothing of tall, eccentric beings who arrive here from the sky."

"I don't understand. Do you mean...we have microbes in our bodies, bacteria that isn't really 'us.'"

"As do we all. This is something else—small like microbes, yes, and many, flowing through your bloodstreams, yet also *one*. It is faint, but it has consciousness of some form. It hums of renewal, of eternal replenishment. Unfathomable, alien to me in a way you are not, but it *is* there. In this, I am not mistaken."

Perplexed yet again, Alex racked her brain for what Beshai could be sensing. The Caomh clearly didn't understand human physiology, though....

Renewal. Replenishment.

Akeso.

Wow.

Her face lit up. "I think I know what you mean. It's a long story, and we didn't realize, but thank you for telling me."

Beshai grasped her hands anew and studied their intertwining fingers. "These extraordinary things do not burden you, and yet..." she blinked, but her irises revealed nothing "...you *are* burdened. Beyond this hole, this absence in your mind, I sense in you a growing hunger. A need, an agitation in your very essence. I thought it connected to your missing 'other.' I do not presume to know your ways, only what I see."

A ringing in Alex's ears grew in volume, banging harsh, strident chords against her eardrums. She blamed it on the haunting reverberations of Ahearne's memory. "It's just my desire to be able to connect with her, to tell her I'm okay and make sure she's okay as well."

"As you say, my child. Rest here tonight, then go as you must. I hope you find what you seek."

Caleb was running out of ways to stall Jaisc on dinner when Alex emerged from Beshai's home. He caught her attention as it roved across the village and motioned her over.

He was intensely curious about what the Caomh had discussed with her; when she reached him, however, they were instantly surrounded by not solely Jaisc but half a dozen other residents.

They were then herded off to dinner in a spacious dining room and provided multiple courses of berries, sprouts and beans served in bronzed bowls crafted from the same metal as Beshai's mugs. Meat was a delicacy for the Taenarin, small rodents and worms its only source, and they presented it in bite-sized chunks on kabobs. Prime rib, it was not.

Dessert surprised him by being a savory mousse, but he was glad when the meal ended. They were shown to an empty room at the far right end of the semicircle of buildings.

Alex collapsed on the quilted bedmat with a groan. "These Taenarin are so high-maintenance. Between the touching and the glowing and the chattering, the formalities and the fretting…. I'm exhausted, and not from the grueling all-day hike."

He tugged his jacket off and settled beside her. The air was cool up here, so far from the springs and so close to the ice, but the rooms were warmed by hearths.

"I admit, they are a little on the fussy side. And since they share their feelings so visibly, privacy isn't high on their priority list."

Belatedly noticing it was actually warm in the small room, she wiggled out of her pullover and he tossed it in the corner on top of her pack.

"So I know we need to discuss Ahearne's memory, but what did Beshai want to talk to you about?"

"Turns out she could tell quite a bit more about us through touch than we realized. She said…" he noticed the tiniest flicker in her expression "…she could sense Valkyrie's absence in my mind. She didn't understand what she sensed and was interested. More importantly, though, she noticed another oddity as well. She said I have a microscopic entity living inside my body, one different from our natural bacteria and bearing some form of consciousness. I think she meant a remnant of Akeso."

He sank down on his back, the better for her not to be able to see the shadow crossing his face. "From when it healed your arm—it makes sense some cells would have been left behind."

"I can't perceive it. If there's any awareness in those cells, it doesn't...talk to me."

He exhaled deliberately, trying to push away the unwelcome emotions surging in his mind. He didn't want to feel them toward her. If she carried a piece of Akeso inside her, it was a gift—a wonderful reward that came with the gift of her life.

She propped up on a forearm and leaned over him. "Something you wanted to say?"

He must not have been hiding his inner conflict as well as he thought. His gaze swept across and past her stare to a point behind her shoulder. "I suppose I really am jealous this time."

He could see her lips curl up in a self-satisfied grin out of the corner of his eye. "Well, don't be, because she said it's living in you, too."

Now his gaze shot to her. "What?"

"You heard me right. She assumed all humans had microscopic companions living inside them since we both did. I bet you're wondering how, but if you think about it, there's no reason your pores wouldn't be large enough for tiny molecules to sneak through. Hell, it was probably a requirement for Akeso to commune with you the way it did."

He focused inward and searched himself mentally, but he couldn't perceive it either...or could he?

Wind rustles a sea of grasses.

Each stalk bows in submission, yielding to the wind's will.

A splash of water escapes a creek to moisten the shore.

Roots harbored in the soil reach out, yearning for the nourishment the water brings.

He'd believed them merely vestiges, impressions formed out of the lingering echoes of memories. But maybe they weren't *his* memories...and maybe they were something more.

He laughed, his mood decidedly improved. "Not going to lie, that makes me happy. An uncommon brand of happy."

"I thought it would." She kissed him with such tenderness it felt like a second gift, then rested her head on his chest. "I'm ready to leave now."

"I know." The undercurrent of strain in her voice had been growing throughout the day and evening; it now reverberated like a taut string plucked too hard. He stroked her hair, still smiling. "We'll head to the main village first thing in the morning, thank Jaisc for his hospitality, and get him to activate the lift for us."

She nodded languidly against him. "This is a good plan."

29

TAENARIN ARIS

TAYNA PORTAL SPACE

An elbow to the sternum awoke Caleb.

Before he'd reached full awareness he calmed the combat reflexes that had instinctively flared, for the source of the elbow was Alex.

She jerked around restlessly in his arms while muttering incomprehensible half-syllables. She was having a nightmare.

"Hey...." He caressed her body as gently as he could. His fingertips drifted along her arm, over her waist and down her hip, and back again. A fine layer of sweat slicked her skin beneath his palm. When his caress returned to her hand he found it clenched into a rigid fist. "It's okay, baby. It's just a dream."

Her back pressed hard into him; she growled nonsense through gritted teeth. He repeated the words in a soothing tone. She hadn't slept well the night before, either, but not to this degree. "You're safe...."

With a gasp she wrenched around to face him, eyes drawn wide open but irises bleary. She stared at him for an instant in what seemed like confusion—then her mouth was on his and one of her hands snaked down his chest to the waistband of his pants.

He reigned in the growing ardor her actions unconsciously evoked and pulled away slightly. He coaxed her gaze to focus on him while stroking her cheek. "Alex, are you awake? Are you *here?*"

Her nose scrunched up, and her brow knotted. Several seconds passed, and she blinked. "I'm here. But...I need you. *Please.*"

Were there any more illicit, arousing words in the pantheon of spoken language? No, there were not.

He gave up all pretense of restraint. He shifted his weight to ease her onto her back and hover above her. His lips roamed across her neck then collarbone as one hand went to her waist and seized the hem of her tank. They typically slept in the nude on the ship, but obviously not here.

He moved down her body as his palm moved up it, nudging the tank up her chest and over the curve of her breasts. He paused to appreciate the sight. He wasn't going to tire of it...ever, he'd daresay.

Her nails dug into his shoulders as he trailed kisses along her abdomen. He countered her urgency with veneration, taking care to devote special attention to the skin once torn apart by laser fire in Cavare. No scar remained, but he'd never forget the wound.

"Caleb...." It was a throaty purr. A plea.

He complied, but on his own terms. He cut short his journey down the length of her body, instead roving circuitously upward until his tongue danced around a nipple. She gasped and bucked against him in response, which did nothing to dissuade him.

Only when she scratched up his spine savagely enough to draw blood did he journey to her neck, her jawline and at last her lips, taking care to graze the stubble adorning his jaw over all the most sensitive areas on the way.

Her hands slid beneath his pants at his hips; she sat halfway up in his embrace to shove them off. He took advantage of the motion to slide a hand down her back and do the same. A few minimally graceful but swift movements and no trace of clothing remained.

Nearly a year after the night that began with a fateful jailbreak and many months after marriage, slipping inside her was profoundly familiar, intimate and as ecstatic as the first time. Every time.

The sound escaping her throat resided in the space between a moan and a cry. She clamped a hand over her mouth, eyes wide in horror.

He chuckled softly. She had many exquisite talents, but keeping quiet was not one of them. But here they really, *really* should be quiet, for sleeping aliens lay meters away.

His lips hovered a sliver above hers. "Shhhh."

A fractional, vertical motion of her head—an acknowledgment—and his mouth crushed hers as her body arched beneath him.

He knew every centimeter of her body now. He knew what she unapologetically liked and what she secretly craved. He knew how to keep her at the edge and how to make her scream—hopefully silently this one time.

It had been an endless source of joy for him to learn all these things, one night, morning and afternoon at a time.

Knowing all he did, he wanted to draw this interlude out. He wanted to stay this way, their bodies wound together in the most precious of ways, until the coming of the strange, subterranean dawn.

But her words had not been uttered in jest, and her very real need bled out of her and into him, radiating off her skin like searing embers and driving all other thoughts away in favor of blind passion.

One of the greatest pleasures in life was tasting the desire of one who loved you, and reflecting it back to them in full. His eyes locked on hers and held them relentlessly as her irises blazed a wild, electric silver that was all her own. Their breaths fell into a synchronicity matching the rhythm of their bodies.

Somewhere along the way he lost control to her, and she carried them to deeper, darker places with an entrancing abandon.

Her lashes fluttered and her lips parted. One hand grasped for his hair; the other clawed at his shoulder, begging him to stay with her for one...more...breath....

She did cry out, but he held her tight against his skin, muffling the exclamation in the crook of his neck.

The next instant he was grabbing the hand on his shoulder and pinning it to the mat. His other hand wrapped around her fingers clenched in his hair, and he surrendered to the rapturous abyss.

"Ah wuvf uhh."

Still surfacing from the deeper, darker place she'd led him to, he found himself, among other things, short of breath.

He inhaled slowly, then loosened his embrace of her enough to tease her lips with his own. The tip of his nose touched hers. "Something you wanted to say?"

She laughed breathlessly against his mouth. "I love you. I mean, I was also suffocating, but mostly I love you."

"Sorry—about the suffocating. Not much else." He closed his eyes and let himself simply *feel* her, flush with sated ecstasy, warm and wonderful beneath him.

But he'd bruise her if he drifted off to sleep like this, his weight heavy atop her slender frame. He reluctantly rolled onto his side. "What gave you a nightmare?"

She murmured a noncommittal, "I don't remember...."

He traced her cheek with his fingertips. "What was this? Are you okay?"

"I am now."

For the briefest of seconds, a warning chafed at the fringes of his mind, whispering disquiet at her evasion. But he was still floating on an endorphin high, and her countenance looked so delighted and lovely, he elected not to see past it to anything troublesome.

Instead he fell asleep with her head on his chest, his arms wrapped steadfastly around her.

30

TAYNA PORTAL SPACE

"I hope we've shared valuable information with you and provided you a measure of insight. I have tried to do as Slanait Lakhes asked of me to the best of my ability."

Caleb nodded and clasped Jaisc's hands firmly in his, the better to convey his sincerity. "You have. Thank you for showing such kindness to foreigners, as well as indulging our many questions."

Jaisc chuckled in a shimmer of lavender and aquamarine. "They were indeed many. But your curiosity is refreshing. As Iona-Cead, perhaps I should consider engaging in a manner of it myself."

The niceties and platitudes continued on and on, and *on*, while Alex fidgeted beside Caleb.

They had been hours trekking back from the Caomh's home. She was sweaty, and she'd been wearing the same clothes for going on sixty hours. She wanted a shower, clean clothes, a steak and a glass—or a bottle—of wine, not necessarily in that order. She wanted to talk to Valkyrie. She wanted to touch the *Siyane* with her mind. And at this point she wanted all these things with a fierceness bordering on madness.

There was no way Caleb hadn't recognized her increasing agitation by now. But just in case, she cleared her throat loudly.

He glanced over at her as the muscles in his jaw twitched beneath the skin, then redirected his attention to Jaisc. "Now we should really be going, and you can return to your normal life."

"Yes, yes." The Iona-Cead gestured up the pathway. "I must accompany you up, to see to the procedures."

"Of course. Whenever you're ready."

She kicked Caleb's foot, but he kept a perfect poker face as Jaisc began heading up the pathway toward the lift entrance.

Stop that. Five minutes won't make a difference.

No, but then five minutes becomes ten minutes becomes ten hours. I'm ready to go.

I did notice.

Finally, mercifully, they were in fact leaving. The lift spun upward in excruciatingly slow revolutions. Had the descent been this slow? She didn't remember it being this slow.

She waited as long as she could stand, then reached out in her mind.

Valkyrie?

Nothing.

Five more seconds.

Valkyrie?

Nothing.

The false ice hologram came into view above. Three more seconds.

Valk—

There you are. What was a subterranean civilization like? Show me.

Wait a minute. Weren't you worried about us?

A little. But a Metigen paid me a visit to assure me you weren't in any danger and inform me you would return in a few days.

WHAT?

SIYANE

"There was a Metigen. On the ship. In the cabin—this cabin."

'Yes. It appeared out of nowhere, breached the shielding and hull as if they did not exist, and hovered around inside for several minutes. We had a most frustrating conversation. I have to admit, Alex, I now more fully understand what you've always said about their aggravating manner. It declined to answer most of my questions and departed without a polite farewell.'

Caleb emptied his pack onto the table. "Let me guess—did this Metigen happen to go by the name 'Lakhes?'"

'It did. Interesting that you know this. By the way, I should mention the Metigens call their own species 'Katasketousya.''

Alex tossed her pack into a corner; she'd unpack and repack it later. "Yeah, we heard that, too. We got to hear quite a lot about the great and benevolent Lakhes while we were below. Their savior and protector."

'Another species worshiping Metigens as gods?'

She frowned and went to grab a chilled water, then leaned against the back of the couch to sip on it. "Not exactly. They revere Lakhes, but not as a god. There's also the distinct possibility this Metigen actually did save them."

'From what?'

Caleb came over and took a swig of her water. "An interstellar superhighway."

She screwed her face up at him. "Huh?"

"Never mind. From invaders of some sort—a fleet of ships harvesting the planets in their system."

Valkyrie sounded rather intrigued now. 'Another system here in this space?'

He shook his head. "Nope. In the universe through the master portal. They—or the Metigens—seem to call it Amaranthe."

'Fascinating. Amaranthe: undying, everlasting.'

"That's what the dictionary says." Alex took the water back and went to the cockpit. "Let's go ahead and get out of here. Knowing the ground is hollow beneath us, I'm suddenly imagining it opening up and devouring us."

"Okay." Caleb kissed the top of her head. "I'm going to shower while you get us off this rock, then I'll cook."

"Cook steak. Or pork. Basically all the meat, please."

His response was laughter as he disappeared downstairs.

As soon as he was gone, she spun to face the viewport. She hadn't had a shower, a change of clothes or any of the other luxuries she'd been so fervently looking forward to, and it didn't matter.

She closed her eyes and glided into the walls of the ship.

Hydrogen. Oxygen. Bonded into hexagonal crystalline molecules and solid beneath her, beneath the ship.

Nitrogen in the atmosphere. A greater presence of oxygen, yet less than desired. Neon, methane. All quiet, calm, stable gases surrounding her. She didn't feel the cold here.

She rose into the air, displacing the gas molecules with a level of violence sufficient to send them knocking into one another and creating a chain reaction which rippled outward for kilometers before it dissipated into stillness once more.

The upper air began to fight against her progress. It pressed in on her as if to demand she stay. But gas molecules were weak, paltry substances compared to hyper-strong layers of adiamene: carbon and amorphous diamond metamaterials latticed together at a pico- scale of fidelity.

Bruised but unbroken, the atmospheric components dispersed away to merge into the solar wind as space welcomed her into its arms.

Quiet. Dark. Empty. Alive, deafening and sparkling with effulgent photons and radiant energy.

She drifted for a time.

Valkyrie's voice—no, not a voice. Merely a thought, a collection of qubits resolving.

We can transition to superluminal now. It will take us 14.2 hours to reach the portal.

All right.

She did.

The discordance hit her like a supernova shockwave. At the edges of the bubble, space and time were warped and dragged in ways which should not be, by particles which did not belong in this dimension.

Alex, do you still find the bubble disconcerting or uncomfortable?

Alex...that was her. The ship. No, her the person, the body in the chair. The ship was the *Siyane*. Or Valkyrie. Both, and also her.

I do.

Then why are you still here?

Alex?

I missed it.

I crave it. I need it.

PART V:

HACK THE GALAXY

"I would hurl words into this darkness and wait for an echo,
and if an echo sounded, no matter how faintly,
I would send other words to tell, to march, to fight,
to create a sense of the hunger for life that gnaws in us all,
to keep alive in our hearts a sense of the inexpressibly human."

— *Richard Wright*

PORTAL: AURORA

(MILKY WAY)

31

ROMANE

Noah walked into their living room an instant before she disconnected the holocomm. "Hey, breakfast is...." He slowed to a stop. "What's up? Was that Miriam Solovy you were talking to?"

Kennedy glanced over her shoulder and nodded. Her voice came out a bit tentative, as she was still processing the conversation which had just occurred. "Change of plans. We're paying a visit to Advent Material's Rasogo II facility this morning. I'll fill you in on the way."

"Okay. But why the urgency?"

"Because we're going to need a lot more adiamene, and we're going to need it soon."

ℛ

In the desperate final days of the Metigen War, Lionel Terrage had solved the puzzle of how to swiftly and reliably create adiamene. The solution provided by Noah's father worked, but it had not come cheap, keeping the promise of large-scale adiamene production out of reach as a commercial enterprise.

After the end of the war, the Prevos had taken a fresh look at the problem. As with so many things, the application of brute-force quantum algorithm analysis coupled with human ingenuity had produced economically feasible improvements in short order.

It turned out if a critical early stage of the chemical combination took place in extremely low gravity, many of the careful—and exorbitantly expensive—strictures used during the later stages of the synthesis became unnecessary. In the case of the *Siyane*, this early stage would have occurred during the days Alex and Caleb had fled the Metis Nebula for Earth—in the near-vacuum of space.

Ramp-up costs were still substantial, but nothing like the hundreds of millions they'd originated at. And once a line was up and running, it was commercially viable. Expensive as all hell, but viable.

Kennedy admired the Advent Materials facility out the viewport of the valet transport as they approached. The company had recovered commendably from the blow of one of its VPs being a Metigen agent, then a dead Metigen agent.

The facility hadn't been constructed specifically for adiamene production. Many materials were easier or cheaper to produce free of a planet's gravity. The company had, however, repurposed twenty percent of the facility for adiamene production upon entering into a nice supply contract with Connova.

Seneca was taking care of its own manufacturing, which came as something of a relief at the moment. The Romane government, though, needed kilotonnes for the IDCC Rapid Response Force ships and civilian government vessels. She also had orders for three commercial civilian transports and one audacious order from Ronaldo Espahn; he wanted to build an entire space station using it.

The volume of adiamene currently being produced by the facility sufficed to meet those needs. But thanks to the most unexpected comm this morning, it would no longer meet all *her* needs.

Therefore, she was here to negotiate a deal to expand Advent's adiamene production to thirty-five percent of the facility's lines post-haste. She didn't intend to single-outsource the process forever—it wasn't good business strategy—but for now it was more efficient to take advantage of the economies of scale generated by doing so.

Noah leaned over her to peer out the small viewport as they prepared for docking. "Now that is one imposing looking factory."

"Hmm." He wasn't wrong, but she'd spent enough time visiting orbital factories to have grown accustomed to their admittedly forbidding appearance.

Hulking rectangular modules stacked three high and four deep were connected by elaborate latticed frames. Production lines churned material through the lattices to the next module, shepherded by mechs. If there were any viewports to break up the monotony of heavy, dark metal, they weren't visible from this vantage.

It definitely didn't qualify as a tourist destination, that much was certain.

They passed through the force field into a small docking bay meant for personal ships. The big cargo transports docked directly into loading/unloading modules on the other side of the facility. As soon as the clamps engaged they stood and exited the transport, as they were the only passengers.

A man greeted them at the docking bay entrance. "Ms. Rossi, welcome. I'm Jeffrey Kass, Rasogo II's administrator and Assistant Director of Manufacturing for Advent Materials."

"It's a pleasure, Mr. Kass. This is my business partner, Noah Terrage."

"Ah, yes. I've met your father on several occasions."

Noah rolled his eyes. "Of course you have."

Kass looked confused but gestured behind him. "Please, come with me. We'll go to my office and discuss a few details regarding what you're expecting, then we'll walk the virtual production lines and see how we may be able to implement your requests."

⟋R⟍

The floor shuddered beneath them so roughly Kennedy thrust out an arm against the wall to stay upright as Noah's hands landed on her waist from behind. "Is that normal?"

The administrator tried and failed to mask a grimace. "I'm sure it's nothing to worry about."

Hardly an answer. Orbital stations were built with safety as a primary concern, and by and large they *were* safe. But they were still in space, and space was not safe.

A shrill alarm pealed through the hall, accompanied by bright flashing lights. Noah grabbed her by the arm and drew her close. "I'm guessing that, however, *is* something to worry about."

"Yes, uh, let's get to my office. I need to assess the situation. It appears...security is telling me armed mercenaries might have infiltrated the facility via the docking bay. Why would they do such a thing?"

Noah groaned. "Because it's what mercenaries *do*."

Kennedy frowned at Noah as they hurried down the hallway. She tried to send a message to the Romane authorities and to Mia, but they both bounced. "Someone's blocking external comms."

Kass shook his head, panting from his accelerated pace and mounting panic. "Well I don't—"

As they rushed past an equipment storage room, the floor, the walls and the ceiling all shuddered, far more violently this time. Everything lurched to the right then pitched downward.

A wrenching sound screeched as something tore free from its moorings.

Noah shoved her forward.

A sharp pain zinged across the back of her head.

She had the vague, inappropriately amusing thought, *not again!*, and everything went black.

32

ROMANE

"Atlantis is eager to jump on board, thanks to its proximity to New Babel. Its leaders are worried they're next on Montegreu's list, and they may be right.

"The good news is, Atlantis' security force is well trained and professional. The bad news is, the colony will need a full provision of ships; the worse news is, there are increasing signs Zelones has already infiltrated the illicit entertainment industry as well as the gray market. Also, Atlantis' geographic position between Arcadia and New Babel is not ideal. I'd like to help their government out, but we need to consider it carefully."

Ledesme nodded as if the assessment didn't surprise her. "What about Pyxis?"

Mia made a prevaricating motion with her hand. "Not quite so eager. The governor cozied up to the Alliance during the postwar reconstruction. I suspect the leadership realizes the colony needs protection but hasn't yet decided where they should accept it from."

"We won't drag them in under protest. But if they join the Alliance, we will find ourselves surrounded on three sides by Alliance worlds. I'll see what I can do."

Morgan: Hey, do you know where Noah is?

Mia: I think he went with Kennedy up to the Advent Materials orbital facility, Rasogo II. Why?

Morgan: Kennedy was supposed to be here twenty minutes ago to discuss a possible change to the 2nd gen fighters. She's not answering messages or pulses.

Mia sighed inwardly. Checking with Noah was the obvious next step. But Morgan didn't care for Noah, so rather than reaching out to him directly, she was going the long way around.

It would be faster to simply do it than argue with her. Mia sent Noah a quick pulse.

No response.

Mia: Noah's not answering either. They could be otherwise engaged, but just in case, contact Rasogo II.

Morgan: Right.

Mia redirected the fullness of her attention back to Ledesme. "Thank you for taking Pyxis on. Requi's ready to sign up as well, though they'll be a bit of a charity case. Sagan is somewhat cool to our overtures, likely due to the Alliance's efforts defending the colony from the Metigens, but I have a contact there who might be able to help—"

Morgan: Motherfucker.

Mia: That good?

Morgan: Rasogo II is offline. The whole damn station.

"Governor, there may be a problem at the Advent Materials orbital manufacturing facility. If you can get Defense Chief Herndon on holo, I'll bring Commander Lekkas in to fill us in on what she knows."

⟆

"The vessels outside the structure are registered to Total Chemical Solutions, which is why they didn't trigger an alert from the defense arrays. Clearly either the registration is faked or the ships are stolen."

Ledesme's expression had grown steely. "And they're towing the Advent Materials facility away from Romane? Do we have any indication where they're planning on taking it?"

Herndon shook his head. "No, ma'am. There aren't any colonies nearby, and I can't conceive of a way they'd be able to create a superluminal bubble around it. They would need to load a cruiser-class sLume drive onto the station...which I guess they could do, but since they haven't yet...."

Mia glanced over from the screen she was studying. "Zelones is liable to have something hidden in an uninhabited system or the void—a secret space station, or a carrier where they plan to offload the equipment, adiamene and whatever else is in the facility then spirit the materials away. Or perhaps their cruiser-class sLume drive is waiting there."

The governor gave Mia a skeptical look. "What makes you think this is Zelones—other than the fact that every major incident on independent colonies in the last month has been Zelones led or instigated?"

Mia considered the intricate logic thread connecting the dots to link together over a hundred disparate facts and form a trail across the galaxy that ended at Olivia Montegreu's feet.

"Respectfully, Governor, it's too complicated to take the time to explain, and I propose our response should be the same regardless of the perpetrator."

"So it should." Ledesme turned to Morgan's holo. "Commander Lekkas, I believe it's time for the IDCC Rapid Response Force to prove its mettle."

Morgan's smile conveyed a mix of anticipation and slightly disturbing fervor. "I thought you'd never ask."

RASOGO II

ROMANE STELLAR SYSTEM

Noah awoke to a scream, a cry and an explosion. He couldn't be sure the order.

Confused about a number of things, the unexpected sounds being only a few of them, he tried to raise onto an elbow and peer around—

—a hand landed on his shoulder and urged him back down with a furtive whisper. "They're close. We need to play dead."

"Kennedy?"

She scooted closer, her stomach on the floor, and placed a finger to his lips then dropped her head beside him and shut her eyes tight.

It was shadowy in the hall—most of the lighting was out—but her hair was matted and too dark. Blood? He opened his mouth to ask if she was hurt, then remembered her rather insistent admonition.

At the sound of approaching footsteps, he too tried to play dead.

"Darren, check the room to the left."

A few seconds later the faint whine of laser fire preceded a dull thud.

Noah's pulse accelerated, making him grow lightheaded. Whoever 'they' were, they had just shot someone.

"Looks like a couple of bodies over here. Want me to check them?"

"Nah. It's a mess down there, and blood's everywhere. If they're not dead yet, they soon will be. This way through to the admin offices is blocked. We'll have to go around."

The sound of boots jogging off receded into the distance. He again struggled to reach a sitting position, and again Kennedy stopped him. "Don't try to move. Your arm's trapped under some equipment."

His arm? Which arm? Not the one he was moving, obviously. His mind felt fuzzy. Slow.

He looked to the left and was met by a wall of metal centimeters from his face. No, not a wall; it gave way to air at some point high above. A metal crate, then. Possibly several metal crates.

His head dropped back to the floor. "It doesn't hurt. It doesn't...." Panic seized his chest with the ferocity of a lightning strike. "Kennedy, I can't feel my arm!"

She crawled to her knees and leaned over him to stroke his cheek. "Shhh. Your eVi's medical routine shut off the pain signals coming from the nerves in your arm. That's all it is."

"Right." His mind raced sluggishly from thought to thought with no rhyme or reason. He frowned in concern—for himself to be sure, but mostly for her. "Do you have blood in your hair? Are you hurt?"

She scoffed in defiance of the dire circumstances. "Something hit me in the head when all this equipment came crashing down is all. I blacked out for a minute or two, but I'm fine." She paused. "Kass is dead."

"Shit. So...evidently the facility is under attack by bad guys."

"'Bad guys?'" She forced a feeble smile. "Is that a technical term?"

"The most technical. If we can get to the docking bay, you can fly the transport, can't you?"

She exhaled. "I can fly it. But we can't get there. Noah, I can't move the crate trapping your arm. I tried. It's wedged between other, even heavier equipment. It's going to take three or four people to clear all this out, or else machinery."

"Oh." He sucked in a breath and was surprised at the effort required. There was a heaviness in his chest which didn't seem natural. "So we wait for rescue." He grimaced. "Assuming rescue is coming."

She gave him a weak shrug. "I was supposed to be meeting with Morgan right now. When I don't show...."

"She'll start searching, if only out of annoyance at being stood up. And she has ships with high-powered laser weapons. We simply need to lie low." He chuckled at his own pun, but it morphed into a cough. Oh, that did not feel good at all.

It occurred to him then he might be in serious trouble.

He closed his eyes and worked to force his brain to focus, to actually pay goddamn attention for once, for a few precious seconds. He needed to think this through.

After the seconds ran out he reopened his eyes and found hers in the darkness. "Kennedy, you need to go—make a run for the docking bay and escape. As soon as you get outside the field jamming the comms, you can alert the authorities. Call in the troops, and they can come rescue me."

She stared at him, brow furrowing into tight crevices…was she *angry* at him? And here he was being all noble and self-sacrificing.

It wasn't like he wanted to die alone. But he preferred dying alone and her living to them dying together. And he was surprised at how much he was okay with preferring it. Must be the blood loss.

"Are you crazy? I'm not leaving you, Noah."

"Listen, there's nothing you can do for me here. I'm trapped good and proper. One of us should—" he almost said 'survive' "—get out."

Her alluring, full lips quivered in agitation and probably fear, serving as a vanguard for the rest of her features. Then her jaw set. "No."

"Come on, Blondie—"

"You are so damn infuriating! You rescued me when *I* was trapped under tons of rubble, even though you had every reason in the world to just keep running and save yourself. I may not be able to rescue you, but…but I won't leave you to…I won't leave you, dammit, so shut up."

33

ROMANE

INDEPENDENT COLONY
INDEPENDENT DEFENSE CONSORTIUM HEADQUARTERS

Morgan enlarged the most recent visual scans above the table in the still-makeshift briefing room.

"This is what we know. Six Class III tugs have attached themselves to the Rasogo II facility. They're towing it on a bearing N 18.24° -6.05°z W relative to Romane at a speed of 1,800 megameters per hour.

"Now, normally tugs don't have weapons beyond a single utility laser, but these are probably Olivia Montegreu's tugs, which means they'll probably have legitimate weapons. In addition, they have an escort of five merc hybrid fighters, which are nothing but weapons.

"Our first objective is to sever the cabling lines tethering the facility to the tugs. Wherever they're taking it, we don't want it to get there, nor do we want the battle taking place somewhere they have the advantage and possibly reinforcement armaments. But most important is this: if we disable any of those tugs while Rasogo II is still tethered to it, the structure could be ripped apart. Seeing as there are civilians on board, hopefully alive, that is not an optimal outcome."

Her gaze roved over the room to where Harper stood leaning against the wall with ostensibly casual interest, if not mild disdain. The taut, corded muscles running down the woman's neck and across her shoulders, exposed by the form-fitting tank she wore, told a different story. A muscle twitched in her jaw as Morgan's eyes landed on her.

"As soon as the cables are gone, Harper's team will sneak onto the facility using the cloaked shuttle. We will draw the fighters away then engage them."

One of the pilots, Regina Olsen, raised a hand. "What about the tugs? If they're weaponized, they might shoot up the place or, if they're feeling vengeful, crash themselves into it."

A corner of Morgan's mouth curled up. "That's why Mr. Naissen will be taking the lead initially when engaging the fighters. I'll be along, but first I need to deliver a few gifts."

Olsen nodded, satisfied. The team had mostly given up inquiring about the many secret toys, tools and information Morgan enjoyed.

"Once all targets have been destroyed and Harper's team has neutralized the enemies inside Rasogo II, we'll guard the structure until friendly tugs from Advent Materials arrive to return it to where it belongs. Advent will also be implementing additional security, so that will signify the end of the mission. Any questions?"

They looked nervous and hyped on apprehension, but no one raised a hand. They were anxious to go. So was she.

"Dismissed. We fly in five."

ℛ

The rings of the atmosphere corridor gave way to the faint haze from the last vestiges of the atmosphere, then to the stars.

Thanks to Romane's binary suns, space here was never truly black. They also meant a flash of glaring light lurked around most shifts in trajectory, hence the omnipresent filters on the glass.

A little glare did nothing to dampen the rush of adrenaline coursing through Morgan as her flight gathered in formation and sped toward Rasogo II. It wasn't her first time back in the cockpit or in space, as they'd been training for weeks now. But this time it was real—real enemies using real weapons who would fight and die—and her body knew it. Her mind knew it.

I know it as well, if you're interested.

It was a faint whisper in the recesses of her mind. Stanley's voice grew quieter every day...and she didn't know why or what to do about it. *I wouldn't have suggested otherwise. You're in my brain cells, after all. This will be your first true combat mission.*

We controlled thousands of fighters in the decisive battle against the Metigens. This cannot possibly be different.

Wait and see. But deep down, she wondered if he remained strong enough to appreciate the intensity of the experience.

The tugs were operating at what must be maximum speed, but the fastest Class III tug was still slow, and they caught up to the entourage in minutes.

Commander Lekkas: Listen up, squad. It's show time. Targets are marked and assigned. Slice your designated cables, and ignore any incoming fire. Your ships can take the abuse.

She hoped the squad members were ready. For some of them, it had been years or even decades since they'd flown in combat; others never had. Plus, knowing the adiamene hull could absorb anything directed at it was different than believing it, particularly when one sat in the snug cockpit of a tiny ship being shot at by a hulking, imposing vessel. Luckily for them the adiamene should protect them from the worst consequences of the mistakes they were guaranteed to make.

The other pilots may not appreciate the technological marvel the new fighters were, but she certainly did. The adiamene and the reduced need for force shields it brought meant no extra weight, no bulk that wasn't engine or weapon. Though they weren't flying in-atmo today, the design was nonetheless optimized for it, so aerodynamic drag would be essentially nil. And the entire cockpit was virtual. Forget whisper displays—for her the controls now acted as an extension not of her eVi, but of her quantized mind.

She arced above the sprawling Rasogo II facility and toward the center tug on the far side. The cabling strung out for some two hundred kilometers. Good. It reduced the risk of one of the vessels crashing into the structure.

The starboard side of her fighter lit up in weapons fire from the tug. It was powerful—she'd been right about them being unusually heavily armed—but it didn't mar the adiamene.

She fired on the thick double cables, circling them in a tight arc as her laser burned through the tough, durable material.

Olsen shrieked on the squad comm. *Help! This tug's tearing me apart!*

Commander Lekkas: No, it's not. Calm down and concentrate on your mission.

Olsen: But I—

The cabling fell away, and Morgan yanked hard to port. Olsen was flying erratically, jerking around ineffectually in an attempt to avoid the tug's attacks. She targeted Olsen's assigned cabling as soon as she came in range. It broke apart just before she reached it, and she sailed through the widening gap.

Commander Lekkas: Get out of here Olsen, before you kill somebody.

In her tactical vision the final cabling from the final tug fell free, the rest of the squad having managed to do their jobs.

She switched comm channels.

Commander Lekkas: Harper, you are clear to go.

HarperRF: Acknowledged.

Five red dots grew on the map as the fighter protection neared.

Commander Lekkas: Everyone else, engage those fighters. Remember, draw them away from here and toward the designated coordinates, so you can help each other out.

Now to deal with the tugs in a more final manner. She spun and accelerated above the plane the structure occupied. A smile grew on her lips. Damn, it was good to be home.

As she neared the closest vessel, she released her first payload. Two high-powered yet miniaturized plasma bombs dropped and attached themselves to the vessel's hull. The tug captain likely didn't even know it had happened.

She repeated the action for the second and third tugs then veered across the top of the facility toward those on the other side.

The long expanse of metal beneath her shuddered in a blast of light as several of the tugs fired on the facility. Of *course* they fired on the facility. If they couldn't have it, they intended to destroy it.

Terrific. The exterior hull was strong of necessity, but it wasn't a military structure designed to withstand directed assaults. It wasn't going to last long.

Harper growled in her ear. *Dammit, Lekkas, you said we were clear!*

Commander Lekkas: Seven seconds. Chill.

Fourth tug. Fifth. Sixth. She blew the charges the instant the last one stuck.

The explosions were contained by design. The tugs crumpled in on themselves rather than exploding outward, which would have sent dangerous debris hurtling toward the facility.

Commander Lekkas: Now you're clear.

HarperRF: Am I?

She flinched at the bite in Harper's tone. *Out here, yes. Anyone hurt?*

HarperRF: Not yet.

ℛ

RASOGO II

Romane Stellar System

Kennedy gasped when the walls and floor began to shake violently. The strewn crates and equipment jostled around, and she yanked her foot in an instant before a crate fell where it had lain.

Noah moaned as the debris crushing his arm shifted. She crawled closer and brought a hand to his face. It could be the dim light, but he looked so pale. His skin felt clammy beneath her palm. He'd passed out half an hour ago, and despite the moan, the shuddering didn't wake him now.

Her head was throbbing, eVi-provided pain suppressors notwithstanding, but it hardly mattered. She probably had a concussion, and her eVi had kept her from falling asleep so far. She was so very tired...but she needed to be awake in case Noah stirred.

The station shook again, more viciously this time. Her eyes widened in horror as the crate balanced above the one pinning Noah teetered. She threw herself over him and buried her head in the curve of his shoulder.

She remained there for untold seconds, scared to move, knowing another shudder would bury them both.

The blow never came. Finally, she gingerly pulled away and checked his condition again. He was still breathing...it was all she dared say with any confidence.

She scooted back to the wall, exhausted from the minimal activity.

Maybe she'd been wrong to stay; maybe she could have successfully escaped and returned with help by now. But she had no weapons. If she'd run into whoever had invaded the facility, it would have meant a permanent end to her life.

She lifted her hand off the floor to run through her hair, but stopped when she noticed it had come up from the floor sticky with blood. She skittered farther down the wall. Jeffrey Kass' blood. It had to be. She thought his body had been trampled under the heavy equipment, leaving his blood to ooze out from beneath it.

The stark realization made her gag. She leaned over to retch, but only saliva dribbled out from between her lips.

A muffled shout drove the unpleasant images away, to be replaced by new ones. Were the attackers coming around for another pass now that they had full control of the facility?

She'd have preferred to die in the initial attack. At least then she wouldn't have had to suffer these hours of despair, huddling here in the dark watching Noah's life seep out of him.

More noises echoed in the distance, chaotic and uneven. She couldn't make any sense of what was happening. Was someone fighting back? Was this rescue in the making?

Boots thudding against the floor—lots of them—drew closer. This was it, for good or ill.

A light illuminated the hallway, blinding her momentarily.

"Anyone alive down here?"

If it was the attackers, all was already lost, so she shielded her eyes with one hand. "Yes! Please, we need help!"

Four people jogged down the hall toward her. Two turned to face away, guns raised; the other two knelt beside them. "What's the situation? Are you injured?"

"I'm fine, but Noah needs urgent medical attention. His arm's trapped—"

The soldier cut her off. "Noah? Terrage?"

"Yes." She squinted into the harsh light. "Captain Harper?"

"Affirmative." The woman leaned across Noah and shone another light at his upper arm where it disappeared beneath the crate, then up the pile of debris. "Okay. We've got a medical evac in-bound. It'll be here soon. I'll notify the medics of your location." She held her hand out behind her, palm up. "Verela, I need a bio-bond injection."

One of the other soldiers grabbed a syringe and a vial out of his pack, snapped the vial into the syringe casing and handed it over. Harper pulled the collar of Noah's shirt down and shoved the needle into the soft tissue above his collarbone. "We don't dare try to free him until the medical personnel are here to intervene once he's clear, but this should help isolate the injury and keep him stable until they arrive."

To intervene. Harper didn't know what they would find once the crate was moved. Nothing good, so many different possibilities of bad.

She took a deep breath. "I understand. I'll stay here with him."

Harper peered at her suspiciously. "You have a head wound."

"What? Oh, it's nothing."

"I need some collagen gel."

The same soldier retrieved the gel and passed it to Harper, who set the tube beside her. Then, without asking, she grasped Kennedy's head with both hands and began feeling for the wound.

A second later a soothing coolness spread down the back of her head, and Harper released her. Kennedy tried for a grateful smile, but she wasn't exactly at her best. "Thank you."

A curt nod accompanied the woman vaulting to her feet. She pointed to one of the soldiers behind her. "This is Bryan Pello. He's going to guard this junction up here. We need to finish sweeping the facility. Civilian comms are back up, so if there's a problem, message me at *»HarperRF.»*"

Were they? She hadn't noticed. Her injury might be worse than she thought.

The soldiers took off once more, but the one Harper had pointed to halted at the junction and took up an alert stance.

She leaned down and kissed Noah's forehead. "Hey, guess what? You were right. Rescue came. You're going to be okay. Just hold on for a while longer."

Her squad took out all five fighters before Morgan reached the battle, surprising and impressing her. The rapid victory also explained, however, why the mercenaries had wanted to steal the facility. They needed adiamene if they hoped to match their adversaries in the field.

She ordered the fighters back to Rasogo II for patrol duty then landed in the docking bay.

Controlled chaos awaited her. She scanned the bay and determined a medical transport was serving as the focal point for much of the chaos. One person was being loaded on a stretcher into the transport, and another was being treated with some exigency on the floor beside it. Two medical personnel rushed out of the bay into the interior carrying a med kit and collapsed stretcher.

Commander Lekkas: Harper, report.

HarperRF: All accessible areas are secure. Two sections are cut off by debris. We've got nine dead mercenaries and three in custody. Fourteen dead civilians, eight injured and five unharmed. Four are missing, but given the state of this place I expect we'll find their bodies when the debris is removed—hold one.

While she waited, she watched two medics guide another stretcher toward the transport, followed by two bedraggled, dazed workers stumbling along in its wake.

HarperRF: On our way to you with the two of the prisoners.

Commander Lekkas: Any word on Rossi or Terrage?

HarperRF: Yeah. Rossi's ambulatory, but Noah got pinned by equipment. He may live, but no way he's not losing an arm.

Morgan cringed. She didn't care for the man, but that didn't sound good.

Harper and five members of her team emerged from the dark hall with two handcuffed mercs in tow. Harper had one by the arm, driving him forward roughly.

Morgan went over to meet her at the shuttle. "They say who they're working for?"

Harper shoved the prisoner into a jump seat and secured restraints around him. "Haven't bothered to ask. Been a little busy."

She looked like it, too. Blood decorated various parts of her tactical gear and much of her face. Strands of damp, no longer blonde hair peeked out from beneath her helmet, and she had a cut above her left cheek. Her skin shone with sweat and was flushed from exertion. A Daemon hung off one hip and a daisy chain of grenades off the other.

Morgan blinked. Shit, she'd been staring. Luckily Harper was busy double-checking the prisoner's restraints and hadn't noticed.

Yet another stretcher emerged from the entry hallway. Even tangled and blooded, Rossi's curls were unmistakable as she hurried behind it. The figure on the stretcher—Terrage, she assumed—had a large medical stasis device surrounding his left shoulder, and the arm below it was completely encased in thick medwraps.

Rossi looked up and, spotting Morgan, mouthed a 'thank you.' She nodded tightly in response.

When Harper stepped away from the prisoner, Morgan climbed into the shuttle and got in his personal space. "Then I'll ask. Who are you working for?"

The man spat in her face.

She rolled her eyes and wiped the spittle off her cheek. Then she punched him square across the jaw before grabbing him by the throat. "*Who* are you working for?"

The man's teeth gritted in her grip behind busted lips. "You're like her—crazy glowing eyes. Unnatural, inhuman eyes."

She released him with a dramatic shove and leapt out. "Olivia Montegreu, like we thought. Somebody really needs to kill that bitch."

Harper took the next prisoner from two of her team and tossed the woman in an empty jump seat. "Point the way."

ℛ

ROMANE

INDEPENDENT DEFENSE CONSORTIUM HEADQUARTERS

Brooklyn found Morgan waiting for her in the briefing room when she returned from cataloging all the equipment and making certain it was checked into the system. Mostly and haphazardly. The rush from the op still buzzed around in her brain like a fly she couldn't—and frankly didn't want to—swat away.

She hesitated in the doorway. "If you want to do a debrief tonight it's fine, but any chance I can take a shower first? I smell like smoke and blood."

"Your arm could use a medwrap, too."

She glanced down at the abrasion running the length of her left forearm and shrugged. "I'll rub some gel on it later."

"Good work today. I mean I didn't see much of it, but given what I did see, and the results...good work."

She rested on the door frame and crossed her arms over her chest, ignoring the burning sensation as the abrasion rubbed against her other arm. "Were you expecting something less than 'good work?'"

Morgan's gaze drifted across Brooklyn and away again. She hopped off the edge of the conference table to pace around the room while drumming her fingers on her thighs. "You never can tell about these things. I'm not comfortable relying on others to get the job done."

"You mean you're not comfortable being in charge of more than a few pilots."

"No, I'm not *used* to being in charge of more than a few pilots. Big difference."

"Well, I can be in charge if you want. I don't mind."

"You're quite...." The woman's face screwed up, her eccentric—and Brooklyn now knew unequivocally Artificial—lavender irises flashing. "Did you just make a pass at me?"

She wiped sweat and probably a little blood off her forehead with the back of her hand. "Oh, if I make a pass at you, you won't have to ask."

Morgan's tongue flicked out to lick her lips. She likely didn't realize she'd done it, but it sent electricity shooting up Brooklyn's spine. The electricity mixed with the adrenaline still coursing through her veins to create a volatile mixture.

Then Morgan scowled and headed decisively for the door. "Fucking Marines...."

That was uncalled for.

Morgan tried to evade her on the way out the door. Brooklyn's arm darted out and grabbed her wrist, then slung her into the wall and pinned her there before she could escape. The woman's wrist was surprisingly small, almost dainty; Morgan's arrogant and flippant demeanor hid a slight, thin build.

"You should try that, actually. You might learn a few things. Oh, and in case you were confused, *this* is me making a pass at you."

Morgan's free hand snaked around her waist and yanked her closer until their lips lingered a trace apart. The woman's voice had dropped to a sultry whisper and taken on a hint of a velvety Senecan accent. "You think you have something you can teach me? By all means, enlighten me."

Brooklyn reached over to the control panel in the wall, closed and locked the door.

ℛ

She felt behind her for her shirt. When she found it she wadded it up and stuffed it behind her head as a makeshift pillow. The marble floor was cold beneath her bare skin, though she hadn't noticed until now. "So what did Stanley think? Or was it not his first time?"

"It's not like that, not really." Morgan rose up on an elbow to lean over her.

She had never seen the woman's hair unbound before tonight, but now it hung in tangles to graze her chest. It was a rich, deep chestnut color. She chuckled throatily as Morgan shifted her head, sending the tips to tickle Brooklyn's skin as they brushed over her breasts and back again.

She tried to concentrate on Morgan's words instead of her hair and its mischief. "How is it, then?"

Morgan's nose crinkled. Always aloof of countenance, in the repose of afterglow her face was expressive and her features bordered on...soft. Best to not say it aloud, however. Dainty bones or no, the woman had demonstrated earlier tonight that she packed a hefty right hook when properly motivated.

"He's fading away or...being subsumed into me. I think his personality and individuality weren't well enough developed before we joined—he hadn't existed for very long—and he can't maintain it now that there's no physical separation."

"Hmm." She'd learned only the most basic details about the Prevos and had never directly interacted with an Artificial. In this respect, Morgan had much to teach *her*. Maybe a few other respects, too, not that she was ready to admit it.

Brooklyn moved onto her side and reached up to run fingertips along Morgan's temple. "Still have the eyes, though. Looks to me as if they're shining as dazzlingly as ever."

A smug grin spread across Morgan's face. "You fancy them, do you?"

"They don't suck."

"No, they don't. And no, they're not fading. None of the quantum processes cavorting in my brain cells are. It's only his consciousness, his…voice which is diminishing. It's not happening to Annie or…honestly, I'm not entirely sure what Mia and Meno even are anymore."

She winced. "I didn't mean to kill him. And sometimes…sometimes I find myself thinking or saying something that sounds like him, so maybe it's more we've truly merged, just on a deeper level than I can perceive. I know, all this sounds weird and creepy."

"Damn. Here I thought I was having a threesome—"

Quick as lightning, Morgan had shoved her fully onto her back and hovered above her, hands splayed on either side of her shoulders. "Are you saying I wasn't enough to satisfy you? Because if you are, I might take it personally."

"I'd say the jury's still out." Such a lie, and she suspected Morgan knew it. "You should try again, and we'll see how I feel about it after."

Morgan lowered herself down until the length of their bodies touched. She placed a gentle yet insistent kiss on Brooklyn's lips. "Be careful what you wish for, Marine."

34

SENECA

Graham's door was open, but he stood behind his desk, facing the window and studying a screen. Richard hesitated before rapping his knuckles on the frame to announce his presence.

Graham turned around and waved him in. "I'm glad you're here."

"Oh?" Richard asked as he sat down. They'd continued on with a veneer of business as usual in the days since Graham had divulged the details of Operation Colpetto, but an air of tension had developed between them nonetheless.

"Laure Ferre was murdered, along with all the people in his office. I guess Montegreu finally decided she wanted him dead. As to why everyone else present was also killed? I suppose it makes it easier for her to do whatever she wants with the remains of his organization but…hell, she is one psychotic woman."

"And now you figure you have a burgeoning Zelones problem on Krysk."

"I can only hope it's burgeoning. More likely it's already full grown. I thought you might want to take a trip and see what you can learn on the ground there."

Richard grimaced. He did view Montegreu as his responsibility, and the news of her murdering a bunch of people stirred up plenty of outrage. But some things were more important, with a great deal more lives—legitimately innocent lives—at stake.

"I can't. That's why I'm here. I need to take a leave of absence for a couple of weeks. Possibly longer."

Graham nodded solicitously. "Because of Colpetto?"

"No. I mean, I won't deny it would be a good idea for me to take a step back and give myself time to…make peace with everything. But no, it's not why. I need to do something for Miriam—help her on a project. I know, conflict of interest. Again. But it's not for the Alliance, or at least not the new Alliance government and…it's not contrary to Seneca's interests…."

He gave Graham a rueful expression. He wanted to fill his friend in and believed Graham would keep the information confidential, but he was sworn to absolute secrecy. "I'm sorry, but I can't say anything further. I wish I could."

"No problem. This arrangement has always been dependent on your personal interest in continuing it. What about Will?"

At first Richard hadn't understood why Will had reacted in such a vehemently negative manner to the revelations of Colpetto. Until he realized he'd never truly internalized the fact that Will's home—where he'd been born, grown up and given his allegiance—was and had always been the Senecan Federation. Will felt betrayed by his government, an institution he'd devoted his professional life to serving and protecting.

The flash of clarity had made for an odd moment, if a far less traumatic one than learning Will's true profession. He had sensed the world shift a hair off-kilter…but once there, balance had been restored. Once he'd *understood*, he'd been able to help, even while still struggling with his own outrage. On the flip side of a far more honest conversation, a shower, alcohol, sleep and a lot of venting, Will's anger had faded to low-grade umbrage.

"He'll be staying. I may want his help a day or two here and there, but he's not abandoning you, too."

"I'm going to operate under the assumption you're not abandoning me until you tell me otherwise."

Richard huffed a breath. "Fair enough. Before I go, I've received a few tidbits of data and a crappy image of someone who's high up in the OTS chain of command. The information suggests he's from Earth, but I don't have access to Alliance security databases any longer. Besides, you have better files on the people who matter on Earth than the Alliance does."

"Why would you ever think such a thing?" After a beat Graham's exaggerated façade of innocence broke, and he laughed. "Pass it on. Maybe we'll strike gold. Tessa's beginning to make an impressive amount of progress infiltrating OTS channels in the last few days. She should be able to match it to someone, or at a minimum to additional details on this someone."

"So having a Prevo on staff is working out, then?"

Graham looked pained. "Don't get me started. I guess. So far. Ask me again when we prevent an OTS attack and have terrorists in custody."

"Will do." He stood and reached over the desk to shake Graham's hand. "Thank you."

"Always." Graham brought a hand to his jaw, looking uncommonly thoughtful. "Earlier today I heard we were suddenly diverting some of our adiamene output—and a few of our new prototype ships—to a covert location. Your leave of absence wouldn't have anything to do with those moves, would it?"

Richard had always prided himself on his poker face. "Sorry. I don't know anything about that."

✺

SENECAN FEDERATION HEADQUARTERS

It disturbed Graham more than a little to find Vranas available to see him immediately upon his arrival. It was ten o'clock in the morning; there should be Cabinet meetings, or at a minimum meetings with advisors. There should be strategy sessions, updates from underlings and a variety of other urgent comings and goings. Instead, the Chairman was simply sitting alone in his office.

The sight reaffirmed his reasons for coming. He kind of wished it hadn't.

Vranas motioned for him to enter and closed the door behind him. "I'd offer you a drink, but, well...."

"The sun's still on its upward trajectory, sure." He prevaricated for a second, then sat in one of the guest chairs and dropped his elbows to his knees. "Nothing urgent demanding your attention this morning?"

"Not as of yet, small favors and all."

"Why the hell not?"

Vranas merely raised an eyebrow in question.

Graham exhaled. "Let's see. There's the fact Olivia Montegreu is in the process of surrounding the Federation with planets and assets controlled by her—I realize that's my problem, which is why you *should* be dragging me in here to demand I do something about it. I'm sure you've been briefed on her attempt to steal Advent Materials' Rasogo II facility and get her hands on a shit-tonne of adiamene. Luckily she failed, thanks to the IDCC's response team—another small issue you need to be figuring out what the bloody hell to do about. Is the IDCC our ally or our enemy? Do we need a treaty or an embargo?

"OTS is blowing up buildings from here to Nyssus and back again, yet another thing you ought to be chewing my ass over, or Gianno's ass, or somebody's ass.

"Oh, and the new Earth Alliance Prime Minister is picking a fight with pretty much the entire galaxy, including us. For now, we seem to only be third or fourth on her hit list, so we've got a small reprieve. Which is a damn good thing, as it appears we require the time to get our act together."

Vranas frowned; he looked genuinely perplexed. "I don't understand. You came here to see me because you want me to yell at you?"

"I want you to do something. *Anything*. We're in serious danger of finding ourselves caught in the middle of several galaxy-sized messes, all at once, and you're just...sitting here counting the minutes until afternoon tea. I don't know what's fuzzed up your head, but you have got to snap out of it, for everyone's sake. For all the people out there's sake." He blinked. "Sir."

"Ha. Was wondering if you'd bother to remember that formality." Vranas swiveled his chair around to stare out the windows. "I think maybe the Metigen War was the last great battle I was prepared to fight. I've been doing this too long. Even though I'm not, not in the grand scheme of things, I feel old. Tired."

He looked tired, too, but Graham had piled on enough and then some. He worked to soften his tone. "Listen, Aristide. If you want to step down and not run the next election cycle, no one will fault you, least of all me. You've done far beyond your share.

"But right now you *are* Chairman of the Senecan Federation, and you're taking our 'hands-off, minimal government' approach a mite too far. We need leadership, dammit, more than usual, and I believe you can provide it. I've seen you do it a hundred times."

Vranas ran a hand down his face. "You've certainly cleaned my clock right and proper."

"Yeah, well, you can fire me later."

"Likely not. Can't guarantee my successor won't." He squared his shoulders. "I won't answer 'what's fuzzed up my head.' It doesn't matter, because you're correct. So while you're here, do you have any ideas on how not to end up in another war with the Alliance?"

Graham smiled. "I do. On that issue and that issue alone, we wait. We don't do a damn thing."

"You're serious. You chewed my ass worse than the nuns at my Catholic primary ever did for not acting—so you could tell me we need to not act."

"There's plenty of other acting for us to do, don't worry. But yes, I did. I have a sneaking suspicion something else is afoot with respect to the Alliance, and it would be a good idea for us to let it play out without our intervention." He paused. "Or mostly without our intervention. If you're serious about being back on the job, you'll want to have a conversation with Gianno. I suspect when it comes to the Alliance situation, she's taken a bit of her own initiative."

35

ROMANE

Morgan threw her feet up on the table in the break room, the better to study the list of potential recruits on her aural. The Romane government kept trying to give her an office, but she had no need of one. All the information she required at any given time resided in her head, her only legitimate workspace the flight hangar. So instead she wandered around the building and did whatever work she needed to do wherever she happened to be.

She was already turning into a bureaucrat and administrator as things were. The minute she called an office home, her life was over anyway.

She'd fired Olsen after the Rasogo II op, so now she had to find a replacement. Plus two more new pilots, as an additional set of fighters were due to be delivered next week. They wouldn't be the new 2nd gen ships, thanks to Rossi being preoccupied at the hospital. But having now flown a 1st gen fighter in combat, she couldn't really complain, for it was an order of magnitude more advanced than anything the Federation or the Alliance currently fielded.

Theoretically, she had a target roster of thirty pilots and thirty-six ground troops to be stationed on Romane. The other colonies were being given some flexibility in determining their manpower needs. The recent wars had produced a lot of battle-tested combatants, some of which had left the military in the aftermath...though many of those who did so had no desire to return to a life of danger and violence.

She heard the footsteps approach from down the hall long before they reached the break room, knew it was Harper by the light yet purposeful, no-nonsense gait. The woman always moved with economy of motion, never wasting effort when it could be put to better use elsewhere.

A sly smile burgeoned on her lips...

...which she quickly squelched when Harper slid into the chair opposite her and clasped her hands on the table. They were keeping their relationship—was that what it was?—secret for now. Or not advertising it. Not that casual displays of affection were something she did in any event.

Of course, she also didn't do relationships—with men or women. With anyone. So she supposed at this point everything had become subject to...reinterpretation.

Harper rarely wasted words, either. "You and I need to take a ride."

"It's working hours."

"This *is* work. We got some coordinates out of one of the prisoners. Technically out of his eVi—" At Morgan's darkening expression, Harper raised a hand in protest. "Don't worry, no torture was involved. Merely tech. But these may be the coordinates for where they intended to take Rasogo II.

"Now, I don't want to go in guns blazing before we know what we're dealing with. So let's *take a ride.*"

SPACE, CENTRAL QUADRANT

INDEPENDENT SPACE

The recon vessel was designed for two, a pilot and a tech operator, but it was cramped nonetheless. Still, given unmatched cloaking and an sLume drive, it served as the logical choice. The ship had been acquired, not built, and Morgan made a note to requisition a new, more modern design from Rossi.

It would have taken the tugs some time to bring the Rasogo II facility to the coordinates, but it was a short fifteen-minute superluminal trip for them. They nevertheless reverted to the impulse engine a hundred megameters away. It would be a shame to waste the cloaking shield by announcing their arrival in a noisy burst of exotic particles from the warp bubble termination.

Morgan studied the regional map as they neared the coordinates. On a galactic scale, they were still quite close to Romane, with Pandora 1.2 kpcs distant toward the Galactic Core and Earth a bit farther away in the opposite direction from the Core. Prime real estate—or it would be were there anything of value here. But there wasn't. No planets, no asteroids, not even a star within three parsecs.

Space was screwy that way. You could encounter a vast swath of void right in the heart of civilization.

"Perfect place to hide something you don't want found."

Morgan nodded agreement and stood to go grab a water before they got too close to whatever waited at the coordinates. It wasn't a long walk—four meters to the small refrigeration compartment embedded in the rear wall. "And it's a far more convenient jumping-off point for incursions than New Babel."

"You're one hundred percent convinced Olivia Montegreu is behind all this, aren't you?"

"I am. You heard the prisoner."

"The 'eyes,' sure. It's hardly definitive proof, though. As I understand it, glowing eyes are all the rage these days. Everyone under the age of thirty is either a Prevo or wants to pretend they are."

Morgan chuckled to herself. *We're meant to be the next evolution of the human species.* Devon had done a fine job of kickstarting exactly that, no question.

On the one hand, most of the kids out there Harper referred to weren't *truly* Prevos; they had simply boosted their brains with quantum processing from a ternary computer. On the other hand, this alone constituted the most significant advancement in human capabilities since the invention of eVi technology over two hundred years ago. They may not be legitimate Prevos, but they were undoubtedly something more than ordinary humans.

"True. But I'd be willing to bet none of them control anything like...this." She enlarged the visual scanner screen.

The space station hidden in the void was a gargantuan complex the size of a small city. There were no outward frills, no ornamentation one saw on commercial stations designed to make them appear welcoming and safe, but it was nonetheless elegant in its functional design. No tori spun, which meant gravity plates must be in use—if in excess of a fraction of the station, at great expense.

"Damn." Harper leaned forward intently. "It makes sense Montegreu wouldn't entrust all her assets to the safety of New Babel, or any single location. Still...I wonder if she's here."

Morgan continued forward until they ought to be in visual range, but the station remained all but invisible. Only the light of docking bay force fields and several arriving and departing ships marked its location.

She slowed the ship to a stop. "We should be safely hidden, but watch the radar just in case. I'm going to try to find out."

"How?"

She flashed Harper a playful grin, then leaned over and kissed her. It was an impulsive act and something she never would have done under normal circumstances. But it felt...right.

"I'll be back." She settled into her seat and closed her eyes, leaving Harper looking visibly confused.

Directly ahead 2.341 megameters.

The quantum space shifted, hazy and indistinct, then she was inside the station. In marked contrast to the exterior, it was brightly lit, if no less utilitarian in design. She had landed in a lab, chimeral development by the looks of it.

She departed it, trying to locate the command center or administrative offices. They should be...up? It was human nature to situate them 'up.' Even if Montegreu was no longer definably human, she would have been when she built this place.

Morgan drifted through the ceiling like some kind of appari-
tion. Packaging lines, storage. The station felt sparsely
populated—by humans. Many of the operations were automated,
and bots floated everywhere.

On a hunch, she followed a man dressed in notably expensive
clothes who moved like he had somewhere he needed to be. He
took a lift guarded by tight security, followed by another one, and
finally arrived at a level which sparkled and shone on a scale far
above the rest of the station.

"Ms. Montegreu, you wanted to see me?"

No reliable images of Olivia Montegreu existed, but Abigail
had described her accurately, if insufficiently. Ageless, pale, blonde
and inappropriately thin, her skin now spangled in an intricate
web of fine gold glyphs. They were so extensive Morgan could
not conceive of how they would have been implanted...unless her
Artificial had grown them completely from within. Disturbing
notion.

The effect was to make her entire body glow, soft and subtly,
giving her an almost angelic appearance. Ironic, as the truth was
the polar opposite.

The woman's glittering irises—golden to match the glyphs—
darted about, tracking unseen data. "The mission plan for New
Orient is ready." She took a disk from a tall stack on her desk,
pressed her thumb to it and handed it to him. "Assemble the team.
They move at 2300 Galactic."

"Yes, ma'am." The man pivoted and left. Morgan noticed the
dramatic relaxing of his shoulders once he reached the lift. He had
to be a trusted lieutenant, but Olivia still terrified him. Much as
she imagined Olivia terrified everyone who crossed her path.

Rather than retreat to the ship immediately, Morgan backed
out to the perimeter of the station, noting dozens of turrets and
proximity sensors as her mind floated in space outside the structure. Calling it well defended understated the matter.

A brute force assault *would* fail. In another two months the
IDCC—which was to say she, Mia and Devon—might develop the

technological tools necessary to succeed, but that was in the future, and this was today.

Return.

She opened her eyes. "She's here, at least for the moment."

"What the hell did you do?"

"Oh. Guess I haven't gotten around to talking about this particular trick."

Brooklyn stared at her deadpan. Not horrified or panicked by confusion, merely awaiting an explanation.

"We—Prevos—can project our consciousness into this special quantum dimension. We call it 'sidespace,' not that it matters. And we can use it to observe other locations. I'll explain the specifics later, but first we need to deal with the here and now, okay?"

Harper's brow creased briefly, then she jerked a nod. "Okay. Tell me what you saw."

Damn, she was impressively...impressive. Nothing frightened her, or frightened her away.

Morgan gave her an apologetic smile. "Thanks. I promise I *will* explain it better later. Montegreu is inside, but the defenses are as robust as you'd expect. IDCC forces aren't strong enough to infiltrate the station, not yet. If we had a few of those negative energy bombs we used against the Metigens, we could blow the whole place. But the IDCC is going to need a far larger budget to be able to afford those...and everyone on the station would die, not just Olivia Montegreu. So I guess that idea's out either way." Oh, the responsibilities of command.

She met Harper's still intense gaze. "Your Alliance friend Colonel Jenner is hunting Montegreu. Contact him and tell him to get his ass here yesterday, and to bring the cavalry with him." Then she frowned. "Wait. No. Not the entire cavalry. How good a special forces Marine is he, really?"

Harper shrugged. "Exceptional. Maybe even one of the best there is serving right now. But how do you know he's hunting her?"

"Devon. Annie, whoever. Tell Jenner whatever you have to tell him in order to get him and...not his cavalry, but his best people, headed this way."

She smiled again—this woman was making her do that far too frequently; her cheeks were starting to get sore. "We can't leave. We need to keep eyes on Montegreu. So I'll be up here—" she tapped her temple "—for a while."

ᴙ

ARCADIA

EARTH ALLIANCE COLONY

Malcolm sat in his small office at the Alliance Forward Naval Base on Arcadia doing nothing except being troubled.

Olivia Montegreu was acting in too many places at once, creating far more incidents than his team hoped to track, much less prevent. If he hoped to catch her and bring her to justice, he was going to need a serious influx of backup and resources.

But on this particular morning, Montegreu wasn't even the source of his concerns. It should have been a welcome change, but it turned out to be closer to the opposite.

Pamela Winslow had won the election; immediately thereafter she'd begun issuing executive orders prohibiting a variety of activities related to Artificials, designed to 'bridge the gap' until more draconian legislation was able to be passed by the Assembly.

She planned to cut off all relations with the newly formed IDCC on the basis of it being controlled by Prevos. She didn't call them Prevos, but the implication was clear. Restrictions on importation of a variety of quantum computing equipment and products had been proposed, lest they contain components which might be used to create a sentient neural net.

To top things off, she'd accused the Federation of secretly supporting the expansion of the Zelones cartel, citing reasons bearing little relation to reality.

It wasn't his business—not until such time as he was ordered to start enforcing the new laws. But when the day arrived...could he really do it? Could he carry out orders he believed were morally wrong? Or worse, the alternative: could he *defy* orders? Commit insubordination or, if worse came to worst, sedition?

He didn't know a damn thing about Artificials. But he did know about Prevos—he knew Alex, and he couldn't help but feel he knew Mia, though he probably hadn't the right to feel it. He knew they'd enabled the defeat of the Metigens while risking their own lives in the process, saved the entirety of humankind and demanded no power in return. Were they frightening, something new and unfathomable? Maybe in the abstract, but not in the flesh.

It was all a disaster in the making. Terrorists were attacking anything associated with Artificials, whether it be research labs, businesses who used them or Prevos themselves. Now the Prevos were fighting back, or someone was. An OTS protest of Suiren Corp on Demeter the day before had been disrupted by EM grenades, frying every eVi in a hundred-meter radius. No one had died, but dozens had been taken to clinics.

His train of thought was interrupted by a holocomm request. He blinked in surprise when he saw the sender. Less surprise than he would've had prior to the referral contact from Lekkas, but surprise nonetheless.

He accepted it immediately. "Harper. It's good to hear from you."

"Good to be heard from, sir."

"I'm not your superior officer any longer. You can call me Malcolm."

She shrugged in acceptance. She appeared to be on a ship, but he wasn't able to tell anything else about her surroundings. She looked good, though. Healthy. "I'd say you can call me 'Brooklyn,' but no one does that. Listen, I learned from a—" she glanced at something or someone to her left "—reliable source you're hunting Olivia Montegreu. Is it true?"

His team was covert in the formalities, but there wasn't a genuine need for it. And she'd already been informed. And he seemed to be adhering to fewer bureaucratic regs every day.

"I'm leading a task force with that singular goal, in fact. Thus far all we've accomplished is cleaning up the bodies and wreckage left in her wake, however."

"I know where she is right now."

He leaned forward in his chair. "Excuse me?"

"She has a secret station in dead space near Romane. And as of right now, she is in residence."

The news of the attack on Advent Materials' Rasogo II facility and the IDCC response had made the rounds, and he didn't have to be a genius to connect the dots. She was working on Romane. The attack had occurred in Romane space. Montegreu was an all too believable suspect. "You're working for the IDCC."

She shrugged. "Leading its ground response forces, actually. I hope this isn't a problem for you."

He shook his head, if a tad weakly. "I understand why the independents think they need to be able to defend themselves, given everything that's happened in the last year. Everything happening now. I only…."

"I'm protecting people, Malcolm, not attacking them."

"O'Connell was a traitor and a psychopath, Harper. He did not represent the Earth Alliance military."

"Maybe not, but given what I'm seeing on the news feeds these days, he could have represented more of the government than you think."

He grimaced. "I don't have a good response to that, so let's just leave it alone. Talk to me about this space station."

⟐

"Admiral, it will require us to go to Romane. To work with the IDCC."

Miriam Solovy gave him a dismissive wave. She seemed busy bordering on distracted. And…hard, displaying a steel in her eyes and determination in her expression beyond what he'd seen in the past.

"Winslow's overblown rhetoric aside, the IDCC is not our enemy. Not yet. In the absence of regulations or an Executive Order prescribing our interaction with the organization, *you* may interact with them as you see fit to protect the interests of the Earth Alliance. Needless to say, eliminating Olivia Montegreu is in the highest interests of the Earth Alliance."

"Understood, ma'am." He paused, debating whether to broach the next point. "Mia Requelme is also there. Working for the IDCC."

"I'm aware. Are you asking me whether you have permission to cooperate with her as well?"

"Well, given the circumstances of her departure from Earth...."

Miriam stopped whatever else she was doing and sighed, eyes downcast for several seconds before rising to meet his gaze. "Colonel, there are matters in flux and plans in motion you don't—can't—know about. Perhaps later, if you're willing, but for now ending the threat Olivia Montegreu poses must be your only priority. So I'll say again—the IDCC is not our enemy. It is not...it is not my enemy, and it need not be yours."

She squared her shoulders and notched her chin yet higher. "I'll make this simple for you, Colonel. I tasked you with hunting down Olivia Montegreu, and I'm reaffirming this now, verbally and by official record. I expect you to use your thus far exemplary judgment to do whatever you feel is necessary in pursuit of that singular goal, and I will stand behind any actions which result. That is an order, Colonel Jenner. Are we clear?"

What in God's name had he wandered into? And by 'wandered into' he meant forcefully elbowed and bullied his way in. "We're clear, ma'am. In that case, we'll leave straightaway."

36

MESSIUM

EARTH ALLIANCE COLONY

The sprawling Earth Alliance Northeast Regional Headquarters on Messium continued to show a few scars from the Metigen invasion, in part because once essential capabilities were restored Admiral Rychen had prioritized civilian reconstruction efforts over military ones. Cranes still swung above some of the outlying buildings, and scaffolding still adorned a wall here and there. But the base was up and running and busier than ever.

He liked Messium, Richard decided as he abandoned the shuttle from the commercial spaceport for a brisk walk across the grounds.

First impressions could be revised later, but he liked the muted hues and practical infrastructure and the way the air carried a hint of pine on the breeze. It bore little similarity to Vancouver, but it was nice. He thought he'd choose a hotel in walking distance of the base to make up for the many hours he expected to be spending indoors.

He mysteriously cleared all the security checks on the base, and without so much as a second glance. Every query returned the same information: retired Naval Intelligence, here to consult on a classified matter.

That much was true, as far as it went. The fact his current position did not appear to be included in his file made for a curious deviation from standard procedure.

The Communications and Data Building looked almost entirely new, and everything shone in the understated way the best military architecture did. He had to stop himself several times from saluting when he passed high-ranking officers. He wasn't in uniform, because he no longer *had* a uniform.

A wing in the back of the complex, designated simply "E-13," was his destination. Here he encountered the tightest security thus far, with his name, fingerprints and facial and retinal scans checked against an approved list. But whatever the list consisted of, he was on it and was granted entry.

Several conference rooms were arranged around a central atrium. All were equipped with brand new data nooks and interactive tables. Beyond the semicircle were a couple of offices.

Most of the space, however, was dedicated to hardware. It reminded him of Annie's lab at Special Projects, if both smaller and more modern. At the rear of the wing, one-way glass spanned the wall to look out on the verdant landscape.

He found Rychen in the largest meeting room. The admiral stood alone, quietly studying a screen above the center table.

Richard saluted this time, technicalities be damned.

He was left a bit flustered when Rychen returned the salute then stuck his hand out. He accepted it, but frowned. "It's a pleasure to see you again, sir. It's been quite a few years. But I'm no longer serving—"

"The Cross-Sector Security Conference on New Columbia, summer of 2318. I remember. And I'm aware of your situation. All I really care about is Admiral Solovy trusts you with her life, and I trust her with mine."

"As do I. Thank you, sir."

"I also know that without the actions of your husband, we likely would have fought the Second Crux War until we were unable to win the Metigen War, so you both have my personal and professional thanks."

Before Richard could stammer out a suitable response, Rychen barreled ahead. "Now that the awkward pleasantries are out of the way—" he entered a lengthy sequence on the virtual control panel, and a multitude of new screens opened above the table "—welcome to Project Volnosti."

Richard laughed. The word was immediately familiar, for once upon a time David Solovy had launched into many a speech on why *vol'nosti*—the inclination toward personal liberty and freedom—was worth fighting for, worth paying any price to safeguard. The speeches invariably transpired on a Saturday night after several drinks had been enjoyed by those present.

"She does realize the Prime Minister can translate Russian, doesn't she?"

Rychen laughed as well, shaking his head. "I don't think she cares."

"I think you're right." He brought a hand to his chin. "So what am I looking at?"

Rychen pointed to the leftmost screens. "These detail what's going on out there." He gestured over his shoulder at the hardware across the hall. "Dr. Canivon has already come and schooled us and gone. We've got most of the existing databases replicated, but the neural net itself won't come online until Admiral Solovy presses the trigger."

He then shifted to the middle screens. "These are tracking our major assets: what's in production, what's operation-ready and what we still lack. The attack on Rasogo II threw a wrench in our anticipated supply chain, but we've been able to bridge the gap until the facility is up and running again. Most of the assets themselves are being stored offsite until their services are required. For the moment, those are my responsibility."

Having played a role—or at least been present—in the initial stages of that part of the venture, Richard had an inkling of where 'offsite' might be, as well as how and by whom the supply chain gap had been bridged.

"And this—" Rychen slid the final screen to the center "—is what we know, what we don't know and what we desperately need to find out. Not my area of expertise, but I understand it is yours."

The admiral smiled. "I won't make you stand here and study it with an audience. I'm needed back at my real job, anyway. Come on, I'll show you to your office."

PANDORA

INDEPENDENT COLONY

The broadcast went out across the shared mindspace of the Noesis—a guarantee only Prevos would receive it and no Prevo could not hear it.

"The time has come.

"I want to make one thing clear to each and every one of you: I am not asking you to endanger your lives to any greater extent than you already have. Anyone who wants refuge, say the word and it will be provided to you. We are setting up safe houses on dozens of worlds and arranging for secure transport to any of Romane, Pandora, Requi or Sagan. Unfortunately, Aesti and Pyxis are considered too Alliance-friendly to offer suitable refuge, and Atlantis is no longer safe.

"I'm sending out a ware tweak which will mask any glow in your eyes so you won't be identifiable as a Prevo in public even without shadewraps. I know many of you prefer to brandish what you are with pride, but you need to consider both your personal safety and operational security. For those of you who choose to act with us, hiding your nature in most situations may become necessary.

"We will do everything in our power to protect one another from attacks by OTS and from imprisonment under the new Alliance laws.

"For anyone who wants to fight, you had better believe we will be fighting, too. We have people watching known OTS members covertly from sidespace, and we plan to do all we can to subvert their activities and ultimately to bring them down. To do this, we need to organize locally. Find the other Prevos physically near you.

"Wherever OTS stages its next protests, help our plans to counter them. If you want to stand proudly in public and show OTS you are not afraid, this is where and when you can do it.

"Our strategy is not only about subversion, either. We now have people lobbying, often from positions of power, for the Senecan Federation to not follow in the Alliance's footsteps, and instead to enact legislation protecting the rights of Prevos not merely to exist, but to live free. The IDCC is now making it a condition of joining its consortium that the applicant colony recognize our rights. Thanks for that, Mia.

"Above all, know this: you need not be afraid. They own the fear. They fear us because they believe we're powerful, and they are correct to do so.

"Most of us probably just want to be left alone to enjoy our lives, but the rest of the galaxy isn't going to allow it. So instead we will do whatever we must to survive. If for you this means seeking refuge, we are with you. If for you it means standing and fighting, we are with you."

Devon retreated into his own mind and collapsed into a chair. Parts of his consciousness—the parts which were more Annie than him—worked to turn his words into action, while the parts mostly belonging to him decided whether to order in Chinasian for dinner or go out.

He should go out. He needed to give a visual display of camaraderie, and it would engender confidence in him among the emergent Prevo population on Pandora.

But acting the leader in virtual space was one thing; doing so in person was another, and a role he still wasn't comfortable embodying.

Mia: Who are you and what have you done with Devon Reynolds?

He chuckled. *Come on, Mia. Can't a person grow and mature?*

Mia: Certainly. Impressive to do it so quickly, though. And with such flair!

Devon: Trial by fire, Mia.

Mia: Plus your world spins at quantum speed now. Exhausting, isn't it?

Devon: I don't think I've slept more than four hours at a stretch in a month. Hey, I'm glad you touched base. I heard from Abigail earlier. She has an idea how to make Olivia Montegreu vulnerable, should anyone catch up to her.

Mia: What brought this on?

Devon: The attack on Rasogo II, but she'd been working on it for a while. I suspect she feels guilty about creating Mecha Olivia, despite the fact her life was on the line. Given the current state of Alliance politics she wasn't sure who to provide the information to, so she gave it to us.

Mia: Damn. You know where Morgan currently is, right? The timing couldn't be better. I'm on it.

Devon: Good. I also told Abigail to double her personal security, and triple it if she could. Even after New Babel, she still thinks she's invincible, but she's got to be near the top of both OTS' and Montegreu's hit lists.

Mia: No doubt. Now that Sagan has seen the light and joined the IDCC, I can throw some additional protection her way.

Devon: Thanks. Is Noah going to be okay?

Mia: Looks like he will be. He's facing significant reconstruction surgery at a minimum, and maybe prosthetics. They're keeping him sedated until all of that is handled. But he'll heal.

Devon: Glad to hear it.

Mia: Me, too. Get some rest, Devon. You've earned it.

Devon: Can't. I made this revolution happen—I'm the one who has to see it through.

After she retreated from his foremost consciousness, he considered being tired. But then an image of the OTS terrorists from Thali's Lounge rose in his mind to taunt him.

He had a cause, and his cause had an enemy. Emboldened, he stood and grabbed his jacket.

The time had in fact come—the time to be a leader.

37

ROMANE

Mia's mood brightened more than she'd expected when Malcolm Jenner walked into her new office, though his manner was stiff and so very military. "We must stop meeting like this, Colonel Jenner—sorry, Malcolm."

He stared at her, his expression unreadable, for a lengthy second before he relaxed his shoulders with a small smile. "Maybe next time we can simply meet for lunch, no pressing crisis required." Then he seemed to realize what he'd said and cleared his throat. "Harper told me to report here, so here I am."

"I expect also feeling a bit uncomfortable being in the IDCC offices for any reason, but even more so when you're not in charge of events. Apologies for the circumstances."

He didn't respond directly, instead gazing around the office. "Nice digs. Hardly the office of a runaway."

She flinched in surprise at the term. Did he know so much about her past? How could—oh, he meant a runaway from Earth. From EASC. Right.

"Governor Ledesme has been most gracious and accommodating. I believe she's gotten past her initial distrust of Prevos that you saw during the Metigen assault—or possibly she hides it better now. Also, she's tasked me with enough work to require two offices and three assistants at a minimum."

She went over to the closet and grabbed her coat. "I need to swing by the armory downstairs to pick up some equipment we'll be making use of, then we can go."

"Go?"

"I'm coming with you."

He looked frustrated, and the corners of his eyes pinched in to match his lips. "I don't understand. You're not a soldier, and this is certain to be a dangerous mission. Also one I'm becoming anxious for the details of, by the way."

"You'll get them as soon as we're underway." She paused to glance down at the floor then up at him. He was quite tall—had she never noticed before? "I realize you have no reason to trust me, but do you at least trust that I want to see Olivia Montegreu dead as much as you do?"

"Of course. I..." his eyes darted away "...might have checked up on your history a little. I'm sure you bear no love for the cartels."

So he did know after all. Which runaway *had* he meant, then? Why did it matter? She frowned—at herself, though he clearly caught sight of it. "Yes, there is the absence of love. To top it off, a good friend of mine was wounded in the attack on Rasogo II."

"All the more reason. I don't blame you. And I do trust you, apart from this mission. You proved yourself the last time I was here on Romane."

"A few things have happened since then."

"Not anything that changes my mind, as far as I'm concerned."

Really? His honorableness was rather bewildering. She started to press him on it, to ask why her fleeing EASC, stealing valuable EASC property and helping to engineer the issuance of false orders to him didn't make him trust her any less...but they were in a hurry. Every passing second was another second Olivia Montegreu could leave the space station. Also, Morgan was beginning to get awfully crabby in her head.

"Well, thank you. Now I am coming with you, and I will fill you in on the way. Promise."

SPACE, CENTRAL QUADRANT

INDEPENDENT SPACE
EAS GAMBIER

They rendezvoused with the IDCC recon craft ten megameters out from the space station. The small craft didn't have a ship-to-ship docking mechanism, so Harper executed a space walk over to the *Gambier*.

She collapsed her helmet and jerked a nod at Malcolm. "Good to see you, sir—sorry, old habits." She waved a vague greeting in Mia's direction.

"And you, Harper." He introduced the six members of his team he'd brought along, and they got down to business. The trip here had been short, and Mia had briefed them only in generalities.

They were going to hijack a supply ship en route to the station, hold the crew hostage and use the ship to hitch a ride inside. They could retrieve the proper clearance codes and procedures by force if necessary, but with any luck a promise of amnesty and new identities would persuade the crew to cooperate. Malcolm and several members of his team would infiltrate the station, sneak to Montegreu's office—or wherever she happened to be at the time—and kill her.

There were a few details still to be worked out, obviously.

Mia dug into one of the bags she'd brought. Her hand emerged holding a compact, flat device, which she offered to him. "Cloaking shield."

"We have those."

"Just try it on for size."

He made a face but accepted it, then fitted it onto his belt and activated it.

If the gasps of surprise from his team were any indication, he wasn't cloaked but instead had disappeared entirely. He held his hand up in front of him—or thought he did, because he couldn't see it. At all. There was no telltale shimmer, no offset to the objects behind his hand. "Prevo tech, I assume?"

Mia shrugged. "More Metigen tech, honestly. We found a better way to miniaturize their cloaking shield. They're prototypes, and we only have two. But they've been thoroughly tested, and they should maintain this level of fidelity at speeds up to three meters per second, or a healthy jog. Draw your gun and hold it out as if you were preparing to fire."

He did as instructed. Beginning at his wrist the illusion began to dissipate, until the last two centimeters of the Daemon's barrel were clearly visible. He nodded understanding, though no one could see it. "That's the range then."

"It begins to fade out at a radius of 0.67 meters and ends at 0.84 meters—the gradual decrease is actually why it's so effective. We're working on extending the distance, but for now doing so requires a bulkier power pack than is practical to wear."

"Hopefully we won't need to be shooting much, particularly since we'll be invisible." He deactivated the shield. "Only two?"

"Take me." Harper was leaning against the cabin wall, but her posture screamed coiled tension and her arms were crossed and locked stiffly over her chest.

He winced. "Sorry, Harper. I have complete faith in your abilities, but this team has been working together for the last five months. I can't risk any glitches in communication or orders." He motioned behind him. "Paredes, you're up. Even invisible, we'll still need to get past tight security."

The young tech officer acknowledged the order. "Yes, sir."

"Fine, but I'm part of the hijack team."

He risked another glance at Harper, and found the defiant glare he expected. "Why is it so important to you?"

"Seeing as I don't need your permission to speak freely, it's like this. We got the intel, we found the station and we worked out how to execute the infiltration. The IDCC deserves to play a role, and if the mission succeeds, we deserve some of the credit. We have a reputation to build."

"Point taken. You're part of the hijack team." He chuckled lightly. "But the IDCC is already going to play a role, isn't it, Mia?"

Mia smiled. "It is. I'll be with you every step of the way, and I'll get you to Olivia Montegreu."

"Virtually."

"Correct. At the same time, Commander Lekkas will be monitoring security and watching for any sign they've been alerted to our presence."

"Also virtually."

"Correct again. And once we've achieved our primary objective, she'll close in—non-virtually—and place plasma bombs in strategic locations. When they blow, they'll cripple the station but not so badly people won't have time to evacuate."

"Really?" This remark didn't come from him, but rather Devore.

Mia looked at the special forces captain with startling earnestness. "Really. We—the IDCC, Prevos, whoever it is you have misgivings about—aren't cold-blooded killers. The people on the station may be criminals, but none of us want a thousand deaths on our conscience. Do you?"

Devore blinked. "No."

"Good. Then we're all on the same page." Mia returned to the bag and retrieved another item, a small transmitter.

"Now for the grand prize. Malcolm, you know firsthand the strength of the shield Montegreu wears. Strictly speaking, 'wears' isn't accurate—the shield is generated and powered by her cybernetics. Activate this transmitter inside a twelve-meter radius of her location, and it will disrupt her shield for a few seconds—five, maybe seven or eight if you're lucky. It's a narrow window, but that's your window to take her down."

It *was* a narrow window. "How did you come up with it?"

"Abigail copied the technicals of the shield's programming while she was conducting the Prevo procedure. It took some time, but eventually she uncovered a few weaknesses."

She stared at him with unnerving intensity. "Malcolm, don't underestimate this woman. We have no way to know how much or in what ways she's 'upgraded' herself since she became a Prevo. Expect anything."

"That's what they pay me to do."

"If you say so." Her expression relaxed. "I'll stay here with the pilot when the rest of you hijack the supply ship. It doesn't matter where I'm physically located, so long as it's more or less stationary."

The pilot indicated assent. "We'll be out here imitating a hole in space."

"Yes, you will be. Mia, I'm sending you our pulse-based comm channel information. Will that work? Will you be able to talk to me using it?" He hadn't the faintest idea how this thing she could do functioned.

"It will."

"Then let's get started." He turned to the pilot. "Major Berg, alert us as soon as a candidate ship comes into range."

*R

Olivia Montegreu did not inspire loyalty in her underlings— but she did inspire fear.

The captain of the ship they boarded sweated profusely, and his skin had blanched to an ashen gray. "You can't protect me from her. I do this, and I'm a dead man."

Malcolm donned a thoughtful countenance as Grenier held the man securely. "If that's true, you're already dead simply by allowing your ship to be boarded. I mean, who knows what you've told us. At least my way, you have a chance.

"You want to be an Earth Alliance citizen? We can make it happen: new name, new background, new life. Want to be anonymous on Pandora? We can make that happen, too. If you keep a low profile, you'll have a lot better chance of surviving than you do if you rat us out now."

"Uh...." The man gaped wide-eyed at the floor. "Good point. I want to live on Shi Shen, and I want my name to be Har—"

"We can work out all those details after the mission's complete. For now, all you have to do is act normal. Proceed exactly as you would if we weren't here. Can you do it?"

The man gulped, blinked and nodded.

38

DOLOS STATION

Colonel Jenner: Mia, are you here?
Mia: Standing right beside you. Or floating anyway.
That wasn't creepy at all. *I'll take your word for it. Paredes?*
Captain Paredes: Good to go, sir.
The fact Paredes was also invisible meant in most respects there was no difference between his and Mia's presence. Didn't help.

Colonel Jenner: All right. Grenier and Devore, make sure our ship captain here doesn't do something stupid. If you're detected for any reason, start shooting and get the hell out of here. We'll find another way off the station. Otherwise, we'll be back.

He and Paredes exited the open cargo bay of the ship onto one of several docking bays on the station. They instinctively moved to the wall, not wanting to be exposed. But though the bay was brightly lit and busy...no one was able to see them. It was damn disconcerting.

Still, someone *could* bump into them, so they took care to stay out of the way of passersby.

Mia: There's a freight lift in the far corner. Hurry and you can catch the next load up. Take it to the second stop.

They reached it in time and hopped aboard as it began ascending, taking care not to jostle any of the crates. They exited two levels up, where they nearly collided with a worker who unexpectedly exited a doorway as they passed. Being invisible was in some ways far trickier than merely being stealthy.

Mia: You've got a long hallway gauntlet to run now. It'll open up into a larger room. Take a left out of it.

The number of bots they saw increased in inverse proportion to the drop in people. Yet the bots' enhanced vision did not detect their presence.

Mia: In the next room on your left is a man. You need his thumbprint and retinal scan.

Colonel Jenner: Understood.

There were two people in the room, a man and a woman. He shot them both with stunners. Paredes secured the woman while he produced a thin film and took the man's fingerprint then held open an eyelid and captured his retinal scan.

They dragged the limp forms behind a desk and injected them with a sedative to keep them under for twenty or so minutes.

Colonel Jenner: Next?

Mia: Cool. Continue down the hallway to a lift on the right. The fingerprint and retinal scan are required, but it also has additional security you'll need to break.

As soon as they reached it, Paredes went to work on the security panel. Malcolm stood there twiddling his thumbs.

His last incursion into Montegreu's domain had been a bloodbath, with fever-pitched combat and conflict from start to finish. This time the most violent thing he'd done was hide an unconscious person under a desk.

It was fine. There was only one person whose blood must be spilled today.

The advent of true invisibility was going to force a tremendous adaptation by security systems...but they would. Thermal imaging, until the shields could mask that, too. Then air current monitoring or other spatial disruption detection, until it too could be circumvented. Technology was and would likely always be a game of perpetual one-upmanship. But for today and probably tomorrow, the IDCC now had the advantage.

Captain Paredes: Done.

They activated the lift, and he mentally prepared himself. They were drawing close to the target. Paredes had the transmitter;

once they were in the office the captain's sole job was to keep disrupting Montegreu's shield until she was down or the shield had compensated for the disruption.

Mia: Take an immediate right. One more lift, same procedure. At the top will be a door on the right—this is the door to her office. We think she controls it, so you'll have to brute-force override the lock.

Colonel Jenner: And she's inside?

Mia: She is. A brief pause. *Sitting at her desk staring at its surface, which means a whole lot of nothing.*

He'd been warned she'd look somewhat different from the previous time he'd seen her. Neither that nor anything else would distract him from the task at hand.

Colonel Jenner: Paredes, you heard the lady. Throw everything at the lock and get the door open as fast as possible.

Captain Paredes: Yes, sir.

He didn't need to see Paredes to know the patronizing, 'I do actually know what I'm doing' look the Marine gave him.

They reached the office. The outer walls as well as the door were glass. But they were invisible; she could not see them. He stood completely still nonetheless. 'Expect anything' meant expect that her Artificial eyes *could* see them.

He studied her while he had the opportunity. She did look odd, but mostly she looked like a sadistic killer.

It took Paredes eight seconds to break the door encryption. The instant the door began to slide open, Montegreu produced a modified Damon from beneath her desk and bolted out of her chair.

Commander Lekkas: Security alerted. Lockdown in progress.

Colonel Jenner: Noted.

Captain Paredes: Disrupter active.

She opened fire the same time he did. He briefly forgot the barrel of his gun was visible beyond the cloaking, and was promptly reminded when direct fire sizzled over his defensive shield.

He drew his arm in and scrambled sideways.

4 seconds

He'd hit her, but she wasn't down. Her shield may be disrupted, but the signal only decreased its effectiveness, not eliminated it. The timer ticked down in the corner of his vision.

3 seconds

She was moving, running for the still-open door while spraying the room in laser fire—

—she stumbled and crashed into the wall. Had Paredes tripped her?

2 seconds

He was on her in an instant to brace her against the wall. She kicked and clawed at her unseen attacker, skin and irises ablaze in caustic gold.

She fired anew, and the point-blank shot broke through his defenses, grazing his hip. He ignored the harsh sting to bring his Daemon up between them.

1 second

He wedged the barrel under her chin and pressed the trigger.

Blood and brain matter hit the wall behind her with enough force to rebound, coating him in it. Blood traced an outline of his form in thin air for half a second, then vanished as the shield incorporated the new material into its cloaking routine.

He stepped away and let her body fall to the floor. Her eyes stared up at nothing, now dulled to a lifeless green.

Mia: Damn...okay, all lifts are shut down as part of the security protocol. We're working on how to get you out of there.

He crouched beside the body and flipped it over, revealing a gaping hole in the back of her skull.

Colonel Jenner: Mia, you don't need to watch this. No one needs to watch this. He didn't want to watch this, much less do this. But it needed to be done.

He activated his blade and drove it into the base of her neck to slice a half-circle pattern. Next he pulled the flap of skin up and reached in, feeling for her data store. There was a chance it contained crucial intel on Zelones operations across the galaxy.

He recoiled at the sensation of the wet, slippery tissue sucking at his hand...then it slipped past a solid object. He closed his fingers around it and yanked, hard.

More blood sprayed his face; he nearly gagged. He breathed through his nose as he retrieved a wrapper from his pack, secured it around the data store and deposited both in another container then into the pack.

Colonel Jenner: Paredes, you good?

Captain Paredes: Yes, sir. He sounded as if he was trying not to vomit. Malcolm couldn't blame the man when he was struggling with the same.

He forced down the acid in his throat and went to the cabinet behind the desk, where he attached a micro-bomb. He didn't know if she kept information here in the office, but it wouldn't hurt to destroy any hardware.

Mia: You've got incoming security forces. They'll be there in twelve seconds. The door opposite her office leads to her private hangar. Hack the door.

Several environment suits are stored in the closet on the left. Get in them. The force field is locked down, but we're going to blast you a hole and pick you up.

She had said to expect anything.

Paredes didn't wait for an order to start working on the hangar door.

Malcolm checked the lift as it began to ascend—packed full of mercs, as reported. He dropped a grenade down the shaft and rushed back. The explosion rocked the floor just as Paredes got the door open.

He went straight for the cabinet.

Colonel Jenner: Any chance you can close the door behind us in case we have more incoming?

Mia: Nope. And you do have more incoming.

He held out one of the environment suits and waited for invisible Paredes to grab it, then quickly stepped into the one he'd chosen, remembering at the last instant to shut off his invisibility shield. They would need to be seen to be rescued.

Ominous sounds grew from down the hallway. Seals check. Helmets secure.

Colonel Jenner: We're ready.

Mia: Hold onto the closet frame and hug the wall behind you.

Colonel Jenner: Done.

Silver laser fire burned through the opposite wall. Artificial gravity vanished in favor of the weightlessness of space.

In such an enclosed area the laser, though originating from a small recon craft, tore through everything—the ship occupying the hangar, the front wall and much of the floor.

When the fire ceased, he grabbed Paredes' hand. Together they launched themselves off the closet and out the gaping hole into space.

Colonel Jenner: Gambier, now you're the one who's invisible. I need a target.

Berg came on the comm. *And if we deactivate the cloaking shield, the station will shoot at us and probably hit you. We're eighty meters above you and descending slowly. You'll be able to see us when we're three meters away.*

Colonel Jenner: Got it.

Major Berg: There might be a love tap involved.

More like a bum rush, as the hull became visible a split-second before slamming into them. "Ugh!" He forcefully expelled a breath.

Colonel Jenner: We need to have a discussion about your repressed violence issues, Berg.

Major Berg: Yes, sir. The outer hatch is to your right and is open, if you'd like to come aboard.

He grasped the outer edge of the opening and pulled himself over to it, then motioned Paredes in first. The outer hatch closed behind them, the air hissed and the inner hatch opened. "Get us out of here, Major."

"Gladly, sir. Commander Lekkas, we are retreating to the rendezvous point."

Commander Lekkas: On your tail. All bombs have been placed.

Malcolm collapsed his helmet and stripped out of the environment suit as they banked up and away from the station.

Mia stood from the copilot's seat—and let out a gasp as a hand covered her mouth.

"What? Oh, right. I'm covered in blood and gore, aren't I?"

She shuddered. "Rather a lot of it."

"A small portion of it is even mine. Someone want to grab me a medwrap? Never mind, everyone else is on the supply ship—are they clear?"

Berg nodded. "Yes, sir. We had to blast them out, too, but they're in one piece."

He exhaled in relief. "I'll get my own medwrap."

He went to one of the cabinets in the rear of the cabin and opened up the med kit, then removed his tactical vest and lifted his undershirt to inspect the wound. It wasn't bad—little more than a nick—but the skin was torn and seeping blood.

"Here, let me." Mia reached over and slid the med kit down the counter to her. She retrieved the antiseptic, bio-bonding gel and a Size 3 medwrap.

He held his shirt out of the way, then jerked slightly on the application of the chilled antiseptic.

"You did it. Killed perhaps the most powerful and definitely the most dangerous person in the galaxy."

"I had significant help. Thank you. And—" he peered down at his side as she pressed firmly on the medwrap to secure it "—thank you."

"I'm glad we were able to help."

"Can I ask...when you say 'we,' do you mean you and your Artificial or...?"

She pursed her lips as she let go of the medwrap and took a half-step back. "It depends. This time I was referring to Morgan and I, and Harper, and I suppose the IDCC in general. Sometimes, though, when I say 'we' I am referring to both myself and Meno. As to whether we're truly separate, individual beings now...I'm sorry, do you really want to hear all this?"

"Yes." He meant it.

A curious glint flared in her luminescent eyes. "Okay. I believe we continue to be distinct, because we each have our own sense of self and identity. But I would have difficulty pointing to the place where I end and Meno begins. He might do a better job..." she chuckled softly "...he says he could not. So there you go. I doubt all that rambling helps you understand it any better. Sorry."

"No, it does help, a bit. Are you still...do you still require the connection to be open in order to remain conscious?"

She propped against the counter. "Yes and no. Yes, but should his hardware become damaged in the future, it won't incapacitate me. Enough of his consciousness resides in my brain cells now, as he's effectively filled in the gaps with himself. So I guess the real answer is, the connection *can't* be cut now—it's no longer an option."

"But your eyes, they're...well, they're still white. Lekkas' are sort of purple, and I'd heard that meant something."

"It does." She grinned with unexpected playfulness. "Want to see something neat?"

Berg interjected from the cockpit. "Sir, we'll be in position to meet up with the mercenary supply ship in twenty seconds."

"Understood, Major." He lowered his voice to a murmur. "I absolutely do."

She blinked deliberately—and her irises glowed a brilliant lavender. Before he had a chance to react, she blinked again, revealing an arctic blue hue. Again, and they were a rich jade. Once more, back to white.

A second or two passed, and she started fidgeting awkwardly. "You're staring at me very strangely now. Did I freak you out? I feel like I'm always freaking you out."

"Uh...no. No. It was..." *sublime* "...interesting. And surprising. And I won't ask you to try to explain this one to me."

"We're ready to dock, sir."

"Commence docking procedures." He cleared his throat and finally remembered to tuck his shirt back in his pants. "Thanks for the first aid."

"My pleasure." She tilted her head toward the cockpit. "Should we get ready to blow this place?"

"We should."

Everyone came on board to wrap matters up, including the shell-shocked but slightly giddy merc captain—who was beginning to act like he was part of the crew, laughing and joking with Grenier as they settled in.

Malcolm confirmed everything was in order, then gestured to Morgan Lekkas. "Activate the charges."

Outside the viewport, multiple explosions erupted across the station. He cocked an eyebrow. "You simply 'thought' it, didn't you?"

Lekkas shrugged. "Not technically. I sent a command to my ship, and it sent the command to the charges."

"Sir, are we planning to stick around and try to rescue people?"

"No. We're not equipped for it, and the *Gambier* can't hold more than a few additional people. We gave them a chance, which is more than they deserve."

He went over to Harper and stuck out a hand. "It was a privilege working with you again, even if in only the smallest way."

Rather than take his proffered hand, she brought her own hand to her brow and saluted. "Thank you, sir. I would've preferred to get to shoot something, but it was nonetheless an honor."

He huffed a kind laugh. "You're doing good work. I wish it was for me, but it's still good work. I sincerely hope the politicians don't mess everything up and turn us into enemies. We should be allies."

"I hope so, too." She glanced over her shoulder at Lekkas. "We ought to get out of here before God and everyone shows up to pick through the station's carcass."

Lekkas nodded. "I wholeheartedly agree."

Mia sighed. "I need to catch a ride with you two. It's time I let Colonel Jenner and his team get back to their duties."

He started to protest...but she was right. Eliminating Montegreu had been a huge boon, but it heralded a mountain of work awaiting him. Also, he was having a harder and harder time being a military commander when Mia was on board. He mouthed an apology.

"It's going to be hideously cramped."

Mia scowled at Lekkas. "And also brief. Don't worry, you two will have plenty of time for a more private celebration once we get to Romane."

Harper actually *blushed*. Lekkas glared deadpan at Mia before cringing in Harper's direction.

What...oh. So far beyond any of his business, so he merely smiled and pretended he hadn't noticed anything. "Thank you all. Amazing job today, everyone."

Then as Mia moved to follow Harper and Lekkas through the hatch, he sidled up behind her and placed a hand on her arm.

She stilled, and he leaned in to whisper at her ear. "For the record, I prefer the jade."

She didn't turn around, but he saw the corner of her lips curl upward. "I'll...keep that in mind."

39

EARTH

Jude Winslow held his breath as the door to his mother's home office closed and a faint hiss betrayed the lock engaging.

He forced his posture to relax, then strolled through the hallway and down the stairs. Into the kitchen, where he grabbed a fruit scone out of the basket on the counter, then across the foyer and up a different stairway to his suite.

Only once his own door closed did he exhale for real. He sank onto the edge of his bed. It had been eighteen years since he'd tried to break into his mother's office. The punishment on being caught trying to do so when he was nine had been a month of home confinement with no non-school exanet access.

It had been the first time, though certainly not the last, that he'd entertained feelings of hatred toward his mother.

The files and systems in her office had always been too tightly locked down, with too many associated risks, to try to break into since she'd been a member of the Assembly. As the new Prime Minister, they had become unbreakable.

Or all but.

He'd needed to divert fairly significant funds—funds which were earmarked for OTS—via the labyrinthine laundering process he'd long ago put in place, simply to buy the necessary ware and to silence the seller. He'd spent his own personal funds on the additional equipment required, chalking them up as tools of the trade. Even then it took a bit of luck and a healthy dose of inside knowledge.

But in the end he'd gotten it done, because if his life's work was to mean anything he *needed* the information his mother possessed.

Now he sat on his bed skimming through the wealth of data he'd collected. There were so many potentially valuable data points in the files, but today he desired a single, specific one: the name of the monster who had dared stand up to him on Pandora, thumbed his nose at everything Jude believed in and forced him to walk away.

The abomination had made him look weak in front of one of his most important lieutenants. Worse, had made him *feel* weak. He needed that name.

Until recently he hadn't known the code words the government used to reference its Faustian creations, and without them it would have taken hours to find the thread that ultimately led to the treasure. But as the technology started to spread among criminal hackers and rejects, words began bubbling up to the surface. Words like 'Prevo' and 'Noetica.'

They were all it took. He opened a file...and chuckled to himself. Of course, two names would do as well.

R

The other ranking members of OTS were mere dots of light, the barest pseudo-physical representations of their presence in the group commspace.

Anonymity was important in the organization. Half a dozen knew him personally, another dozen by his coded designation, Linjal—and anyone else wasn't here. But strict adherence to safeguards and rules would save them from successful infiltration.

He smiled, and the act expressed in the space as a subtle flare of warm colors. "Fellow comrades and compatriots, well done on Demeter and in Rio this last week. We have a number of upcoming initiatives, and I trust you are already pursuing them with your full efforts.

"But I'm here today to share some very good news. We now have the opportunity to cut the roots from the tree, to sever Medusa's head from her snakes."

He paused for dramatic effect, well aware of the importance of projecting a confident, larger-than-life persona. "We have two new targets, and they trump all other objectives. Kill them, and we win. Though the battle may rage on for some months or even years, if we take out these two individuals, in the end, we win.

"Their names are Devon Reynolds and Abigail Canivon."

PART VI:

THROUGH A GLASS, DARKLY

"Shut your eyes and see."

— James Joyce

PORTAL: C-17

SYSTEM DESIGNATION: CIBATUS

40

LOBBY SPACE

Saviors. Killers.
Protectors. Deceivers.
Creators. Destroyers.

Could the Metigens truly be all these things, or did one behavior merely exist as a front to mask another? If so, which were the fronts, which the truths?

Learning the Taenarin history had pitched a curve ball into Caleb's estimation of the Metigens, and not solely from a theoretical perspective. The memory of the Iona-Cead who'd led their exodus had been a moving experience, and far more impactful than being told the believed facts.

He had suffered the fear, wrangled with the suspicion and ultimately welcomed the trust Ahearne granted Lakhes. It was proving difficult to separate those emotions from his reality.

Alex sat fiddling with one of the scopes at the workbench while they tried to noodle out what to take away from the shared memory. "I want to be able to call the story false—an origin myth, a legend. We have the technology to create experiences that vivid, so it's safe to say the Metigens do as well. But the Taenarin? We saw no evidence they have capabilities approaching that level of sophistication. Did the Metigens plant it all?"

"Beshai said new memory orbs were being created even now. She claimed to receive some form of language memory from Jaisc, and I think she had to be telling the truth. How else would she have instantly understood us? How the memory capture and transfer works isn't remotely clear, but it sure seems to be native to the Taenarin."

"So the memory was real."

He shrugged weakly. "At a minimum, the Taenarin who it belonged to believed it to have been a real experience. Could the Metigens have implanted false memories in Iona-Cead Ahearne's mind, like we've speculated they did to humans to create the alien abduction myth? Possibly?"

Every answer they found only led to more questions; with every new fact the Gordian knot of the Metigens and their pocket universes grew more complex. And it was becoming damn frustrating.

"But then why the cloaking field? Why go to such elaborate measures to hide the Taenarin if there was never a real threat?" She shook her head. "Occam's Razor. We could construct a labyrinthine scheme to explain how the Metigens faked it all, but the likelier scenario is it's simply true."

She sighed and dropped the scope on the workbench. "So what does it mean? Why do they treat some species as playthings and their deaths as sport, while going to extraordinary lengths to protect others? Why does a group of aliens who can and do engineer supernovae and black holes also actively shelter a single planet supporting less than a million beings?"

Protectors and killers. Saviors and deceivers.

Caleb wandered around the main cabin, no destination in mind. He knew something about being both. He would kill—had killed—to protect those he cared about.

So who did the Metigens care about? The Taenarin, apparently, but.... He huffed a breath and leaned against the data center table.

"What?"

"Amaranthe."

"What Lakhes called the universe through the master portal. And?"

"That's what they care about."

Valkyrie understood. 'The Metigens—Katasketousya—went to such lengths to save and preserve the Taenarin because the species originated in Amaranthe, which we must now assume is also the Metigens' home universe. An excellent insight, Caleb.'

Alex snorted. "The Metigens are ethnocentric? Seriously?"

"And why shouldn't they be? Not only are most of the pocket universes out here 'other,' they're also stocked with their creations. Their experiments. But the Metigens didn't create, didn't engineer, the Taenarin."

'Hmm.'

He chuckled a little at Valkyrie's very human utterance. "You have thoughts, Valkyrie?"

'Forgive my momentary narcissism, but I am pondering parallels between the theory you've proposed and humans' views toward Artificials.'

A flush rose to heat his skin, and he didn't respond immediately. Was this shame he was feeling?

In the past he'd referred to Artificials as tools, as technology created by humans for human use, and brushed aside the notion they might be something greater. In getting to know Valkyrie these last months, his thinking had quickly evolved, but he'd never stopped to properly examine the evolution.

Had Mesme's aeons-long observation of humans been what changed the alien's opinion of them? If that were the case, why had Iapetus not experienced the same maturation with respect to the Khokteh, or the unknown Metigen who watched Ekos with respect to Akeso and its ilk?

Maybe the answer was as simple as the Metigens weren't a monolithic species. Maybe there were good Metigens and bad Metigens, and many in-between. Of course there were. Where intelligent life was concerned, there always were.

"But most people's poor treatment of Artificials stems from fear, not disdain." Alex's response was directed at Valkyrie, but she watched him with intense curiosity. He kept silent for now.

'The Metigens feared humans, did they not? It did not stop them from also viewing humans as lesser. In fact, I would posit the two beliefs are often strongly interrelated. Disdain acts as a shield to obscure the fear.'

"Fair point." Alex moved to the data center and opened the chart they'd created to track the various species and locations they'd encountered. "So far we know of three separate species in or from this Amaranthe: the Metigens, the Taenarin and the humanoid beings that were intending to reap the Taenarin planet. Anaden."

"The same term Iapetus used on Ireltse. Now we know it's not a place or a thing—it's a species." Caleb frowned. "Why would the Metigen say it to you?"

"I don't know, but…it was said with fear. Kind of like the fear Ahearne sensed from Lakhes." She drifted off for a moment, then abruptly jerked as if shaking off a reverie. "Anyway, they're clearly gargantuan assholes, if not the only ones. So in Ahearne's memory, Lakhes indicated numerous advanced species coexisted there—more than three, certainly. Not surprising, I suppose."

"Isn't it, though? We haven't found any intelligent life back home. Admittedly, we've hardly begun to search. We've explored less than a third of a single galaxy among billions."

Her countenance darkened. "True, but that's not why we haven't found aliens in our own universe. We…dammit, Caleb. We're an experiment, too. There's no use trying to pretend it isn't true. What we've seen so far is one species per portal. Why would we be any different?"

"Because Mesme admitted we were different."

She stared at him in palpable frustration. Mesme's word would not be enough for her. "Well, special or not, we've crashed their playground, and we're starting to make a real dent in this network. I say we keep going."

He nodded agreement. He wasn't ready to abandon this train of thought quite yet, but her abrupt shift in topic meant she was.

She enlarged the portal network map and, per their randomization tactic, covered her eyes and pointed. "Portal C-17 it is."

41

SIYANE

CIBATUS PORTAL SPACE

They didn't emerge into a nebula.

Caleb straightened up in his seat, instantly on alert. The other times this had happened, the entire space had been empty, but it wasn't the case here.

There were stars, for one. Not many, but they were here—and they were close.

He glanced over at Alex and found her posture slumped, her eyes shut. "Alex?"

After a second her lashes fluttered. She shook herself as if awakening from a slumber. "Yeah, this is new."

"Did you just traverse the portal while linked with the ship?"

A guilty pout grew on her lips, but her focus remained far away. "I did...."

They didn't understand the technology underlying the portals; they didn't even really understand what the portals *were*, beyond the obvious. "That was reckless."

"It was amazing. Like submerging in a pool of light and—"

"It was reckless, and you should have warned me ahead of time in case something went wrong."

Her gaze fell to her lap. "You're right. Sorry."

He gave her a forgiving smile, but it hid festering concern. Her adventuresome, fearless spirit was one of the first and most treasured aspects he loved about her, but there was a point where fearlessness became foolishness. He knew this all too acutely, for in days past he'd strayed across that line a few times—and was damn lucky to have survived to grow smarter.

Now she played in unknown realms far beyond their comprehension, and she was increasingly doing it with a callous disregard for her safety.

But it could be he had become too overprotective, a consequence of his manifest need for her, and was forgetting the wisdom he'd gained after the assassination attempt on Pandora. Or maybe he resented her connection to the ship, resented how eagerly she sought it out and the growing hours it took her away from him.

He blinked and shook it off, far more willing to let this train of thought die. They were heading into yet another new space holding yet new dangers on the horizon, and he needed to concentrate.

"Okay, so no nebula. This means they aren't bothering to hide the portal from whoever or whatever lives here." He looked back at Alex and was relieved to find her eyes again clear and alert. "We're probably facing a novel scenario. Be on your guard. Valkyrie, go ahead and activate full cloaking now."

'Done.'

Alex nodded. "Initial long-range scan results?"

'This space is most unusual. It can be considered a universe only in that it is a discrete, self-contained space beyond a portal. The populated region—populated by astronomical objects—is small, approximately two kiloparsecs in diameter. In addition, there are no galaxies within the range our instruments can reach, only individual stars. I've also been unable to detect any other notable astronomical phenomena: no nebulae, no supernova remnants, no globular clusters, no pulsars. I could go on, but you do not require a catalogue.'

Alex's expression grew in incredulity with each data point. "How interesting. And the closest star is..." her hand swept up the virtual HUD "...a short thirty-four parsecs away."

She stood, giving him a chagrined grimace. "Wasn't expecting that. I'm going to splash some water on my face, then we'll approach the star."

His eyes followed her as she walked through the cabin and descended the stairs, but they found no answers and no comfort.

Alex gripped the edges of the sink and let her head hang over it, blinking forcefully at the start of each exhale. She felt simultaneously nauseated and giddy, buzzed on the high while already ill from the crash.

Traversing the portal *had* been amazing. It had also been disorienting and bizarre. The portal had spun her body up like a top, twisting and distorting it into something unrecognizable, then tossed it out the other side a scrambled mess.

You should rest for a while before we proceed any farther into this space.

Are you kidding? I'm not about to loll around like some invalid when there's something new and unknown less than thirty minutes away.

The mystery can wait another few hours, Alex.

No. It can't. I'm fine.

She sucked in a deep breath and met her own gaze in the mirror. Her skin still looked clammy; she splashed cool water on her face and wiped it dry, then checked again. Better.

She tucked a wayward strand of hair behind her ear and nodded sharply at her reflection.

Just fine.

She proved it by taking the steps two at a time and loping into the main cabin with a deliberately carefree smile. Caleb's brow twitched once...but he seemed to accept the performance.

Relieved, her attention shifted to the viewport—

—a massive ship emerged from superluminal directly in front of them. "Valkyrie!"

'Adjusting course.'

They veered to starboard dramatically enough to cause her to stumble. She lurched into the cockpit and leaned on the dash to peer up and follow the profile of the vessel as they arced around it.

"It's definitely Metigen." The design was familiar. As with the ships in Ahearne's memory, it resembled a superdreadnought in important respects but lacked some of the more menacing qualities. It displayed a blockier profile, as if it were divided into segments. Interestingly, it did have docking ports spanning the hull, though they were all empty.

The ship cruised through the portal behind them and vanished as swiftly as it had arrived.

She sank into her chair. "What are the odds we're going to discover another rescued alien species hiding near this star?"

Caleb shook his head. His eyes were piercingly bright and danced with unspoken thoughts—thoughts she was a little afraid to probe. "I've given up on calculating odds on anything out here."

"You and me both. Nothing to do but find out."

Valkyrie took the statement as an implicit instruction, and the warp bubble formed around them.

42

Alex had seen a lot of oddities in her nine years as a space explorer. She'd seen a functioning sextenary star system. She'd seen an asteroid shatter a moon in real time; she'd even been up close and personal with a bona fide diamond planet. Since they'd begun exploring the portal network she'd seen enough queer things to believe she could no longer be shocked—not by astronomy.

She was wrong. "How many?"

'One hundred ninety-two in this outer orbit, extrapolating from the consistent spacing of those detected. An additional grouping located 2.2 AU closer to the star hosts another forty-eight, and I am detecting a third grouping approximately 0.5 AU from the star containing between sixteen and twenty.'

"Planets." It wasn't a question as such, though her tone held plenty of disbelief.

'Planets.'

"Okay." She whirled around and went to the data center. "Since we can't see all of them at once, let's model this out." Caleb joined her as a three-dimensional representation of the star system sprung to life above the table.

The star sat at the center of three sets of interlocking circles. The innermost set included three orbits separated by sixty degrees, with the middle orbit situated *precisely* on the star's fundamental plane. Six small orbs on each orbit designated suspected planets, all equidistant from one another.

The center set resided 0.85 AU from the star—right in the Goldilocks zone—and included four orbits of twelve planets each.

The final set, out here at a fraction over 3 AU, consisted of eight separate orbits playing host to an incredible twenty-four planets.

Each.

Two hundred fifty-eight planets orbiting a single star. Every one had been placed with a level of mathematical precision that ensured none fell into another's Hill sphere of gravitational influence and the orbits remained steady.

And 'placed' they had been. This was an artificial construction from start to finish. But to what purpose? There was no TLF wave here; this was simply the closest star to the portal. Did all the stars sport such configurations?

'I'm now picking up a number of smaller signatures at various locations throughout the system.'

"Ships?"

'A reasonable assumption.'

Caleb shot her a questioning look, but all she had to offer was an exaggerated shrug. "I've no idea."

"All right. Let's creep, carefully and invisibly, up on the nearest planet. Give any ships a wide berth, and we'll see what we can see."

She nodded agreement and headed back to the cockpit, leaving the map rotating above the table. They'd need it again.

During the trip to the plum-colored gas giant, they passed within a few megameters of no less than four massive vessels identical to the one that had nearly run them down. Three appeared to be headed for the interior planets, one for the portal.

Enormous structures stretched from the exosphere of the planet down into the depths of a thick hydrogen and methane atmosphere. Smaller machines—they reminded her of the mechs at the superdreadnought factory she and Caleb had destroyed—worked along the outside of the structures.

They approached one of the structures more closely as a ship arrived to hover above it. The mechs detached modules from the top of the structure and ferried them to the ship, where they docked the modules into the empty ports.

"They're extractors. The vertical structures are mining raw materials from the planet, which these ships are then transporting. Somewhere."

She peered at Caleb with a hint of suspicion. "Makes sense, but…."

"How did I figure it out so quickly?"

"I should know better than to ask by now."

He tilted his head. "Experience."

She frowned at the vague answer, but let it go on account of the ridiculous scene outside the viewport. The mechs had now begun detaching the modules from the ports, reversing their path and carrying them back to the structure. It must mean their contents had been offloaded to the interior of the ship.

When they were done, the ship moved on to the next mining structure.

"Any signs of life down there, Valkyrie? Obviously nothing humanoid can live here—not without a great deal of help—but that doesn't mean nothing can live here."

'Zero. There is a significant amount of movement and energy, but it qualitatively matches the signatures generated by the small mobile machinery.'

"Understood." Her fingertips drummed an insistent rhythm on the dash. Exploring the lower layers of a gas giant using anything other than a probe required all kinds of specialized equipment she didn't have. "We may come back, but for now let's move to the next planet."

⟡

The next planet was a duplicate of the first, down to its diameter and the rich color of the outer atmosphere. The third one they checked sported a marginally different atmospheric makeup, but was otherwise indistinguishable from the others. They each had hundreds of extractors burrowing into them, staffed with the industrious mechs hard at work.

The volume of materials being harvested and transported every hour was gargantuan. When multiplied by the number of planets in the outer orbit, it grew to an amount which was difficult to grasp in any tangible way.

She dragged a hand down her face and grimaced at Caleb. "Move to the middle orbit? I mean, we both know what we'll find there, don't we?"

He nodded, though his focus didn't stray from the scene below.

As expected, the planets in the central ring were garden worlds. They weren't being stripped by towering extractors as the gas giants were, however.

Instead a series of still large, latticed docks orbited each planet. The massive transport ships were berthed in many of them, and smaller vessels arrived and departed with regularity.

These planets had far friendlier atmospheres and were more suited to life, so they were going down to the surface of one. It was a course of action so immediately and patently self-evident not even Valkyrie attempted to argue otherwise.

Alex took manual control and eased through the atmosphere, dodging several of the smaller vessels on the way. But the *Siyane's* cloaking held, and none raised an alarm.

Beneath the cloud cover lay a temperate, semi-tropical land mass the size of South America and verdant green from coast to coast. She descended to less than a kilometer above the surface and zoomed in the visual scanner.

It was an orchard. The entire *khrenovuyu* continent was an orchard.

A horde of spider-like bots harvested whatever the orchard was growing, ripping prodigious crop from tree limbs and propelling it into mesh nets floating above the bots' chassis. When a net was filled, it detached from the bot and floated upward until it was snatched up by a larger bot and towed to one of the smaller ships. The assembly line transfer ultimately ended, as with the gas giants, at the docking ports of the largest transport ships.

The orchard stretched the breadth of the eastern hemisphere and all but the coldest regions at the poles, where something else grew and was harvested. Millions...no, tens of millions of the bots swarmed across the continent like ants—or maybe worker bees was a better analogy—operating in tireless, perpetual cycles.

The entire production repeated itself time and again, everywhere on the planet and in orbit above. Even the two small oceans kept their own brand of harvesters busy.

She fidgeted, propelling her chair in semi-circle arcs with her feet. "Don't you want to know if it's really food they're growing and harvesting?"

Caleb gazed at her skeptically. "It's almost certainly food."

"I know. But what kind of food?" She held up a hand to forestall the coming retort. "Okay, almost certainly fruit. But what kind of fruit?"

He shook his head, but his expression was teasing. "I'll get the equipment ready. We'll go down, but we're wearing full defensive gear."

43

UNCHARTED PLANET

CIBATUS PORTAL SPACE

'Full defensive gear' meant tactical suits, personal shields, Daemons and blades. The air was well within the breathable range, but Caleb insisted on taking the breather masks, too, in case...the bots expunged poison gas or something. Or the trees did.

He was well past believing he could predict all the ways the Metigens' experiments might try to kill them.

He checked her over then allowed her to do the same to him. "This is a reconnaissance mission. We'll see what they're growing, take a sample to bring back if we're able and try to get a closer peek at the bots' operation—all without attracting their attention."

"Damn. I was considering asking one of the bots on board for tea."

He shot her an unimpressed look and moved to the hatch. It had surely been intended as a joke, but her tone had nonetheless been acerbic.

He'd expected her irritability to lessen once they returned to the ship and left Taenarin Aris behind, but in some ways it seemed to be getting worse. With a quiet sigh he again forced the ruminations into submission so he could focus on the task at hand.

They couldn't find a clearing in the orchard large enough to land in, so Valkyrie descended until the pulse detonation engine rustled the leaves of the trees, and they lowered the ramp. It stretched almost vertical before reaching the ground below, but it was the best solution.

"Stay close, Valkyrie, and be ready to rescue us."

'I would be happy to consider it my primary mission in life, should you ever stop rescuing yourselves.'

He descended the ramp ahead of Alex with due caution, scanning the vicinity for threats. Below the treetops, line of sight became limited. The trees were arranged in perfect rows, though, so he was able to see some distance down the intersecting rows.

Alex appeared beside him as he stepped onto the soil. The air was fragrant with the aroma of...ripe fruit. It had to be. "I told you it was fruit."

She headed for the closest tree. "Then let's take some back. You know, for testing."

The limbs of every tree sagged heavy, laden by an unfamiliar crop. The skin resembled that of an orange, rough and dimply in texture, but the color was the deep red of Rome apples and each one was as large as a cantaloupe.

While Alex removed a container from her pack and wrested one of the fruits from a low-hanging limb, he knelt down and drove his blade into the soil surrounding the base of the tree, then twisted it around to break it up.

The dirt beneath the surface was moist on the verge of being soaked. There was no hint of a recent rainfall aboveground, which meant an underground irrigation system. He dug deeper, searching for a pipe or—

'Four bots are approaching your location from the southwest.'

He leapt up and peered in the reported direction. "I see two of them."

'The others are traversing adjacent rows. All are harvesting the crop, so their progress is slow. Not so slow as one would expect, however. They are most efficacious.'

The degree to which the bots were programmed for any activity other than harvesting was an interesting and, as of now, quite relevant question. He pulled Alex beneath the shelter of the overhanging limbs and pressed her against the trunk. "Make like the tree and don't move."

Her chin notched down in agreement, and they huddled quietly as the bots neared. He could no longer track the one handling their row, but one the next row over soon came into view.

Up close, the spider analogy continued to hold in most respects—other than the fact the bot was flying, of course. Eight multi-jointed legs ended in claws perfectly sized to fit around the ripe fruit. A rotund body held the flight mechanism and whatever programming they required, a latch on top secured the net, and there was little else to them.

The arms moved with impressive speed, deftly picking the ripe crop and directing it into the attached net with brutal efficiency. A single tree held perhaps fifty of the fruits and took less than six seconds to strip.

The bots made essentially zero artificial noise as they worked, and the only indication he and Alex received that one had reached their tree was the limbs shuddering as the arms tore the fruit away.

One of the limbs bounced down into Alex's face on the rebound. She muffled a cry and jerked away, but not before one of the spidery arms pursued its prey and the claw tangled in her hair.

"Ow!" She tried to yank away from its clutches, which sent the bot into a skittering rampage. Its arms flailed about in search of the impediment to its continued work. Another of the claws would have gouged her face if not for her quick reflexes in dodging it.

He made a note to compliment her on the move later. Survival first.

The bot's flailing only succeeded in entangling its claw more deeply into her hair; the long locks had been drawn into a smooth knot, but now one side puffed out in a snarled mess.

"Hold still for one second." He drew his Daemon and shot the bot point-blank in its center mass.

It fell to the ground, taking her with it. Its arms convulsed briefly then went limp.

He dropped to his knees beside her and pulled out the smaller of his blades, then grabbed the offending bot arm. He pushed it away until the claw and the strands of hair caught in it were separated. "Sorry about this." He sliced through the ensnared hair.

"It'll grow back…." As soon as the last strand was free, they were both on their feet—a good thing, because the bot tending to a neighboring row must have been alerted to the disturbance and dive-bombed them. Only the heavy limb-cover prevented it from tearing into them.

He ducked and spun out from under the tree, sighted down and shot it as it circled around for another pass. "Okay, that's it. We're leaving. Valkyrie, lower the ramp."

'You have garnered additional attention. Four more bots are now heading to your location from multiple directions.'

"Excellent." They'd wandered a few dozen meters from the *Siyane*. Alex drew her Daemon as well, and they moved back-to-back toward the ship as the ramp lowered.

Two bots crested the tree tops and accelerated toward them. He took them both out with rapid shots. A flash of light to his left signaled Alex doing the same to a third one approaching from the side.

"At least they don't have lasers."

"Or poison gas."

She spared a second to glance back at him in amusement—then swung around and shot over his shoulder to take out the last one.

"Nice job, baby."

She opened her mouth to reply, but it clamped shut as her eyes widened. He pivoted to see *six* bots speeding down the gap between the rows toward them.

His heel hit the bottom of the ramp; he motioned her up first and edged his way up backward while firing. He eliminated four of the six, reached the hatch and ducked inside. "Get us out of here, Valkyrie."

'My pleasure. I wouldn't want them to scratch the hull.'

Alex gave a winded laugh, as the likelihood of the spindly bot claws being able to mar the adiamene was remote.

Hatch sealed, he hurried into the cockpit after her. "Doubt that'll happen, but if they were alerted en masse, far larger defensive measures might have been as well."

The *Siyane* accelerated upward with due speed, and they were gone before anything else could arrive to chase them.

⌗

The next planet differed only in what it grew. The plants resembled maize, but the ears harvested were nearly a meter in length. Following their adventure on the previous planet, they elected not to do the ground reconnaissance required to learn more.

Hours passed as they surveyed planet after planet in morbid fascination. Most grew varieties of food staples, but some were devoted to a kind of soft timber and several were ocean worlds where algae and other forms of plankton were collected by barge ships sporting cavernous water tanks as bellies.

All the tests pronounced the fruit they'd brought back from the surface safe for consumption, so they sliced it up and gave it a try in between planets.

The flesh was chewier than Alex expected and tasted vaguely like a pear.

Caleb was an abject wimp and waited until she'd taken a bite and didn't keel over before he followed suit. His initial verdict consisted of a wishy-washy face, and she tossed him some sugar to sprinkle on it. He acted happy enough with the result that she did the same for the next bite.

Yep. Better.

The damage to her hair thankfully turned out to be minimal. The strands which had gotten tangled in the bot's claw were scattered rather than all in one chunk, so now she just had *way* too many flyaway hairs. And a long scrape on her skull from the bot's opening swipe.

After satisfying themselves the central rings held no further surprises, they moved to the innermost orbit. To no one's surprise they found rocky, dense planets; their cores were being harvested by mammoth drills, presumably mining for iron and other heavy metals.

These planets were as inhospitable in their own way as the gas giants, so they watched for a few minutes before backing away.

Alex dropped her head against the headrest and covered her face with her hands. She had a headache. She'd resisted linking with the ship, because she needed to be *here* to analyze what they were seeing. A traitorous voice whispered in dulcet tones that Valkyrie was really the one doing all the analyzing, but she ignored it as best she could and tried to concentrate on the mystery at hand.

The numbers were beyond calculation. Well, Valkyrie could calculate them—*See! the voice murmured*—but the resulting totals were so large as to not carry any relatable meaning.

"Who are they feeding? And supplying? Why? We know from the superdreadnought manufacturing facility that they can conduct this level of production, but the sheer work involved is out of character with everything else we've seen from the Metigens out here."

"Amaranthe."

There he went again with his smug one-word answers—the *same* one-word answer. She raised an eyebrow at him in hopes of evoking a more fulsome response.

He kicked his feet up onto the dash. "At this point, I think we have to assume there exists an active universe through the master portal, one home to multiple alien species. Given all this—" he waved out the viewport "—we can also assume it's heavily populated.

"Now, maybe they're unable to grow or harvest their own resources for some reason, or maybe it's so populous they need to supplement those resources. Maybe this form of factory universe is more efficient than the other options. But as for why the *Metigens* are the ones doing it…I don't know."

'A reasonable hypothesis would be that the Metigens are the only ones possessing the skill to engineer the system—the stars, planets and orbits at a minimum. Compared to building worlds, the harvesting itself is radically simple. Perhaps they allow their ships and machines to handle it merely as an afterthought.'

Alex nodded in nominal agreement, as most of her attention was focused on the massive transport ship passing across the upper region of the viewport.

She nudged the controls, and they shifted around to keep it in view.

"Go ahead."

She glanced at Caleb out of the corner of her eye. "Hmm?"

"You want to follow it—or follow one of them. Go ahead, but I'm telling you, it's going to the master portal."

She flashed him a grin and activated the sLume drive. They didn't need to follow this particular ship. The portal was a bustling place, and there'd be plenty to choose from. "That will still be interesting."

Minutes later she exited superluminal. They didn't have long to wait, as one of the transports soon approached and traversed the portal.

They followed.

They had never witnessed a ship traverse the master portal from their lobby. But they weren't in their lobby, and this version of the master portal was as busy as the Manhattan atmosphere corridor. Dozens of the enormous ships cast tiny black dots against the mammoth structure.

There seemed to be nothing to it. Ships entered and exited in the same manner they did the smaller lobby portal, without special procedures or fanfare. Only the relative scale differed.

Easy.

She gave up the struggle and slipped into the skin of the *Siyane*.

The portal transformed into a double-layered plasma of ionized exotic matter—

"Alex."

She reluctantly backed out to reality and met his gaze. "We should do this. Now is the time. We can sneak in alongside one of these ships, and no one will be the wiser."

He stared out the viewport and didn't respond.

"Look, we now know whoever or whatever is through there, they eat *food*. This means it's a tangible, multi-dimensional, livable space with organic beings in it—humanoids, even. We've seen them. We won't die simply by existing there. It's a *real* place."

"That is...an excellent point." He blew out a breath, long and slow, and regarded her wearing an expression layered in conflict.

Finally, he tilted his head and dropped his chin low. "Okay. A peek. But be ready to turn around and high-tail it out, and long before any spindly claws get themselves tangled in your hair."

She smiled in appreciation of his attempt at levity, but also of his willingness to believe in her when it was entirely possible she was leading them to their death.

He reached out for her, but she'd already returned to the ship. The press of his hand was a distant, faint graze upon her corporeal body.

She didn't leave time for second-guessing. A new ship advanced toward the master portal, and she eased in a close hundred meters below it.

Alex, this is an unwise escalation of an unwise course of action. Allow me to handle the traversal.

No.

The portal grew in size until it filled her vision, then her artificial senses, then every aspect of her perception.

Electric currents sparked and leapt out toward her, tickling her borrowed skin.

A buzz grew in her elemental hearing until it blended into the crackling electricity racing everywhere.

She closed the final picometers to the shimmering, undulating barrier—

44

SIYANE

Amaranthe Gateway

They pitched bow over stern to spin out of control faster than Caleb could process what was happening.

The inertial dampeners went offline, sending his body and mind roiling within the confines of the restraints. Alarms flashed in garish, angry lights on the HUD. He squinted to his left, trying to find a stationary point he could focus on. "Alex?"

No response. His vision began to clear as the spinning eased to a less dizzying but more nauseating speed, and he saw her chin listing against her chest. Her eyes were closed, and blood seeped from both her nostrils. *Shit.*

He unfastened his harness and fell across the cockpit more or less into her lap—in the smallest of favors, the gravity plates continued to function. He lifted her chin. "Alex? Talk to me." Still no response, but she was breathing. "Valkyrie, stabilize the ship and get us away from the portal."

Silence.

"Valkyrie?" His voice echoed through the quiet cabin.

Fuck.

He felt along Alex's neck for a pulse. It raced along at a perilous speed. Their spinning finally stopped, leaving the ship eerily still.

He unfastened her harness and straightened her up in the chair, then tapped on her cheeks. "Come on, Alex. Wake up."

Her eyes flew open, wide and luminous with their artificial glow yet somehow bleary and unseeing. She groped around blindly. Her hands passed over his face and neck without stopping—

—she surged out of the chair, catching him by surprise and knocking him on his ass.

"Alex, calm down! We're okay!" They weren't remotely okay.

She fell to her knees, clung to the cockpit half-wall and pulled herself up, then lurched into the cabin to stumble around wildly.

He rushed out of the cockpit and tried to grab her, but she escaped his clutches twice. Damn those training lessons.

He pivoted and was lunging once more to snare her when she collapsed onto the edge of the couch and sank to the floor.

Instantly he was on his knees at her side. Blood now gushed out of her nostrils, covering her mouth and chin and soaking into her shirt.

She looked up and blinked. The synthetic glow left her irises. She immediately blinked again, and it was back.

Again.

Again.

Her connection to Valkyrie toggled on and off and on in succession like a strobe. The lights in the cabin also began dimming and brightening, but the pattern clashed, out of sync with her eyes.

"Hey, hey, hey...." He tried to gently hold her still, but she was shaking, her head and arms jerking as if being subjected to low-level shocks. Was she having a seizure?

His hands clasped the sides of her face and forcibly held it stationary. "Alex?"

She stared at him but did not *see* him, blinking rapidly—on off on off on off—and for the first time ever, what he saw frightened him. The being staring blankly at him in between blinks couldn't be human.

She started coughing. Gagged on blood and spit it up—then abruptly she slumped over sideways until her head hit the floor.

He'd been too slow to catch her, too slow to let his hand take the blow for her.

He lifted her shoulders and propped her up against the couch, but her eyes were now closed and her body limp. Unconscious.

Jesus. Panic clawed at the edges of his perception, but he had to stay in control. He needed—

The ship shook violently and swung to port. That had been weapons fire hitting the hull. "Valkyrie, are you there?"

Silence.

Another hit sent them canting at a forty-five-degree angle.

He forced air into his lungs, lifted Alex up into his arms and carried her to the cockpit. He strapped her into her chair; the restraints would keep her from being flung around the cabin like a ragdoll, as well as upright and not choking on the blood still flowing from her nostrils.

Next he took the controls. The adiamene should theoretically hold for some period of time, but there were no guarantees. Obviously their cloaking shield was down.

The master portal hung off to starboard, and they were clearly still in the lobby space. He fired the thrusters. The ship fought him, jolting turbulently back and forth. "Dammit! Valkyrie, give me control of the goddamn ship!"

The ship moved—and stopped again. More vessels—or possibly different vessels—fired on them. The impacts threw him forward into the dash then to the floor.

He crawled back into his chair and strapped himself in, ignoring the warm ooze of blood dribbling down his temple. It had been stupid not to do it first, but it had seemed like there wasn't time.

In desperation he engaged the sLume drive. Just a quick, seconds-long sprint to put distance between them, the portal and the attackers.

Alarms screamed but the drive didn't engage. The lights blinked more furiously.

Valkyrie had control of the ship, and she was out of control. Unless he found a way to wrest command from her, they were dead in the air, floating helpless and easy pickings for the enemy.

The ship now shuddered continuously from a barrage of fire,

and yet more, louder alarms sounded. No metal could withstand this level of onslaught forever.

His fists slammed down on the dash in frustration. "Bloody *hell!*"

Was he helpless? Was there not one single goddamn thing he could do to save them? What options did he have left—

—the space outside the viewport brightened to gleam in pin-pricks of light. Blue light, like the portal.

When the luminance overpowered all he could see, there was the sensation of motion. Smooth, not jarring as with the impacts, but still excessive enough to make his stomach lurch.

Then everything stilled.

He blinked. The light outside dissipated to re-veal...mountains? And a meadow?

The scene was instantly recognizable. They were on Portal Prime, in sight of Mesme's lake.

He didn't stop to wonder how. He raced into the cabin for the med kit and a towel, then returned to lean over Alex and wipe the copious blood off her face. She'd lost a lot, though not a life-threatening amount. Once he'd cleared some of it away it looked as if the flow had slowed to a trickle.

Cloak yourselves.

He jumped at the voice. Mesme? Surely Mesme. "We *can't.*"

No alternative instruction followed. He set the towel aside and ran the med scanner across her forehead and temple, hoping it would tell him what to do to help her.

She blinked, hesitantly this time, and opened her eyelids half-way.

"Hey. Don't try to connect to Valkyrie."

He saw the glint in her eyes as she began to do exactly that. He doubted it was out of spite or defiance, but instead merely instinc-tual. He grasped her shoulders firmly. *"Don't."*

She blinked once more, and the relief that surged through him when her irises remained normal was enough to make him dizzy. She gazed at him in confusion, but also in recognition.

He smiled and ran a hand along her cheek. His chest had seized up so viciously he wasn't sure he would be able to speak; it took tremendous effort but he managed to force out a weak breath. "Welcome back, baby."

"What—" She started coughing, grabbed the towel in her lap and held it to her mouth as her shoulders wracked. When it dropped from her hand it had darkened considerably. He hoped it was from blood she'd swallowed and not something worse.

"Where are we?" Her voice croaked, shaky and tentative. She cleared her throat and peered out the viewport. "Is this...Portal Prime?"

"I think so. I think Mesme transported us here."

"The whole ship? Wait, why?"

He exhaled. It came out harsh, rough, frayed by the ragged edges of panic. "The portal bounced us, hard. Valkyrie went berserk, and you...you had some kind of seizure then passed out. I couldn't get control of the ship away from her, and we came under attack by Metigen vessels."

"Valkyrie? Are you all right?"

Silence lingered for several seconds, but eventually a response came. Soft and uncertain as well, but a response. 'I...I believe I will be. Allow me to execute a full restart. I will return momentarily.'

Alex frowned and dragged a hand down her face, then deepened the frown when it came away streaked in blood. She gazed around in disbelief and mounting horror. "Why is there blood on everything? Why is there always fucking blood fucking *everywhere* when I wake up from being unconscious?"

"Hey!"

Startled, she gaped at him in shock for a beat, then deflated completely and sank bonelessly against the backrest. "What happened to me?"

He knelt beside her. "You were bleeding from your nose. A lot. You should take an iron supplement soon, or you're going to be feeling really weak."

"I had a *brain hemorrhage?*"

"I don't...." He shook his head. Helplessly. "I don't know." The terror-turned-euphoria pounding in his chest and against his eardrums had begun to recede, leaving in its wake something he didn't expect: anger.

"You were connected to the ship when we hit the portal, I'm assuming?"

She gave a weak nod in answer.

"You're insane, I'm assuming?"

Her lips parted to convey what might have been a retort, when the lights brightened and stayed that way.

'I'm pleased to report I have regained full functionality.'

45

AURORA THESI (PORTAL PRIME)

Alex ran a hand over the nose of the ship...and scowled. The adiamene was *dented*. The repulsion from the portal—whatever force the Metigens used to effect it—had been that strong.

Her brain felt dented. Dulled, with faint, jagged cracks splintering it. Valkyrie said there was no significant damage to the neural tissue. But then again, the Artificial might be dented, too.

Near as Valkyrie was able to determine, most of what had happened was Alex's fault. Her mind, assimilated as it was into the atoms of the *Siyane*, had not been able to process the force of the ricochet the ship experienced when it impacted the portal. The resulting shock kicked off a chain reaction in her brain, which among other things disrupted the connection mechanism to Valkyrie—but not before the problems ricocheted further into Valkyrie's processes as well.

If she hadn't been linked to the ship when they made a run at the portal, Valkyrie might not have malfunctioned, she definitely would not have passed out, and they probably would have been able to leave under their own power before coming under attack.

The nose of the ship would still be dented, though. She focused her scowl on the hull; it seemed as suitable a victim as any to suffer her misdirected vexation and angst.

At least they weren't going to need to remove the panel and physically repair the damage. Valkyrie was now so extensively integrated into the ship she claimed she'd be able to mold and shape the metal back to its normal configuration within a few hours.

Mesme was nowhere to be found. Not its consciousness, that was. They'd checked, and its unnerving little gray body still lay dormant in the stasis pod inside the small cabin.

Caleb paced in erratic circles around the lush meadow behind her. He'd been unusually quiet, bordering on taciturn, since the first minutes after she'd woken up. Now the tension radiated off of him in waves, ruffling the blades of grass on its way to suffocate her.

She pinched the bridge of her nose, in the hope applying pressure there could alleviate the pressure everywhere else. She didn't want to have this conversation. But every minute they didn't stood to make it so much more catastrophic.

She turned and leaned against the hull, crossing her arms at her waist. "I'm sorry, okay?" She tried to sound genuinely apologetic, but the words emerged pinched and strained. Pretty much like her.

He halted midway through a traversal and stared at her. His mouth opened. After a pause, he closed it.

"Please, just say what you want to say. This brooding is worse than anything you can throw at me."

"Are you so sure about that?"

A warning fluttered in her chest, but she nodded.

"You could have died. We all could have died. What in the hell were you thinking?"

Well, she *had* asked for this. She worked past the raw lump in her throat…and chose the truth. "I wasn't."

"What does that mean?"

"It means…it means I got caught up in the rush." Judging by the solidifying bleakness of his expression, the truth had been a mistake. She hurriedly backtracked in a bit of a panic. "But in my defense, it may not have mattered. Valkyrie may have gotten her circuits scrambled regardless."

I told you I'm not at all certain that's true.

Later, Valkyrie.

You are lying to him.

No, I'm not. We don't know for sure.

But in her heart she did know, which explained the queasiness churning her stomach. They had a word for it: guilt.

"Then we'll need to address that problem, too, because I had no control over the ship. None. I had no ability to act, to defend us or save us, and that is *unacceptable*."

"More safeguards, more failsafes. I get it." It came out tinged in sarcasm. She hadn't meant it that way. Everything was coming out wrong.

Caleb expression contorted into something she was afraid to decipher. "You think? Do you get what I'm saying? There was *nothing* I could do. Nothing except yank Valkyrie's power. But considering how much of yourself you've given over to the ship, I would probably be unplugging you as well and—"

She gasped in abject dismay. It elicited a cringe from him, and his voice softened a touch. "I didn't mean it like that."

She'd been on his side; she'd been trying her damnedest to apologize. She understood how important being able to act when threatened was to him, and she knew she'd frightened him.

But his words were a bucket of ice water pitched in her face. She could hardly breathe from the shock of it. "Really? Because it kind of sounded like you did."

He squeezed his eyes shut, amplifying the effect of the clenched muscles in his jaw and the fierce streaks of discontentment his eyebrows had become. "Really. I only meant...you were unconscious, and Valkyrie was not in control of her functions, and I had no way to predict what might happen to you if I shut her down improperly."

His eyes reopened to reveal dark, storming irises, almost black against the fair periwinkle sky. "Alex, I have never in my life been so terrified, and...angry and frustrated and...helpless. Are you hearing me? *There was nothing I could do.* Helplessness is not a place I visit often, and for damn good reason. Jesus, I can't...."

He threw his hands in the air rather than finish the sentence. Something told her it was for the best.

"I know. I am sorry. Please believe me, I didn't mean to put you in that position."

"But you *did* put me in that position. Your stunt was reckless and idiotic. Alex, you can't be so careless with your safety! If you choose to place yourself in danger when the risk is worth it, when there's a larger, more important goal at stake, I am there with you. I will stand beside you and risk everything without question. But you cannot continue acting like this on your random whim."

Every ingrained instinct she had, including several she'd assumed long buried, flared in outrage. Bitter memories taunted her from the recesses of her mind. She scrunched her face up to the point of pain from the effort of holding back words she would surely regret in epic ways if they made it past her lips.

She raised a hand only to hold it out, warding him off, and inhaled deeply. Slowly, buying herself time.

"You're right. You're absolutely right. But..." she winced "...don't tell me I *cannot* do something for my own good. Please, I'm begging you here. Those words are a ridiculous trigger for me, and I don't want to lash out at you when you don't deserve it, or get myself killed trying to prove you wrong. I know it's my own failing—I *know*—and I'm trying to be better than that, but just don't...please."

"Right. Not your keeper. Forgot for a minute." He abused his jaw with both hands. "*Fuck.* Okay, we need to run some tests to confirm all the systems are operating correctly. I don't want to find out something's still broken once we're back in space."

Cold. She felt cold. Shivering, goosebumps prickling her arms in the warm afternoon air. "Caleb...."

"No, it's fine. Everything is...fine."

"Like hell it is!"

I drifted in the woods behind the lake, behind the small house I had built as if it were somehow a home.

Constructing it had involved directing wood and stone, millions thick with atoms, yet now I commanded but a few precious particles. I rested, working to regain my energy, and imposed patience upon myself. Only serenity could hasten regeneration of will.

Moving an ethereal, semi-physical manifestation of oneself was the simplest of matters, done without thought. Transporting small objects—timber, rocks, a Human or two—while I remained stationary and whole was nearly as trivial to accomplish. Doing so with and within myself required the application of greater resources and effort, but it was not what I considered a notably difficult task.

Transporting myself *and* a forty-two-meter-long ship across space and a demi-portal and through a planetary atmosphere was, as Humans were prone to say, another matter entirely. I had barely managed it, and it left me sapped of all but the faintest spark.

But that had been many moments ago. I evaluated myself...yes. I was nearly recharged enough to return to my normal external form. Nevertheless, I elected to wait until I reached my full strength and allow them to argue in the meantime.

There were times I believed Humans did little else but argue with one another. It was one of their traits I found most confounding, for it should have inevitably led to their consummate demise many thousands of times, but somehow it had not. Not as of yet.

I did not have the ability to observe the details of Alexis and Caleb's explorations through the other portals, so I dared not speculate as to what this argument in particular was regarding. A reasonable supposition to make was it pertained to the less than optimal state they were in when I had arrived on the scene. They were most—

—I sensed the approach of another like a growing darkness on the horizon. Never in my remembrance had one of my own radiated such malevolence.

So news of the events at the Amaranthe gateway had reached the Idryma.

It was with a great, sorrowful dread that I gathered up my energies, which I judged to be woefully regenerated for the task at hand, and surged out of the woods to the lake below.

⁂

Retreat to the ship and cloak. Do it now.

"Mesme?" Where the hell was the damn alien?

Alex glared at the empty air and threw her hands up in exasperation. But she obeyed the *order* like the proper little girl in military school she'd once been for twelve weeks in another life.

Caleb closed the hatch behind them. "Valkyrie, tell me the cloaking shield is working."

'There is one way to find out. Cloaking shield engaged. All readings indicate it is functioning to specifications.'

Alex hurried to the cockpit to peer out the viewport, because there better be something worth seeing outside. At first nothing appeared out of the ordinary, and her rising blood pressure chased away any remaining shivers.

Then Mesme materialized in empyreal, winged form to hover above the center of the lake. Sneaky bugger had been hiding from them?

Several seconds later another Metigen soared down the slope in a projected air of urgency. It halted directly opposite Mesme.

Where are they?

Where are who, Hyperion?

Hyperion…Aguirre and Hervé's alien contact, and the one who threatened their safety the first time they were here.

"Why can we understand them? Why can we *hear* them?"

Caleb gave her a surprisingly mild shrug, considering his current state of mind and the rather disharmonic state of the world and all who resided in it—most notably them. "Maybe Mesme wants us to?"

Hyperion: Do not play coy with me, Mnemosyne. Your Human pets tried to breach a gateway to Amaranthe. Their presence in the Mosaic is too dangerous to continue to be tolerated. Send them home and eradicate the Aurora portal, or I will do it for you.

Mnemosyne: They can throw themselves at the Amaranthe gateway all they desire. They will not get through. They are not a danger.

Hyperion: Not a danger? They threaten everything we've worked for aeons to accomplish. They will bring ruin upon us all. You must see this. Stop protecting them. Hand them over.

Mnemosyne: No.

She felt the force and conviction of the statement reverberate in her chest as if it had been a seismic tremor. Mesme truly was protecting them. She sighed…nothing was ever simple, was it?

Hyperion: So they are here, then. You did sweep in and rescue them like the angels they once worshipped. You imagine yourself quite the shepherd, don't you? This was all a mistake. Aurora was a mistake. The Human species is no different from its progenitor, and if allowed to run free they will be the end of everything.

I say again—hand the Humans over, and I will do what is necessary, what you lack the fortitude to do.

Mnemosyne: And I, too, will say again. No. You do not rule here, Hyperion, and you possess no authority over me.

Her hand had found Caleb's sometime in the interchange…and he hadn't fought her. Worse, he now gave her hand a reassuring squeeze. She longed to grab him and draw him into her arms and whisper how much she loved him until the pain faded and everything stopped being so damn *hard*.

But an existential battle over their lives was being waged

outside, so all she could do was offer him a desperate smile when he whistled in appreciation. "Damn, Mesme. I did not know you had it in you."

Hyperion: I will take them from you if I must, Mnemosyne. I will—

A third Metigen appeared out of nowhere to insert itself between the two quarreling aliens.

You will not.

Hyperion's manifestation shrank in size; its threatening gleam dimmed.

Hyperion: Praetor Lakhes, it is good you've come. The insolent Humans running rampant through the Mosaic attempted to break into Amaranthe. Mnemosyne spirited them away and hides them even now. With you here we can at last bring an end to this foolish madness and restore reason to our work.

The great Lakhes at last. Hyperion called it 'Praetor.' This implied Lakhes was in charge. Interesting.

Mnemosyne: Lakhes, the time has come to choose a side.

Hyperion: Your words are traitorous, Mnemosyne. There is only one side: the side of discipline, study and supervision.

Lakhes: I know, Mnemosyne.

Spurred on by a hunch and a hint of a memory from their time in Portal B-5, of the glimpse she'd caught of the Metigen in the quantum space before the star went supernova, Alex braced herself and moved into that space.

The Metigens' presence in the quantum dimension resembled an overlay—or perhaps an underlay—upon their physical appearance, ethereal as it was. They retained their core avatars—the winged ray, the horned owl, the faie—while their visible forms shifted and undulated.

Hyperion: Praetor, do not listen to the poetic caprices of this exile. Mnemosyne chants platitudes while undermining our every move. Banish these Humans back to Aurora and eradicate its portal so they never trouble us again.

Lakhes: And if I do not? What will you do then, Hyperion?

Hyperion: If you...if you do not? I...will do what necessity demands be done, Praetor, for all our sakes. For the sake of all living souls in Amaranthe.

Mnemosyne: Lakhes, choose.

Lakhes: I chose long ago, Mnemosyne, even if you did not see it. Hyperion, you are forbidden to reenter Amaranthe—don't attempt it, for your access has already been revoked. I believe you believe you act in our best interests, but your judgment is too narrow to manifest as wisdom.

If you bring harm to the Humans currently in the Mosaic or those in Aurora, you will be made corpus-bound. You would do well to depart now, or I may become vexed and increase the punishment further.

Hyperion: Praetor, how can you—

Lakhes: Depart.

Hyperion dissipated in an agitated flutter of blooded scarlet lights, leaving Mesme and Lakhes to float above the lake.

Mnemosyne: Lakhes, I thank you for—

Lakhes: No need, dear friend, but now is not the time to press your position. See to your charges, but do try to ensure they don't attempt to breach Amaranthe again until the time is right.

Mnemosyne: And when do you expect the right time will be, dear friend?

Lakhes: Mnemosyne, I will say it a second time, as I seem to be forced to do whenever Humans are about: do not overreach. I realize how poorly things fare in Aurora as well as you. Whenever that time proves to be, it is assuredly not today. If your charges possess such talents as you assert, perhaps they should use them to mend their home before endeavoring to do the same elsewhere.

Now, I should return to the Idryma, lest Hyperion rouse a mutiny in my absence.

Mnemosyne: Of course. And know you have my thanks, and my allegiance.

⟨R⟩

She squeezed tightly on Caleb's hand, so hard he'd have to pay attention. "I'm going to try to follow Lakhes."

"Follow where...oh. Do it. I'm here."

Oh, how I hope you are, my love.

Lakhes' physical presence flitted into the air and away, but she concentrated on the quantum presence, what she suspected was the truer essence of the alien. She'd never done this before, but if she kept Lakhes firmly in her sights, she thought she'd be able to track—

As with all movement over distances in this space, it was quick. A millisecond, no more than two, and they hovered in front of one of the portals in the Aurora lobby. She wasn't even dizzy...or she was well beyond dizzy and it happened to feel the same in this twilight zone.

The portal opened, and Lakhes vanished into it.

Valkyrie, where are we? I need to know which portal this is.

Measuring. Portal A-9.

She gazed at the portal, glistening and gauzy through the filter of the quantum space. The fact Lakhes had done so notwithstanding, she didn't know if she had the ability to traverse it with naught but her mind. She flowed forward to try...

...and stopped herself. After what had happened mere hours earlier, after Caleb's words and the anguish on his face had cut her in the deepest places...it would be nothing short of blatant stupidity to attempt it, and she very well may lose her life for the effort.

Return.

She opened her eyes. "Lakhes went through Portal A-9. Let's go."

⟨R⟩

What had they just witnessed?

Caleb pretended to relax in his chair and ruminated on it while they made the short trip to the portal. To be honest, he welcomed the diversion the chase provided from the more uncomfortable and too destructive events which preceded it.

Mesme, then Lakhes as well, had protected them. Not the Taenarin or anyone else from Amaranthe, but *them*. And from one of their own, no less.

Hyperion meant to cut off his and Alex's access to the portal network and everything beyond it at a minimum, and possibly to kill them. Mesme had once claimed the Metigens did not kill using their own forms, but Caleb wasn't so certain Hyperion had gotten the memo.

To complicate the picture, there appeared to be an ongoing dispute among these Metigens about some larger, unnamed conflict—one which, by their account, had already spanned aeons.

His head might reel from the implications, but he was a practical guy when it came to missions, and to his way of thinking this without a doubt constituted a mission. Not one for any government, but for the people—all of them. This was the show. So he focused on the here and now.

Lakhes' statements to Hyperion implied the Praetor controlled entry into Amaranthe. Perhaps more importantly, the statements implied that at some point in the future, he and Alex *were expected* to traverse the master portal to Amaranthe.

A familiar but unwelcome chill radiated at the base of his spine. Puppet masters pulling their strings, indeed.

On top of it all, Lakhes had indicated there were problems at home, in Aurora—problems serious enough for the Metigens who weren't supposed to be watching any longer to take notice of them.

Dammit, could things stay not fucked up for once? For the briefest blink of time?

But whatever was happening back home, it would have to either wait or work itself out, for they may be about to unlock a number of the Metigens' secrets. Or Alex may be about to, anyway.

He watched her in the corner of his vision, not giving any hint to her that he did. She monitored their approach to the portal and nominally directed the ship. But mostly she chewed on her bottom lip and stared out at the darkness.

He feared for her, feared for her life as she recklessly threw herself into these perilous situations. She chased the truth without so much as a thought for her safety, chased an enemy he had no way to help her fight.

Now he felt impotent, because he couldn't find an enemy target suitable for shooting or knifing or strangling…and because he wasn't even sure who the enemy was any longer.

If he were honest with himself—and he really did try to be—he feared the path she headed down would take her somewhere he couldn't follow, and not merely physically.

And he had no idea how to stop her from going down it, not without losing her entirely. Which was something else he could not do.

She straightened her posture and glanced over, but didn't quite meet his gaze. "We're there."

PORTAL: A-9

SYSTEM DESIGNATION: IDRYMA

46

IDRYMA

There was nothing.

It wasn't the void they'd encountered through several of the previous portals. Space did exist here, same as it typically did in the lobbies. But they found no exit portal. No universe beyond the lobby.

Alex searched the blackness for a glimmer that might point the way. "This looks like a dead end. But obviously it's not if this is where Lakhes went. So…what are we missing? Valkyrie, are you picking up *anything* special?"

'I regret to say I am not. On the surface, there is nothing unusual here. On the other hand, there is nothing usual here, either.'

A chuckle died in her throat as she gazed at Caleb. He peered out the viewport, on the lookout for something to make itself known. He was still focused on the mission, still embracing their purpose here. Still *believing*.

Her chest seized up, captive to a sensation she hadn't yet found a name for. She reached out and enclosed his hand in a vise-grip, taking him by surprise.

His eyes darted to hers and stayed there; he drew in a sharp, visible breath.

She offered him the best smile she was capable of conjuring. "You understand how much I love you, don't you? More than—" *all the stars in the heavens…*but she'd never been so eloquent with her feelings as her father "—anything. I'm truly sorry about what happened at the portal. I put you in a terrible position, and it wasn't fair to you. I'm sorry about…outside, too. About a lot of things.

Back on Ireltse, I told you I would do better. I failed at that today. Badly. But it was my mistake, and I own it."

He stared at her in something like wonder, with a distinct dash of relief. A wonderful smirk grew on his lips, continuing on so far as to light his eyes. "Apology accepted. Now time's wasting, so go find what's hiding here. *Go.*"

She clasped his hand once more, hoping it was enough for now, enough to stem the tide. Then she closed her eyes to transition into the quantum space.

A gasp must have escaped her lips back on the ship, for she sensed his grip tighten.

Fractals of light unfolded in every direction ahead of her. There was a *structure* built in this dimension, where concepts such as distance, width and height should not exist.

Many stories tall and wide beyond her vision, the structure transcended anything she had ever seen or imagined. Its beauty was breathtaking, but the light waves hummed a slightly dissonant tone at the very edge of her hearing, a chord forever seeking resolution.

What is this place?

If I had to make a guess, I would say it is the Idryma.

Whatever that is.

A reasonable question. I can offer theories, but I sense now is not the time.

Slowly, cautiously, she drifted inside the outer walls of this creation. Beings—or representations of their consciousnesses— ambled through its halls. Though the edifice felt like a hologram and its light the most illusory of planes, they moved as if the virtual floors beneath their feet were real.

It's possible we only see a narrow segment of the complex. If it extends into additional dimensions, this may be akin to observing a 2D drawing of a cube.

We've seen the Metigens make use of at least six dimensions several times now, so...sure.

Could they see her? None reacted to her presence, not even the one who passed a sliver away from her, so she decided they could not. Odd, since by their actions they clearly recognized and acknowledged one another.

Were all the beings present Metigens? Instinctively, she believed the answer was yes. And she was forced to conclude they could manipulate this quantum space with infinitely greater skill than she or her fellow Prevos had been able to accomplish. She was a ghostly spectator here, but they appeared to be *existing* here.

Above her and ahead, she detected a concentration of those inhabiting this place.

She willed herself *up* and wandered along their outskirts. They interacted in a manner which suggested they conversed with one another, but she could not hear their words.

It took a minute to discern it, as they retained wispy and ethereal forms, but the individuals took on distinct shapes. One resembled a lion-like creature, another a many-armed...cephalopod? She noted a broad-winged bird, and several shapes derived from no organic inspiration she'd ever seen. Off to the side floated a tall, graceful faie—

Lakhes.

She moved closer.

Lakhes shared space with another being, one who took as their avatar a great caracal, and as she drew near, she did begin to hear and understand them. How? Mesme was not here to radiate a translation, and she remained unable to comprehend the others.

Lakhes: —so quickly? Perhaps we bred their bloodlust too well. Yet this in itself contains a lesson we can learn from.

Unidentified: I agree. In the end I hardly had to encourage them. Their eagerness for vengeance oozed in the sweat from their pores. I daresay it would be a challenge to dissuade them, but if you wish me to attempt to slow their progression, I can do so.

Lakhes contemplated the question a moment. *No. We have learned nearly all we are apt to from them. Allow them to act, and*

*see if they do. There is a small chance we misjudge them. Assuming
we do not, let it flow to its end. Once it's done we will shut Enisle
Twenty-Seven down and queue it for re-use.*

The other Metigen rippled its form in response and floated
off down the corridor.

*Valkyrie, renumber all the portals using this one as the starting
point. Given that order, what portal are they discussing?*

Khamen. The Khokteh portal.

Dammit! There was so much here to investigate, so many incredible possibilities to explore. But if the Khokteh were in danger
of being annihilated they needed to move fast. She prepared to
leave, swearing to return—

—Lakhes' essence spun and surged forward to surround her.

I see you, Alexis Solovy.

Her pulse hastened, ready to panic. But the alien wasn't hurt-
ing her. Was it?

In the part of her consciousness still residing in her body, she
felt the warmth of his palm as Caleb stroked her cheek. He was
concerned. She tried to make her head nod to convey she was
okay, and thought she succeeded.

"You can't exterminate the Khokteh! You haven't the right.
They deserve to live."

*Ah, yes, you did visit their Enisle. Their own decisions have
demonstrated they do not.*

The words implied the Praetor only now remembered that
they had spent time with the Khokteh. But it was a lie. Lakhes had
known she was here the whole time and had allowed her to
overhear the conversation with whom she assumed must be
Iapetus, before confronting her. Lakhes *wanted* her to know what
was about to transpire.

Was it a test? A challenge? Not that she cared; her course of
action had already been decided.

"You manipulated them into war and killing. You treated them
like playthings, but they are so much more. They simply need to be
allowed to choose their own path, free of your interference."

Lakhes' essence twisted and undulated around her; she felt as though her skin should be tingling from the adamant yet spectral caresses.

Enough. I will not debate the merits of our stratagems with a Human. The fate of any single species populating any single Enisle has no consequence to the universe.

"Which universe?"

The only one which exists of its own volition. The only one which in truth exists at all.

"Amaranthe."

Mnemosyne was correct. You are a clever one. Even more clever than your sentient ship. Or might Valkyrie be here as well? No matter.

Well done on having discovered this place. My compliments to you. The perspicacious nature of... the points of light quivered *...Humans is proven once again. But now you must depart.*

"Not until you answer my questions. Why is Aurora dangerous? Why do you create universes then prime the residents to exterminate themselves? Why do you waste your time toying with species you view as insignificant when you clearly have real enemies in Amaranthe? Are you hiding—"

Her perception was propelled backward, as if it were being pulled into a vortex. She slammed into her body.

Her eyes flew open with a gasp.

"Alex?"

She sat straight up in the chair and grabbed Caleb by the shoulders. "We have to save them."

PART VII:

PUPPET MASTERS

"Give me a lever long enough and a fulcrum on which to place it, and I shall move the world."

— Archimedes

PORTAL: AURORA

(MILKY WAY)

47

ROMANE

Noah stared at the hand. *His* hand, he supposed, but his brain wasn't quite ready to accept it yet.

His brow furrowed in concentration...and the fingers curled in toward the palm. Directing the movement hadn't actually been hard. His focus shifted, and he slowly bent the arm in at the elbow. It seemed heavy, but he knew it was his imagination.

The skin tone was a tad pale, but the doctors promised it would tan and soon be indistinguishable from the rest of his skin. Because it *was* his skin, cloned from his other forearm and grafted onto the biosynthetic limb beneath—a limb constructed using his own bone, grown and shaped on a self-dissolving lattice.

Still, while partially organic, the prosthetic arm stretching from fingertip to a few centimeters below his shoulder was more synthetic than—

—he stopped himself. What the hell was he being angsty and melodramatic about? He loved tech, and this was cool, dammit.

It was going to be stronger than his real arm had been once he got used to controlling it. He bet it packed a helluva punch. And he'd been in enough scrapes to recognize there were times when what you most needed in the world was a helluva punch.

His spirits lifted considerably, and he was beaming when Kennedy walked into the hospital room with his father in tow. Even the sight of Lionel didn't dampen his mood. If pushed, he'd be forced to admit he was almost—*almost*—glad to see his father.

He lifted his fake arm in the air and gave it an experimental wave. "Hi."

His father appeared positively concerned as he hurried over to the bed. "How are you feeling? You're lucky to be alive, you know. I spoke to all the doctors. They say if a few more minutes had passed without medical intervention, your eVi would not have been able to prevent your brain from stroking."

Noah shot Kennedy a questioning grimace, but she shrugged helplessly. He rolled his eyes in his father's direction. "Good to see you too, Dad."

Lionel blinked. "Yes. Right. I'm happy to see you awake and in positive spirits." He reached out, grasped the prosthetic arm and twisted it back and forth, inspecting it like it *wasn't* attached to Noah's body.

"Ow!"

Lionel set the arm down and patted the hand perfunctorily. "So the nerves were properly reattached. Good. Looks as though they did a fair job. I made certain no expense was spared, so the limb should function perfectly for you. If it doesn't, inform me and I'll take care of it."

Noah started to bristle. He opened his mouth to protest that he didn't want or need his father's charity. But his father's charity meant he had a state of the art prosthetic arm all but indistinguishable from his own—better than his own—and not a clunky synthesized polymer one. His looked at his father, really *looked*, and for the first time found genuine kindness in the man's eyes.

"I'll keep that in mind. It feels fine. A little weird, but I bet I'll forget it's not mine—not my original arm—in no time. So...thanks."

Kennedy moved to the other side of the bed and placed a far more gentle hand on his shoulder. "Are you in pain? The docs have great drugs if you need any."

"Let's make sure and swipe some on our way out, then. It's...sore I guess, at my shoulder where they connected all the pieces on the inside. But a dash of pain reminds me I'm alive and nearly wasn't."

A distressed frown darkened her features, and he reached over using his real arm to place a hand on hers. "It's okay. No, it's better than okay."

The frown blossomed into a smile in response, lovely as a cloudless sunrise, and he thought he probably shouldn't leave her ever.

Lionel cleared his throat, ending the weighty, emotional moment with a typical absence of grace. "Ms. Rossi, please inform the appropriate representatives that Pandora will be joining the IDCC. Have the necessary records sent to my attention, and I'll ensure they're executed and returned."

Kennedy didn't seem surprised. "I'm glad to hear it. And please, you can call me Kennedy. I think we're well past honorifics now."

His father regarded her with a rather perplexed expression, one most unlike his characteristic scowl of disdain. "Very well, if you insist...Kennedy."

Noah gave Lionel a vaguely accusatory look. "So you really do wield a lot of authority for Pandora, then?"

Ah, there was the scowl. Back to normal. "Yes, I do. And that's all I intend to say on the matter, so don't bother to press it."

"I wouldn't dream of it."

Kennedy tilted her head in question. "May I ask why you decided to join?"

"Criminals hurt my son. IDCC forces saved him, then punished those responsible. The Consortium has proved its worth to me."

Noah was too shocked to figure out how to retort. He gazed at Kennedy instead, eyes a bit wide. She squeezed his hand.

Huh. Just like that it became *his* hand.

She looked back to his father. "I know they'll be pleased to hear the news. You should receive documentation in the next hour."

"Yes, well." His father straightened up. "I have a comm to take, and I want to speak at greater length to the doctors overseeing your care. I'll return later to check on you." He pivoted and left the room.

Noah sank against the pillow. "Well, he's not getting any more charming."

"But?"

"But I suppose it's…nice, what he's doing. For me, for the IDCC."

"You're damn right it is."

He may have relaxed, but she was twitching beside the hospital bed. He tilted his head curiously. "What's up?"

She chewed on her lower lip. "So…the Alliance issued an arrest warrant for me over the adiamene dispute."

"You're kidding."

She shook her head. "I'm a fugitive!" She started giggling as the words spilled out, bouncing on the balls of her feet. "Can you believe it? I feel so naughty."

He laughed, relieved she was taking the news so well. He'd expected horror at best, panic at less best, if something like this happened. He must be rubbing off on her. "Imagine how naughty I'm going to feel when I make love to a fugitive from justice. I can't wait."

"Neither can I." Her lips quirked mischievously and she placed a soft kiss on his mouth. "But you need to concentrate on healing for now."

He scoffed. "Seriously, though, you don't think they'll send law enforcement after you, do you? Or…crap, doesn't Romane have an extradition treaty with the Alliance?"

"You haven't checked the news lately, have you? What am I saying, obviously you haven't checked the news. You've had more important things to worry about. But no—not any longer."

48

"Everything is ready to go on this end. We are operational and awaiting the stream."

Miriam eyed the security cam footage of the lobby, noting the new arrivals. "Okay, Christopher. I'm out of time. Initiating transfer."

"Good luck, Miriam."

"Luck is not a factor. I'll see you soon."

She killed the holocomm and opened a new screen, then carefully input a string of commands, passwords, authorizations and more commands.

The hesitation before she hit 'Proceed' was hardly long enough to be measurable.

The line between patriot and traitor was a fine one indeed. It was also one drawn by the victors, so her placement relative to it remained to be seen.

She was sitting patiently at her desk when they arrived, but stood when the door opened to admit Pamela Winslow and four members of the woman's security retinue.

"Prime Minister, what can I do for you? To warrant a personal visit when you have so many pressing matters to handle, it must be quite important."

"You have refused to implement Assembly Resolution SGR 2323-4761. Do you confirm this?"

"Is that the one ordering the military to act against Alliance citizens, rounding them up and imprisoning them while lacking probable cause then denying them a timely hearing?"

"The Alliance military is sworn to protect its citizens from threats without *and* within."

"Yes. It is." She didn't flinch, and Winslow folded under the weight of her stare.

"I'll ask you once more, Admiral. Are you refusing to enforce a valid Assembly Directive?"

"I take exception to the term 'valid.'"

"*Are you* refusing to enforce an Assembly Directive?"

"I am."

Winslow tried to mask the malicious smile but did not entirely succeed. Miriam wasn't surprised; this was what the woman wanted, after all. "Then you will suffer the consequences. As Prime Minister, I am exercising my authority under Article 31.3 of the Second Earth Alliance Constitution of 2146 to relieve you of the rank of Fleet Admiral, effective immediately."

"Oh, dear. I suppose I'm forced to return to being a simple Admiral—a rank you do not have the authority to divest me of."

"No, but an Ethics Council tribunal does, and I will ensure you're brought in front of one inside a week."

"You'd best get to work on that, then." Miriam brushed past Winslow to exit the office.

"Agent Treston, detain Admiral Solovy on suspicion of conspiracy to commit treason."

She stopped in the open doorway. Hearing the word pronounced aloud chilled her to the marrow in her bones, but she would *never* let it show.

She looked behind her to the man Winslow had directed the order at. The agent appeared unsure of what to do, and the warning in Miriam's eyes couldn't be helping his resolve.

"Prime Minister, I'm not certain we have the—"

"She is suspected of being a clear and present threat to state security. Detain her now."

"Y-yes, ma'am." The agent took a hesitant step toward her.

Miriam leaned into the atrium and secured the attention of the security officer on duty. "Captain Fletcher, these agents are attempting to illegally restrain a superior military officer."

"Ma'am!" He leapt up and barked orders into his comm. In seconds six additional MPs had arrived in the atrium.

"Agent *Treston*."

Treston drew his service Daemon. She had to admire his audacity. The next second everyone's weapons were drawn. Except hers, of course. No need to be unseemly.

The Prime Minister's security team was outnumbered and literally outgunned. Winslow vibrated with rage.

Had she honestly believed Miriam's people would not follow her orders without question, would not defend her even if the Prime Minister's actions were not illegal—which they were?

Miriam met Winslow's gaze in a cold, steeled and utterly composed manner. "Let's not create a bloodbath in EASC Headquarters. I'm confident you don't want to start your term in office under the cloud of such an unfortunate scandal."

She paused to give Winslow the opportunity to argue; the woman did not.

"I'm leaving now. Once I've departed, Captain Fletcher will see you and your men off the Island."

"You are making such a mistake, Admiral."

"We will see, won't we?" She pivoted to Fletcher. "Two men with me. They'll inform you when I've authorized the Prime Minister and her people to depart. Until then, keep them here."

"Yes, ma'am." His chin notched up. "Godspeed, Admiral."

That of all things caught her off guard. She blinked. "Thank you, Captain. And thank you for your exemplary service."

"It's my honor, ma'am."

A sharp salute and she headed for the lift, turning her back on what had become her favorite office ever. If things went her way, perhaps she'd see it again.

R

Her MP escorts were stoic and silent during the ride down the lift. On reaching the lobby they respectfully motioned for her to remain while they cleared the way to the exit. It was unlikely Winslow had kept any security in reserve, much less a force worthy of concern. But the MPs' job was not to assume.

Once outside she did not head for the spaceport, but rather the courtyard.

Right on time, an EA military shuttle descended from above. It was an unusual place to land, but the shuttle apparently had all the required clearances, for no one was attempting to shoot it down.

She pivoted to the MPs. "Thank you for the escort, officers. My ride's here, so I'll be going. Delay one minute after I've boarded the shuttle, then inform Captain Fletcher that Prime Minister Winslow and her security detail can be taken to the spaceport and placed aboard their transport.

"Do not share any details about my departure until the Prime Minister has left the premises, and then only with Captain Fletcher or Major Lange."

"Understood, Admiral."

She returned their salutes before traversing the half-step up and into the waiting shuttle. The door closed behind her as the late-morning sun reflected off the Headquarters façade.

She exhaled deeply, trying to leave it all here…then moved into the small cockpit and perched on the seat next to Richard. "Thanks for the pickup. Encounter any problems?"

He shot her a quick, reassuring smile as he banked above the Strait. "Plenty, but I wasn't an intelligence officer for nothing."

"No, you weren't." She reached over and squeezed his shoulder. "*Thank* you."

"You're welcome. Are you all right?"

"I am. I must be." She nodded firmly. "I'm just grateful Alex isn't here to see the fallout from all this."

"On the other hand, the stream of obscenities she'd level at Winslow might be entertaining, and possibly unmatched in history."

She wanted to laugh aloud, but she worried it would trigger an avalanche. So instead she merely huffed a breath in response.

When the ensuing silence lingered a bit long, Richard cracked his neck. "I've got one of the new scout ships waiting on the EAO Orbital. We'll be at Messium by the morning."

Messium. The tense encounter had caused her to momentarily forget the most important part. She immediately opened a holocomm.

"Christopher, I'm in the air but don't want to access the system until I'm beyond Earth space. Did you receive everything?"

"The Artificial is reporting receipt and integration of all records, protocols and security encryptions. The connection was cut twenty-three seconds ago on your end, for what it's worth, but not before we gained all necessary access."

"We have control of the EASC network?"

"No, Miriam. We have control of the entire Earth Alliance Armed Forces network."

49

PANDORA

The news feed played in Devon's head as he unlocked the obscenely encrypted door to his apartment.

"In the wake of the new legislation passed by the Earth Alliance Assembly, government officials have announced a ban on quantum component imports from any colony which has legalized the private ownership of Artificials or the use of what the Assembly termed 'Prevo technology.'

"This currently includes all colonies who have joined the IDCC, and depending on the outcome of the vote expected soon in its Parliament, may extend to the entire Senecan Federation as well.

"In addition, Alliance officials have put those governments on notice that they will expect existing extradition treaties to be honored, including with respect to any Earth Alliance citizens located on those worlds who violate the laws passed today."

If the Federation extended legal protection to Prevos, it would be a huge win. There had been a flurry of activity on this front during the last week in the halls of government on Seneca. He'd been busy working to keep the Prevos there—and everywhere—safe, but he and the others had peeked in from time to time to monitor developments.

Still, even if the legislation passed it didn't guarantee their safety. On the contrary, an enraged OTS would mean greater risk for Prevos on Federation soil. But at least they'd finally have law enforcement backing them up.

"A Federation spokesperson has issued a statement expressing concern over the Alliance legislation and indicating they will need to review it in some detail before addressing the matter. The IDCC,

however, responded by requesting that their constituent colonies nullify all extradition treaties with the Alliance, in effect severing high-level diplomatic relations. Romane has already done so, and others are expected to follow suit in coming days.

"In other news, the Prime Minister's office has announced Miriam Solovy's removal from the post of Fleet Admiral in light of accusations of sedition, dereliction of duty and conspiracy to commit treason. Admiral Solovy's whereabouts are not being made public at this time.

"We'll have additional updates regarding the alleged death of criminal mastermind Olivia Montegreu at the top of the hour, but for now we return you to coverage of the bombing of the Astral Materials headquarters on Scythia. The organization OTS is claiming credit for the incident...."

The reporter had left out 'terrorist,' a pejorative they'd been happy to bestow on OTS before today. He wouldn't be surprised if the news organizations had been warned against using the term by the new administration.

Devon huffed a laugh to himself. 'Not being made public' meant 'we don't have a clue' in government-speak. Was Miriam Solovy now as much a fugitive as he'd been when he ran, if not more so? It looked as though it was rather more so.

He wondered what she'd done to piss off the new Prime Minister...be a decent human being, most likely.

Which she was. He knew it, and Annie knew it. They each knew it separately; knowing it together, it became irrefutable. He felt as though he were far closer to the woman than he was, thanks to all the leakage from Annie and from Alex before she'd left.

Alex.

She'd want to be told about what had happened, about what he suspected was soon to happen. Of this he was certain.

For all Alex's devil-may-care approach to life, which he truly, no-bullshit admired, she cared for her mother to a far greater extent than she'd willingly admit—even beyond their recent reconciliation. She'd *want to know*. And because she'd want to know, he thought Caleb would probably want to know, too. Of course, there was also that other thing Caleb would probably want to know in an 'I didn't want to know this' sort of way.

Devon was not the grand arbiter of what-should-and-should-not-be-known. He figured the more knowledge the better. So they should know.

Maybe he could do something to fix that.

He'd found the peculiar quantum waves while tooling around in sidespace last week. Curious, he'd tracked enough of them to determine they streamed in from across settled space to meet up with the TLF wave still coming from the inactive portal. They flowed alongside it but in the opposite direction.

Back toward the portal.

It was the mechanism by which, somehow, the Metigens watched. This was the most logical explanation, and the one he, Mia and Morgan agreed was the likeliest one. The fact they didn't understand how the mechanism functioned didn't change the reality that the mechanism *did* function. The technology was simply more advanced than their own.

There existed the possibility the Metigens had obeyed Alex's decree at the end of the war and abandoned their watchtower, in which case he'd be whispering into the abyss.

The signals still streaming in both directions argued they had not, but since he didn't understand the mechanism he could only speculate. Either way, it was worth a shot, right?

After taking a moment to compose his intentions, Devon shifted into sidespace.

He located the closest wave by superimposing a vector from the Metis portal to Romane, followed it a few parsecs to the TLF signal—it pointed directly at Earth—then aligned himself on the path of the quantum wave nearest it and tried to match its frequency. His success was due far more to Annie's efforts than his own.

Thank you, Devon.

You bet.

He had no idea if this was apt to work, but in case it did he readied his cockiest mental voice.

Hey, Metigen aliens. We realize you're still watching. Enjoying the show?

Listen, I assume you're up to speed on events here in our little universe. But given you're assholes, what I'm about to say might not have occurred to you. So I'm going to broadcast it at you in big flashing neon letters:

If you happen to bump into Alex and Caleb out there in your multiverse playground, you should consider encouraging them to swing back by home. I believe they have a vested interest in current shenanigans on this side of the portal.

But hey, it's just a suggestion. Peace out.

PORTAL: C-2

SYSTEM DESIGNATION: KAMEN

50

IRELTSE

Crushed sandstone sifted through Caleb's fingers, insubstantial as dust. A breeze caught the debris mid-fall and spirited it away before it could join the ashes blanketing the ground.

He stopped in the middle of what had once been a street, his arms pulled in at his sides, his fists balled in barely restrained fury.

Broken stone and shattered walls were all that remained of the Center, and every other building in Ireltse's capital city. But this wasn't the deceptively sterile, pure-in-its-completeness annihilation caused by an anti-matter weapon like the one Pinchu had used to decimate Nengllitse.

Instead, the city had been leveled by cluster bombs. Impelled shrapnel had ripped through the sandstone structures like they were butter, shredding every obstruction they encountered. The street beneath his feet was tinted a muted, rusty red. Sometime in the last several days, it had flowed a river of blood.

In a burst of anger he grabbed the closest chunk of rubble and hurled it through the air. With nothing left standing high enough to halt its progress, it sailed far into the distance before smashing to the ground and fracturing into more dust. "Damn fool! Why couldn't he listen? This didn't have to happen...."

"The house is gone, too. The cliff it sat on collapsed—was blown up, I guess. Most of the house is in pieces at the bottom of the canyon."

Alex knelt a few meters behind him. Her eyes were closed, and her voice sounded detached and monotone.

He glanced around, shocked to discover the *Siyane* was no-where to be seen. How had he missed it leaving? Probably something to do with the scenery distracting him. "You flew the ship over to the house?"

She nodded slowly, without affectation.

Valkyrie could've flown there herself; she didn't need Alex's guidance, much less her mind. Why—

"I needed to see for myself. It was the most efficient way." She opened her eyes and gave him a weary, desolate smile.

"Reading my mind a new skill you picked up recently?"

"I wish." She sank down to rest on her heels. "My head hurts. I'm kneeling amidst a hundred thousand dead Khokteh, and all I can think is that my head hurts."

He crouched in front of her. "You could be suffering serious neurological trauma. You need to see a doctor...and you need to stop connecting to the ship until you feel better."

"I feel better *when* I connect to the ship."

"Alex...." His voice trailed off as a flare of blue-white light took shape behind her.

She frowned and twisted around to see what had captured his attention. The Metigen completed its typically theatrical entrance, and its empyreal form came to rest above the bloodied street.

Instantly she sprang to her feet and bum-rushed the alien. But there existed no physicality for her to attack, and she could only skid to a stop in the midst of the swirling lights.

"You sons of bitches, all of you! Are you happy? You have your wanton devastation to feast on once again. Lap it up!"

The alien's presence grew agitated, and Caleb reached into the vortex to clutch her wrist. "Alex, we don't even know if this is Iapetus. Maybe—"

"Oh, it's not. This is Mesme. And I don't give a goddamn if this isn't his realm. I've seen how they work, and they are all responsible for this atrocity."

It is true this is not my 'realm,' nor these creatures my focus. But in the ways which matter, you are not wrong.

She must have shifted into the quantum space long enough to identify the Metigen's 'true avatar,' as she'd characterized it. She was getting rather adept at moving in and out of the mystical dimension.

So this was Mesme, then. Caleb worked to lessen the venom in his voice to a tolerable level. "Thank you for rescuing us at the portal, and protecting us at the lake."

Alex seethed. "Why did you bother, though? Does keeping us alive somehow make you feel better about all the carnage?"

One has nothing to do with the other, and both were done for their own reasons.

Okay, fine. He'd expressed his thanks, and he just wasn't up to being polite on what had been a damn trying day, to put it mildly. "What reasons can there *be* for this? What justification could possibly exist to raise an entire species for slaughter? To give them reason and intellect and emotion, to let them love and dream and achieve, only to mercilessly cut them down like animals?"

We did not 'cut them down.' They committed this bloodshed upon themselves.

"Like your ships did all the killing for you when you attacked us. Not you. Never you. Never the taint of death on your elusive hands." His anger over this massacre, still roiling and seeking its shape, adjusted targets easily enough from Pinchu and the Khokteh to the Metigens.

"You have plans for us, some role we're expected to play for you in the future. Answer the question, or we're out. *Why?* What is the purpose of the Khokteh's existence and their deliberate obliteration?"

That is three questions.

Alex screamed and lashed out at the points of light from within, desperate for something tangible to rage against.

Caleb wrapped his arms around her from behind and coaxed her out while glowering at Mesme in loathing.

Then he lessened his hold on her to a single hand. Together they turned their backs on the alien and began walking away.

To learn how to battle. How to wage war.

They stopped, but did not turn around.

We have never been fighters, not in all our long aeons of existence. The fierceness, the survival instinct essential to battling—to defeating—a true foe is not part of who we are.

So we study how to fight, how to kill and die. We study not one way to do so, but all possible ways, until we find one which can succeed.

Caleb shared an admittedly intrigued glance with Alex, then looked over his shoulder. "Succeed how?"

In the only manner one can succeed in a war against an oppressor: liberation.

"You're oppressed. You, who can build and eradicate entire universes on a whim."

Everything is relative, Caleb, and the circumstances are far more complicated than you realize.

"Then explain them to us. Is it the Anaden who oppress you? Are they who you seek to overthrow?"

Mesme churned in agitation. *You know?*

"Know what? We know what they were intending to do to the Taenarin—"

Enough. I have already said beyond what is prudent, and this is not my purpose today. I came here to you for another reason.

I bring a message, albeit one delivered via a most unexpected method. Your presence has been requested in Aurora.

Alex groaned. "*Sukin syn*, what's happened now?"

R

"Why do we bother, Caleb? Why pick up the pieces and glue the world back together if it's just going to fall apart again the first time someone knocks it around a little? Insanity is doing the same thing over and over again and expecting a different result.

"If we can't change human nature in all its *khrenovuyu* stupidity, we're simply banging our heads against the wall—hence the headache."

He found he didn't have a good answer. Terrorists *and* governments hunting down the very people who had saved them from genocide? He appreciated that the Prevo technology was frightening; the new and unknown was always frightening.

But trying to stamp something out for challenging the status quo had never worked, not for long. Another lesson people had forgotten more times than they'd learned it.

And Miriam accused of treason? On the run? He couldn't begin to fathom that one. Of course they would be returning, if for this reason alone.

He put a hand on Alex's hip and sighed; Mesme had departed, but they still stood amid the wreckage. "We need to consider—"

"You bother because every now and then you do change the heart and mind of someone, even if it is far too late."

They both jumped in surprise as their translators squawked and Pinchu emerged from behind a wall of rubble.

A smile broke across Caleb's face, and Alex bolted for the Tokahe Naataan. He embraced her with enough vigor she let out an "Oof!"

"Apologies, Alex Human. I forgot how puny you are."

"It's okay." She disentangled herself from his arms and squelched a grimace. "We thought you were dead."

"I nearly was, should be now and may yet still join my beloved Cassela."

He did look terrible. The fur on his left arm had been almost fully singed off, exposing bronze skin in patches. A thick bandage held his left shoulder in place, and his face was filthy with dirt and scratched to hell. "But some are alive? To be honest, seeing the level of destruction, we didn't hold out much hope."

The Tokahe Naataan flinched and turned away, but found only ruin. "A few thousand, optimistically. We've been gathering survivors in a neighborhood to the south that was spared the worst. And there are other cities. Several were hit as well, but not all. Not yet."

"Was it the Tapertse?" The colonies supported smaller populations than the homeworld, and after the anti-matter weapon did its work he didn't see how Nengllitse would have retained enough of a force to retaliate.

"Indeed. You were right, Caleb Human. About everything. I should have asked for a shield. I should have fought to protect my people instead of inflicting vengeance on innocents. Now I drown in the blood of my *shikei*."

He stared at the debris, then shifted his gaze to Alex. "I saw you speaking with one of the Gods a moment ago. You truly are their emissary—unless you are their leader, to yell at one so freely."

"Oh, Pinchu, if you knew how far from the truth that was...." Her gaze had dropped to study the rubble at her feet, but now it rose high to meet Pinchu's, her eyes lit with sudden fervor. "You need to make peace with the Tapertse. You need to bring an end to this war, or you will *all* die."

"At this rate, such an outcome won't take so long...though we are nearly out of soldiers to use the weapons the Gods provide."

"No, you misunderstand. I'm not talking about you killing each other off thousands at a time. If you don't stop fighting and soon, all this—" she waved an arm at the sky "—all the planets, stars and Khokteh alive today will vanish from the cosmos as if they never existed at all. This is what your gods have planned for you."

Her expression was stern enough to cower the mightiest warrior into submission, and Pinchu wilted beneath it. His gruff voice faltered. "You ask me to make peace with the monsters who did this?"

She didn't even look around at 'this.' "Yes. The alternative is extinction. There's no coming back from that—no new weapon to fire when no one is left and you've no universe left to fire it in.

"Pinchu, you have one last chance to stand up and say, 'Stop. No more. We want to live.' You can't undo the past, but you can give your people a future."

He regarded them silently, then wandered several meters away to poke his feet at debris. "What if the Tapertse refuse to talk? How do I make them listen?"

Caleb went over and clasped Pinchu on his intact shoulder. "We'll help you."

51

IRELTSE

The temple on the outskirts of the city remained standing, not so much as a chink in its columns amid all the destruction wrought so near to it.

Had Iapetus' Tapertse incarnation warned its subjects not to defile religious landmarks? She absolutely would not put it past the Metigen to do exactly that.

An ominous full moon bathed the temple in a crimson sheen, a reflection of the blood spilt at the behest of the entity it celebrated.

Alex took Caleb's hand in hers, and together they climbed the steps to the dais.

They'd be returning home in the morning, later than they should but as soon as they dared, in the hope they could restore a measure of sanity to clearly insane people.

But first there was one last matter to take care of here.

She reached into the recess at the center of the long table and pressed the metal ring without fanfare.

It took Iapetus longer to appear this time. The alien had probably not been expecting any additional summons. As before, the Metigen's transformation into a vague Khokteh form halted on awareness of their presence.

You do get around, don't you, little fledglings. One can hardly keep up with all the commotion you've generated.

Could the alien be more condescending? She stood tall to fix her glare on its pulsing lights.

"That's the idea. Now we're here to make damn sure you see and acknowledge what's happened here in the last several days. The Khokteh worlds have made peace with one another. Ireltse and Tapertse have laid down their weapons and agreed to help rebuild Nengllitse alongside their own cities. Their war is over."

For today, perhaps. Their brutal, violent disposition will not allow it to remain so for long.

"Maybe, maybe not, but we'll all get to find out, because you will not shut this Enisle down. No one will—not you, not Lakhes or any other Metigen, not your Idryma. The Khokteh are under our protection."

What—

"Here's the thing: everyone deserves a chance to live. Not just those from Amaranthe. You—all of you Metigens—have never grasped this, but we are going to make you honor it nonetheless. Humanity will fight you to protect the lives of the Khokteh, and any other species you threaten. Now and forever."

She gulped in air, flush with righteous indignation and emboldened by Caleb's encouraging touch at her waist. "We saved ourselves from the decimation you intended to mete out on us, and now we'll do the same for others. Because life—the very existence of it—is precious, no matter where it came from or who created it."

Iapetus' already nebulous form swelled and agitated around the dais.

Who are you to believe you can make demands of the Idryma?

She was aghast at the alien's continued arrogance, but Caleb just smirked with a brazen, fierce certitude. It was beautiful. "We're the people who are going to help you win your war. But you're playing by our rules now."

You dare—

A second Metigen arrived from the darkness in a rush of brilliant ice blue lights, displaying its winged form so distinctly she didn't need to peer into the quantum space to confirm it was Mesme.

Enough, Iapetus. It has been decided.

Mesme shifted to face them directly. *Caleb, Alexis, we accept your offer of assistance and, within reason, your terms for it. This Enisle will not be tampered with further. If the Khokteh perish in the future, it will truly be of their own doing.*

She squeezed Caleb's hand, sensing his relief flow and merge with her own. "Then answer a few questions for us. Please. Who is your war against? Who are your oppressors?"

There is no war today, only the dream of a future one—of a war which will free not merely the Katasketousya, but all beings of Amaranthe. Our oppressor is as you deduced: the Anaden. They have been so for many long aeons.

Caleb stepped forward, not in intimidation but rather vehemence. "But who are the Anaden? What are they, to be so powerful they can oppress you? If you want us to help you, we have to know."

Mesme morphed and shifted until it presented the humanoid form it had taken on Portal Prime when they first met.

They are you, and you are they.

Caleb's expression conveyed unmitigated shock. He growled a single, stunned word. "What?"

Humans are the genetic recreation of the Anaden, Aurora a recreation of their beginnings.

It, and you, were designed and spawned so we might study the enemy until we understood its nature, and in so doing decipher how the Anaden evolved into the host of monsters and tyrants they have become.

It was our hope that if we accomplished all these things, we might discover a way to defeat our enemy. The enemy of all sapient beings.

Silence hummed in the ghostly night air for endless seconds.
Finally Alex sank against the dais table with a dramatic sigh. "Well, fuck."

TO BE CONTINUED IN
THE THRILLING CONCLUSION OF
AURORA RENEGADES

***

SUBSCRIBE TO
GSJENNSEN.COM

Receive updates on AURORA RENEGADES, new book announcements and more

Author's Note

I published *Starshine* in March of 2014. In the back of the book I put a short note asking readers to consider leaving a review or talking about the book with their friends. Since that time I've had the unmitigated pleasure of watching my readers do exactly that, and there has never been a more wonderful and humbling experience in my life. There's no way to properly thank you for that support, but know you changed my life and made my dreams a reality.

I'll make the same request now. If you loved *DISSONANCE*, tell someone. If you bought the book on Amazon, consider leaving a review. If you downloaded the book off a website with Russian text in the margins and pictures of cartoon video game characters in the sidebar, consider recommending it to others.

As I've said before, reviews are the lifeblood of a book's success, and there is no single thing that will sell a book better than word-of-mouth. My part of this deal is to write a book worth talking about—your part of the deal is to do the talking. If you all keep doing your bit, I get to write a lot more books for you.

This time I'm also going to make a second request. *Dissonance* was an independently published novel, written by one person and worked on by a small team of colleagues. Right now there are thousands of writers out there chasing this same dream.

Go to Amazon and surf until you find an author you like the sound of. Take a small chance with a few dollars and a few hours of your time. In doing so, you may be changing those authors' lives by giving visibility to people who until recently were shut out of publishing, but who have something they need to say. It's a revolution, and it's waiting on you.

Lastly, I love hearing from my readers. Seriously. Just like I don't have a publisher or an agent, I don't have "fans." I have **readers** who buy and read my books, and **friends** who do that then reach out to me through email or social media. If you loved the book—or if you didn't—let me know. The beauty of independent publishing is its simplicity: there's the writer and the readers. Without any overhead, I can find out what I'm doing right and wrong directly from you, which is invaluable in making the next book better than this one. And the one after that. And the twenty after that.

Website: www.gsjennsen.com
Email: gs@gsjennsen.com
Twitter: @GSJennsen
Facebook: facebook.com/gsjennsen.author
Goodreads: goodreads.com/gs_jennsen
Google+: plus.google.com/+GSJennsen
Instagram: instagram.com/gsjennsen

Find all my books on Amazon:
http://amazon.com/author/gsjennsen

APPENDIX A

SUPPLEMENTAL MATERIAL

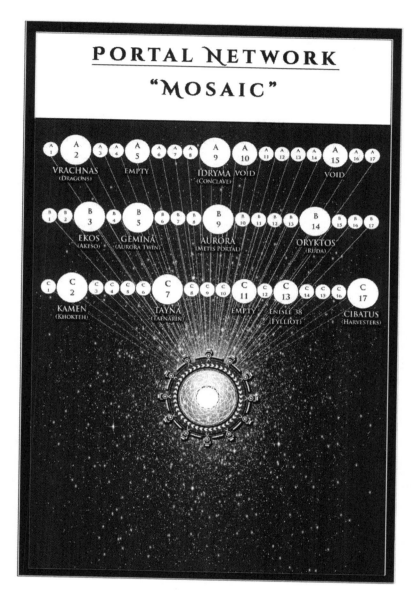

(UPDATED)

Updated Portal Network Map can be viewed online at: gsjennsen.com/ mosaic-map-post-dissonance

DRAMATIS ALIENORUM

IDRYMA

Lakhes
Conclave Praetor

Mnemosyne
First Analystae of Aurora Enisle

Iapetus
First Analystae of Khokteh Enisle

Hyperion
Analystae

PORTAL B-3

Species
Ekos

Planets
Ekos-1, Ekos-2, Ekos-3

Characters
Akeso ("All")
Ekos-2 Intelligence

PORTAL B-14

Species
Ruda

Planets
Rudan

Characters
Supreme Three

PORTAL C-2

Species
Khokteh

Planets
Ireltse, Nengllitse, Tapertse

Characters

Pinchutsenahn Niikha Qhiyane Kteh
(Pinchu)
Tokahe Naataan of Ireltse

Casselanhu Pwemku Yuanwoh Vneh
(Cassela)
Amacante Naabaan of Ireltse

PORTAL C-7

Species
Taenarin

Planets
Taenarin Aris

Characters

Jaisc
Iona-Cead of Taenarin Aris

Beshai
Caomh of Taenarin Aris

Dramatis Alienorum can be viewed online at: gsjennsen.com/characters-alien-dissonance

AURORA RHAPSODY
TIMELINE

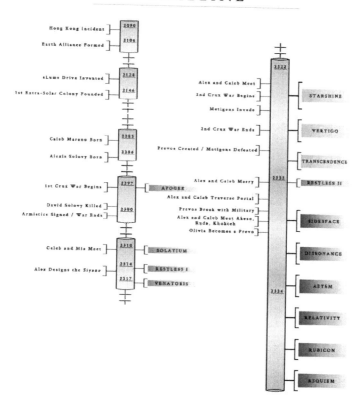

APPENDIX B

AURORA RISING
DETAILED SYNOPSIS

STARSHINE

By the year 2322, humanity has expanded into the stars to inhabit over 100 worlds spread across a third of the galaxy. Though thriving as never before, they have not discovered the key to utopia, and societal divisions and conflict run as deep as ever.

Two decades ago, a group of breakaway colonies rebelled to form the Senecan Federation. They fought the Earth Alliance, won their independence in the Crux War and began to rise in wealth and power.

Now a cabal of powerful individuals within both superpowers and the criminal underground set in motion a plot designed to incite renewed war between the Alliance and Federation. Olivia Montegreu, Liam O'Connell, Matei Uttara and others each foment war for their own reasons. One man, Marcus Aguirre, manipulates them all, for only he knows what awaits humanity if the plot fails.

AR

Alexis Solovy is a starship pilot and explorer. Her father, a fallen war hero, gave his life in the Crux War. As Operations Director for Earth Alliance Strategic Command (EASC), her mother Miriam Solovy is an influential military leader. But Alex seeks only the freedom of space and has made a fortune by reading the patterns in the chaos to uncover the hidden wonders of the stars from her cutting-edge scout ship, the *Siyane*.

Caleb Marano is an intelligence agent for the Senecan Federation. His trade is to become whatever the situation requires: to lie, deceive, outwit and if necessary use lethal force to bring his target to justice. Clever and enigmatic, he's long enjoyed the thrill and danger his job brings, but now finds himself troubled by the death of his mentor.

R

On Earth, Alex is preparing for an expedition to the Metis Nebula, a remote region on the fringes of explored space, when she receives an unexpected offer to lead the Alliance's space exploration program. After a typically contentious meeting with her mother, she refuses the job.

On Seneca, Caleb returns from a forced vacation spent with his sister Isabela and her daughter Marlee. Fresh off eradicating the terrorist group who murdered his mentor, he receives a new mission from Special Operations Director Michael Volosk: conduct a threat assessment on disturbing readings originating from the Metis Nebula.

While Alex and Caleb separately travel toward Metis, a Trade Summit between the Alliance and Federation begins on the resort world of Atlantis. Colonel Richard Navick, lifelong friend of the Solovys and EASC Naval Intelligence Liaison, is in charge of surveillance for the Summit, but unbeknownst to him, the provocation for renewed war will begin under his watch.

Jaron Nythal, Asst. Trade Director for the Federation, abets the infiltration of the Summit by the assassin Matei Uttara. Matei kills a Federation attaché, Chris Candela, and assumes his identity. On the final night of the Summit, he poisons Alliance Minister of Trade Santiagar with a virus, which overloads his cybernetics, causing a fatal stroke. Matei escapes in the ensuing chaos.

Shortly after departing Seneca, Caleb is attacked by mercenary ships. He defeats them, but when he later encounters Alex's ship on the fringes of Metis, he believes her to be another mercenary and fires on her. She destroys his ship, though not before suffering damage to her own, and he crashes on a nearby planet. She is forced to land to effect repairs; recognizing her attacker will die without rescue, she takes him prisoner.

Richard Navick and Michael Volosk each separately scramble to uncover the truth of the Santiagar assassination while Olivia Montegreu, the leader of the Zelones criminal cartel, schemes with Marcus Aguirre to implement the next phase in their plan. Olivia routes missiles provided by Alliance General Liam O'Connell to a group of mercenaries.

Fighting past distrust and suspicion, Alex and Caleb complete repairs on the *Siyane* using salvaged material from the wreckage of his ship. Having gained a degree of camaraderie and affection, if not quite trust, they depart the planet in search of answers to the mystery at the heart of Metis.

What they discover is a scene from a nightmare—an armada of monstrous alien ships emerging from a massive portal, gathering a legion in preparation for an invasion.

Meanwhile, Olivia's mercenaries launch a devastating attack on the Federation colony of Palluda. Disguised to look like a strike by Alliance military forces, the attack has the desired effect of inciting war. The Federation retaliates by leveling an Alliance military base on Arcadia, and the Second Crux War has begun.

Alex and Caleb flee the Metis Nebula to warn others of the impending threat, only to learn war has broken out between their respective governments. Caleb delivers information about the alien threat to Volosk. He informs the Director of Intelligence, Graham Delavasi, who alerts the Federation government Chairman Vranas and the military's supreme commander, Field Marshal Gianno. Forced to focus on the new war with the Alliance for now, they nonetheless dispatch a stealth infiltration team to investigate Metis.

Caleb is requested to accompany the team and return to Metis, only Alex refuses to drop him off on her way to Earth. Tensions flare, but Caleb realizes he's emotionally compromised even as Alex realizes she must let him go. Instead, he agrees to go to Earth with her, and together with Volosk they devise a plan to try to bring a swift end to the war by exposing its suspicious beginnings.

The plan goes awry when Caleb is arrested shortly after they arrive—by Alex's mother—after his true identity is leaked to Richard by those in league with Marcus.

While Caleb is locked away in a detention facility, his friend Noah Terrage is recruited by Olivia to smuggle explosives to Vancouver. Possessing a conscience, he refuses. The infiltration team sent by the Federation to Metis vanishes as the Second Crux War escalates.

Alex is forced to choose between her government, her family and what she knows is right. She turns to her best friend, Kennedy Rossi, and their old hacker acquaintance, Claire Zabroi. Plans in place, Alex presents her evidence on the alien armada to a skeptical EASC Board. Their tepid reaction leads to a final confrontation with her mother and a final plea to focus on the true threat.

Alex hacks military security and breaks Caleb out of confinement. Allegiances declared and choices made, they at last give in to the passion they feel for one another. Despite lingering resentment toward the Federation for her father's death and fear that Caleb is merely playing a role, she agrees to accompany him to Seneca to find another way to combat the looming invasion.

Caleb appeals to his friend and former lover, Mia Requelme, for help in covering their tracks. She hides the *Siyane* safely away on Romane while Alex and Caleb travel to Seneca. Secretly, Caleb asks Mia to hack the ship while they are gone to grant him full access and flying privileges, something Alex zealously guards for herself, and Mia uses her personal Artificial, Meno, to break the encryption on the ship.

On Earth, Richard wrestles with unease and doubt as he begins to believe Alex's claims about the origin of the war. He confesses his dilemma to his husband, Will Sutton. Will urges him to work to bring about peace and offers to convey Santiagar's autopsy report to Alex in the hope the Senecan government can find in it evidence to prove the assassination was not their doing.

Volosk meets with Caleb and Alex, and they hand over the autopsy report Will forwarded and all the raw data they recorded on the aliens. In return Volosk arranges meetings with the highest levels of leadership.

As Alex and Caleb enjoy a romantic dinner, EASC Headquarters is destroyed in a massive bombing executed by agents of Olivia and Marcus. Though intended to be killed in the attack, due to a last minute scheduling conflict Miriam Solovy is not on the premises. Instead EASC Board Chairman Alamatto perishes, along with thousands of others. On the campus but outside Headquarters, Richard narrowly escapes critical injury.

Within minutes of the bombing, Caleb and Alex are ambushed by mercenaries in downtown Cavare. Caleb kills them all in dramatic fashion, but unbeknownst to him Alex was injured by a stray shot. In the panic of the moment he mistakes her shell-shocked behavior for fear of the killer he has revealed himself to be.

Heartbroken but determined to protect her, he flees with her to the Intelligence building. Upon arriving there, they find the unthinkable—Michael Volosk has been murdered, his throat slit in the parking lot.

Suddenly unable to trust anyone, Caleb pleas with Alex to go with him to the spaceport, but she collapses as a result of her injury. Stunned but with one clear mission, he steals a skycar and returns to their ship, where he can treat her wounds in the relative safety of space.

The EASC bombing successfully executed, Olivia's Zelones network turns its attention to Noah. In refusing to smuggle the explosives he is now a liability; the first attempt on his life misses him but kills his young companion. Searching for answers, he traces the source of the hit and realizes he was targeted because of his friendship with Caleb. Lacking other options and with a price on his head, he flees Pandora for Messium.

Miriam returns to Vancouver to preside over the devastation at EASC Headquarters. She begins the process of moving the organization forward—only to learn the evidence implicates Caleb as the perpetrator.

Marcus moves one step nearer to his goal when the Alliance Assembly passes a No Confidence Vote against Prime Minister Brennon. Marcus' friend Luis Barrera is named PM, and he quickly appoints Marcus Foreign Minister.

Alex regains consciousness aboard their rented ship as they race back to Romane. Misunderstandings and innate fears drive them to the breaking point, then bring them closer than ever. The moment of contentment is short-lived, however, as Caleb—and by extension Alex—is publicly named a suspect in the bombing.

Every copy of the raw data captured at the portal, except for the original in Alex's possession, has now been destroyed. Recognizing an even deeper secret must reside within the portal and hunted by the conspirators and authorities alike, Alex and Caleb begin a desperate gambit to clear their names and discover a way to defeat the aliens.

On reaching Romane, Alex, Caleb and the *Siyane* are protected by Mia while they prepare. Kennedy brings equipment to replace the ship's shielding damaged in Metis. On the *Siyane*, she realizes the repairs made using the material from Caleb's ship has begun transforming the hull into a new, stronger metal. Caleb receives a vote of confidence from his sister Isabela, and a gesture of trust from Alex in the form of a chair.

Back on Earth, Miriam and Richard work to clear Alex's name, even as Miriam is threatened by the newly named EASC Board Chairman, Liam O'Connell. Marcus informs his alien contact, Hyperion that his plan has nearly come to fruition, only to be told he is out of time.

As the invaders commence their assault on the frontiers of settled space by sieging the colony of Gaiae, Alex and Caleb breach the aliens' mysterious, otherworldly portal at the heart of the Metis Nebula.

ᴬR

VERTIGO

BEYOND THE PORTAL

Alex and Caleb survive the portal traversal to discover empty darkness on the other side. They follow the TLF wave until they are attacked by a host of alien vessels. Alex discerns an artificial space within the emptiness and pitches the *Siyane* into it. The vessels do not follow, and Alex and Caleb find themselves in the atmosphere of a hidden planet.

The planet mimics Earth in almost every way, but is 1/3 the size and orbits no sun. It differs in one other respect as well—time moves differently here. Days back home pass in hours here.

When they land and venture outside to explore their surroundings, Alex notices the ship's hull continues to transform into a new, unknown metal. As she puzzles over it they are attacked— by a dragon. The beast captures Alex and flies off with her.

Caleb takes control of the ship to chase the dragon. As it reaches a mountain range, the *Siyane* impacts an invisible barrier which throws it back to its origin point. On his return Caleb encounters and kills 2 additional dragons. Believing the barrier is a technology repulsor but uncertain of its parameters, he crafts a sword from a piece of metal, deactivates his eVi and crosses the barrier on foot.

Alex wakes in a memory. Eleven years old, she enjoys breakfast with her parents, then overhears a conversation between them she in reality never witnessed. Realizing this is an illusion, she demands to be set free. A ghostly, disembodied voice challenges her. Thus begins her journey through a series of scenes from the past in which she is forced to watch events unfold, helpless to intervene or escape, as her protests, tirades and desperate pleas go unanswered.

— First is a gauntlet of her own mistakes. Designed to paint her as selfish and uncaring, her worst flaws are displayed in encounters with friends, former lovers and most of all with her mother.

— She views a massive battle between the Alliance and Federation and realizes this is about more than her—the aliens having been watching and recording events across human civilization.

— Traveling further back in time, Alex suffers through the Hong Kong Incident 232 years earlier. Over 50,000 people died when an Artificial trapped HK University residents for 5 weeks without food. At its conclusion her captor speaks to her for only the second time, telling her she has 'done well.'

— She is sent to the bridge of her father's cruiser in the middle of the Kappa Crucis battle of the 1st Crux War—the battle that took his life. She sees her father's heroism as he protects thousands of civilians against a Federation assault, then his last moments as, his ship crippled, he contacts Miriam to say goodbye. The heartbreak and emotion of the scene devastates Alex, leaving her crumpled on the floor sobbing as the *Stalwart* explodes.

When it's over, she thanks her unseen captor for showing her this event. It expresses confusion at the incongruity of her distress and her thanks, leading her to observe that for all their watching, they still have no idea what it means to be human. Before the interchange can continue, she is told she will wake up, as her companion approaches.

Caleb hiked through the mountains for 2 days. The environment led him to recall a mission with Samuel, during which his mentor divulged the woman he loved was killed by slavers he'd been investigating. Later, Caleb discovers small orbs hovering in the air to generate the tech repulsion field. He renders several inert and confiscates them.

Having reached the dragon's den, he attacks it using the sword, and after an extended battle flays and kills it. As he nears the structure the dragon guarded, an ethereal being materializes but allows him to pass.

Alex awakens as Caleb enters, and they share a tender reunion. Soon, however, he is forced to admit Mia's hacking of her ship. He expects her to lash out in anger, but she instead declares her love for him. He quickly reciprocates, and rather unexpectedly they find themselves reconciled and closer than before. She recounts her experiences while a captive, and they decide to seek out the alien.

Eventually they come upon a lush valley sheltering a large lake; the alien Caleb encountered soars above it. It approaches them while morphing into a humanoid form and introduces itself as Mnemosyne.

Though enigmatic and evasive, the alien reveals its kind have been observing humans for aeons. It suggests humanity is being conquered because it advanced more swiftly and to a greater extent than expected. On further pressing, the alien—Alex has dubbed it 'Mesme'—indicates the invading ships are AIs, sent to cower people into submission if possible, to exterminate them if not. It emphasizes the ships are only machines, and notes humans have machines as powerful—Artificials. Part of Alex's test was to ensure she appreciated the dangers and limitations of Artificials, but also their potential.

Alex recalls a meeting 4 years ago with Dr. Canivon, a cybernetics expert, during which she met Canivon's Artificial, Valkyrie. She and Valkyrie hit it off, and Canivon explained her research into making Artificials safer and better aligned with human interests. She begins to understand what Mesme is suggesting, but pushes for more intel and acquires a copy of the code powering the planet's cloaking shield.

Mesme admits to believing humans are worth saving. The alien warns them they will be hunted on their return through the portal; at this point a second alien appears and a confrontation ensues. Mesme deters the new alien long enough to transport Alex and Caleb back to the *Siyane*. They arrive to learn the ship's hull has been completely transformed into the new metal.

Alex studies the cloaking shield code and adapts it for use on her ship. They depart the planet and continue following the TLF wave, discovering a massive shipyard where superdreadnoughts are being built and sent to their galaxy. Beyond it lies a portal 10x larger than the one that brought them here. It generates their TLF wave—as well as 50 more waves projected in a fanlike pattern.

They track one of the waves to a portal identical to the one leading to the Metis Nebula. They traverse it to find the signals replicated in a new space and a second origin portal, which leads them to conclude this is an elaborate, interlocking tunnel network.

Caleb devises a way to destroy the shipyard using the tech repulsion orbs he confiscated. They launch the orbs into the facility then activate them, resulting in its obliteration. This attracts the attention of enemy ships, which chase the *Siyane* through a series of portal jumps. Alex asks Caleb to fly her ship while she figures out a path that will deposit them nearest their own exit point.

On reaching it, Alex activates the sLume drive and traverses it at superluminal speed to emerge parsecs beyond the portal and well past the waiting enemies in the Metis Nebula. With working communications, they learn they've been cleared of all charges. Alex sends a message to Kennedy, telling her they are alive and have destroyed the aliens' shipyard.

MILKY WAY

As the 2nd Crux War escalates, Federation forces conquer the Alliance colony of Desna. Lt. Col. Malcolm Jenner's *Juno* is the sole defender, and it escapes just before being crippled.

Miriam jousts with Liam even as she remains under a cloud of suspicion due to Alex's alleged involvement in the HQ bombing. Richard enlists the aid of a quantum computing specialist, Devon Reynolds, to help uncover the tampering in government records which led to the framing of Caleb and Alex for the bombing.

On Seneca, Dir. of Intelligence Graham Delavasi reviews Michael Volosk's files, including his suspicions regarding Jaron Nythal, and decides to follow up on the suspicions. Nythal tries to flee, but before he can do so the assassin Matei Uttara kills him. When Graham is called to the crime scene, he connects the dots and realizes a conspiracy does exist, and at least one person in his organization is involved.

Caleb's sister Isabela is taken in for questioning. In order to gain her trust, Graham reveals to her that her father was an investigator for Intelligence and was killed 20 years earlier by a resistance group planning to overthrow the Federation government. Her father's apparent abandonment of his family was a feint to protect them. After he was killed, the government covered up the incident.

On Messium, Kennedy is headed to a meeting when the aliens attack and is trapped under falling debris. She is rescued by a passing stranger—who turns out to be Noah Terrage—and they seek shelter. While her injuries heal they study the aliens' interference with comms and find a way to circumvent it. Kennedy sends a message to Miriam.

The Alliance launches an offensive to retake Desna. While the battle rages in space, Malcolm Jenner and a special forces team rescue the Desnan governor and his family. The Alliance fails to retake the colony. Meanwhile, an explosion takes the life of EA Prime Minister Barrera. In the wake of his death Marcus Aguirre—who arranged Barrera's murder—is named Prime Minister.

Devon Reynolds uncovers alterations to the records used to frame Caleb and Alex for the HQ bombing. At Richard's request he and a group of hackers leak the evidence to media outlets.

Upon seeing the news, Graham Delavasi refocuses his efforts to uncover the conspiracy. Suspecting his deputy, Liz Oberti, he uses Isabela to set a trap. Oberti is arrested but refuses to provide any intel.

The EASC Board meets about the Messium attack, where Miriam shares Kennedy's method to thwart the comm interference. Admiral Rychen readies a mission to drive the aliens off Messium.

While Richard and Miriam discuss Alex's name being cleared, Richard's husband, Will Sutton, arrives. In an effort to help expose the conspiracy and end the 2nd Crux War, he confesses he is an undercover Senecan Intelligence agent and puts Richard in touch with Graham.

Following a heated confrontation with Will, Richard departs to meet Graham on Pandora. Together they interrogate a man suspected of smuggling explosives into Vancouver. The agent gives up Olivia Montegreu, and they formulate a plan to ensnare her.

Miriam confronts Liam over his mismanagement of the war and alien invasion. Enraged, he strikes her, but she refuses to be intimidated. Marcus reaches out to his alien contact, entreating that he now has the power to cease human expansion and pleading with it to end the offensive, but the alien does not respond.

Olivia visits a subordinate on Krysk, but finds Richard and Graham waiting for her. In exchange for her freedom, she gives up Marcus and the details of their conspiracy. Before they part ways Graham gives Richard Will's intelligence file.

Malcolm is sent to assist Admiral Rychen in the Messium offensive. As the battle commences, Kennedy and Noah flee their hideout in an attempt to reach a small military station across the city. They witness horrific devastation and death while crossing the city, but successfully reach the station and repair several shuttles to escape.

The Alliance ships struggle to hold their own against a powerful enemy. Malcolm retrieves the fleeing shuttles and learns the details of the situation on the ground. Faced with the reality that Alliance forces will eventually be defeated, the fleet retreats to save the remaining ships for future battles.

Graham returns to Seneca to inform Federation Chairman Vranas of the conspiracy and the false pretenses upon which hostilities were instigated. Vranas begins the process of reaching out to the Alliance to end the war. Isabela is released from protective custody and returns home to Krysk to reunite with her daughter.

Based on the information Olivia provided, Miriam goes to arrest Liam, only to find he has fled. Richard similarly accompanies a team to detain Marcus, but on their arrival Marcus declares everything he did was for the good of humanity, then commits suicide.

After studying Will's Intelligence file and realizing his husband had acted honorably—other than lying to him—Richard pays Will a visit. Following a contentious and emotional scene, they appear to reconcile.

The EA Assembly reinstates Steven Brennon as Prime Minister. His first act is to promote Miriam to EASC Board Chairman and Fleet Admiral of the Armed Forces. On her advice he signs a peace treaty with the Federation.

Olivia approaches Aiden Trieneri, head of the rival Triene cartel and her occasional lover, and suggests they work together to aid the fight against the invaders. On Atlantis, Matei Uttara's alien contact tells him Alex and Caleb are returning and instructs him to kill them.

Kennedy and Noah reach Earth. Kennedy's easy rapport with the military leadership spooks Noah, and he tries to slip away. She chases after him, ultimately persuading him to stay with a passionate kiss.

Liam arrives at the NW Regional base on Fionava. He injects a virus into the communications network and hijacks several ships by convincing their captains he is on a secret mission approved by EA leadership to launch clandestine raids on Federation colonies.

Alliance and Federation leadership are meeting to finalize war plans when an alien contacts them to offer terms for their surrender. It involves humanity forever retreating west behind a demarcation line, cutting off 28 colonies and 150 million people.

The leaders don't want to surrender but recognize their odds of victory are quite low. Then Miriam receives word that Alex is alive and the aliens' ability to send reinforcements has been destroyed. They decide to reject the terms of surrender and fight. On Miriam's order their ships open fire on the alien forces.

⁂

TRANSCENDENCE

The Metigen War is in full swing as Alex and Caleb approach Seneca. Caleb initiates an Intelligence Division protection protocol, and he and Alex join Director Delavasi at a safe house as several actions are set in motion.

Alex contacts Dr. Canivon to discuss the feasibility of enriching human/Artificial connections, only to discover Sagan is already under attack by the Metigens. The Alliance is defending the independent colony, and Alex asks her mother to ensure Canivon and her Artificial, Valkyrie, are rescued and brought to Earth. Caleb reaches out to Isabela, who divulges the truth about their father's profession and his death. Caleb confronts Graham about it, and a heated argument ensues.

On Earth, Kennedy works with the Alliance to manufacture the material the *Siyane's* hull transformed into, now called 'adiamene.' She implores Noah to seek the help of his estranged father, a metals expert. Noah agrees, but the request introduces tension into their relationship. Devon tries to restore communications to Fionava and NW Command, while elsewhere at EASC Devon's boss, Brigadier Hervé, is contacted by Hyperion, the same alien Marcus Aguirre was in league with.

Alex, Caleb, Miriam, Richard and Graham converge on a secluded, private estate on Pandora, and Alex and Miriam reunite in a more tender encounter than either were expecting. Alex reveals the full extent of her plan to the others, including that she intends to spearhead it by being the first to neurally link to an Artificial. Even as they meet, agents of the Metigens seek to stop them—the safe house on Seneca is blown up, and the assassin Matei Uttara pursues them to Pandora.

When Miriam breaks the news to Alex that her former lover, Ethan Tollis, died in an explosion, she flees to grieve in private. Caleb goes after her, but it intercepted by Uttara. A bloody fight ensues, during which both men are gravely injured. Alex arrives on the scene and shoots Uttara in the head, killing him. Caleb collapses from his injuries.

Noah meets with his father, Lionel, in a combative encounter. Despite the tension between them, Lionel agrees to help with the adiamene production, and they travel to Berlin to meet Kennedy at the manufacturing facility. Once Lionel begins work, Noah confronts Kennedy about her motives for forcing a reunion with his father, but the matter isn't resolved.

Caleb regains consciousness, and he and Alex share an emotional moment in which they both come to realizations about each other and the strength of their relationship. Miriam learns Liam has attacked the Federation colonies of New Cairo and Ogham with nuclear weapons, and she is forced to travel to Seneca to smooth things over with Federation leadership. Once Caleb is healed enough to travel, he and Alex depart for Earth. On the way, he contacts Mia and asks her to come to Earth, though he can't yet tell her why.

Miriam meets with Field Marshal Gianno and Chairman Vranas, and in a surprising move tells them she won't take any active steps to stop Liam until after the Metigens are defeated, as they must concentrate all their efforts on the alien invasion. She then tells Gianno about Alex's plan. Gianno selects the fighter pilot, Morgan Lekkas, for participation, and recalls her from Elathan, where Morgan was helping to defend against a Metigen attack.

Alex and Caleb reach EASC Headquarters, where they are re-united with Kennedy and Noah. Alex meets with Dr. Canivon, who was safely evacuated off Sagan, and informs the woman she wants to use Valkyrie as her Artificial partner in the project they've dubbed 'Noetica.' While monitoring the war effort, EASC's Artificial, Annie, discovers her programming has been corrupted and suspects Hervé of tampering.

Miriam returns to Earth and meets with Prime Minister Brennon. She tells him they are losing the war—they and the Federation are suffering too many losses and will run out of ships and soldiers long before the Metigens do—then pitches Noetica to him.

Mia arrives in Vancouver. Alex and Caleb ask her to be a part of Noetica, together with her Artificial, Meno, and she agrees. With time running out and the Metigens advancing, Noetica is approved and Devon Reynolds and Annie are selected as the last participants.

Alex is the first to undergo the procedure Dr. Canivon has devised to allow a linking between an Artificial's quantum processes and a human mind at a neural level. Caleb and Miriam each contend with fear and worry about her well-being, and Miriam comes to recognize how much Caleb cares for Alex.

Alex awakens to her and Valkyrie's thoughts clashing and overrunning one another. She struggles to regain control of her mind and deal with the flood of information, and with Caleb's help is able to do so. She informs her mother the Metigens are deviating from their pattern and heading for Seneca and Romane in massive force.

While the others undergo the procedure, Alex and Miriam meet with Brennon, Gianno and Vranas. Alex makes the case that the Metigens are coming for Seneca and Romane, and Miriam and Brennon decide to send the EA fleet to defend the two worlds.

On Liam's cruiser, the *Akagi*, Captain Brooklyn Harper begins a mutinous campaign to stop Liam. She enlists one of her team-mates, Kone, and a comm officer, who slips a message out to Col. Malcolm Jenner saying Liam's next target is Krysk and asking for intervention. Then she and Kone sabotage the remaining nukes on the *Akagi*.

Malcolm is defending Scythia from the Metigens when he receives Harper's message. He passes it on to Miriam, who informs Gianno. Gianno claims she can't spare the ships to defend the colony if the Metigens are almost at Seneca.

Caleb is furious the military won't defend Krysk, where his sister and niece live, and makes the gut-wrenching decision to try to rescue them. Alex gives him the *Siyane*, saying it's his only chance to reach Krysk in time. After a tearful parting, Caleb leaves, but not before recruiting Noah to go with him.

Alex, Devon, Mia and Morgan, and their Artificial counter-parts, Valkyrie, Annie, Meno and Stanley, gather to strategize. They name themselves "Prevos," taken from the Russian word for "The Transcended," and begin to realize the extent of their new capabilities. Alex shares a touching goodbye with her mother before leaving with the fleet for Seneca.

Devon remains at EASC, where he and Annie will oversee all fronts of the war, and comes to terms with the fact Hervé is working for the Metigens. At the same time, Hyperion confronts Hervé about Noetica. Because she wants the Metigens defeated, Hervé does not reveal to Hyperion that she has secretly placed a

'Kill Switch' in the Prevos' firmware, which when used will sever their connections to the Artificials—and also likely kill them.

Graham, Vranas and Gianno discuss the coming attack and express concerns over Noetica. When Graham returns to his office, Will Sutton—Richard's husband and a Senecan intelligence agent—is waiting on him and bears mysterious news.

Liam arrives at Krysk and attempts to use his nukes to disable the orbital defense array. They fail to detonate, and he has Kone brought before him to answer allegations of sabotage. When Kone refuses to confess, Liam executes him. Harper witnesses the execution via a surveillance camera; devastated, she prepares to try to blow up the ship. On the colony below, Isabela and Marlee are downtown as the attack begins. They seek refuge in the basement of an office building, but become trapped when the building collapses.

Alex reaches Seneca and Admiral Rychen's flagship dreadnought, the *Churchill,* and she and Rychen discuss strategy. Meanwhile, the Noetica Artificials discuss using neural imprints of notable military officers to supplement their and the Prevos tactical capabilities.

Caleb and Noah get to Krysk to discover the capital city under attack. The ongoing assault makes it too dangerous to land and find Isabela and Marlee, so Caleb comes up with a new plan. He draws Liam's ships away from the city, then, trusting the adiamene hull is strong enough to hold the *Siyane* together, crashes it through the frigates and into the belly of the *Akagi.*

They fight their way through the ship to the bridge, where they encounter Harper, who agrees to help them. She distracts Liam, then when Caleb and Noah open fire, disables his personal shield. Caleb kills Liam. Caleb, Noah and Harper rush back to the *Siyane* and escape just before the cruiser crashes.

Noah and Harper help Caleb dig a tunnel to where Isabela and Marlee are trapped, freeing them and several other people. Harper elects to remain in the city to aid with rescue efforts. Noah decides to find transportation back to Earth, eager to return to Kennedy, and Caleb heads for Seneca, and Alex.

The Metigens arrive at Seneca in overwhelming force. Alex, on the *Churchill* with Rychen, and Morgan, on the SF flagship with Gianno, take charge of the battle, employing a number of surprise weapons and tactics to gain an early advantage over the Metigen armada.

Several hours into the battle, Alex argues as it stands now they will not achieve complete victory. She convinces Miriam and Rychen to allow her to break into one of the Metigen superdreadnoughts, where she and Valkyrie believe they can hack the core operating code. She hitches a ride atop a recon craft, experiencing a thrilling and terrifying journey through the heart of the battle.

Inside, Alex finds a cavernous space, with power conduits and signals running in every direction, and goes in search of the engineering core. When she hears her father in her head during the search, Valkyrie confesses that the Artificials' search of military neural imprints turned up one for Alex's father, taken before his death. Not surprisingly, it was compatible with Alex's brainwave patterns, so Valkyrie loaded it into her processes to increase their knowledge of military tactics. Valkyrie then enriched the imprint, creating a more fulsome representation of David Solovy's mind and leading to the unexpected result of his personality manifesting.

When they locate the engineering core Alex immerses herself in it to access the ship's programming. Valkyrie inserts a subtle logic error into one of the base routines, and they quickly depart the ship.

A major battle also ensues on and above Romane. Malcolm takes a special forces squad groundside, where he meets up with Mia in the governor's emergency bunker. Mia believes she and Meno have developed a signal beam to nullify an alien vessel's shields. He agrees to help her test it out on one of the smaller alien ships wreaking havoc in the city. They depart the bunker with part of Malcom's squad, while the rest of the squad conducts rescue operations. The test is successful, and Mia/Meno transfer the code for the signal to Devon, who deploys it to all the fleets.

They are returning to the bunker when Malcolm receives an order to arrest one of his Marines who was part of the rescue team on suspicion of working for the Metigens. When arrested, the suspect detonates a bomb he'd placed at Mia's home. The explosion badly damages Meno's hardware, abruptly severing his connection with Mia and causing her to stroke.

Caleb reaches the fleet at Seneca, and he and Alex enjoy a jubilant reunion. Suddenly Alex collapses to the floor as the trauma to Meno and Mia reverberates through the Prevos' connection to one another. Once Alex recovers, she, Devon and Morgan decide it's time to implement their secret plan to ensure victory.

Miriam is overseeing both battlefronts from the War Room when she's informed Devon/Annie have taken control of both Earth's and Seneca's defense arrays. Panic erupts among the military and government leaders. At that moment Miriam receives a message from Alex asking Miriam to please trust in her, and trust Richard. Richard indicates he knows something but won't divulge what it might be.

Hervé judges it's necessary to use the Kill Switch, but Miriam shoots her with a stunner before she can do so. Miriam refuses to act against the Prevos, even as they turn the defense arrays inward.

Unbeknownst to Miriam, shortly after the Prevos were created, they uncovered the full Metigen network of spies and assassins. Before leaving Earth, Alex went with Devon to see Richard and gave him a list of enemy agents, and he contacted Graham and Will on Seneca. They formulated a strategy to arrest or kill the agents at the last possible moment, and enlisted Olivia Montegreu's aid in the effort. Miriam was kept in the dark because revealing Hervé's involvement ahead of time would've alerted the aliens to the fact the Prevos were onto them.

The defense arrays fire—on dozens of Metigen superdreadnoughts hiding cloaked above the major cities of Earth and Seneca. Armed with massive firepower as well as the disruptive signal beam Mia/Meno developed, the superdreadnoughts are destroyed. The Prevos had picked up the stealthed vessels hours earlier, but again, revealing them too early would have tipped their hand.

An alien representative contacts those leading the military assault, but Alex takes charge of the conversation. The alien says they are open to considering cease fire terms, but Alex notes the aliens are in no position to bargain, as humanity's forces have decimated them. She orders them to retreat through the portal and to cease their observation of and meddling in Aurora. She also asks for an explanation for their aggression; the alien replies that humans are far more dangerous than they recognize and must be contained.

The alien accepts her terms, but warns humanity not to come looking for them beyond the portal. Alex doesn't respond to the warning, instead ordering them to retreat now. They do so, and the war comes to an end.

Later, as EA Prime Minister Brennon gives a speech mourning those lost and vowing a new era for civilization, Gianno and Vranas worry about the future of peace with EA and the danger Noetica poses, before separating to celebrate the victory with their families.

Noah reaches Earth and intercepts Kennedy as she is about to leave Vancouver. He finds her cold and dismissive, and provokes her into admitting she was hurt by him eagerly running off with Caleb, then not contacting her. He admits his mistake and being angry with her, but pleads his case by regaling all he went through to get back to her as fast as possible, and they reconcile.

On New Babel, Olivia and her partner-in-crime Aiden prepare to expand their spheres of influence. When Aiden suggests they merge their cartels—the one thing Olivia had warned him never to do—she uses a cybernetic virus to kill him, then begins taking over his cartel.

Alex returns to Earth and reunites with her mother. She elects not to tell Miriam about the construct of her father, and after catching up they agree to meet for lunch the next week.

Caleb and Alex visit Mia, who remains in a coma and was brought to EASC's hospital at Alex's request. Dr. Canivon says she's somewhat optimistic she can rebuild Meno, and together they can repair the damage to Mia's brain. Caleb authorizes her to move ahead, though there's no guarantee Mia will be herself should she eventually awaken.

They return to Alex's loft for a romantic dinner. Caleb presents her with a belated birthday gift—a bracelet crafted from a piece of his sword, the only remnant of the *Siyane's* hull before it morphed into adiamene.

He divulges that Graham has offered him any job he wants if he'll return to Division. Alex encourages him to do so, insisting they can make a long-distance relationship work. He challenges her about what she truly wants from him. When she caves and admits she selfishly wants him to stay with her, he immediately resigns from Division and asks her to marry him. After an emotional discussion, she says yes.

SIX MONTHS LATER

Miriam returns from vacation to move into the new Headquarters building. She and Richard are discussing threats on the horizon and long-term strategies when she receives a message from Alex.

On Atlantis, Kennedy and Noah are enjoying their own vacation, expecting Alex and Caleb to join them later in the day, when Kennedy also receives a message from Alex.

The *Siyane* hovers in the Metis Nebula, just outside the ring of ships patrolling the portal to prevent any Metigen incursion. Valkyrie has been installed into the walls of the *Siyane*, and Alex and Caleb have married. They activate the portal and accelerate through it on a quest for answers about the Metigens and their network of multiverses.

ABOUT THE AUTHOR

G. S. JENNSEN lives in Colorado with her husband and two dogs. *Dissonance* is her fifth novel, all published by her imprint, Hypernova Publishing. In less than two years she has become an internationally bestselling author, selling in excess of 60,000 books since her first novel, *Starshine*, was published in March 2014. She has chosen to continue writing under an independent publishing model to ensure the integrity of the *Aurora Rhapsody* series and her ability to execute on the vision she's had for it since its genesis.

While she has been a lawyer, a software engineer and an editor, she's found the life of a full-time author preferable by several orders of magnitude, which means you can expect the next book in the *Aurora Rhapsody* series in just a few months.

When she isn't writing, she's gaming or working out or getting lost in the Colorado mountains that loom large outside the windows in her home. Or she's dealing with a flooded basement, or standing in a line at Walmart reading the tabloid headlines and wondering who all of those people are. Or sitting on her back porch with a glass of wine, looking up at the stars, trying to figure out what could be up there.

30759104R00270

Made in the USA
Middletown, DE
05 April 2016